Murder on Bogey Island

The Life, Loves and Times of

a Golfer Who Solves Crimes

Brian Hill

A Tom Colt Mystery

From Off the Grid Productions

ISBN# 978-0-9740754-6-4

Cover design by germancreative

Note from the Publisher: This is a work of fiction. The character Tom Colt, his golf career and detective exploits, are inventions of the author's imagination. In certain scenes, the golf tournaments depicted are based on actual events. Certain scenes also depict well-known business establishments that existed at the time this work of fiction takes place. Apart from those scenes, any resemblance to persons, living or dead, locations, events or business establishments, is purely coincidental. The persons and business establishments depicted have no relation to any person or business establishment with the same name or names.

Off the Grid Productions
Box 1210
Tonto Basin, AZ 85553
writers@offthegrid-productions.com

For information about our other books, book series, and screenplays please visit: www.briananddee.com

<u>Acknowledgements:</u>

I want to thank my father for introducing me to golf when I was 6 years old. He also took me to many professional golf tournaments, including US Opens, when I was a young lad. The excitement of attending those events inspired me to write these books.

One of the most memorable was the storied 1972 US Open at Pebble Beach. I was there when Jack Nicklaus hit that epic shot into the teeth of a gale on the 17th hole to seal the victory. Unfortunately, I was in the porta-potty over near the 16th hole and didn't witness the shot. As they say, when you gotta go…

My dad saw the shot, though, and told me it was magnificent.

Brian Hill

Somewhere in Arizona, June 2023

What is a Bogey?

(also bogy or bogie)

1. An evil or mischievous spirit; a hobgoblin
2. A cause of annoyance or harassment
3. Sports
   a. A golf score of one stroke over par

(Source: American Heritage Dictionary)

Part One
"Laughter would be bereaved if snobbery died."
--Actor and writer Peter Ustinov

Chapter One
--December 1962
Paradise Valley, AZ
At The Boyle Mansion, Evening

So fast it all happened…

Elwood "Red" Boyle, wealthy industrialist and real estate magnate, 66, when he woke up later that night at the hospital, couldn't be certain that his fall down the stairs at his home was an accident. Or was it an attempt on his life—the third such incident in the last year. Three 'accidents'? And in that short a time frame. Not likely.

Fortunately, Boyle's only injuries from his tumble down the stairs were a mild concussion, a sprained left knee and a gash above his right eye.

A young Phoenix PD officer named Rudy W. (his last name was a long Polish one starting with the letter "W" that few of his fellow officers could spell or pronounce) was sent in to interview Boyle at the hospital about the incident. Rudy had sandy hair, a befuddled expression, and a partially successful light moustache. Red Boyle thought he looked about 12.

Rudy was skeptical of Red's suggestion that he may have been pushed down the stairs. Officer Rudy thought most likely Red, a portly gentleman of 275 pounds, had simply stumbled and fallen, possibly under the influence of alcohol.

That, Red knew, was precisely what the wagging tongues of the wealthy set in Scottsdale, and probably his three children as well, would think.

You couldn't tell now, but Red was once a nimble, strong, thin athlete. He aspired to, but failed miserably, at being a professional golfer. Then he aspired to, and succeeded admirably at, being a rich, rich man. As he gained wealth, he also gained weight. His body shape now resembled a large ripe pear.

After Officer Rudy W. left the hospital room, Red sat up in the bed, listened to his throbbing head, and went over the night's events. All he remembered was getting up from his Eames chair in the living room and padding across the plush carpet on silk-stockinged feet to the wine cellar door. He wanted to finish his evening with a small glass of port. He remembered the squeak of the door on his hinges as he opened it, then BOOM! He was at the bottom of the stairs groaning in pain.

The clueless copper was wrong, thought Red: *someone wants me dead.*

When he was discharged from Doctors' Hospital, located on 20th street in Phoenix, and driven home by his faithful butler Duxbury, he thought about the course of action he should take. Did someone really want to kill me? Or want to scare me? Was it a business rival—and there were many of those—who wanted to send me a message?

Red was somewhat lax about security at his 3,250 sq. ft. 6-bedroom home, just off Lincoln Drive in the wealthy community of Paradise Valley. This was a time in Phoenix, Arizona, when we left the doors unlocked during the day, and left the windows open at night, to let in the cool night air of the desert, a blessing indeed after the typically scorching Arizona days. It would not have been difficult for an intruder to gain entrance to Red's home.

The previous night had been the staff's day off. Red, divorced, was home alone.

Given the cops didn't seem to believe his story, and Red thought cops were generally useless anyway, he pondered a course of action. He had to put a stop to this, these threats. He had too much to do over the next few months to open his new golf resort/hotel on an island in the Bahamas—which he owned--on schedule. This was to be, after all, the crown jewel of Red's vast real estate holdings.

Red was a bully and a tyrant to work for, but his employees were remarkably loyal. Some had been with his company for 25 years. The reason? Red paid them extremely well. That secured their loyalty, even though he treated them like crap. Ah, the things we do for money.

He treated his three children just as badly but didn't compensate them nearly as well. He made them beg for nearly every cent.

The answer to Red's dilemma was right in front of him. He smiled as he thought of it, as they passed the huge property owned by his lifelong friend and fellow Princeton alum Judge (ret.) Roy Wilkinson. He knew Roy had a young protégé, pro golfer Tom Colt, who did private investigation work for the

Judge, helping his friends out of the kinds of messy personal and financial situations they often found themselves in.

The young Colt even helped the Phoenix PD solve the widely publicized murder of Lisa Luck, the wife of state Sen. Richard Luck, last year.

As part of the Grand Opening for his resort, Red Boyle had scheduled a Pro-Am golf event to showcase the beautiful course he had built there.

Red thought, *I'll call Roy and ask him to have Tom Colt play in the Pro-Am and attend the Grand Opening. He can be kind of undercover detective, snooping among the guests to see if one of them was the cause of all these dangerous near-misses I've been experiencing.*

Red chuckled when he thought of something else…his silly youngest daughter Patagonia (Patti) had kind of a crush on Tom Colt. She saw him win his first tournament in Las Vegas the previous year and was quite taken by him.

But his mood darkened quickly. Red Boyle's instincts told him another attempt on his life was likely to happen the week of the Grand Opening.

He was certain of it.

The following day, when he telephoned his old college buddy Roy Wilkinson and explained his concerns, the Judge reasonably asked, "Any idea who?"

"Hard to narrow it down. I know I'm an asshole, Roy. It's just…I enjoy it so much."

Red was wrong about the would-be assassin being in his home that night. He merely tripped on a loose floorboard and fell down the stairs. But he was correct that someone was plotting his demise at that exact moment. In fact, more than one someone.

He had a good idea of who these enemies might be. He decided to invite them to the Grand Opening of his resort. Why not force their hand, he thought. Red Boyle, throughout his life was a man who loved to make things happen.

Chapter Two
--March 10, 2005
Scottsdale, AZ
At Valley Vista Country Club

My name is Brooks Benton. I am honored to be your narrator for this story. I am a golf journalist, regarded as a near-legend in my profession and now twice the winner of the Writer of the Year Award presented by the Golf Writers Association of America. Who regards me as a legend? I can't share any specific names, but I'm sure they're out there.

For the last 20 years, I've been a Senior Managing Writer (i.e. ink-stained wretch) for *Championship Golf Weekly* magazine. I've also been an occasional contributor to the *New Yorker, Esquire* and *Playboy.*

I am 51 years old, born and raised in Brooklyn, NY. I am told I retain the characteristic abrasiveness of New Yorkers. I moved out west 20 years ago and fell in love with the wide-open spaces and deep blue skies.

I am one of the better golfers who write about golf. On a good day, I can break 80. I work out regularly to keep my waist trim and my arms strong. I have a full head of dark, wavy hair, a nose that is too bulbous for my liking, and I wish I were taller than my 5'6". Now you know enough about me. Probably more than you wanted to.

On to our real story, which was recently shared to me by Tom Colt. After much arm-twisting on my part, last year Tom agreed for me to help him write a series of books about his detective adventures, his life as a pro golfer, and the many romances he has had. What a life it's been! And he's still going strong today, believe me.

In his 20s, he was an impoverished young golf pro struggling to make it on the tough, competitive professional golf tour. This was the era that many believe was the Golden Age of Golf. Greats like Ben Hogan and Sam Snead were still strong competitors, and new stars like Arnold Palmer, Jack Nicklaus and Gary Player were emerging.

To earn extra cash, Tom Colt gave golf lessons to the affluent members of the posh Valley Vista Country Club in Scottsdale, Arizona. When one of his golf students was murdered, Tom assisted the Phoenix PD with solving the crime.

Chief Homicide Detective Ed Mathers was impressed with Tom's ability to solve the puzzle of the murder. As was Judge (ret.) Roy Wilkinson, one of the most powerful members of the Phoenix business community. He took the struggling young golf pro under his wing, inviting him to live rent-free at the spacious guest cottage located on his estate, and generously giving Tom expense money to play in pro golf tournaments.

There was just one catch: the Judge asked Tom to serve as a kind of private detective, helping the Judge's wealthy friends get out of the kinds of trouble rich folks often get into—money and sex troubles, usually.

Tom, who was raised, along with his tart-tongued twin sister Caroline, by his single mom after their dad was declared missing in the Korean War, had faced financial difficulties all his life. The Judge's offer was too good to pass up.

But Tom would learn the lesson so many others have, that a deal that seems too good to be true often comes with strings attached. Troublesome strings, even dangerous strings. Strings that create moral dilemmas for an earnest young man like Tom Colt.

Tom was a powerfully built man, 6'2" in height. He had strong shoulders and forearms, large hands—a great set of tools for a golfer. His hair, which he wore long for the times, was sun-streaked blond. He had an engaging smile and eyes that betrayed his personality: he had the Look of the Rascal.

Even with the Judge's generous financial assistance, as a pro golfer, Tom's success was spotty at best. He won just six pro tournaments (and two on the Senior tour) in his entire 30-year career. But his crime-solving career was amazingly successful. He and Det. Mathers teamed up to solve some of the most high-profile murder cases among the rich and famous of that time.

The reasons for Tom's tepid success on the golf tour were simple: he had trouble concentrating on golf for a full 18 holes. He had an active mind that could be easily diverted from focusing on such things as selecting the perfect club for a shot or remembering to keep his swing tempo slow.

He was known as one of the longest drivers of the ball in professional golf, so much so that the driver, the #1 wood, he used when he played the golf tour was on the display in the Golf Hall of Fame. It had been custom made for him by Judge Wilkinson, who named it the Colt .45. Unfortunately, Tom was never known as one of the most accurate drivers of the golf ball. His tee shots found many lonely places.

His other weakness was with the shortest club in the bag, the putter. He was never consistently good enough with putting to be a consistent performer as a pro golfer.

The Judge not only helped Tom financially but mentored him in the art and science of acquiring great wealth in the stock market and in real estate in the rapidly growing city of Phoenix, Arizona. Incredibly, the young man who started out as an impoverished assistant golf pro at Valley Vista Country Club, became the owner of that Country Club later in his life. I have hardly ever heard of an American success story that compelling.

Financial success never spoiled Tom. He remained humble and unpretentious. He lived in a modest condo along the 1st hole of Valley Vista CC, even though he could easily afford one of the mansions developers were plowing up the desert to build in north Scottdale. He told me living in his condo kept him close to the game he loved.

I will be telling you about young Tom Colt in the 1960s, and Old-Er Tom in 2005. Both men were fascinating characters, for different reasons. Setting Tom's story on paper has caused me to consider the questions: Do we really change as we get older? Hopefully we learn. But do we grow? Are we wiser?

I got to know Tom Colt when I joined Valley Vista Country Club five years ago. He was one of the most intriguing people I had ever met. And despite our completely different backgrounds, Tom's philosophy of life and mine were surprisingly similar.

The first book in the series we wrote together, *The Mystery of the Golf Club Murder*, as I write this, has just been released. The book has stirred up considerable controversy among the rich and pompous golf-y set that Tom and I wrote about. They took umbrage at how we portrayed these wealthy and powerful families in our book. But we told the absolute truth. As Scottish poet Robert Burns said,

> *O, wad some Power the giftie gie us*
> *To see oursels as others see us!*

But more about that later. Let's have Tom begin our next tale of his golfing and detective exploits, in his own words—with some expert editing by Your Narrator of course.

--January 1963

Tom Colt Continues Our Story:

Rich men love to collect expensive things--and people. Some collect wives or mistresses, or both. Some collect works of art and display them in their homes. Even if they are the only ones who ever get to see and enjoy them. Some wealthy men collect businesses, for the love of making money, for notoriety within the business community, and the sheer joy of having subordinates to order about.

You and I might be content with adding an 1895 Indian Head penny we've been looking for to our coin collections, or picking up a coffee mug from each of the places we visit, but The Rich possess a grander vision about collecting.

Elwood "Red" Boyle collected real estate properties: houses, hotels, golf courses, shopping malls. At the zenith of his house-collecting career, he owned 12 of them in the US, the Bahamas, Europe and the UK. It is reasonable for us to comment, you can only live in one house at one time, so what's the point?

The point, as with all avid collectors, is immortality. As long as you continue collecting, acquiring, building, you will never die. At least that's what the rich like Red Boyle believe. The auction houses that handle estate sales for the families of the rich know better, or course. It is the act of acquiring these things that brings these rich men the greatest joy. Possessing them is secondary, as odd as that may sound.

'Things' are very important to the rich. Sometimes important enough to kill for.

My name is Tom Colt. I am certainly not a rich man, far from it, but a keen, fascinated and often appalled observer of them. I am 28 years old, a professional golfer by trade. I compete on the pro golf tour and teach golf to the wealthy people who play at the exclusive—snobby, I mean--Valley Vista Country Club in Scottsdale, Arizona.

I also moonlight as a Private Detective, sometimes helping these same wealthy people at the Country Club to extricate themselves from trouble of a financial or personal nature. Trouble they almost always created themselves.

Judge (ret.) Roy Wilkinson, who got me started as a Private Investigator, and my mentor in the business world, once told me that many rich men are surprisingly stupid. I would add they are often arrogant and frequently careless, sloppy at covering their tracks. My investigative work involves a delicate balancing act because Judge Roy Wilkinson often hires me to help his rich friends escape legal troubles or even arrest, from my very good friend Det. Mathers of Phoenix PD—who expects me to assist the cause of justice.

I am valuable to both the Judge and Det. Mathers because of my position as a golf pro. The wealthy club members I give golf lessons to often take me into their confidence. The golf pro is somewhat like a psychiatrist—or perhaps like a priest taking Confession. The Club Members share their secrets with me. Even when I don't particularly want to hear them. You will be shocked by what they share.

In early 1963, I was to learn shortly that Elwood "Red" Boyle, his family, his friends, his enemies, had many, many secrets.

***

Brooks Benton Continues Our Story:

A Tuesday afternoon in January 1963. The weather was miserable, dismal. The slate grey sky wept cold drizzle onto the verdant, normally cheerful golf links at Valley Vista CC. January in the Arizona desert isn't necessarily as sunny as the Chamber of Commerce tells the prospective tourists from the Midwest in travel brochures. The few Club members who showed up that day to attempt a round of golf had long since retired to the warm clubhouse for drinks and sandwiches and boasts about how well they played.

The exception were two souls who had persevered all the way to the 18th hole, Tom Colt, 28, golf professional and Det. Ed Mathers, 38, of the Phoenix PD. They might seem unlikely friends, but over the course of the last two years had become best buddies—and teamed up to solve several crimes, including murders.

Mathers was a medium-height, stocky, nearly pudgy guy. He had dark thinning hair slicked down with a greasy hair tonic brand called Kreml. Think of a man who's a classy dresser and then think of the opposite—that was Mathers. Mismatched colors, baggy trousers and shirts. He spent very little of his cop's salary on wardrobe. When Tom first met him—Mathers signed up for golf lessons with Tom—he would not have believed that Mathers was the most brilliant detective on the Phoenix police force. He was a friendly, non-intimidating, unassuming guy—until he was prepared to make an arrest.

Tom and Mathers shared a passion for golf. When Mathers began taking lessons from Tom, he had possibly the worst golf swing Tom had ever seen: a brutal lunge at the ball followed by a gouging effort at the soft turf. With his iron shots, the divots often went further than the ball. The shame of it was that Mathers was muscular and coordinated. Tom quickly diagnosed remedies for the most glaring of Mathers' swing faults. The improvement in Mathers' swing was immediate and surprised even Tom.

Completely by chance, Tom also helped Mathers solve a crime—a bank robbery—while they were having lunch at a restaurant downtown. It was Mathers' turn to be shocked; his young golf instructor had a knack for deductive reasoning. A few months later, one of Tom's golf students from the Club was murdered at her home. Mathers was assigned to the case and immediately asked Tom for help because as an employee of the Club, the members often confided in him. They teamed up to solve the murder.

Mathers worked to transform Tom into a detective, just as Tom worked to transform the detective into a good golfer. Both efforts were succeeding, though works in progress in 1963.

As they trudged up the hill to the 18th green—they were both carrying their bags of clubs—no electric golf carts for these men--Mathers, as he often did, brought up a case he was working on.

Mathers was a cop who could seldom be found at the Police Headquarters in downtown Phoenix. He thought detectives do their best work outside of the office. His motto was, "Confined spaces lead to confined thinking." You were as likely to see him hiking in the desert, horseback riding, boating at Theodore Roosevelt Lake east of Phoenix or on the golf course. Wherever he was, his active mind was at work trying to put clues together.

As they finished their round of golf that day, Mathers told Tom, "One of the members here, guy named Elwood Boyle, Red he goes by, claims there have been attempts on his life. Three, in fact. We looked into the last one and couldn't decide if his claims had merit. He took a tumble down the stairs at his home. Says he was pushed."

"I've never met Mr. Boyle, actually," Tom said. He still, by force of habit, referred to the rich people in his orbit as Mr. and Sir.

"Very rich dude. Hotels, golf resorts, fertilizer plants, cattle ranches—all sorts of stuff he owns."

"Fertilizer plants…didn't know there was big money to be made in packaging and selling manure," Tom mused.

"It's not an easy business. You really gotta know your shit." Mathers smiled. Tom chuckled.

"Why does someone want him dead?"

"I thought you might have picked up some gossip about that in the locker room. Guys like that, it's either people they've screwed over in business, women they've screwed and then dumped, or their kids they've screwed up since childhood and want the parent dead to get their inheritance."

Tom laughed. "You paint such as pleasant picture of the rich."

"You know I'm right about them. They're usually up to no good."

Mathers wiped the drizzle off his face with his handkerchief and smiled. His dark hair was flopping down his forehead into his eyes. Tom and Mathers both looked a mess. They were soaked, cold, weary—an exhilarated from taking on the dual challenge of this extremely tough course and the tough weather. Golfers are a strange breed, pro or amateur.

For the record, Tom shot an even par 72 that day in the cold drizzle, Mathers managed an 84.

"Do you want me to do some sleuthing?"

"Yes. My gut feeling is, there's nothing to old Red's concerns, but sometimes my gut feelings are the result of the enchiladas I ate the night before and washed down with too many Dos Equis cervezas."

"I know someone who knows the Boyles well. I'll start with her."

"Good man."

***

Excerpt From *Gentleman Golfer Monthly* magazine – January 1963 edition, page 15

Our year-end review of the 1962 golf season would not be complete without mentioning Tom Colt, one of our game's most accomplished men-about-town. Though, sadly, not one of our game's most accomplished players.

Tom was inexplicably absent for most of the second half of the '62 pro tournament schedule, after he teased us again with flashes of brilliance early in the year, winning the Las Vegas Winter Fling Invitational in dramatic style with an eagle-2 on the final hole.

*At **Gentleman Golfer**, we wonder what amorous adventures Mr. Colt embarked upon later in '62 that took him away from tournament golf for so long.*

On second thought, perhaps we don't want to know. Ours, after all, is a publication for the whole family.

All kidding aside, it's a shame this talented young man isn't more dedicated to his golf career. If we were to grade Colt's performance for 1962, we would award him a B+ for skill, D- for attendance, C for effort, and of course A+ for fan engagement, particularly from female fans, as we have observed before.

Time to get your act together, Thomas J. Colt. You're not getting any younger. And great new players emerge each year, like young Jack Nicklaus in '62, winning the US Open for his first pro victory.

***

Caroline Colt, Tom's twin sister and partner in their fledgling private investigation firm, fumed as she tossed the magazine aside. She was seated on the green leather sofa in the home she shared with Tom. The home was the guest house on Judge Wilkinson's estate, which the Judge gave to Tom rent-free in return for his assistance as a part-time private detective.

Caroline moved in with Tom last year when she had a disagreement with her landlord. He believed she should pay the rent on time. She disagreed.

The design of the guest house echoed that of the main house on the Wilkinsons' property. Tom called it Southwest Modern. It had a dark red tile roof and white exterior with rust colored trim.

The color scheme of the guest house's interior was blue— Tom's favorite color, the exception being a large plush green leather sofa in the living room. Everything in the guest house looked brand new. Tom wondered if anyone had lived there before him.

The two bedrooms looked out to a small swimming pool and to Tom's delight when he moved in—a putting green—with a surface as true as the greens at Valley Vista Country Club where Tom worked.

The Judge made it his business to know everything about the people in his orbit. He knew Tom's favorite color and installed a putting green knowing Tom needed to work on that aspect of his golf game.

Part-time detective Tom was in the kitchen preparing their lunch, roast beef sandwiches on Kaiser rolls, with lots of tangy mustard dressing.

The young Colt twins loved to eat well, a trait they inherited from their mother, who owned one of the most popular, and consistently delicious, catering businesses in Scottsdale. Their mom catered to the same rich clientele Tom did with his golf lessons.

Caroline once had lovely shining brown hair and an attractive figure. She had the same interesting pale-blue eyes Tom had. She and Tom both had near-genius IQs. She had a beautiful singing voice and considerable acting talent; she had been the lead performer in high school musicals and dramas.

All this changed when their father disappeared in the Korean War. Caroline, who idolized their dad, lapsed into a lifestyle that included drug abuse and depression—and failure at several crappy jobs. Now, at 27, she was rail thin and looked older than Tom. Even her brown hair looked flat and tired. But to her credit, she was battling back—with lots of encouragement from her brother.

Caroline said, "Do the monkey brains who write this rag not know you were recovering from a near-fatal bullet wound. Can't you sue them for libel?" Caroline's voice had a dusky quality, as though her vocal chords were lightly sandpapered.

Tom brought the sandwiches out, gave one plate to Caroline. "Forget what they said. I think that writer is jealous. His nickname among the golf pros is The Warthog. Probably doesn't get a lot of dates."

Caroline took a big bite out of her sandwich. "This roast beef is yummy!" She took another large bite. "But I still think you should call our lawyer. Reporters are so full of themselves."

"Dear sister, you can't sue over an opinion. And second, I don't give a shit about his opinion. And third, we don't have a lawyer. Up until recently we couldn't afford one."

"Why is it called *Gentleman Golfer* when it is a bunch of assholes?"

"A magazine called *Assholes Talk Golf* probably wouldn't attract a wide readership."

Caroline grinned. She marveled at Tom's ability to take life's vicissitudes in relaxed style. She, on the other hand, tended to want to throttle people.

***

In early '63, Tom's current girlfriend was Katrina Stern. We must draw this careful distinction—current—because Tom's romantic situation could and did change suddenly and frequently. The romantic forecast for young Tom Colt was always stormy weather.

Tom and Katrina had both played for the college golf teams at Arizona State, but at that time never became friends. A chance meeting in '62 at the driving range in Tempe, Arizona, near their alma mater, resulted in a series of dates that culminated with a romance. Katrina was more accomplished as a pro golfer than Tom was, having already won three tournaments on the ladies' tour compared to Tom's single victory on the men's.

She was tall for a golfer, and trim. She had a runner's body, with great strong legs and calves. She had long, shining black hair.

She was an intense, extremely focused young woman who took her golf much more seriously—perhaps too seriously—than the easily distracted Tom. In competition, she had a steely glare; and off the course she often had face set in a frown. On the rare occasions when she did smile—her face was lovely, with pretty laugh lines and shining green eyes. She was one of those young women who are beauties and don't yet realize it.

Tom and Katrina helped each other immensely with their respective careers. Katrina helped Tom to become more focused during tournament rounds, to practice more, and to work on physical fitness. Katrina was a pioneer in recognizing the value of fitness in pro golf, like Gary Player was on the men's golf tour.

She also got Tom to quit smoking, which probably saved his life. In the early '60s, it was common for athletes to smoke, and even be pitchmen for tobacco company advertisements, as strange as that seems today.

Tom, for his part, advised Kat on lengthening her golf swing to add distance off the tee, which enabled her to win a tournament in Tucson in dramatic fashion in 1962. He also helped her to see the value to interacting with the fans and becoming more popular as a result, including wearing cuter, sexier clothes. His advice worked. She signed with agent Morty Fine of Mighty Fine Management, the same agent that represented Tom, and got several commercial endorsement deals.

The latest was sunglasses. In the early '60s, Cat Eye sunglasses were popular. The frames had an oval shape with wings on either end that sorta resembled how cats looked.

Morty got a deal for Kat with a manufacturer of sunglasses, logical since golfers often wear them. They came out with a "KAT-EYE" brand in her honor. The endorsement deal was lucrative. The only downside was she had to wear the ugly things at least one round at every tournament. She thought they looked hideous. Morty told her how great she looked in the frames. Like all great agents, Mr. Fine was skilled at the art of bullshit.

Katrina would never admit it, but she loved the attention she got from being in the sunglass advertisements. After writing about golf for twenty-five years, I can assure you that pro golfers have the large egos of entertainers whether they admit it or not.

In her love life, conflict perpetually bubbled and churned in Katrina's proud heart. The voice of tradition told her she should get married and settle down to produce between 3-5 kids. But her fiercely independent streak drove her to totally commit herself to being a golf champion.

Tom Colt as a potential boyfriend was a delightful compromise. She loved their days on the golf course together, practicing, sharing golf tips, encouraging each other, helping each other with their games. He was so handsome; she couldn't really believe he would want to be with her as boyfriend-girlfriend. But she sensed he did, and it excited her and made her feel almost beautiful—something she never had felt before.

Her older sister Ingrid was always regarded as the beauty in the family, with long blond hair and a great figure—she looked like a shapely maiden in a German beer hall--and an outgoing personality to match. Kat was the quiet, relentlessly determined girl who devoted herself completely to her golf career.

Kat had been born in Germany just before World War II. When she was still very young, the family emigrated to Brazil, then pulled up stakes again and moved to America. All this early upheaval left its mark on Katrina.

Achievement was like her fortress. Her protection. Having to leave everything behind—twice—scarred her. As did all the death and destruction she saw in the war. Lives ruined. Parents and kids separated. Families driven from their homes.

She was not sure she wanted to take the conventional route of marriage and kids. She had seen how in the blink of an eye you could lose everyone dear to you, lose all you've earned, lose your home. She came to believe life was a kind of marathon race and you had to stay ahead of everyone else. She was afraid if she relaxed, let up on her relentless pace to achieve, she could lose everything again.

After the hot and heavy romance blossomed with Tom in the middle of '62, Kat was starting to have reservations about their relationship. Theirs was not destined to be a blissful romance. Two things about Tom she couldn't accept: 1) She knew he would continue to see (read: have sex with) other girls; 2) His new career as a Private Eye scared her to death. She had two uncles who were in law enforcement. She knew the dangers of confronting criminals on a frequent basis.

Her first instinct was to cool it with Tom. But then he invited her to be his partner in a tournament sponsored by millionaire Red Boyle for the Grand Opening of his new resort in the Bahamas. She thought that perhaps being together for a week, on and off the golf course, at a romantic setting like an island, would give her clarity about their relationship.

Their schedules were also an obstacle on the path to true love. The tournaments they played on their respective golf tours took them out of town for weeks at a time. As the 1963 tournament season began, it was difficult for them to see each other for more than a day or two between events.

Another complication had arisen at the end of '62. Tom's friend (and Kat suspected his sometimes lover) wealthy divorcee Jilly Flannery, had introduced Kat to Stan Barker, the young energetic CEO of his family's successful sausage making company in Milwaukee. Stan was as golf crazy as they come. He belonged to a wonderful country club in Wisconsin, Blue Mound Golf & Country Club, and played four or five times a week during the summer (in Wisconsin, summer means the two weeks before and after the 4th of July).

At the ladies' pro tour event in Milwaukee the previous summer, Stan followed Kat all three rounds and invited her to dinner the Sunday night after the tournament concluded. She politely declined that night. But Stan was not easily put off.

He opened a processing plant in Phoenix, seeing the population growth that was coming to the southwest. In the 50s, Midwesterners had discovered Phoenix and its splendid winter climate as an escape from the cold, icy, dark places where they grew up. He also joined Valley Vista Country Club.

Spending time in Phoenix gave him the opportunity to pursue his interest in Katrina.

Stan looked pretty much like you'd expect a sausage-maker from Milwaukee to look. He had a happy, jowly face, dark hair trimmed short (you don't want hair falling in the knackwurst mixture) and was on his way to becoming pudgy. He tried to conceal a two-pack-a-day smoking habit; he believed smoking might help keep the weight off.

Serious-minded about his career, Stan was developing frown wrinkles on his forehead. He had the kind of strong, commanding voice many business leaders have. Stan was so enthusiastic about his business it was endearing to Kat. She had the same kind of fierce dedication to her golf career.

Stan was a sausage nerd: his passion in life was to work magic with the simple ingredients of meat and spices. At 39, he had remained a bachelor. His status as a young successful business owner gave him many opportunities to date lovely, lovely women, but so far nothing stirred his passions as much as grinding meat, fat and spices and tightly squeezing the resulting mixture into flavorful animal intestines.

Until he met Katrina Stern.

What drew Stan to Katrina? EVERYTHING ABOUT HER. The rhythm and power of her golf swing, the cute frown on her face when she was concentrating over a golf shot. And her German accent stirred deep ancestral feelings in Stan, whose family's sausage making skills were acquired in Bavaria.

Katrina's slender body and long, long legs particularly enthralled Stan. Possibly because he had always dated hefty Midwestern girls before. It never occurred to him that perhaps consuming his company's sausage products was partially responsible for the weight issues these young women faced.

The 1960s were a time when many people experimented with mind-altering drugs. Stan managed to make a product with the most potent drug from the '60s that you probably never heard of, which he named Barker Spicy Brazilian Bratwurst.

This Barker bratwurst had a secret ingredient. Only two people knew what the secret was, Stan and his plant manager in Waukesha, Wisconsin who had been working for the Barker family for 40 years and would never divulge what it was.

Many thought the secret ingredient was cannabis, because consuming the sausage did give you a feeling of bliss. Others got an elevated mood from eating it, so they guessed it might have cocaine, like Coca-Cola once did.

The secret was a Brazilian spice that Stan had imported. It arrived in a tightly-sealed package once per month. Only Stan and the plant manager were allowed to open it, and they added it to the sausage mix themselves during the meat grinding process.

The spice was…a powerful aphrodisiac.

The effect of the drug was to fan the flames of desire for both men and women, making them see members of the opposite sex as more attractive than perhaps they are.

If you've ever gone out on a Friday night, after a tough week at work, and drunk much more than you should have, then awakened the next morning next to someone very strange, and thought, *why did I do this? Why? This isn't like me.*

This was pretty much the effect of the Barker Spicy Brazilian Bratwurst.

For both men and women, it numbed that part of the brain responsible for Good Judgment.

***

Tom Colt was the most popular assistant pro Valley Vista Country Club ever had. The members, particularly the females, loved his charming, positive personality, his boyish, blond good looks, and his powerful golf game. Even though his success on the pro tour was spotty, Tom had on element of his game that impressed everyone: he was probably the most powerful, longest driver of the ball on tour at that time. He could even outdrive powerful young Jack Nicklaus by more than 10 yards. To see him blast a tee shot on a wide-open Par 4 or Par 5 was a thrill for golfers and golf fans of all ages and both sexes.

Tom was also a fabulous golf instructor. He had a knack for spotting flaws in a club member's swing and showing them how to correct the flaws in easy-to-understand terms. For some reason about 75% of his lesson clients were female...

Tom wasn't quite as popular with the management of Valley Vista Country Club, who paid his salary as assistant pro. He was a bit too brash, a bit too modern, for the stuffy men who ran the Club. So, it surprised him when The Club President, Wesley Stoneman III, asked him to select a new piano player for the sedate and stuffy main dining room.

Tom Colt Continues Our Story:

Stoneman had a left-to-right combover hairdo on his egg-shaped noggin, one of the guys who use the thin remaining strands to try to disguise the fact they're bald. Never works, but they keep trying. He made his fortune in the cement biz and his views on most every subject were set in concrete, too. He wore thick glasses with wire rims.

After I sat down in his office, he said, "I asked you to do this chore because you like music and shit. I don't know why we can't just play golf at a golf club. Now, it seems the members demand I provide needless and expensive entertainment. What's next? A swimming pool for the kiddies? Not on my watch. Anyway, show me the guy you picked."

I handed Stoneman a file folder with a photo and resume of the musician I selected. His name was Raymond B. Lasalle.

Stoneman scrutinized the file with narrowed eyes. Raymond was slight of build and had those long, beautiful fingers needed to play piano. He had short-cropped, stubbly dark hair. In the photo he was dressed nattily in a dark, pin-striped suit and silver tie.

"A young guy...23 it says here. Hope he's not one of those Rock and Rollers. Egad they're insufferable."

"He's classically trained on the piano and knows show tunes and all the favorites from the American Songbook. I heard him play a few selections at a jazz club in Phoenix. He's great. Even composes tunes."

"No, no. Not some jazzbo from south Phoenix. That won't go over at Valley Vista."

"Maybe don't look at where he came from, but what he can do. Just an idea, sir."

Being insubordinate to Stoneman, or stonebrain as I called him, was always great fun for me.

"I see Roy Wilkinson has given you his long-winded speech about not lumping people into groups, we're a nation of individuals, each of us unique, and that's what makes us successful, blah, blah."

"Yes, and I agree with the Judge. There's no more individualistic profession than mine, pro golf. We dig our livelihood out of the ground, by ourselves, every day."

"Of course you agree with Judge Wilkinson's views. He is grooming you to be his son."

"I don't--"

"His boy Drew, whom he worshipped, was killed in a plane crash. You are, like, the replacement. And you lost your father in the War. You fill the gaps in each other's life. Why else would he spend all this money sponsoring you on tour. You're far from the best young golfer out there, and the Judge always seeks out the best. I mean, the young Englishman Rodney Burkett has already won 5 events. You've only bagged one win and as I recall it was mostly luck."

My response was the shrug of complete indifference.

Stoneman closed the file. "Okay, we'll give your individualistic piano player Raymond a chance."

"Thank you, sir."

"But I completely disagree with you and Roy Wilkinson: where we come from tells the whole story."

I nodded. Didn't want to argue with this fool.

"Never let it be said that Wes Stoneman III doesn't change with the times."

"The thought never entered my head. And sir, I tried to get Ed Ames or Perry Como, but the Club couldn't afford them on a nightly basis."

"No need to be snide, Tom. Remember no matter how popular you are with the female members, you're just an employee here. And a lower level one at that. Not part of management like for some reason you think you are."

I nodded with a level expression, thinking, *oh, I remember, every time I pick up my puny paycheck. Last year I earned twice as much being a part-time detective.*

Stoneman tossed the file down on his desk. "Have this Raymond guy go to personnel to sign an independent contractor contract."

"Thanks, sir. I promise you won't be disappointed."

"Good. But tell him no Rock and Roll crap. Soft, quiet dinner music. Music that is good for digestion. I don't like surprises."

I nodded again, thinking, *Won't you be surprised when I own this Country Club someday.*

Chapter Three
Are You Game, Tom?

Brooks Benton Continues Our Story:

One of the coolest features of the Guest House where Tom and Caroline lived, thanks to Judge Wilkinson, was the practice putting green in the back of the property, located adjacent to the other cool feature, a heated swimming pool.

Poor putting was the feature of Tom's golf game that kept him from reaching his full potential on the professional golf tour. He was unable to consistently make the 15-foot putts that the great champions make when the game is on the line. Tom frankly did not have the calm nerves required for good putting.

Now he faced an added complication. His nerves were even jumpier after he had been shot in the shoulder last year. He physically recovered quickly—the bullet passed right through with minimal damage to nerves, muscles or blood vessels. The mental damage unfortunately was much more severe.

In the early events on the '63 golf tour, Tom had played well enough to be encouraged for the upcoming Phoenix Open, his hometown event. He was hitting the ball long and straight. The one issue he faced was his nerves. He flinched whenever there was an unusual noise, and at crowded golf tournaments there are always noises. The worst experience was at the Palm Springs tournament when a car backfiring caused him to knock a ten-foot putt twenty feet past the hole.

That night in early February, he went outside to the little putting green behind the guest house and practiced his stroke by the light cast out from the porch. His mind turned not to thoughts of golf, but thoughts of girls. Katrina was wonderful. He loved so many things about her. He smiled when he recalled the great fun they had on the golf course, and in bed.

But he couldn't help reflecting on his wild romance last spring and summer with Julia Wilkinson, the Judge's daughter, an aspiring singer and accomplished femme fatale. He looked up at the lights shining brightly from the Main House, as the Judge called it, and wondered where the well-traveled Julia was, when she would be returning home.

Nothing in Tom's young life could compare to the excitement of when he met Julia. She and her singing group,

The Loose Impediments, were performing at a party after last year's Phoenix Open.

When she took the stage, Tom's life course was altered forever. When a man sees an extraordinarily beautiful woman for the first time, his reaction can be centered in one particular organ. Or his entire body can become animated with renewed energy, quickening hopes. For Tom, it was the latter.

She had wavy blonde hair styled with an exciting flip where it kissed her shoulders. It was rose-gold colored hair that shone exquisitely in the lights above the little stage. She was wearing a soft white turtleneck sweater, without a bra, to the delight of the gentlemen in the room. Her breasts were, well, awesome, with a bounce that matched the rhythm of her songs.

She had deep blue, expressive eyes. Her face was perfectly proportioned. High cheekbones. Lush lips. No flaw worth mentioning except a small scar on her chin. Her dark blue skirt was well above the knee. Her legs were as lovely as the rest of her.

A cute touch for this all-girl band was that they wore golf shoes with the spikes on the soles removed.

The other girls in *The Loose Impediments* band were attractive. But Tom saw only Julia. He believed every love ballad she sang that night was just for him.

He probably fell in love with Julia Wilkinson that night.

Overly optimistic Tom soon jumped to the conclusion that Julia was falling in love with him as well. That notion was blown to bits one night when Tom returned from a tournament in Florida a day early and found a naked Julia making love to her boyfriend, a wealthy mining heir named Derrick Rhodes, in of all places the little swimming pool behind the guest house where Tom lived.

Julia later acted like it meant nothing, but even Tom at 27 was not that naive.

Fortunately, Katrina entered his life and healed his broken heart. But Julia's life was full of crisis and drama, and Tom was drawn in again when the boyfriend and Julia got into such a violent argument, provoked by the guy severely beating her due to ironically, jealousy over her relationship with Tom, that she stole Tom's private investigator gun and threatened to kill Derrick.

Tom arrived just in time to defuse the situation, but not before Julia—accidentally we hope—shot Tom in the shoulder, ending his golf tournament season for 1962.

Julia went off to New York to stay with the Judge's sister until the scandal died down. Tom lied about what happened to protect Julia. Det. Mathers knew he lied but reasoned that you can't ask a man to send his dream to the slammer.

Part of the reason for Julia's erratic behavior was that she suffered from a mysterious mental disorder, with few treatment options in the early '60s, what we know now as bi-polar disorder. She had tried several different medications to cope with it, with only partial success.

Tom was forbidden by the Judge to mention Julia's role in his being shot, but a country club is a nest of gossips and many people suspected what happened. He struck a shrewd deal with the wily Judge, especially for a young man not experienced in business. In exchange for his silence, he was to receive a 5% interest in several of the Judge's upcoming real estate projects.

In one of life's strange twists, Tom being shot by a girl he thought he was falling in love with sparked the beginning of his success in business, and his journey from poor boy to affluent man.

Tom stopped his putting practice and gazed up at the serpentine path Julia had taken one memorable evening from the Main House to the Guest House, wearing only a short nightgown, and they made love on the green leather couch in the living room.

It was, and would always remain, one of the Top 5 moments in Tom Colt's life.

We would be reasonable to call Tom Colt a fool for love. Julia had visited Tom that night with the sole objective of offering him her perfect body. Tom did not know at the time the other side of the transaction was that Tom would be available to help her when the next crisis arose, and the one after that.

The Wilkinsons, Judge and Daughter, were transactional people. They never gave anything away.

***

Tom Continues Our Story:

All good detectives need solid, reliable information sources. One of the best for me was Jillian (Jilly) Flannery, a wealthy divorcee 17 years my senior. No one was more wired into the whispers, gossip and scandals of our little golf-y community than she.

And with Jilly an added bonus was that we had great sex while she was dishing on the wealthy set she was an integral part of, and I was still on the periphery of.

I met her in the summer of '61 when she started taking golf lessons from me. We got on great and quickly became friends. She and I had remarkable chemistry despite our very different stations in life. Jilly was gorgeous, with a curvy figure and a smile that simply sparkled.

She attended every party that mattered, and her presence immediately made the party a memorable one. She didn't walk into a room, she effervesced. Her personality was so bubbly that she seemed tipsy even before she sipped her first Manhattan of the evening. She wore her glossy brown hair in a short bob style with gold highlights. The effect was much like an elegant lampshade.

Jilly spent a fortune on stylish clothes, but oddly enough enjoyed taking them off as much as putting them on.

These days, we might call Jilly a cougar. But in 1963 I just called her a hell of a lot of fun.

And I should mention she was an excellent golfer. She frequently paired with her best female friend Missy Gould in local amateur team tournaments, and those two frequently won.

She started out shanty Irish in Chicago and achieved a meteoric rise to wealth. Continuing our theme of the rich collecting things, Jilly collected rich old men as husbands. By 1963, she was lace curtain Irish.

When I began giving Jilly Flannery golf lessons the previous summer, she was already a fine player. I just gave her game a bit of a tune-up. One night at a party she and I ended up in an upstairs guest bedroom at the hosts' house. We found we were compatible in bed as well. Our relationship was pure fun. Neither of us had expectations about our being together forever—or even the next day.

One night at dinner Jilly explained it to me this way, "You and I would never work out as a couple. And not because I'm slightly older than you are. As much as I love young strivers like you, I need a man who's already made it, who's already there. I don't want to relive the struggles I had to rise to the position I am at today. Also, you'll want children, and I don't at all. Never have. I know that is an odd thing for a woman to say."

It surely was in 1963.

Our conversations in bed were always lively—she bounced from subject to subject and challenged me to keep up. She was bouncy during sex, come to think of it.

One morning I was lying next to Jilly Flannery in her ocean-liner sized bed, with the frilly rose comforter and the fluffy pillows. We were naked, as we almost always ended up when we got together. Her head was resting on my shoulder.

"Where did the term hard-boiled detective come from?" Jilly asked me out of the blue.

"World War I. Some sergeants were considered 'good eggs' by the enlisted men, others, the rougher ones, were termed 'hard-boiled'."

From then on Jilly called me The Soft-Boiled Detective. As she put it, "Over easy. At least in my bed."

Then she bounced to: "I'm from Chicago. We're all born Democrats. There's a little D on the bracelet they put on your tiny wrist in the hospital. I was one of the few who broke away and voted GOP. My older half-brother, the Phoenix Police Chief, the honorable James Flannery, was furious with me when he found out. I told him, 'I like IKE. Deal with it'. He backed down. Men aren't as tough as they seem, you know. Even police chiefs."

I nodded in complete agreement with that sage observation. I would never describe myself, for example, as tough.

Soft-Boiled Detective. I chuckled at that one.

Brooks Benton Continues Our Story:

Later that same morning...

"Could you do me a favor?" Jilly enquired.

"Anything within reason, or perhaps a little beyond."

She giggled. "Stand over by the window, with that beautiful morning light shining on you."

Tom got a quizzical look, then pulled off the covers, got out of the bed and complied.

"Turn just a little bit, please," she added. He did. She'd seen him without clothes many times, but that one time made her gasp with wonder. The light bathing Tom from the bay window was like out of a Renaissance painting.

"You want to take some Polaroids?" he joked.

"I could sell them for a lot of money in the Ladies Locker Room at The Club. But then again I already have a lot of money. So much I have trouble keeping track of it all."

Seeing that gorgeous man, young Tom Colt standing there, completely naked, meeting her warm smile with one of her own, was a wondrous image Jilly would never forget.

She said, "No, I think I'll keep you, keep your body, all for myself."

You are my reward, for all the difficult things I've had to do, she thought as her eyes roamed over every inch of his body, stopping a few times at one spot. Not even the bullet scar on his left shoulder could mar his beauty to her. It somehow enhanced it. Jilly had been hit by many shots, metaphorically speaking, over the course of her life.

Jilly was not a woman who paused to appreciate what she had. Whatever she had, she always wanted more. But seeing Tom standing by that window, illuminated by the brilliant desert sunshine, was one of the few instances when time stopped. For a moment, she was totally satisfied.

"If I had clay, I would make a sculpture of you. Of course, my sculpture would feature a larger--"

"I'm sure that would be the most prominent feature."

They both laughed.

Jilly, her eyes still fixed on Tom's chiseled form, stopped a few moments to consider what she was most enamored of, Tom Colt or Tom's cock. Both, in equal measure, she thought affirmatively. And she intended to have both as long as she wished.

Tom's skill at getting people to tell him their secrets, extremely valuable for a private detective, extended to his social life. Jilly told Tom Colt things she told no one else, not even her bestie Missy Gould. Those two girls shared everything, even the sordid details of her husband Sterling Gould's many affairs with women less than half his age.

Jilly said, in a wistful voice, "One day my first husband called me and made me drop everything I was doing to go to his office to give him a blow job. He said he was having <u>such</u> a stressful day. He made me kneel behind his desk. I felt like his degraded whore. I've hardly ever felt worse in my life than that day."

"I'm sorry..." Tom said, not knowing what else to say, other than wishing he could go back in time and punch the bastard's lights out. But he also wondered about Jilly, *why did she do it?*

"Every hot round in bed with you wipes away another bad memory like that one. But you know, I've realized those awful memories are how I got all these Things." She swung her hand softly to indicate the Things. "I couldn't bear working as a secretary or a stewardess. I wanted these Things."

Jilly's words, "I wanted these Things," would haunt Tom throughout 1963. The upscale people's need for Things would lead to several murders. Tom had trouble relating to their obsession with money. Not that long ago, he lived in a bare apartment on 16th street with a sagging sofa, a dining room table with wobbly legs, and his golf clubs in a corner by the front door. And he was fine with that, then. If he was teeing it up the next day on a challenging golf course, he was happy. Tom in his twenties had not yet discovered the magic of Things.

She gave Tom a sweet kiss on the chest. It was soft and warm.

"Speaking of the Wilkinsons..."

Tom chuckled because the conversation had just been re-routed, Jilly style.

"You told me once that Julia paid you this huge compliment--that she admired how you were grateful for all the good things you have. To me, she's just big breasts, no brains, but she nailed that one. I admire you for the same reason."

She turned and sat up in bed, the sheet falling away. She looked at Tom with that sparkling smile of hers. "Golly, gee whiz, wow, hot damn---you make me feel wonderful."

She sighed and leaned back on the pillows momentarily, then an idea showed on her face. *What is our next topic going to be?* Tom wondered. Jilly frequently caused conversational whiplash.

"Any new cases going on?"

"Yes. The Judge asked me to go to the Grand Opening of a golf resort. The owner is a friend of the Judge's, the guy thinks someone is trying to kill him."

"Red Boyle."

"How'd you know?"

"I'm invited to the Grand Opening, too. So are half the members of Valley Vista."

"Can you think of anyone who might want to kill Mr. Boyle."

She laughed, loudly. "I can't think of too many people who wouldn't. He's what I call a GPM, Gross Pig Man. He's deliberately rude, he's a glutton, he jerks people around for the hell of it, and he also has uncontrolled flatulence."

"He farts?"

"All the time. He's had some gastric condition since his early 30s. Major Stinko. See what I mean, GPM."

Jilly let Tom puzzle over that cryptic remark. Then pulled the covers off and hopped out of bed. "Well, I guess we can't just lie here all day in a romantic dream. Wait, why the hell not? I'm rich!"

He tossed a playful pillow at her. "You are such a goof!"

"Let's take a shower—together of course—then I'll fix you a big manly-man breakfast. And we'll go out and play some golf. I feel like I could birdie every hole today."

She started for the bathroom, then turned back to Tom. Her body was always a thing to behold: curvy hips, breasts prominent and proud, a cute and taut backside. And a sparkly, confident smile that showed she knew she was beautiful.

"You are such a good listener, I feel like I can tell you everything, bare it all to you."

"Evidently," he said.

She giggled. "Thank you, Thomas J. Colt. For making me so happy. See, I'm learning to be grateful, too."

After their shower, Tom sipped coffee and sat at the kitchen table while Jilly cooked breakfast. She was a skilled chef. She was pretty much skilled at everything she set her mind to. She popped 4 thick, aromatic sausage links into a skillet.

"This is a new flavor of Barker brand sausages, Barker's Spicy Brazilian Bratwurst. Haven't tried them yet. They better be good. They cost a fortune, like 20 bucks a package. The label on them says, 'You Must Be 21 or Older to Purchase This product'. Kinda weird, eh? Special order only. Test marketed to the country clubs like Valley Vista. Stan bought a mailing list of the members. I think he did it just to appeal to the biggest snobs."

"So you bought three packages at least."

"Yes, of course, what's your point?"

She tried to frown but it turned into a smile. They greedily consumed the sausages, with a parmesan cheese and mushroom omelet. They both loved the Barker Spicy Brazilian sausages--never had a sausage quite like it.

"You and I should team up in Red Boyle's tournament at the Grand Opening."

"Oh, sorry. I'm paired with Katrina Stern."

"Right, your non-spicy Brazilian."

"Please retract the cat claws. And Kat is German, she and her family only lived in Brazil for a bit, after the war."

"Enough about her. Anyway, the week on Red's little island should be a blast. My gossip hotline tells me there may be some strange happenings unrelated to golf."

"Would you care to explain?"

"Surely. The chickens may be coming home to roost for Red, old bastard that he is. He thinks I'm in love with him or something, so he's told me some juicy bits about his business career, but I think he's repulsive."

"That's not really elaborating."

"Okay, okay, Sam Spade. Back off with the interrogation." She had a wry smile. "He's done a lot of people wrong. You know what I say about Roy Wilkinson being manipulative—it goes double for Red Boyle. His business practices could be described as sharp, sleazy and occasionally lethal. He takes special joy in ruining other businessmen."

"Swell guy…"

"I also know he has a thing for young actresses at his Boyle Academy of the Performing Arts. Not worth it for a girl to get free tuition if you ask me. Some of things he asks them to perform on him wouldn't qualify as Arts. Ha!"

"Great info," Tom said, finishing off his eggs. "Amazing the things you find out."

"Think of me as your undercovers agent."

Tom got the joke and chuckled.

"But that's all I can say for now. You know how I hate spreading gossip."

"Yes, you're the soul of discretion."

"Sometimes I get the feeling you are making fun of me."

"Never. My admiration for you knows no bounds."

"Or at least for certain parts of me."

"Can't get enough of those parts…"

Tom helped Jilly clean up the kitchen after breakfast. When they finished, they both had a sheen of sweat on their foreheads even though Jilly kept the household temperature quite cool.

They turned to each other at the identical moment and both got a look of feverish passion in their eyes. They both laughed and smiled. They both had the overwhelming urge to make love again. Tom couldn't explain why. He felt like he was losing control…

The clothes they had just put on were strewn on the carpet as they raced back to the bedroom.

"What's gotten into us this morning?" she said as she tore the bedspread off and they tumbled onto the soft sunshine-yellow sheets.

"I felt so warm, kind of like hot lava was rising in me."

"Yes," she exclaimed, "like I'm ready to erupt."

"Maybe it was the sausages."

She nodded furiously, exclaimed, "I'll buy more tomorrow."

***

At the Guest House at the Wilkinson Estate the Next Day...

Tom Colt Continues Our Story...

A firm knock was heard by the budding detective, me, on the sliding glass door that led to the patio. I got up from the red bar stool by the kitchen counter and glanced over. It was Judge Roy Wilkinson.

The Judge was an older man when I met him in '62. He was born in 1899. But he had an ageless quality, like he's always been there, and always would. Two qualities struck me when we met: he was a man constantly in motion, doing deals, planning deals, building, transforming the little desert city of Phoenix into his hoped-for metropolis. The second was his chain smoking. I hardly ever saw him without a cigarette in his hand. Smoking had given the Judge's voice a rough quality, which made him seem even more formidable.

He was just under 5'9", but to me he seemed much taller. He wore his iron-grey hair cropped short in a military-style haircut. His smile was one of his unique features—it never seemed to have joy or mirth behind it. It was just a display of small chisel-like teeth. The Judge had that quality of gravitas to an extent I had never encountered before or since.

Some in the Phoenix business community said Judge Roy Wilkinson ran the city of Phoenix. That was an exaggeration of course. No one man could run a city as large, and rapidly growing, as Phoenix.

Except the Judge sorta did, everyone agreed.

The Judge was in one of his affable moods that morning. He was a nice fellow unless facing a threat to his business empire. Then, look out.

I opened the door, and the Judge came inside. He was casually dressed in shorts and a tee shirt, having just finished mowing his lawn. Yes, this rich, rich man still did routine chores like that, saying it reminded him where he came from and how hard he must work to keep all he has earned.

He noticed the *Gentleman Golfer Monthly* magazine on the coffee table.

"The best approach to dealing with your enemies is to say snarky things about them, just short of spreading vicious rumors, if possible repeat things that damage their standing in the community or their workplace. Then forgive them completely for what they did to you. Then forget them. Never let your adversaries occupy valuable real estate in your head."

I thought it remarkable that buried somewhere in the Judge's harsh advice was Jesus' admonition to forgive your trespassers.

"You told me the author of that negative piece about you has the face of a warthog. Just repeat that every chance you get, and others will be repeating it as well."

He paused to light up a cigarette. Now a non-smoker, I never liked the smell of smoke in my house, except that in this case, technically, it was his house.

He continued: "Don't give a moment's thought to what those piffle peddlers say, son. Because they don't give much thought to what they publish. And never accept criticism from someone whose advice you could not trust."

"I'll remember that." I remembered everything the Judge told me down the years. That's how formidable a figure he was in my life.

A quick puff on the unfiltered Pall Mall, then he said, "I have something much more important for my resident detective geniuses to work on. A case... And this time you're going to prevent a murder, not investigate one..."

He paused, looked at me with that odd smile of his.

"Are you game?"

Chapter Four
--March 8, 2005
Scottsdale, Arizona

Brooks Benton Continues Our Story...

Yes, Tom was game. And what a case it turned out to be.

I joined Valley Vista CC five years ago and over that time have gotten to know Tom Colt as well as I know my own brothers. Even before we began our book collaborations, I played golf with him at least once a week. You get to know a fellow when you golf with him regularly. The long intervals between shots in our great game allow for revealing conversations. And you can see relatively quickly whether your playing partner is a gentleman or a boor—or perhaps even a jerk that should best be avoided.

Well, Tom is a true gentleman. By any standards he is a huge financial success, but he remains as unpretentious as when he was a struggling young assistant golf pro. He has also been able to remain physically young—he looks at least 20 years younger than his age. Still has the narrow waist, strong arms and proud posture he had back in the '60s. His powerful arms and shoulders were developed from a night-and-weekend job he had in high school after his father was lost in the Korean War. He worked at a high-volume produce packing plant on the west side of Phoenix, carrying 100 lb. crates of fruits and vegetables to delivery trucks.

His blond hair has a touch of grey in it, but that's the only notable evidence of age on the guy. Remarkable! I'm only 51 and I look older than Tom does. I do my best to not be pissed off about this.

One of the things that amazed me about Tom Colt was how people are drawn to him. He has that ineffable quality of charisma. At Valley Vista Country Club, you can find him every Saturday night on the casual dining porch that looks out over the 18th hole of the golf course. He orders the same entrée each Saturday, a medium-rare strip steak with a garlic-sauteed mushroom cap. He drinks several glasses of red wine and socializes with the members and their guests who want to meet and hear about the remarkable adventures Tom had over the course of his life.

Since I am nearly 20 years younger than Tom, one of things that rankled me about him is how young, beautiful women are still attracted to him. When he and I dine, they pay great attention to him and very little to me. I know I'm not handsome, famous or rich like he is, but I am, after all, a legendary sportswriter. Writing, as you know, is a rare and marvelous skill.

This disparity in our popularity used to bother me. But after working on the first book collaboration with Tom, I came to understand he richly deserved all the attention, all the adulation. He was the most generous person I ever met. When he read the finished manuscript for our first book, he was so effusive with praise I almost cried. And I am a tough kid from New York City. I never cry.

Instead of being jealous of Tom and all the fans he had, all the ladies who adore him, I decided to study how he did it, how he gave absolutely no thought to the passage of time. This is what I came up with:

Tom Colt's Secrets to Staying Young
1. Drink red wine but avoid all hard liquor.
2. Fortify your physical strength by eating red meat.
3. Fortify your mental strength by reading at least two improving books per week.
4. Populate your life with beautiful, intriguing, complicated women.
5. Avoid politics—and politicians—as much as possible. They are toxic.
6. Play Golf Every Day, even the rainy ones or the cold ones. No wimping out.
7. Tell those close to you how much you appreciate them.
8. Be grateful for every blessing that comes your way. That guarantees you'll attract more blessings.
9. Be financially generous with those friends who need your help. You can always make more money, but good friends are hard to come by.
10. Be open to all new possibilities, including the possibility of falling in love.

One of the blessings—and possibilities--that has come Tom's way is named Carmen Lopez. She is the Head Waitress, and Captain of the Waitstaff, at Valley Vista, a position of considerable responsibility given how hard to please rich people are.

Carmen is a beauty, a stunner, probably in her mid-30s I would guess, and divorced a number of years ago. She has long shiny dark hair, warm expressive eyes, a bright smile, and possibly the loveliest legs I have ever seen. The waitress uniform at Valley Vista features short enough skirts to show these legs off to great advantage. It's not just they are shapely, it is how Carmen moves, with a casual, elegant grace.

I could watch her all day. Carmen's amazing legs, those shapely calf muscles, came from horseback riding. She grew up on a ranch in New Mexico, I learned, intrepid investigative reporter that I am.

As Tom once told me, she's the Princess of the Country Club. Every man between 21 and 81 wants to be with Carmen. And the junior boys want to hurry up and turn 21, with the hope they could ask her out before their dad does.

Well, as you guessed, Carmen only has eyes for Tom Colt. They have a strong friendship that I would say probably blossomed into love at least two years ago. But to my knowledge, they have never even gone out on a date. Their difference in ages might seem the obvious reason for this, but Carmen, I found out thorough the staff grapevine at the Club, gave this no thought. Tom, however, did. Their relationship existed only at the Country Club where both put in 50+ hours per week, happily put in the hours I should add.

They looked at each other so fondly, it really amazed me they never tried to take their relationship outside the Club. I couldn't understand what held them back. I almost wanted to play matchmaker, but my own efforts at romance have been so ineffective, I might botch it up for them. And I must confess I had a notion that Carmen and I...well, you can guess.

That night, I was dining with Tom when Carmen stopped by our table and sat down.

Carmen spoke in a warm, soft, reassuring drawl, the voice of a true Westerner. Not a slow drawl, though. When she got excited, her speech had the pace of a Ferrari.

The men of Valley Vista CC heard many different things in Carmen's voice. For Tom, the sound of her voice held deeper meaning: it meant all things were possible for him, even now.

Her voice to me conveyed an inner strength. She was up for any and all challenges in life.

She turned to me, "I just finished reading your book! I loved it. Brooks, you are one hell of a great writer. The way you told the stories of Tom's life. It's like I was there. It was...one of the best books I've ever read. And I've loved to read, ever since I was a little girl. Writers are so amazing!"

I thought, *screw Tom Colt. I'm in love with this girl. We leave for Las Vegas later tonight. One of those all-night wedding chapels. Yes, that's the ticket. Carmen Benton is a lovely name, don't you think...*

But then Tom took her hand in hers as we talked. She leaned in close to him. Their faces softened to a warm glow when they looked at each other. One does not need a PH. D in romantic psychology, or even be a skilled romance writer like Nora Roberts, to recognize these obvious signs of love. Dammit.

"I want to warn you both that some of the members are on the warpath. They all have been reading the book and some of them don't like how their relatives were depicted."

"It was all true," I said.

"Yes, but they are rich. They are not used to anyone calling bullshit on them," Carmen said.

Tom nodded, in agreement with her. Then she leaned over and kissed Tom. "You were brave to tell your story."

"Don't I get a kiss? I was brave, too."

"You <u>might</u> get your wine glass refilled." She smirked, got up and walked back to the kitchen. I didn't care that she had just turned me down flat. I admired those legs as she walked...oh, my, that girl. I wish she'd realize that writers make the best lovers because they have such great imagination...

Tom and I finished our desserts, chocolate fudge brownies with a raspberry liqueur sauce, and I begged off for the evening. The publisher had a series of calls set up for me with news outlets to promote the book. I arranged for Brooks Benton to do most of the publicity. Not Tom Colt. I'm vain, I admit it.

As I got up from the table, Kathleen Prentiss-Valenzuela walked over to Tom's table, and he pulled out a chair for her to sit down. She was mentioned in our first book, the daughter of a woman who was murdered, Lisa Prentiss Luck. This became the first murder case Tom and Det. Mathers solved together.

Kathleen never knew her mother, who had put her up for adoption. A wonderful and prosperous family in Mexico, the Valenzuelas, adopted her and did a terrific job raising her. Kathleen learned later on about what happened to her mother and Tom Colt's role in bringing the killer to justice. They had been friends ever since.

Kathleen was a gracious woman who looked very much like her mother, I had heard. Seeing her always caused Tom to pause and briefly go to a distant place in his mind...

We exchanged greetings.

"I don't want to interrupt," Kathleen said, nervously, it seemed to me.

She handed Tom a small envelope. Looking puzzled, he took it in his hand.

"I need to talk to you about something important. Something I've been wondering about for a long time."

Tom was even more puzzled. Kathleen's expression was unusually serious.

"Please read this note and reflect on the two questions I asked."

"Okay," Tom said vaguely. And Tom was seldom vague.

"Thank you," Kathleen said with great warmth and sincerity and then, still exhibiting nerves, walked out the door and back into the clubhouse.

"See you tomorrow," I said, and gave Tom a friendly pat on the shoulder. I followed Kathleen out the door.

Tom stayed and ordered another glass of wine, then opened the envelope. The two questions were not a mystery, not a surprise, but they certainly qualified as important.

***

On the south wall of the Gentlemen's Lounge (barroom) at Valley Vista CC, there is an enlarged photo of Tom Colt in his 20s, holding the trophy from one of his pro tournament victories. His smile was triumphant, beaming. His face was a boyish, thinner version of the face Tom shows to the world today. You can also clearly see mischief in his eyes: that Look of the Rascal that Tom was known for. He retained that look to this day.

Carmen Lopez, stopping by the photo on her way to the kitchen, wagged a testy finger at the smiling 28-year-old Tom Colt in the photograph, holding the tournament trophy he won in '63.

Softly, she said to the photo, "Young Tom, I wish you could speak to your older self and tell him that he and I would be great together. He doesn't take my word for it. I've practically thrown myself at him. He's stubborn, your older self is. I'm here every day and sometimes I think he doesn't even see me.

I sign up for extra hours so I can be near him. He takes my breath away when he smiles at me."

Not realizing her voice was getting louder, she added, "Talk to him for me, PLEASE! This is going to drive me crazy!"

Wise old piano player, Raymond B. Lasalle, who played piano there since the '60s, and was the second biggest rascal at Valley Vista CC after Tom himself, changed what he was playing to a jazzy tune of his own composition: *Doctor says, There's No Cure For Love.*

"My my," he said, smiling, remembering young Tom and how stubborn he was back in 1963, too.

Later, Tom stopped as he was walking by that same photo.

Tom Colt Continues Our Story:

It's strange to look at your younger self, particularly at a moment of triumph like this from so long ago. I doubt anyone even remembers this tournament I won. I remember it well. I suppose people think I'm disappointed in the results of my golfing career—just 6 tournament wins and 2 on the Senior Tour over a nearly 30-year time span in competitive golf. But I'm not in the least disappointed.

If I could go back in time and talk to my 1963 self, I'd tell the young lad in this photo: *Enjoy every moment out there, kid. Enjoy the fans, the spectacle of the tournaments, enjoy being around Hogan, Snead, Palmer, Nicklaus, Player, Casper and all the rest. You are privileged to compete during the Golden Age of Golf.*

I'd advise him, that if anything, he's trying too hard. If young Tom Colt could've just relaxed, he would have won many more tournaments.

It's hell to be poor, like we were when I was growing up. Absolute hell that seemed impossible to escape. I put tremendous pressure on myself to make money, so I would never be visited by poverty again.

Young Tom with your whole life ahead. I wished I looked like you. I've found the most wonderful girl. She is so beautiful I can't take my eyes off her. I'm certain she's the girl Caroline told me I would find someday. Remember that night, when she said that, the night we were almost killed by gangsters in Mexico and Caroline saved me?

This girl, Carmen, would fall in love with you in about a minute, young Tom. You're the perfect guy for her. But I guess our age is the one thing we can't do anything about.

I forgot I was in the lounge and said aloud, "It's a shame, Young Tom, it really is. I feel like I let you down."

Brooks Benton Continues Our Story:

Raymond the piano player smiled again, with the acquired wisdom to know exactly what both Carmen and Tom were thinking as they gazed at the photograph.

Softly, he said, "And by the way, TC, you haven't changed at all. And you sure as shit have never let anyone down."

Tom went over to the bar, poured two glasses of Merlot and brought them over to the piano, giving one to Raymond.

Raymond had become one of Tom's most enduring friends down the years. Both being rascals, they understood each other.

"Congrats to Ray Jr. getting admitted to Stanford. Sometimes I wish I'd gone to a fine university like that. Princeton, maybe. Judge Wilkinson talked about his college years like they were the best years of his life."

Ray played a few soft notes on the piano, his mode of stimulating thinking, like Tom gripping and re-gripping a golf club.

"Our job was to work our butts off so we could help the next generation go to a fine university. Think about all those kids you helped with the Laura Colt Scholarships."

Tom nodded.

"Cool of you to name the scholarship after your mom. Nice lady, that one. I'd say, one of a kind."

Tom leaned on the grand piano and sipped his Merlot. He nodded, just a bit emotionally.

Tom looked over at Raymond and smiled.

Raymond said, "I've seen a lot from my vantage point at this piano bench at this particular Country Club. I should have written a book about these people and all the mischief the rich get into...but you beat me to it."

"For a private detective in need of cases, the rich never disappoint."

"Would you please take that girl in your arms and never let her go. I've been sitting at this piano for 41 years waiting for you to find a woman who loves you with all of her heart. I saw you with Julia Wilkinson—no good, she only loved herself. Not Jillian Flannery—she mainly loved money. Not Katrina Stern—she's too hard on everyone, especially herself. And there were all those others." He smiled. "Not Paige

Lawson, the pretty beancounter girl. She saved me a ton of money on taxes, I gotta say. But the girl's name is Carmen Lopez."

"I'm glad you hung in there with me all this time. You might have given up."

"I'd be obliged if you finally made your move, sir. I'm not getting any younger."

"You don't have to call me 'sir', Raymond."

Raymond grinned. "I did back in '63, when you got me this job. A steady—easy--gig like this is what every musician dreams of. The members here don't even notice what I'm playing half the time. I play the wrong cords in a song sometimes just to test them out."

Tom chuckled.

"So I'm just keeping up the tradition. It's important for all of us to remember where we came from. Even if some of the memories are painful. How long did you call Judge Wilkinson 'sir'?"

"Until the morning I was a pallbearer at his funeral and said good-bye."

"Exactly."

"Do you think that's what's holding me back? The bad memories."

"I do, Tom." Raymond smiled.

He resumed playing…

"I've been watching you and Carmen dance around each other for four years. You've all but worn out the carpet in here. You see, beating young golf tour hotshots 40 years younger than you like you do all the time when they show up here, is hard. Falling in love with Carmen should be easy. A lot of us have fallen for her. But she isn't looking for an old piano man or even one of the young rich snob members. She's looking for someone like you."

"Yes, but—"

Raymond shook his head in disagreement, knowing what Tom was thinking. "Time and age and such are a prison this world tries to lock us into. We're told our race is already run. But the good news is we can break out of that prison. Dreams are still possible at our age." Ray played a few more tender, tinkling notes on the piano.

"Look at me. The Wilkinson Estate gave me a $50,000 bonus for my years of service here, and a recording contract with Red Dog Music. Imagine, finally getting my music heard outside this room. Yes, at my age."

"That's great news! Congratulations."

Ray opened an envelope. It was artwork for the cover of an album titled, *An Evening with Raymond B. Lasalle.* He was wearing a tux, sitting at the piano. He showed it to Tom who responded with a broad smile.

"Odd, too. Judge Wilkinson and his haughty daughter barely ever said 'boo' to me all the years I performed here. You know any reason the Judge's Estate would do this for me?"

"I would guess Roy Wilkinson loved your music. He wasn't one to pass out compliments. Kind of a hard man. But, I finally decided, the day he died, a truly great man."

Another reason might be, when the Judge passed away in 1982, the Trustee for the Wilkinson Estate became Thomas J. Colt. Under Tom's direction, the value of the Estate had doubled. Roy Wilkinson's ambition was to be the first self-made billionaire in Arizona. Twenty years after his death, his dream came true.

Ray continued, "When you started making serious money, I was worried you'd turn into one of these condescending jerks like we see at this Club. But you didn't. Why is that?"

"I'm still a poor boy, Ray. Still hungry."

"I'd be honored to play this piano at your wedding reception."

Raymond's words grabbed at Tom like few words ever had in his life. He had to look away for a moment.

The conversation with Raymond B Lasalle, piano playing philosopher and 65-year-old debut recording artist, gave Tom lots to think about—as it always did.

***

Tom Continues Our Story:

It was another cold, cloudy day, almost too cold for me to go out to the golf course and play. Almost.

For reasons I never fully understood, the tourists flocked here in January, February and March, when the weather was fickle and often cold or wet. And then these 'snowbirds' departed before Easter, when Arizona had the best weather on earth. Just shows us you don't have to be smart to be a tourist, just willing to pay way too much for a tiny hotel room and mediocre meals.

I was in my office going over Valley Vista's financial statements. They didn't look any better than the last time I reviewed them. I continued to be amazed--and dismayed--how much it costs to run a world-class country club. Could this have to do with the impossible task of trying to please arrogant, always demanding, millionaire members, male and female?

I tossed my pen down in discouragement and returned the financial spreadsheets to their file in my desk. I vowed to look at them again soon, perhaps sometime in the fall of next year.

It might seem easy to turn a profit at a club where all the members are affluent, most are filthy rich. But it's not. They got rich by holding on to their money, not spending it. Every increase in the restaurant prices, bar prices, greens fees and especially monthly club dues was met with stiff resistance.

But I didn't purchase the Club for the financial returns, I purchased it because I loved that incredible golf course, and cherished the memories that resided there.

One of the memories was the last golf lesson I gave Lisa Prentiss Luck before she was murdered. I can still see how lovely she looked that day, how happy to be with me, a nobody golf pro at the time. She was one of the few people I met in this country club set who judged a person by who they are, not how fat their bank account was.

Lisa was a lissome blonde with stunning large violet eyes, beautiful long tanned legs and a soft voice like the breath of springtime. She exuded 'class' but in a quiet unassuming way.

I opened a drawer on the right of my desk and pulled out the note I had received from Lisa's daughter, Kathleen Prentiss-Valenzuela. I had taken it out five days in a row and tried to craft a suitable reply. I failed all five days.

The note had two questions: *You knew my mother. Given the circumstances, I wondered if she ever considered having an abortion. I mean in those days it would have been an unimaginable scandal for a woman married to a Phoenix politician to have a baby fathered by a nineteen-year-old boy in Mexico.*

I took out a piece of Valley Vista CC stationary with my title, 'CEO and Owner' on it—which still startled me to see--and wrote:

"She would have never given that a thought. Lisa wanted you more than she ever wanted anything. She would have endured any hardship to see that you were born. I see her face every time I look at you."

Question #2 was: *Tell me about you and my mother. How did you feel about her? I have this feeling you were special to her. I've asked people who know you and they don't seem to be able to tell me a thing. Is it some kind of secret what happened between you two?*

I wrote: "Not a secret in the least. If she had lived, I would have fallen in love with Lisa Prentiss. When I knew her, she was at the lowest point of her life, and she was still kind, gracious, caring, and fun. She had a quality that is difficult to explain. It was like, we spent so little time together and yet knew everything about one another."

I took the note and my response with me when I left the Club and drove to the Memorial Park in North Phoenix where Lisa was laid to rest more than 40 years ago. I put them in a small notebook I carried with me, which had memories I cherished and still served to inspire me.

I considered the possibility that Lisa was meant to be the love of my life, but we of course never got the chance to see. But I could feel, the last time I was with her on the golf course at Valley Vista, that we had formed a strong friendship, one of trust and affection. Lisa, who was so troubled and trapped in a bad situation, relaxed and felt safe when she was with me.

We both felt the stirring of something strong, perhaps it was love. A big gap existed in our social status. I was an impoverished golf pro, remember. I was too afraid, or lacking in confidence, to tell her how I felt. It may have been the thing I regret most in my life. And I carry a lot of regrets with me.

She told me how she felt in a note she sent to me the day before she died. I carry the note with me in the little notebook:

> *...and Tom, our friendship means more to me than you know. I may have started out as just a golf student to you, but you were something more to me. And I hope you feel the same...*

I wondered, as I closed my little notebook and went back to my car, *if these feelings for Lisa, who lies there in a grave, are still real and alive, if she could have been my true love, what does that say about the rest of my life? Will it be a hopeless search for someone like her?*

***

Brooks Continues Our Story:

The note from Lisa that Tom carried with him wasn't the original, just a photocopy. The original had nearly crumbled to dust, Tom had read it so many times.

As Tom sat on the patio of the Guest House that evening under the dome of sparkling stars and a clear desert night, he wondered, as he had done many times before, which of those stars watching over him was Lisa Prentiss, a woman he would always love and never forget.

He looked up at those stars and said, "Lisa, I believe you and I could have had a wonderful life together. I'm sorry we weren't given the chance to find out. I'm so sorry."

He had the Ladies' Locker Room attendant put the note to Kathleen in her locker the next morning. He got to the Club early, 6:30 AM, and began his day with a ritual that never failed to cheer him up, hitting two buckets of practice balls on the driving range. His everlasting ability to hit a golf ball longer, straighter, truer than almost anyone alive always brought him out of whatever worry or despair he felt. Perhaps it was time he let Lisa Prentiss Luck recede into the distant past.

And perhaps the dead would like a chance, a final chance, to communicate with us, and assure us that we, at the time, did the best we could for them. Eternity probably provides one with needed perspective.

***

Tom Continues Our Story:

You might wonder why I worked so hard on keeping my golf game in shape, given I was technically retired from tournament competition. It was because I played challenge matches at Valley Vista on a regular basis against young hotshot golf pros who showed up in the hopes of beating Tom Colt.

Lifting a few grand out of their wallets was a thrill I never tired of.

The prize money on the professional golf tour has grown exponentially since I played. Was I envious? Absolutely. But it makes beating these youngsters when they show up here all the more satisfying.

After I left the driving range and returned to my office, I saw that Brooks Benton had left a stack of copies of our book, *The Mystery of the Golf Club Murder,* on my desk, in case I got requests for autographed copies.

My office door had 'Tom Colt International Enterprises' stenciled on it. I really didn't do any business overseas, but I thought it sounded cool.

I was curious what the members of the Club would think of our book. I had written about real people. Real rich people. Real rich people who were used to everyone truckling to them.

It turned out I wasn't quite prepared for the backlash.

Brooks Benton Continues Our Story:

Sterling and Missy Gould were featured prominently in Tom's narrative of Valley Vista members and their shenanigans in the early '60s. Sterling, 65 then, was a weathered, outdoorsy gentlemen with a shock of silvery hair. He had an enormous belly that he tried to conceal with expertly tailored suits. Sterling had the searching eyes of the big game hunter, but the game he pursued most avidly was the attractive female under the age of 50.

His wife Missy, 51 at that time, was a former beauty queen who was still exciting and vivacious—and a terrific golfer. Her figure was still remarkable. She wore her silver-frosted dark hair in the pixie cut actress Audrey Hepburn popularized.

The Goulds' grandson, Ronald "Rusty" Gould, who had a large gut reminiscent of his Grandpa Sterling's, stormed into Tom's office. His face was flushed with anger or perhaps from the exertion of walking up a flight of stairs. His jaw clenched so tight Tom thought it might shatter.

"How can I help you?" Tom said with welcoming cheer in his voice.

Rusty had a copy of *The Mystery of the Golf Club Murder.* He slammed it on Tom's desk, which accomplished nothing except make his own hand sting.

"Damn you! In your book, you made my grandfather sound like a serial adulterer."

"And a fat one at that." Tom mentally chided himself for enjoying this so much.

That teed the lad off even more.

"You wrote about my grandpa in the shower at the locker room, and I quote, 'with rolls of fat flapping halfway down to his dick'."

"And that day he confessed to having an affair with a beautiful 30-year-old married woman who was murdered a short time later. And when your grandfather heard about Lisa's murder, his major concern was to make sure the cops didn't suspect him."

"It was bad form to print that." He said 'bad form' as though it were a crime punishable by stoning.

"Old Sport," Tom commented.

"What?"

"You mean, bad form, Old Sport."

"You humiliated my grandmother, who was so kind to you over the years, when you were a nobody."

"Missy came up to my office this morning and planted an energetic, wet smooch on my cheek. She said she loved the book. And it's not easy for her to get around just a month after that hip replacement and all."

"She kissed _you_? I don't believe it."

"Ask her. It was sweet and lovely kiss from a lovely lady."

"You go to hell! This isn't over!"

"You're right. Brooks Benton and I are working on our next book."

Tom couldn't help grinning. If anything, he had grown to be more of a rascal over the years.

After Ronald stormed out, Tom only had 10 minutes peace until a nephew of Carter Vonessen's, Timothy Barron Vonessen III, stormed in. Quite the august title for a guy about 5'2". He was on the Club's Board of Directors.

Carter also had been a stalwart on the Club Board, for thirty years. He was a perpetually angry guy who loved to pick a fight. He was built like a brick wall. Strong chin, aggressive expression, a blocky head perched on massive shoulders. He took golf lessons for Tom for several years and never followed any of Tom's instruction. He was one of those businessmen who think they know everything. The nephew had inherited Carter's sweet personality.

"Colt, I have called for an emergency Board Meeting to vote on ousting you from the Club."

Tom didn't look even slightly perturbed.

"As you wish. Go ahead and try. I'll just dissolve the corporation that owns and manages the Club and turn Valley

Vista into a public course. You can stand in line for a tee time like everyone else."

Tom smiled and took a drink from a glass of iced tea on his desk.

"You can't do that…"

"Read the Articles of Incorporation. Yes, I can. I hold the most voting shares, more than the rest of you combined."

The nephew pounded his fist on Tom's desk. Desk was fine afterward, fist not so much.

"You made us, the Club Members, sound like wastrels, snobs and bigots."

"No, I only made the wastrels, snobs and bigots sound like wastrels, snobs and bigots."

"A number of us were opposed to you and your investment group buying Our Club. We still are."

"I know. That makes owning it such a blast."

Poor Timothy couldn't find the words. He made a few guttural angry sounds, turned and left.

Tom made a mental note to ask Brooks Benton what 'wastrels' were. Apparently not a good thing.

***

Tom Continues Our Story:

My next cheery guest was Jilly Flannery's young relative, Sean. He had the characteristic Flannery Irish temper. I'm half-Irish myself so I know whereof I speak. Fortunately for me, my twin sister Caroline got most of the famed Irish temper in my family.

Sean threw his copy of my book across the office. It knocked over a vase of yellow roses, a thank-you gift from Missy Gould on publication of my book.

"You wrote about having sex with my Great-Aunt!!! You are a scoundrel!!"

I leaned back in my chair. "Let me explain the 1960s to you. Throughout the '50s, even discussing sex had been forbidden, let alone doing the act. But this all changed in the new decade. Men and women discovered sex could actually be fun. It was a sexual Revolution, really. And Jillian Flannery was at the forefront. She was a true-blue American Rebel, a pioneer. She still is."

Sean softened. He sat down and stroked his chin thoughtfully with his right hand. "She was? Great-Aunt Jilly?"

"Yes siree. She's no bubblehead. She's the most loyal friend imaginable, and gutsy as hell. Keep reading my books. I have some stories to tell you about your Great-Aunt that will make you stand up and cheer."

I leaned over and picked Sean's copy of his book off the floor.

Sean said, "Could you autograph this for me?"

I picked up my pen—a gold one I had just purchased for book signings--and obliged.

I rose from my chair and picked up the pieces of the broken vase, tossed them in the waste basket, then said, "Be proud of Jilly. And by the way, heightened sexual vitality is a hereditary trait—it's passed down the generations."

Now Sean brightened. "Really?"

"Absolutely. I read it in *Scientific American.* They gave me a free subscription to that magazine when I renewed my *Gentleman Golfer Monthly* subscription for three more years. Anyways, you owe Jilly a debt of gratitude."

"*Scientific American.* You're certain. I've never thought of myself as..."

I smiled brightly and nodded.

Sean became agitated and stood up. "I'm sorry I bothered you, Mr. Colt. I better be going. I have to meet..." He rushed out the door.

I called out, "What's your girlfriend's name?"

"Sally Barrington!" he answered back enthusiastically as he got to the elevator and banged on the buttons.

I remembered seeing her at the Club pool. Nice little body, but kind of a long horse-y face and a horse-y laugh to match. But her daddy owns offshore oil wells in Louisiana, so it's all good.

***

Brooks Benton popped into my office just as Sean had departed. He noticed something new on my desk, a gold doubloon from the 18th century pirate days, in a Plexiglas display. I had brought it in from home; it had spent the last 40 years in a dusty box of memorabilia.

He examined it and asked, "How did it go with the members?"

"Just fine. The members I like, liked the book. The ones I don't like, didn't."

Brooks laughed. "The book is selling great. I think it's high time we started the next one, *Murder on Bogey Island*. The publisher is anxious to get the manuscript."

I indicated the doubloon. "That's why I brought that in. To inspire us. It was found on the Island. Quite possibly, there is still a fortune in treasure on that island."

"So we have a murder mystery and a treasure hunting story."

"Yes. Including one murder that was never solved and treasure that was never found, but a man was killed trying to find it."

"Let's start this afternoon, after lunch. I'll bring my tape recorder."

"Let's."

Chapter Five
The Four Horrids!

Brooks Continues Our Story:

As Carmen Lopez walked from her car to the clubhouse staff entrance, she got that familiar twisting feeling in her stomach. That feeling of dread she always got on Wednesdays. That was the day she would have to serve lunch on the casual dining porch to the foursome of women she had termed, The Four Horrids.

They were little old ladies who played 9 holes of horrid golf in the morning each Wednesday, then came in to have lunch, where they were horrid to the club staff members who waited on them. The Four Horrids were Felicity Greyhawk, 82, former Western movie starlet who was briefly married to Tom's uncle Steven. Daphne Hedgerow, 80, widow of Basil Hedgerow who had been Club General Manager in the 1960s and '70s (and the mother of the current GM Nigel Hedgerow). Virginia 'Ginny' Bland, 84, widow of the former US Senator Robert Bland, and none other than Jillian Flannery, who refuses to disclose her age for this book.

Carmen, being the Head of the Waitstaff at Valley Vista CC, took it upon herself to wait on the Four Horrids, fearing that the less experienced, more emotionally fragile waitresses might sustain permanent psychological damage from serving these nasty, demanding old ladies. And Carmen of course vented her frustration to Tom after the ladies departed in their limousines after lunch.

The Four Horrids teed off precisely at 9AM each Wednesday. They finished their 9 holes around 12:30PM, meaning it took them 3 ½ hours to finish. In other words, a full 18 holes would be a 7 hour+ adventure. They were possibly the slowest foursome in the history of the game of golf, which extends back hundreds of years to the Scottish moors.

Tom Colt and Katrina Stern, playing the same course, required no more than 3 hours for a full 18 holes.

The casual dining porch afforded a great view of the long, uphill 18th hole. Around noon, Carmen walked to the large picture window and watched with apprehension as the Four Horrids made their way, slowly, like primordial ooze, up the fairway to the green. They insisted on using caddies, not golf carts, which slowed the proceedings down even more.

Carmen, good with numbers since a young girl when she counted cattle for her father on the family's ranch, ran some rough calculations through her head. From the Ladies Tees, the course was 6,500 yards long. Each of the Horrids hit the ball around 75 yards (save Jilly who could still hit a ball twice that far), so over 9 holes they needed 45 strokes just to reach the greens. Forty-five times four is 180 strokes for the Horrids combined. Assume they 2-putted each green that's another 72 strokes. Or 250 strokes for 9 holes!

The Four Horrids weren't content to wreak havoc out on the course. The minute they sat down to lunch they set about tormenting the club staff. They were nitpickers of the worst sort, hyper-critical of everything. And cheap tippers, although their combined net worth exceeded the Gross National Product of many small countries.

Their demands began with insisting on Table 6 by the window. Carmen had to turn the chairs around at that table so no one else could sit there until the Horrids arrived. They always drank two vodka tonics each, which unleashed their nastiness, always ordered the Daily Special and criticized the heck out of it.

"This isn't a foursome, it's an abomination!" Carmen half-screamed to the sympathetic ears of Tom Colt when she took her break on the back patio, where he was enjoying an iced tea.

"The only one who can hit the ball at all is Jillian Flannery, and she must be 100 years old."

Tom handed Carmen an iced tea to cool her off. A whiskey with beer chaser would have done the trick much better.

"Jilly is about 87, I believe. And quite a character. I heard she had a brilliant golf instructor when she was younger. Must be why she can still play."

Tom smiled to himself. There was much more to Jilly's game than just golf.

Tom added: "Gary Player has a great piece of advice for duffers like these, "Quit the game for a fortnight, then quit it altogether."

Carmen didn't laugh. "Oh, and did I tell you it takes them two hours to have lunch, during which time they call the waitress, me, over approximately 50 times. One of their favorite complaints is that I don't know how to position the glasses and the silverware on the table. I've worked in food service since I was 15—we catered cookouts for upscale tourists who visited my family's dude ranch. Anyway, why do they care? They usually get tipsy and knock over the glasses. Except for widow Bland, who's a Mormon I think."

Carmen paused to take a long swig of iced tea.

"Today, one of them tugs on my sleeve—I hate it when customers grab me—and pulls me over to her wrinkled cheek and says, 'Don't give up on love, my dear.' And then flutters her hand in this weird way."

Tom displayed a quizzical expression.

Carmen continued, "Then Widow Hedgerow chimes in with 'though you aren't much of a waitress, you have the kinds of physical assets men like. So I'm sure you'll find a rich guy soon'. Can you believe the gall, the audacity--"

"Brooks Benton would say, the 'effrontery'," Tom said with a grin. Then, after Carmen scowled, tried to be serious. "What did the first lady look like?"

"Dark, weathered skin. Wears a ton of Indian jewelry, like ten bracelets, seriously—she sounds like a wind chime when she swings at the ball."

"Oh, no. Felicity Greyhawk." Tom rolled his eyes. "She's an actress who played Indian maidens in B-Westerns in the '40s and '50s. She was briefly married to my uncle Steven. Her real name is Florence Plotnik."

"So then Jillian beckons me over, and pulls me so I'm leaning in, looking right into her bloodshot little eyes. She says, 'Darling, my fifty years of life experience has taught me that life is pretty much like the 12th hole at Valley Vista. The choices can be daunting, but risk-taking is always worth it'."

"Evidently her life experience didn't begin until she was 37."

Carmen finally smiled. "I had no idea what she meant. I nodded politely and left. Pretty soon a limo driver walked in, the signal for the Horrids to totter off, to my great relief. I felt like tipping the driver myself."

Carmen got up, retrieved the iced tea pitcher, and refilled both of their glasses. She sat down. Crossed her lovely legs and allowed her skirt to ride up a few inches, which Tom appreciated. Sometimes there are sweet rewards for being a patient listener.

"So, back to the par-5 12th, the sharp dogleg right, the one with the lovely waterfall behind the green."

"Yes! I know it, seeing that I own the course and all."

"You are being a smart ass today. I think you are enjoying the story of my ongoing misery."

"Not at all. It's just, remember, I had to give these same horrids golf lessons for thirty years, and their horrid husbands, and their children who were little apprentice horrids. I feel your pain."

"In that case, you're excused. I was working a split shift that day, with three hours off in the afternoon. So I walked out to the 12ᵗʰ hole. I sat on a bench on the tee box and hoped for insight. What did those silly women mean? I still had no idea."

Tom took Carmen's hand in his. They both felt that jolt of electricity they always got when they touched.

"Two ways to play it. You can hit three easy shots to the green by going down the spacious left side. No rough, no trees, no water hazards, no worries. Or, you can try to cut the corner and place your tee shot atop the narrow ridge on the right side, then go for the green in two and possibly score a spectacular eagle-3. And hear in your mind the cheers that all bold players, all winners deserve. But if your tee shot drifts into the trees, you'll need *Bagger Vance* and a chainsaw to get outta there."

A new light shone in Carmen's eyes. It was the light of understanding. "Can I come over to your condo Thursday after work? I get off at 7:45. I have something important to tell you."

"Yes. What might this be about?"

"I will know for sure by 7:59 when I'm knocking on your front door. I finally got what the Horrids meant. The old dears."

***

Tom Continues Our Story:

I was sitting at my office desk, with I must confess a nervous feeling about what Carmen was going to tell me at 7:59 that evening. The clock on my wall said 4:45.

I was worried she was coming over to tell me she had found another job. I knew she was far too talented to remain at Valley Vista forever. I had that sinking feeling that I had missed my chance with her. Of all things, I, Tom Colt, had not pursued her boldly enough.

But then, as she had so many times over the years, the warm, sweet, fragrant breeze known as Jillian Flannery blew into my office and distracted me from these discomfiting thoughts.

Her semi-serious facial expression suggested she, too, had something significant to tell me. This was unusual. Jilly never seemed completely serious.

"I wanted to let you know, at lunch today I gave you a ringing endorsement to young Carmen our waitress. She is completely besotted with you."

I indicated the couch in my office. She sat down. I joined her.

"She does everything wrong as a server, by the way. The place settings are incorrect. I know a person from her background isn't likely to know where to place the silverware and the glasses. The presentation of the dishes are dreadful. And the service is so slow. I know it's partially the Chef's fault."

"Jilly, I brought him over from a Donald Trump resort."

"That's precisely my point."

She fiddled with the doubloon on my desk. Jilly was a key participant in the strange events at Bogey Island in '63.

"I never thought you might end up with a Mexican girl who works as a waitress."

"She's from western New Mexico. Her parents own a small cattle ranch there."

"They raise small cattle? I get it. That's where petite filet mignon come from."

We both laughed, but I wasn't sure I liked where this conversation was headed.

"She's an American girl, talented and on her way up. Don't lump her into groups. Carmen is a unique individual, like you, like me."

I wanted very badly to change the subject.

"How about you...are you going to get married again?"

"Oh, I hope so. It's what I do best, besides shopping."

In the intervening years from when I met her in '61, and she was a sexy divorcee, she had been married and divorced once more and had another husband who passed away--all men in the retail real estate development business. She now owned shopping malls in 5 states. *Forbes* magazine listed her net worth at half a billion dollars. She was probably the wealthiest woman in the Southwest.

From the change in her expression to a pensive frown, and the way she hesitated before speaking, I knew I wasn't going to like what she was going to say next.

"I don't think she really loves you. I think she loves the fascinating life you've had. She hopes she'll be swept along in whatever amazing and dangerous adventures you embark upon next."

My turn to frown. "Well--"

"Please let me finish. Being with you will give Carmen the self-confidence she needs to fly under her own power. And she will fly away, I would bet on it. Where will that leave you, Tom?"

"Most likely, on the golf course shooting one to four strokes under par and lifting money from the wallets of the smug young pigeons from the pro golf tour I'm playing against. Followed up with a fabulous dinner at our Club. And perhaps meeting a fascinating woman..."

"I suppose that's true. You have always landed on your feet. But I know you too well. Better than anyone, probably. I don't think you'll recover so quickly if Carmen were to leave."

***

Brooks Benton Continues Our Story:

Carmen arrived at Tom's door looking nervous, which was out of character for calm, controlled Carmen. It was 7:59PM.

He welcomed her inside. And tried to read what her emotions were.

She breathed a big sigh and began:

"I want to tell you something."

Tom braced himself. He had a strong feeling this was bad news.

"I'm getting engaged," she said.

Those words, together, were one of the worst blows Tom had ever sustained, far worse than the three times he had been shot when he was a private detective.

Wanting to scream out NO! Tom instead remained stoic.

"Who's the lucky guy?" he asked, smiling but with a breaking voice.

Carmen sighed again. Her anguish was evident.

Tom thought, *it flashed in my mind that my life was over. Not the physical, sentient part perhaps, but the joyful, expectant, wondrous part. The part where dreams can come true.*

Tom Colt, who was so fearless, reckless perhaps as a golf competitor, and as a detective facing danger on a regular basis, had lost his last chance at true love because he, was too *afraid* to tell Carmen how much he loved her. For 5 years.

His life had involved so many ups and downs, stumbles and comebacks. He had met so many wonderful women, but as Raymond the Piano Man wisely pointed out, none of the relationships were quite right, none suited both Tom and his romantic idealism enough to be permanent. And the sting of the failure of his marriage to Mandy when he was in his 20s, still remained. He had told Carmen once, regarding their romance, "I saved the best for last."

He wanted a do-over. He wanted to wind the clock back to the first day Carmen had come into his life, when she took the job at Valley Vista Country Club.

But life is not golf; life does not grant us any convenient Mulligans.

Tom Colt, for all his success and fame in life, all the exciting adventures, his triumphs in golf tournaments and as a heroic crime solver, on that momentous March night in 2005 felt defeated, like he had failed.

Chapter Six
--We Return to February 1963
At Valley Vista CC, Scottsdale, AZ
Tom Tangles with a Wildcat

The start of the 1963 pro golf tournament season had been so busy for both Tom and Katrina Stern that they barely saw each other, even though her home course, thanks to efforts by Tom with the Club President, was now Valley Vista CC. Golf pros are said to "play out of" a certain Club, and the name of the club is included when they are introduced on the first tee of a tournament. Having a top pro playing out of your Club adds prestige to the Club. Playing out of a top Club adds prestige to the golfer.

Tom finally ran into her on the practice range. She was about to depart for Los Angeles where she would be filming a series of golf matches with other lady pros for TV.

Tom said, "Red Boyle has rescheduled the grand opening Pro-AM until March 10 because he was injured in some kind of accident at his home. Can you still make it?"

Kat thought for a few moments. Tom could see reluctance on her face. *Were they drifting apart already?* he wondered.

"I'll do my best. So much going on at the start of the season. I think I can have my best year ever. I've never hit the ball so far." She paused a few moments. "Because of the help you gave me, I should add." The warm smiles they exchanged reassured each of them that there was nothing to worry about: their budding romance was proceeding apace.

"Good luck in the Phoenix Open next week. You should play great at Arizona CC. Suits your power game really well."

"Thanks." What Kat said wasn't really true, but Tom, not the most confident of pro golfers, appreciated any encouragement he could get.

Kat walked back into the clubhouse. Tom headed to the practice range to work on said power game. What he really needed to work on was his shaky putting stroke.

Kat turned and hollered back to Tom: "Yes, I will be your partner in the Pro-Am at Bogey Island! I'll make my schedule work."

Tom beamed. Kat waved.

***

Tom Continues Our Story:

The 1963 Phoenix Open was played at Arizona Country Club, a suburban layout on the margin between Phoenix and Scottsdale.

It was the 6th event on the pro tour schedule that year. The winners of the first five resembled a Who's Who of professional golf in the '60s and beyond: Arnold Palmer, Gary Player, Billy Casper, and the previous week in Palm Springs, young Jack Nicklaus. An older pro, Jack Burke Jr. a former Masters Champion, won the Lucky International Open in San Francisco, played at a public course, Harding Park Golf Club. Lucky Lager Brewing Company was one of the sponsors of the event. You didn't need to be particularly lucky to be invited to play.

As for Tom Colt, I was my usual inconsistent self in the two events I had played, the Los Angeles Open and the Palm Springs Golf Classic. I finished 18th and 23rd, respectively. Not really up to my expectations. I felt great. No lingering effects from the bullet I took in the shoulder the previous year. I was locked in a pattern of making a bunch of birdies and a bunch of bogies every round. The net result was mediocre scores.

Kat taught me how to look back after each tournament round and analyze each shot, what I did right and what caused a poor score on an individual hole. For me, the over-par holes were 50% the result of wild shots off the tee and 50% missing makeable putts from 15 feet and in. Both weaknesses would bedevil me my entire career.

On to my hometown tournament, the Phoenix Open. The Wednesday before the tournament began, a pro-am event was played that allowed local businessmen and other notables to play with the pro golfers. Judge Wilkinson, a leader in the Phoenix Thunderbirds, a local business booster organization that organized the tournament, arranged for me to be paired with Chandler Boyle, one of Red Boyle's children. He was about 35, I guessed. He was already acquiring a large gut like Red Boyle's and had red hair with the texture of steel wool, like his dad's when a youth.

The Judge thought I might learn about the Boyle family dynamics by playing with Chandler. The Judge was of the mind that you can learn a lot about a person's character by watching them play golf. For an amateur, the pro-am was an especially good test because they are not generally used to playing in front of crowds. Their nerves often get to them and they reveal their true selves.

The other factor was, as Det. Mathers always said, when a rich guy believes someone is going to knock him off, the first suspects to look at are the spouse and the children in line to inherit. Boyle was divorced and his ex-wife was remarried and living in Florida, with an even wealthier husband, so in this case the Boyle children were the ones to keep an eye on.

My overall impression of Chandler Boyle that day? He was a phony. He was on his best behavior when the eyes of the spectators were on him, but quickly became surly and self-centered when we were by ourselves out on the course away from the people.

I especially could not abide displays of temper like throwing a golf club or slamming the club down, which can damage the tender turf the greenskeeper works so hard to keep looking perfect. Young Mr. Boyle was guilty of both. What told me a lot about him was when a little kid, maybe 10, was seeking autographs and innocently asked Chandler if he was one of the pros. "I am much more than a golfer," he snarled at the kid, who was quickly frightened away.

On the next tee, he spotted a journalist with a camera, and quickly shifted into Mr. Nice Guy mode, or perhaps it was consummate salesman mode, smiling and preening. When we finished our round, Chandler walked to the door to the players' locker room, was asked by security to present his players' badge, and said to the man, "You mean you don't know who my father is, boy!" To bottom line it for you: Chandler Boyle was a two-faced jerk.

I played well in the pro-am, carding a smooth 68. But keep in mind, the score that counted was the next day's. As I walked from the 18th green to the locker room, there was the familiar sight of a large crowd gathered around Arnold Palmer, waiting for his autograph. Unlike rude Chandler Boyle, Arnie, the #1 most popular golfer and defending champion of the Phoenix Open, patiently signed every piece of paper that was shoved in front of him, particularly those from youngsters.

Palmer was astute enough to realize those youngsters would grow up to be his fans for life. They did, and they numbered in the millions.

In the past we had a small base of loyal Golf Fans, very knowledgeable about the game and appreciative of its rich history, but as a group relatively small in number compared to the fan bases of other sports like Major League Baseball. Arnold attracted Sports Fans in vast numbers. They were not nearly as knowledgeable, and they could get a little rowdy at the tournaments when they discovered the concession stands sold unlimited quantities of beer, but their enthusiasm transformed professional golf. There was a buzz of energy, of excitement at every event, not just the major tournaments like The Masters.

To these new golf fans, most of the other players, including the stars of the previous era, were viewed as vague, black and white sketches. Arnie, as his fans called him, was seen in glorious 1960s Technicolor. His Palmer Charge, the act of coming from far behind in the last round to win the tournament, or at least put a scare into the guy who did win, became a staple of the tour events at that time. No matter how far Palmer was behind the leaders, his fans never lost hope that he could make a patented charge and prevail. His charges were achieved with a risk-taking style of golf that captivated the fans—and the media covering our sport.

A few of his possibly envious fellow pros have said that Palmer lost as many tournaments with his risky style of play as he won—but his heroic defeats endeared him to his fans all the more.

My own style of play involved taking risks as well, though I was not nearly as skilled as Mr. Palmer. My risk-taking many times ended in disaster. But I was addicted to the thrill of trying. As a result, I had to hunt for my golf ball in a lot of strange and exotic places. If I had been a Boy Scout, I would have earned my Explorers Merit Badge several times over.

Even Palmer's fellow competitors could be swept along in the excitement of one of his charges. In the Colonial Invitational in Ft. Worth, Texas, one year, I was playing in the group behind Palmer. When Palmer began rallying from behind, I found myself watching what he was doing more than paying attention to my own game. What Arnold was doing was much more compelling, for the fans and for me. I have to admit I was rooting for him to win...

I understand the psychology of rooting for an athlete or a team. It takes you out of your own difficulties and lets you inhabit the seemingly more exciting and glamourous life the athlete leads. Your troubles are temporarily secondary to the critical issue of the athlete succeeding that day.

As the Phoenix Open's first round approached, I wondered if Palmer could win the event for the third year in a row. I doubted it. That was hardly ever done in the highly competitive world of pro golf.

Could Tom Colt win? I doubted that even more. I wasn't at all satisfied with the state of my golf game going into my hometown event. But golf is a game that seldom offers satisfaction.

I didn't like playing my hometown tournament. There's a lot of extra pressure playing in front of your friends and acquaintances. And for some reason having Judge Wilkinson, my sponsor and benefactor, watching me play made me even more nervous.

The other issue was weather. January and February, when The Phoenix Open was typically played, are rainy months in the desert. March and April, on the other hand, are gorgeous, warm and sunny. You could count on rain, cold rain, interrupting at least one round of the Phoenix Open.

In the first round on Thursday, Gary Player, Jack Nicklaus and Jay Hebert shot fine 67s for the lead. In second place were Arnold Palmer, Julius Boros, Cary Middlecoff and one local boy, Tom Colt. I thought my name looked rather nice on that giant leaderboard near the clubhouse. I wasn't at all certain, however, that I could keep my name among the leaders for a full four days.

I tried to keep my work as a private investigator as quiet as possible. On the first tee of the second round, though, the announcer who introduced the players said, "Now on the tee, the winner of last year's Las Vegas Winter Fling Invitational, and a brilliant private eye as well. Please welcome Sam Spade—I mean Tom Colt."

Golf fans are unfailingly polite. They never boo players they don't like. They just remain eerily silent when the player is introduced. For some reason I got a more enthusiastic welcome from the fans than usual. Maybe they were excited I might apprehend a criminal at the tournament like I did last year in Vegas.

My sleuthing probably would have been more interesting for the fans than the golf I played over the next two rounds. I fell all the way to a tie for 30th place to start the fourth and final round. After 3 rounds, Arnold Palmer was in the lead at 203 strokes, Gary Player second at 204, tied with Jack Nicklaus.

In the fourth round, my inconsistent play continued. My gloomy attitude reflected the clouds that were gathering over the course. I recalled my boastful statement on New Year's Eve, that 1963 was going to be My Year, and I was going to win at least two tournaments. I decided right then to get out of the prediction business.

My caddie, Sheboygan, decided to give me one of his patented pep talks.

Caddies on the pro golf tour are colorful characters—often more colorful than the golfers they work for—and Sheboygan was no exception. I hired him at last year's Phoenix Open when I faced an emergency need for a caddie after I fired my regular caddie, a foul-tempered old guy, for coming to work drunk.

Sheboygan was a mountain of a man, at least 6'5" and more than 250 pounds. He wore his sandy hair in a bristly crew cut. He was enormously muscular. The golf bag he toted looked absurdly small when he was carrying it. He had a battered nose that looked to have been involved in several fights, some that he evidently lost.

He proved to be a fine caddie, though extremely quiet, almost secretive. I eventually learned the details of his troubled background. He was a promising college football player with professional football aspirations until he blew out his knee. He drifted around and fell in with a bad crowd that was involved in selling dope. Although he did not participate in anything illegal, when they were arrested, so was he. He did time in prison and then faced the problems all ex-cons face when trying to rebuild their lives and careers.

Would I have hired him if I knew his background?

Yes. My father cautioned me about judging people. He said, "For most of us, life is a series of mistakes. If we're lucky, we survive them."

Brooks Benton Continues Our Story:

On the third hole of the fourth round, Tom hit one of his characteristic wild shots off the tee. It sailed out of bounds and struck a tall metal trash container in the driveway of one of the beautiful homes that dotted the course. The metal clanking sound was pronounced enough to cause a few spectators to laugh.

Tom dejectedly held out his hand for Sheboygan to give him another ball. With the penalty stroke, he would be playing his third shot, on his way to at least a double-bogey 7 on this par-5 where he hoped to make a birdie 4.

Sheboygan said, "It's early days, Mr. Bond."

In golf speak, he had told Tom that it was still early in the fourth round. Plenty of time to rally.

Tom brightened. "Very good! That's from the golf scene in *Goldfinger.* I love that book!"

"Caroline told me you wished you were a cool dude like Sean Connery. Thought I'd toss you a bone. And your golf game kinda stinks today."

Tom thought, *Remember when Sheboygan would hardly say a word during the round? Good times those were.*

"They're making a movie based on the novel. It's sposta come out in '64."

Tom's face registered skepticism. How did a caddie know this?

"I read the Hollywood trades. *Variety* and *Hollywood Reporter.* I'm studying to be a screenwriter at Boyle Academy of the Performing Arts. Read a whole bunch of books on the subject. Can't tote golf bags forever."

"You're a multi-faceted dude, Sheboygan."

"And beautiful in my complexity."

Tom shook his head. "Look at me. I'm a golfer stuck in a rut of mediocre play week after week. Tied of 39th place right now."

"Yes. Let's look at you, Thomas J. Colt. How many golfers in this country?"

"I think about two million."

"And every damn one of them wishes he could trade places with you. Your office is a beautiful golf course. You work outside in the sunshine. At least most days. I know today's forecast is for rain later on. But you could be in a cubicle pushing papers all day for some asshole of a boss."

"So what's your point?"

"So let's start playing is my point. Maybe you should recognize how lucky you are to be out here."

"And one more thing, Hoss, sometimes you think too much over the ball. Make up your mind about what kinda shot you wanta make, step up to the ball and hit it."

Tom Continues Our Story:

He was right. I birdied four of the next six holes and vaulted into 14th place. I had that rarest of feelings: momentum. For an hour I could do no wrong. I began thinking about how great it would be to win a tournament in my own hometown, in front of my friends—and particularly in front of Judge Roy Wilkinson whose financial generosity had taken so much pressure off me.

There was new spring in my step. I made each swing with confidence. I could almost taste victory...

And just as my confidence was soaring, the skies opened up, the winds roared, and hail the size of marbles bombarded the course, the golfers, the spectators. The TV broadcast tower was blown over, along with many of the concession stands.

Fans and players quickly scattered under the sting of the hailstones. The wind gusts were at least 50mph. Winds damaged the roofs of the expensive homes that ran along the fairways.

Sheboygan and I hustled toward the nearest shelter we could find: the porch of one of these houses.

The threesome of Don January, Johnny Pott and Gary Player, all in contention to win the tournament, took shelter on the porch of a kindly homeowner, who turned out to be the Governor of Arizona, Paul Fannin.

In '63 political figures were less haughty than they are today. They still called themselves public servants, if you can imagine such a thing. By the 21st Century, the politicians had decided we serve them.

How does it feel to be pelted by marble sized hailstones? Hurts! Not as bad as being hit by a bullet, but close. Sheboygan and I sprinted across the fairway, looking for shelter, any shelter. He noticed someone, a female, waving from the porch of a large ranch style home.

We made it under the porch roof just before even larger hail stones started to fall. They made a terrible racket on the metal roof of the porch. It sounded as though the whole structure was going to collapse. They don't build homes in Phoenix with the soundness of structures, say, in the Midwest. We generally don't have severe weather. Just hot, blistering weather. The building materials used in home construction have to be impervious to melting or burning, like houses in hell.

The girl who beckoned us to safety turned out to be Monique Jones, daughter of Montgomery Jones, CEO of Intercontinental Security Bank and Trust Company of Arizona (evidently the longer the name a financial institution has, the more stable it seems to depositors).

Sheboygan remarked. "I know her. Her name's MoniQue. She capitalizes the Q when she signs her name so she can seem unique. Gotta warn 'ya. She's very shy. We take screenwriting classes together. She hardly ever says a word in class. Quietest woman I've ever met."

Monique brought us two bath towels when we reached the porch. We took them with grateful expressions and dried off.

"Hi, Oshkosh!" she exclaimed to Sheboygan. The two of them shared a laugh. Apparently being mistaken about Sheboygan's Wisconsin-based nickname was their private joke.

"Hi, Q!" he replied.

This Miss Q didn't seem particularly reserved to me. She was a dark-haired girl wearing loose beige cotton slacks held up precariously by a slender drawstring, and a pink short-sleeved button-down shirt, rather snug and revealing a nice shape. She had remarkable dark eyebrows and expressive brown eyes. Her mouth was the shape that invited kisses. Her eyes were sharp and wise.

I noticed the remains of a backyard Phoenix Open tournament-watching party that had been shut down by the hailstorm. There were hamburgers and bratwurst sitting forlornly on a hail stone covered grill. I saw the package labels for the sausage were the famous Barker Spicy Brazilian Bratwurst that everyone seemed to be eating in our upscale golf-y community.

I had learned that savvy marketer Stan Barker was selling these sausages only to select clients, who had to be over 21 for some reason, and for 6 times the price of his regular brands of brats. With the wealthy, when you make something difficult to purchase, they will pay almost anything for it.

I can't wait 'til I'm wealthy.

MoniQue said hospitably, "Are you hungry, Sheboygan? I got most of the food inside before the storm really hit. Go in the kitchen and help yourself."

"Don't have to ask me twice," he said as he dropped my golf bag and hustled inside.

I picked the bag up and moved it further onto the porch, out of the range of the rain and hail. Sort of like a caddie is supposed to do for the player.

My faithful caddie had left me with this supposedly shy girl. I had no idea what kind of small talk to make with her. It was unusual to be studying screenwriting back in '63. Nowadays as you know there are three types of individuals living in California: Those who have written a screenplay, those working on a screenplay, and those with an idea for a screenplay they are sure is destined to be a blockbuster—if they could only find a Hollywood agent to sell it. If only...

But MoniQue seemed surprisingly bubbly for the shy sort. She seemed like a Jilly Flannery-lite girl. The pink button-down shirt was nice and tight, showing off the outline of her lovely breasts, apparently untethered by a bra.

MoniQue took my hand. "Come inside, Tom. Let me show you our humble abode."

The abode was about four times the size of the Guest House I lived in and six times the size of the bungalow where I grew up.

The house tour was a brief one that seemed to lead inevitably to her bedroom. "Isn't this nice," she commented, and not in a shy way, as she undid her dark tresses and let them tumble down her shoulders.

Oh, no, thought I, Tom Colt. There was something familiar about this scene. MoniQue looked hot and horny, like Jilly did that morning she and I had a plate of those Barker Spicy Brazilian sausages for breakfast. I recognize the symptoms of frenzied sexuality: The flushed face, the almost manic eyes, the panting. I knew I was at a crossroads here.

I knew this when she grabbed me and planted a nice wet kiss on my lips. It was a very nice, not the least bit shy kiss. What was in that bratwurst? Did MoniQue really want me or was she under the influence of a controlled sausage substance?

She kicked off her sandals and padded over to the four-poster bed. "Oh, Tom! Come here! Think of me like a short par-5 and you're the longest on tour. You can reach me easily, Tom."

"What about your dad?" I enquired.

"Forget him, The master bedroom's in the back of the house. Old Monty is screwing my stepmom's brains out. Although in her case, that shouldn't take long. Some nights I put in ear plugs when I stay here."

I marveled at the deep abiding respect rich children had for their parents. How they appreciate all the advantages they've been given in life...

"So, you are an aspiring screenwriter. I admire writers—"

She flung herself on the bed and stretched out in a most welcoming way.

I attempted to bail. "Come over here, Q. Maybe we could play kissy face for a bit until the storm lets up."

"Ah, to heck with kissy face. I saw you birdie three holes in a row out there today. Do you know what that does to a girl? I love golf, Tom. And I have hot Lebanese blood." She pulled on the drawstring to her pants. "Take me, Tom!"

Shy? Is Sheboygan daft? Blind? He left me with a certified wildcat. And I don't mean a University of Arizona graduate.

I walked over to the bed, like one might approach a thirsty vampire that just woke up from a few centuries' sleep. I gently helped her off the bed and I re-tied the drawstring.

She grabbed me and kissed me again. Then tore at the collar of my shirt and ripped it open. She laughed—a bit manically—and tore the buttons from her shirt as well. The lovely pert, ivory-white breasts spilled out and were in full view.

"But that's such a pretty pink Izod shirt."

"Daddy can buy me a hundred more! At the Club I heard you've been banging old Jillian Flannery. Thought you might like to try something younger…"

She pulled on the pants drawstring again. This time the pants fell to the floor. I really didn't want to look, but kind of had to. Force of nature and all. The panties were blue satin and see-through. A delicious glimpse of dark rich thatch.

Time to be cool under pressure, Tom, like you never are in golf tournaments. Think! With that thinking device in your cranium, not the other less reliable reasoning tool located down below. I wondered if setting a small fire might put out a large one…it works with forest fires, they say.

I took MoniQue in my arms and kissed her. She responded. We continued this through perhaps two dozen or so beautiful smooches. To my great relief, she began to relax. Her eyes took on a normal color and sheen, not a bewitching lustful glow. Her breathing became regular.

"Mmmmmm," she purred. "You're a wonderful kisser. You taste like bratwurst."

Then she seemed to, well, I'm not certain what happened, but it appeared she woke up from the sex-crazed trance. She looked at my torn shirt, then looked down at hers. The shadow of shame fell over her dark and lovely brow.

"I am so sorry. I don't know what came over me. I sort of attacked you. And you were The Perfect Gentleman."

That was the first and only time in my life I had been called The Perfect Gentleman.

She looked down at her pretty, pink-polished toes. I thought she was going to cry.

I put a kind hand on her shoulder. "No worries. You just got excited watching the golf tournament, and then one of your golf heroes walked right into your house—after he had just birdied three holes in a row and was in striking distance of the lead. This couldn't be helped."

Her lovely lips twisted sideways into a frown. "You're not exactly my hero. I like Doug Sanders best. Gary Player is my second favorite. The Black Knight they call him. After that I'd say--"

"Anyway, it was a pleasure meeting a friend of Sheboygan's. Good luck with your screenwriting career." I really, really wanted to escape in case she had a romantic relapse. Or I found out I was only her 15th favorite golfer.

"Whatever. How hard could it be to write a movie. Most movies are lousy."

She took my hand again and led me out the same way she had led me in. Sheboygan was standing in the porch doorway, consuming the biggest pile of meat I had ever seen placed between two slices of rye bread.

"Stooooomsver," he said as he chomped through the meat. I think that was meant to be 'Storm's Over'.

He finished destroying the sandwich. "Thanks for the little snack, Q. See in you in class next week. I think we're analyzing Bogart's film, *The Big Sleep*. That's a good one. Story 'bout a <u>real</u> detective, Phil Marlowe." He cast me an ironic glance.

He finally noticed that an exciting side-view of her breasts was available through her torn shirt. He nodded to me like, Good Job, Dude. I scowled back at him. I was on the moral high road, not at fault for that afternoon's debauchery.

"Bye, guys," MoniQue said in a shy little voice, pulling the edges of her torn shirt back together modestly. "And good luck the rest of the tournament, Tom. I'll be rooting for you." She fluttered her fingers at me pleasantly and shyly.

No you won't, I thought. I'm not even in your Top 10. "Thank you for your hospitality, Miss Jones. You have a lovely...home."

Sheboygan picked up the golf bag and we walked back onto the course, which was a mess of melting hailstones. All the gaily attired spectators, hail-hammered golfers and pissed off concessionaires had vanished and headed home. No more golf that day for sure.

"What happened in there, man?"

"I briefly tangled with a wildcat. She said she had hot lesbian blood or something like that. She also said she loves golfers. MoniQue is uniQue."

"You sure brought sweet little Q out of her shell. She never pays any attention to the guys in class. Maybe you are James Bond."

"No, no. I don't have the energy, my friend."

"I didn't think so."

***

Next day, we were able, finally, to get the fourth round completed. But the magic was gone for Tom along with the fickle thing called momentum. I was back to my erratic self—a couple of birdies, a couple of bogies. I finished 24th.

On the 6th green, while he was waiting to putt, a cheeky bee flew onto tournament leader Arnold Palmer's ball. Then it flew off, possibly causing the ball to move an imperceptible distance. But golfers being the scrupulously honest, self-policing souls they are, Arnold asked for an official ruling whether he should be assigned a penalty stroke because his ball may have moved. The call went all the way to United States Golf Association Headquarters in New York.

Arnold extended his lead to 3 strokes by the end of the first 9 holes, but Gary Player tied him at 14 under par after 15 holes. The impending bee ruling from Gotham City was critical to the outcome of the event...

On the 18th hole, Gary Player had a short putt for a birdie that would tie Palmer for the lead. Player was anxious to step up to the ball and hit it; golfers hate having to wait to stroke a crucial putt—too much time to fret.

Laconic Texan Don January putted first. His ball hung on the lip of the cup, tottering like it might fall in. January waited and waited, an eternity it seemed to poor Gary Player, before tapping the ball into the cup for a par. The wait seemed to rattle Player, who missed his putt.

The call came in from New York that Arnold Palmer <u>did not</u> incur a penalty stroke from the bee-influenced ball. He had won his third consecutive Phoenix Open with a four-round score of 273, 15 under par.

The bee had flown hurriedly off and could not be reached for comment, but was undoubtedly relieved, probably worried about incurring the wrath of Arnie's Army for putting their hero's victory in jeopardy.

Player was second at 274. Jack Nicklaus shot a 71 in the fourth round to finish third at 275. These great champions were referred to as The Big Three. This was a rare occasion when they finished an event 1-2-3.

Palmer won $5,300 for his victory.

At the trophy presentation ceremony, I noticed the two Charter Founders of the Tom Colt Fan Club, Jillian Flannery and my dear sister Caroline, watching Arnold Palmer adoringly as he was presented with his check and trophy. I didn't know they had come out for the fourth round. I never saw them in my gallery that day when I was playing.

Come to think of it, I didn't see UniQue MoniQue either.

And so thankfully I completed yet another tournament in my hometown, surrounded by all my dear friends, fans and well-wishers.

I imagine if it had been me, the bee would have stung me on the hand, I would have yelped in pain, accidentally swatted my golf ball, incurred the penalty and lost the tournament. Yep, that's about it.

***

Chapter Seven

Brooks Benton Continues Our Story:

Tom Colt, out of long-standing habit still careful with money despite the improvement in his financial position, courtesy of Judge Wilkinson, finally had broken down and purchased a television set in late '62. It was a modest sized console, not the heavy models that took up half the living room of a middle-class home.

One advantage to the vintage TV models was that the weight and bulk of the consoles made it more difficult for looters to carry them out of the stores after breaking in. Because if the looters were willing to do the heavy lifting involved in actual work, an actual job, they wouldn't be looters.

One evening Caroline was watching her favorite TV show when Tom returned from his day of giving lessons at Valley Vista CC.

"HA-VA-YAN AYYYY!" she sang along with the opening credits of the popular series *Hawaiian Eye*, that ran from 1959-1963. The show opened with the cast members surfing into shore.

The announcer then intoned: *Brought to you by the new Dentu-Crème!*

Tom made a mental note to brush his teeth more often.

Caroline was a huge fan of *Hawaiian Eye*. If you grow up in the desert, you dream of the ocean. We always want what we don't have.

Tom walked in and saw she was glued to the TV. And fussing with the rabbit ears antenna on top of the console to try to bring in a clearer picture.

He enquired: "Do you love the intricate plots on this show or just seeing Robert Conrad without his shirt on."

"I pick up detective tips about how to get the perp to spill the beans. Robert's bare, tanned, muscular chest is merely a bonus."

"The show's in black and white. How do you know he's tanned."

"Chicks know these things." She rolled her eyes like I must be dim. "I've been thinking about our detective business."

"I'm all eagerness to hear what your ideas, dear sister."

"Good. You can get us two beers from the fridge then, dear eagerness."

I did as told. We each took a swig from our bottles of Blatz.

"Sultry, dangerous dames who need a PI can't find us. In the movies, the best cases come when a sultry dame, a looker like Veronica Lake with a seductive lock of hair that tumbles down over one eye—strolls into the gumshoe's office."

"*It was a blonde. A blonde to make a bishop kick a hole in a stained-glass window*," Tom quoted Raymond Chandler's novel, *Farewell My Lovely.*

"Exactly. I have an idea. Valley Vista CC must have some unused office space they could let us have on the cheap until we start making the big bucks. Let's ask Roy. That would be so cool. Hawaiian Eye works out of a night club at a resort. We could work out of a Country Club."

"I doubt the Judge would go for that. I'm sure he won't. He wants me to work on the PI stuff very quietly."

"Only one way to find out." Caroline got up and walked out the patio door, took the winding path up to the Main House. Tom followed, shaking his head.

The Judge, leaning against his massive desk in his home office, listened carefully to Caroline's pitch for office space.

He frowned. "That's quite an unusual request." He thought for a few moments. "But for you, my wonderful Caroline, I will make it so. We have some space available on the third floor."

Caroline beamed and hugged the Judge. Tom winced. Judges don't usually go in for hugs.

"We didn't hire as much administrative staff at Valley Vista as we thought we'd need when we expanded the clubhouse in '58. It's been a challenge to attract new members the last two years. Kennedy's economy isn't as buoyant as they promised. But what do we expect from politicians? Now he says he's going to lower the corporate tax rate to spur economic growth. I'll believe it when I see it. Why didn't he do that in '61?"

Tom and Caroline, not the most politically-minded individuals, shrugged their shoulders in identical fashion.

"Kids, I heard a great Kennedy joke the other day. He was hosting a group of business leaders at the White House and started talking up how well the economy was doing under his leadership. The guests didn't agree of course. The President said, 'You know gentlemen, if I weren't President, I'd be buying stocks right now'. One of the business leaders replied, 'If you weren't President, I'd be buying them, too'."

The Judge guffawed. Tom and Caroline dutifully laughed as well, though they didn't get the joke at all.

"So, tell me exactly what you want for furnishings in your office and I'll get Marjorie to order it."

Caroline, of course, had this all thought out before she walked over. "Keen! We need a blocky grey metal file cabinet with paint chipping off. A beat-up pine desk with cigarette burns marring the wood. Some chairs on rollers that squeak when you sit in them. The desk needs two drawers, just two. One where the gumshoe keeps the half-filled bottle of cheap whiskey to offer clients, and another where he stashes his .38 gun."

The Judge was amused. "Sounds very *Mike Hammer.*"

"But Caroline, neither of us drink whiskey," Tom commented reasonably.

"Don't matter. Sultry Dames do. They can toss whiskey down with the best of 'em. They're our potential clients. Try to keep up with me, Tom."

The Judge sat down and pondered a few moments. "Let me go over this with Marjorie. She always has inspired ideas regarding how to decorate. Would it be OK, Caroline if she is in charge of the project?"

"Absolutely!" She tried to hug him again and he made an effective dodge. For an older gentleman, the Judge was quite nimble.

"Let me go fetch her and we can make plans." He walked out of the room.

Caroline stuck her tongue out at Tom. "He likes me best, Tom. That doesn't happen very often to Mr. Popularity on the golf tour, does it?"

Tom smiled.

Two weeks later, Tom, Caroline, Marjorie and the Judge walked into the finished office suite for Colt & Colt Confidential Investigations, on the third floor, the top floor, of the Valley Vista Country Club clubhouse. Theirs was the first and only PI firm to be headquartered in a country club.

Marjorie was introduced to Tom as the Judge's personal assistant. He eventually developed enough savvy to realize she was his live-in lover and part-time personal assistant. *Tom Colt, the streetwise detective, at your service,* he remarked to himself.

Everyone liked Marjorie Cluff. She was a gracious woman of about 50, known for wearing long flowing skirts and colorful silk blouses in southwest colors. She attacked any task the Judge gave her with enthusiasm and positive energy.

The Judge and Marjorie had huddled about Caroline's wished-for furnishings and came up with compromise solution. He called a friend of his who was a producer at Paramount Pictures in Hollywood and asked if he could purchase furniture from the set of a detective movie that had just wrapped, a recent adaptation of an Agatha Christie novel. His friend quickly obliged and shipped the set to Scottsdale.

The office furnishings were not those of the struggling down-on-his-luck gumshoe that Caroline envisioned, but a beautiful art-deco suite of desks, rugs, artwork showcasing the upscale, successful detective that was depicted in the Paramount film. Cool blues for the upholstery, light grey rugs. Rich, medium-brown toned wood on the furniture. Mid-century modern is what the look is termed now.

The Judge opened the door and Caroline walked into the suite first.

"Outta sight!" she exclaimed, her eyes wide. "It's like Gumshoe Modern."

The Judge pre-empted Caroline deftly. "So glad it's satisfactory, Caroline, but no need for a hug." Too late, Caroline grabbed him, tighter than the previous hug.

"Marjorie, Judge, this is wonderful!" Tom said.

After the look of shock from the latest Caroline hug left his leathery face, he smiled. "It was my pleasure, son. I'll let you get settled in."

After the Judge and Marjorie left, Caroline sat behind one of the desks. "This is better than the set-up on *Hawaiian Eye*. I am so stoked about our detective biz!"

"Lots of our clients will come from this very Country Club. The members here get into trouble on a regular basis."

"That's what rich people do. They can't seem to help it."

Tom said, "You hugged The Judge. No one grabs and hugs The Judge."

"He's not THE JUDGE. He's <u>My</u> Roy."

Tom, getting comfortable, sat at his desk and put his feet up. He thought, *My sister continues to amaze me, every day. In a weird way, Judge Roy Wilkinson needed her. Perhaps because his life had been about navigating through the business world, which is full of deceit, venality and sometimes treachery. I had already found out that rich people are seldom what they seem. There is always an element of their character they keep in the shadows.*

The Judge had the task of finding exactly what was hidden, so he could do business with these people without falling victim to their deceit.

My sister's directness, her total and complete honesty in all situations, was so different from what the Judge was used to, he welcomed it. No artifice at all, Caroline was always what she seemed.

"Roy called you 'son'," Caroline observed.

"I heard that. Nothing wrong with my hearing."

"Do you think the wealthy and important Judge Wilkinson might consider adopting us?"

"We're not orphans."

"I am."

Tom shook his head in mock dismay.

"He's probably the most powerful man in town and you've always resisted, even hated, authority figures. You didn't even like our first-grade teacher, sweet little Miss Hazlett."

"She had bad breath, like stale coffee and cigarettes. When she leaned over my shoulder to check my work, I felt like retching."

"OK. Name another authority figure you respect. Take your time. I have all day. We don't seem to have any sultry but troubled dames coming into the office with a retainer check in hand."

Caroline scowled, thought for a few moments.

"Detective Mathers. There, are you happy?"

"Very. He's one I respect, too. And I deduced that you're perhaps a little sweet on our Detective."

Caroline worked hard on maintaining an impassive expression.

***

Tom Continues Our Story:

Back at the Guest House that night, Caroline and I grilled New York Strip steaks, drank beer on the porch and chatted happily about the prospects for our detective business. I saw that, already, having a new career had improved her attitude.

Caroline said, "I want to think with absolute clarity, if I'm going to be a detective."

I nodded, not certain where the conversation was going.

"I realize pot and pills don't help me think the Big Thoughts. They just fool me into believing I'm thinking Big Thoughts. I really thinking dope-y thoughts."

She took four bottles of pills from her purse, went inside and washed them down the sink. Then did the same thing with three marijuana cigarettes.

In the '60s, a segment of the nation's youth resorted to taking drugs to seek relief from the post-WW II prosperity, peace and the rise of consumerism. Shopping can be such a drag, man. So can paying off department store charge cards.

Caroline's youthful bouts with drugs had already taken a toll on her health. She was much thinner than she had been even two years before, and tired out too easily for a young person. But it was her emotions that seemed fragile, too, not just her body.

Both of us could tolerate alcohol just fine, oddly. We, as twins, shared a nervous temperament that was soothed with a few bottles of beer. We always enjoyed beer and wine, never hard liquor though, and never really got drunk.

When Caroline returned to the porch, I said, "I...am proud of you. This world buried you in bullshit and you clawed your way out of it, with great strength of will. Hooray for Caroline!"

She sat down with a sigh. I couldn't tell what she was thinking. Finally she said, "That means so much to me, Tom. But why do I suddenly feel the need to take a long shower with Lava soap?"

The moment between us was sweet, but awkward. We were both more comfortable with playful combat than outwardly sentimental warmth. But I knew, mess with Tom Colt and Caroline Colt was liable to throttle you.

This was a milestone evening, to be sure. But with Caroline I had learned there was a good chance that she would lapse back...I hoped and prayed not.

***

Brooks Benton Continues Our Story:

Colt & Colt Confidential Investigations, the newly stenciled sign on the door read. Tom looked at it proudly as he opened the door for Caroline the next morning at 9am sharp.

Caroline busied herself with making a list of office supplies they needed. The detectives sat at their respective desks, stared out the window at the golf course, and learned a basic fact about the detective biz: It can get very boring waiting for a potential client to walk in.

Tom said, "I've been thinking I need to learn how to talk tougher, like the private eyes in the movies."

"Oh, no," Caroline said with a look of alarm.

"Let me run some phrases by you. 'Try that shit with me, mister, and you'll be taking your testicles home in a paper sack'."

"No, Tom. Don't use tough-guy detective language. You're a harmless golfer boy, remember. Let Bogart, Alan Ladd or Bob Mitchum be the tough guys."

"How about, 'Try that again mister, and I'll give you something to remember me by, and it won't be my business card'."

Caroline made a lemon-sour face. "That was worse. As I always say, I think you should let me be the tough guy. I'm not sure you have the capability to intimidate anyone, beyond, say a bunny rabbit with limited street experience."

"I'll keep practicing," Tom said cheerfully.

"You do that." Caroline picked up her purse from her desk and left to purchase office supplies. A few minutes later, the first guest to their new office was Katrina Stern.

Tom sprang out of his chair to greet her.

"So what do you think of the place?"

"Impressive..." she said, but the frown on her face betrayed what she was really thinking. "So you and Caroline are really doing this, the PI thing."

"Yes, and you are the first one to visit Colt & Colt Confidential. How could we be of service?"

He beckoned her to a couch near his desk. "Please tell me your story, Ms. Stern."

He flashed a smile and she sat down. Tom's smile always reassured her that all would be well.

"Just to make sure, you aren't a German spy are you?"

Kat became surprisingly angered. "That's not funny."

"I'm sorry," Tom said, not knowing why she was upset.

She waved away her own words. "Forget about it. It has nothing to do with you, with us, with today."

Tom didn't explore this further. Kat's family escaped Germany at the end of WWII and relocated to Brazil. She never talked much about her time in Germany. She kept all except the basic details private.

"I'm still opposed to you being a detective."

"I promise never to get shot again." Tom tried to make light of Kat's concern and failed. "We can talk about it on the island. Let's team up and win that tournament…"

"We're absolutely going to win."

She fidgeted on the couch a moment, then got up.

"I'm got some errands to run before I head out to San Diego. Just wanted to congratulate you on opening your office."

Tom got up and they embraced. "Thank you. Good luck in the tournament this week."

She smiled and walked out.

Tom, even early in their relationship knew he and Katrina were most likely soul mates. Both believed their romance was going full steam ahead to the next level. What's a more romantic place than a tropical island to make that kind of magic happen?

Neither had any inkling of how fate was going to intervene and disrupt their plans.

***

Tom Continues Our Story:

When I left the Club that day, I was walking to my car and saw just the person I didn't want to run into, my ex-wife Mandy, now married to Marco Greene. He was reputed to be 'an organized crime figure', although a friendly, outgoing one. The cops called him, among other things, The Merry Mobster, The Happy Gangster, The Joyous Gee, the Good Yegg. Their inability to pin a crime on him led them to pin nicknames on him.

Mandy had a cute figure and a pleasant face with dimpled cheeks that appeared when she laughed. She wore her light brown hair medium length to just above her shoulders, with attractive bangs that swept down her forehead.

Mandy and I had been married for just over a year, when we were in our early 20s. The marriage was one of the major regrets of my life; we were not a good match. Mandy wanted financial security from a husband, and I was not able to, as a struggling golfer, give that to her. We divorced, amicably, and she soon met Marco Greene.

Marco was the leading purveyor of prostitution in Phoenix in those days. He also owned four strip clubs. His venture capital was reputed to have come from the Chicago Mob.

He had a unique business model. He would purchase run-down hotel/motel properties, refurbish them (slightly) and then set up his "working girls" in them. He charged the women a high daily rate to occupy the room. Just like they were any other hotel guests. In this way he couldn't be busted for being a pimp. He did not get a share of the "revenue" they generated in the rooms. Pretty smart, that Merry Mobster.

In addition, because the room fees he charged his girls, termed Average Daily Rate in the hotel industry, were so high, when he sold one of the hotel properties, he received a premium price.

Mandy and I married in haste. Why did we do it? We were a temporary cure for a loneliness we both felt. And she was jazzed about having an up-and-coming golf star as a hubby. She had no idea that the coming up part would take so many years, and quickly tired of the perennial financial struggles we faced.

Money problems were the most compelling reason for our divorce, but we would have split up anyway, given time. Mandy's penchant for pouting, whining and complaining quickly got old.

She also had a penchant for blowing up little problems into big crises; but I eventually understood that she wasn't being dramatic, she believed they were huge crises.

Mandy and Marco's marriage always reminded me of an old saying, He/She who marries for money ends up having to earn that money over and over and over.

That afternoon, as I approached my car, Mandy was walking their cocker spaniels, Luci and Desi, on a hiking trail that went from the parking lot up into the desert that ran alongside the Valley Vista course. Forty years later, the whole sprawling area, even up top the low hills, were full of luxury homes.

She looked mopey. Mandy almost always looked mopey. She saw me, unfortunately, and waved enthusiastically. Sometimes I wish I didn't drive a bright red T-Bird that everyone noticed. Maybe switch to a mud-brown Oldsmobile with a blotchy paint job.

I walked over to her, sporting a fake smile of joy at seeing my ex. She said a brief hello, then launched into her favorite subjects, Mandy, Mandy and Mandy.

"I'm afraid Marco is having a relationship with his secretary Luiza. She's a total floozy. It's just the two of them in that office all day. Some days Marco is there from 7AM to dusk.

He doesn't have that much work! His business runs itself. I mean his biggest moneymaker is the prostitution business segment, and there's always strong demand for that."

"And the hookers who work for him do all the strenuous work," I couldn't help adding.

The pout bloomed into a mask of worry.

I made a skeptical face. I didn't see an affair happening. Marco was devoted to Mandy.

"You're the detective. What do you think is going on?"

"Probably nothing. I've met Luiza. Marco has better taste in women that that. I mean, he married you."

"You are so sweet. You always make me feel better. But what can I do to get this out of my head?"

"Take Marco an afternoon snack."

Mandy's eyes narrowed. "I don't understand."

"You said he loves your cooking and he loves to eat. If an affair is happening, it's probably in mid-afternoon when most of the meetings and the day's work is over. You show up with a tasty snack, stay a few minutes and chat. You'd be able to sense if any hanky-panky is going on. You are remarkably intuitive."

"You are just the smartest guy in the whole, wide world!"

"Thank you. I would tend to agree. Anyway, after consuming some of your great cooking, Marco forgets all about Luiza's gorgeous figure."

"You think her figure is gorgeous? OH NO! And by the way, you are no longer the smartest person in the world."

"I was just kidding. Cheer up, kiddo."

"You're right. I'll make a platter of gourmet cheese wedges and some sausage—Marco loves sausage." She exhaled with profound relief. "I feel so much better, thanks to you."

That's me, I thought. *Tom Colt: Champion Golfer, Golf Instructor, Detective, Marriage Counselor.* But I wondered whether I was any good at any of these occupations. At the time all I was certain of is that I was a damn good golf instructor.

"My pleasure to help, Mandy. You and Marco make such a cute, albeit Mafia couple."

"No need to be mean, Tom. Marco is just a businessman."

Who's quite proficient with a Tommy Gun, I imagine, I thought but did not say.

At that point Desi the Cocker Spaniel peed on my new Florsheim shoes. First time I'd worn them.

***

Brooks Benton Continues Our Story:

A golf pro is very much like a psychiatrist. Tom's golf lesson clients often told him things that they really shouldn't. Things that were secrets, things that even made Tom blush. Perhaps it was the relaxed, cloistered atmosphere of a private club, causing them to let down their guard. His early morning lesson with Carter Vonessen was a good example of this.

Tom was a brilliant golf instructor, as the now much improved Det. Ed Mathers would heartily attest, but there were some clients who simply did not listen or employ Tom's golf swing advice.

Vonessen's golf swing, painful for Tom to watch, was a flail followed by a gouge, and many times a grunt.

Vonessen, Tom learned, was also invited to the Grand Opening at Red Boyle's Bogey Island resort.

"Have you ever wanted to kill someone, Tom?"

"I've never had the occasion to get that angry at someone. I understand it, though, the impulse."

What he was referring to, but didn't express, was the night he intervened when Julia Wilkinson, unhinged by anger, wanted to shoot her abusive ex-boyfriend. The result was she 'accidentally' shot Tom in the shoulder and Derrick Rhodes, the wealthy boyfriend, walked away unscathed.

"Well, it's been a year since my dear sister Elizabeth went out one sunny morning on Red Boyle's boat and drowned in Roosevelt Lake. I can't get rid of the anger I feel. It's like I carry it with me everywhere."

"May I make a suggestion, Sir."

"I know, I know. Swing more slowly. Let the club do the work...blah, blah..."

"Not about golf, Sir. Perhaps don't go to Red Boyle's Grand Opening week. Seeing him day after day could be a most unpleasant experience for you, a trigger for your anger so to speak."

"You're afraid it'll be a trigger for my Smith & Wesson .44. I'll kill the sonofabitch and dumb his fat ass in the deep blue sea."

"Yes. And it won't get your sister back. And yes, you need to swing more slowly."

Tom noticed Carter's face getting crimson with anger. He swung even harder. He hit well behind the golf ball, which dribbled about 20 yards down the practice range.

"I can't promise anything, Tom. A golf swing is like an extension of your personality, your real self."

"With that, I would completely agree sir."

Tom thought as he walked back to the clubhouse after the lesson, *I already have a prime suspect and the murder hasn't even been committed yet. This detective BIZ is certainly easier than trying to win golf tournaments, especially the way that young Nicklaus kid is playing so far this year. The competition gets tougher all the time.*

***

At the end of the work day, Tom often took a long shower in the Men's Locker Room at the Club. It was his way of washing off the unpleasantness he often experienced as a humble golf instructor for the rich and fatuous.

The Men's showers in those days were just one big area lined with shower heads, no partitions, like the showers in a high school locker room. Tom wondered if that was because men enjoy comparing anatomy.

He chuckled as he recalled his parking lot meeting with Mandy, until he remembered a detail that had been turning over in his mind:

Mandy said she was going to serve sausage at Marco's office. What if she serves the Barker Spicy Brazilian Brats? Disaster for sure. He thought of calling her and warning her about the effects of that special sausage, but she would have already brought them to Marco's office that afternoon.

OH CRAP! Tom thought, dropping the bar of Dial soap on his little toe.

He didn't hear what happened until he ran into Mandy at the Club dining room the next week. Yes, she had served those special Barker Spicy Brazilian Brats…

Marco was not there when she delivered them to the office, Mandy told Tom. He was running late from a meeting. Mandy chatted with the clueless Luiza a few moments, determined quickly that her savvy husband would not waste any time romancing a ditz like that.

She left and Luiza, after consuming three Barker Brazilian Brats, ended up having sex with the Dentist down the hall, Dr. Ira Shenkman, after sharing the brats with him. Yes, The

Dentist. I began to understand just how powerful those Bratwurst were.

Marco had to let Luiza go from her job the next day. He muttered about the declining morality of young people today. It wasn't so much 'cuz she had sex on his couch in the office. It was with A Dentist. There was a perfectly good accountant in their building she could have chosen.

But there's a happy ending: Marco hired her back a week later. Marco Greene was perhaps the most soft-hearted gangster in the history of organized crime. Her first day back, he noticed the tiny chip she had in one of her front teeth, which Marco found distracting given that otherwise Luiza was a perfect beauty, for a floozy, had been repaired by Dr. Shenkman. Gratis.

Mandy again thanked Tom for his sound advice. Her beloved Mafia husband was completely faithful to her.

Pleased with himself, Tom considered adding 'relationship counseling' to the list of services offered by Colt & Colt Confidential.

***

Chapter Eight
The Continuing Financial Education of a Poor Boy

Judge Roy Wilkinson invited his young protégé Tom Colt to a Friday night party at a rich guy's home high atop Camelback Mountain in Phoenix. The Judge didn't know it, but this was the same luxurious home where Tom had worked as a busboy at a catering gig with his mom, ten years earlier.

Tom on that night ten years ago, surveying the twinkling lights of the fast-growing city of Phoenix, made a pledge to himself that, "Someday this will all be mine." It was the sort of impractical, unachievable pledge most highly ambitious young men make when they are 17—even those currently employed carrying dirty dishes to a kitchen.

Now, ten years later, so much had changed for young Tom Colt. The Judge enjoyed showing Tom off to his friends. Tom was now a mini-celebrity for helping Phoenix PD solve the Lisa Luck murder—and winning his first professional golf tournament the same year. The other highlight of Tom's remarkable year of 1962, being shot by the Judge's daughter Julia—accidentally we all hoped—was never brought up by the Judge. It was as though it never happened.

The Judge was driving his sleek black Lincoln Continental up the gradual, winding incline to the home near the top of the mountain—driving too fast Tom thought. The Judge had his left hand on the bottom of the steering wheel. His right hand, as per usual, was occupied with a cigarette.

On the way there Tom, who struggled to make small talk with this mighty man that he all but idolized and certainly feared, asked the Judge if he ever took a day off to relax by his beautiful pool at home.

The Judge shook his head. "Not a productive use of my time. I try to utilize every moment I have of every day, to advance my goals. Sitting in a lounge chair doesn't get me anywhere. But you and Caroline are welcome to use the pool whenever you want. They say swimming is good exercise."

He puffed on a cigarette and commented, "If you have no vices, how can you tell you're still alive? Being a saint was never one of my ambitions."

Anytime Tom was alone with Judge Wilkinson, the Judge couldn't help instructing Tom on how to achieve great wealth. He assumed that was something Tom was keenly interested in. I mean, isn't everyone? He also liberally shared his political philosophy.

As they neared their destination, a brilliantly lit home near the top of the mountain, the Judge said, "We're a nation of individuals. That's our strength. Collectivism is the plague of mankind. It enslaves people under the idea the government is helping them. It is best to free the individual to go as far as his talent and drive can take him. We separate ourselves by striving, achieving. Collectivism demands that we're all going to end up in the same place. That's garbage, idiocy. Socialist ideas are abhorrent to me."

Tom could see the brightly lit mansion looming near the top of the mountain.

"Our Creator made each of unique. Politicians try to lump us into groups so they can direct us how to vote as groups. Don't fall for it. There's only one Tom Colt. And there's only one Roy Wilkinson in the entire world."

Which the Judge's business and political adversaries would have been relieved to hear, Tom thought.

Tom made an earnest effort to understand, and embrace, the Judge's philosophy of the preeminence of the individual, as the Judge called it. Most days, though, preeminent is not what Tom felt. How would he go about achieving it?

The Judge generally didn't seek out a comment from Tom about his views. He looked over at Tom several times to make sure he was listening, then continued his mini economics lecture.

"America is one of the great success stories of mankind, perhaps the greatest since Our Creator put us here. And our success is the sum of all the individual successes of each of us. What we accomplish as individuals adds up to our prosperity as a nation. That's why each of us must do our part, do our best every day."

Tom nodded in agreement. He strove to do his best, every day—but some days didn't believe he was up to the task. Success in life was much harder than he believed it would be when he was a teenager.

The Judge continued: "The unproductive sector of society, the government agencies, in their vast and ever-expanding arrogance, believe that they can police the private sector—us, American industry, the builders, the creators, the movers, the shakers.

"Much better I think, is we police ourselves. Consider golf, there isn't an FBI agent lurking behind every tree, watching you in tournaments to see if you cheat. Golfers are honorable gentlemen, and we police ourselves."

Tom thought, Except for Rodney Burkett, whom he had seen cheating several times.

Tom nodded. He was never confident enough to question and certainly not argue with the Judge.

"Now, before we get to the party, let me tell you what your assignment is tonight. My old friend from college Red Boyle will be there. He thinks, as you know, that someone wants to kill him. This is a good time for you to meet him. I got you the invite to his pro-am in March so you can investigate. Take Caroline as your caddie. That's your 'cover' as the private eyes say, so no one suspects why you're there. I'd keep an eye on his children. Red is a great businessman but not so good a father."

"You think one of them might actually want to kill him?"

The Judge stopped the car long enough to light up another cigarette and think about Tom's question, then resumed driving. They approached the gate to the property where the party was being held.

"Yes," the Judge said as he coasted the car up next to the awaiting valet parking attendant.

The party was mostly inside the ranch-style house that night, but a few scattered guests wandered outside to the pool area to enjoy the incredible view of one of the fastest growing cities in America, Phoenix. Tom and the Judge were among them, the Judge with a scotch in hand, Tom with a bottle of Blatz beer.

Judge Wilkinson introduced Tom to a gracious man named Paul Fannin who happened to be the Governor of Arizona, who served between 1959 and 1965. He wasn't the typical bumptious politician, the Judge commented to Tom. "Most likely because he was a successful small businessperson, then entered politics. In business you serve the customers' needs to succeed, put their needs first. Career politicians often forget all about their customers, the voters, the minute the election is over."

Fannin was a friendly man, greying at the temples just enough to convey quiet authority.

It really struck Tom how far he had come in the last ten years when he shook hands with the Governor of Arizona—and the Governor knew who he was.

Tom and his mentor continued mingling. Tom knew several other of the party attendees, members of Valley Vista, but there were also other businesspeople the Judge took the time to introduce Tom to. It was all planned on the Judge's part: he wanted to build Tom's circle of social contacts for future use in business. The Judge knew Tom couldn't play professional golf forever.

"Look at this, Tom. Look at what we're building here. Can you feel the pulse of it all—the industry, the ambition, the rising prosperity?"

Tom nodded affirmatively, but at 28, he didn't really feel a part of it yet. He was still a struggler, a striver, in his own mind at least.

The Judge continued: "Mankind's condition for most of history has been poverty, want, starvation and disease. But our modern age has changed all that. Each light you see down there represents a dream—a dream that can be possible now. Life will be spectacular, and The West, specifically Phoenix, Arizona, specifically people like you and me, will lead the way."

Tom nodded affirmatively again. That's just what you did when you were an ambitious young man and Judge Roy Wilkinson spoke.

"I love my city, Tom."

"Where did you grow up, sir?"

The Judge looked off in the distance a few moments.

"Oh, it's not important. Just a place. This, Phoenix, is what's important."

Tom wondered why the Judge seldom talked about his life before he moved here. But that's the way it was with many people then. Phoenix meant the chance for a fresh start, to put the past behind you and never bring it up again.

Tom glanced over at his mentor, this mighty man. It almost seemed like Roy had an authentic smile, of joy, on his face as he looked out over the array of lights spread before them. Usually his smile looked forced—a social grace that was expected but the Judge didn't really mean.

He took a nice slug of his scotch. The city lights, his city, and alcohol had combined to inspire and animate the Judge. He normally was reserved, as though he was analyzing those he talked to in order to calculate their potential to help him become wealthier. But that night Tom saw a different side. He was expansive, his eyes shone with a kind of idealism Tom had not seen before.

Alcohol consumption left Tom in an expansive mood as well. At that moment in Tom's 28th year, as he looked at the

Judge standing by the native stone wall with all the beautiful lights spread out below him, Tom regarded him as the King of the Earth—a man who could get anything done, any time he wanted to.

"I'm not sure I ever told you why I chose to be your financial sponsor on the golf tour. It wasn't because I was convinced you were going to be the next great champion. It was because I saw the spark of ambition, of desire, in you I had when I was young. With my help, you are going to do great things well beyond playing great golf."

"I appreciate everything you've done for me, and for Caroline, sir."

Roy smiled at the mention of Tom's sister. This smile did indeed convey warmth.

"All I ask Tom is that you never doubt me. There will come a time when I ask you to do something...difficult. Something that makes you uneasy and causes you a moral dilemma. Just work through that. That's what it takes to acquire great wealth, which I know is what you want."

Tom's eyes narrowed. He had been warned about the Judge by several members of Valley Vista. Not that they thought Judge Roy Wilkinson was crooked exactly. More like so determined that he didn't view obstacles as significant. He thought he could, and would, knock them down. These obstacles, in human form, felt like they had been run over when Roy got finished with them.

Tom thought he heard the unmistakable sound of someone...farting. He frowned.

"That's Red, your client. He has a problem with uncontrollable flatulence."

"Not very classy of Mr. Boyle, is it. Farting up the place in front of the Governor of Arizona!"

Tom's mom would have been proud to see how her lessons in decorum had been successfully instilled in Tom. She had told him, when you start off with less money and prestige than other people in your social set, one way to fit in is to have the best manners and a winning personality.

The Judge said, "Don't give it a worry, Tom. Gov. Fannin's used to dealing with stinkeroos every day in the state legislature. Remember Sen. Richard Luck...that asshole. Can't believe he stayed in office after the scandal."

Tom enjoyed how the Judge hated politicians. He was starting to become of the same mind after his experience the year before helping solve the murder of the state senator's wife.

The Judge introduced Tom to Elwood "Red" Boyle. Red complimented Tom on all he had accomplished and oddly, dissed his own children as being lazy. They chatted about Tom and Caroline coming to the Bogey Island Grand Opening Party, to do some sleuthing into the danger he may be in.

"I've never been a man who's afraid of anything—but I have to tell you, this time I'm, if not scared, very concerned. The Judge says you're the man for the job. And I believe him implicitly."

Red gave Tom a slap on the back.

"See you there, at my island, young man. Gotta mingle now. Want to invite the Governor to my Grand Opening event. He won't go, but politicians like being asked. And you never know when I might need a favor. Roy can tell you all about me. He knows where the majority of my skeletons are buried. Not all of them, though." Red wandered off.

The drive home involved a continuation of Tom's Continuing Education.

Tom was careful to never point out to the Judge when he repeated one of his political lectures, which he often did.

"You met the Governor tonight. You were excited, I could tell. He's a good man. But not all politicians are like him. The dangerous politicians are the ones who seek public office as a means to get rich—because all of the dark dealmaking that goes on in Washington DC. Never put your faith in the federal government. Have faith in God and in yourself."

Tom nodded.

"I'm sorry. I sometimes tend to make a speech. I don't mean to lecture you. I'm not your father, after all. It's not my role to instruct you."

"I enjoy hearing your views, sir."

Tom didn't add, but the Judge knew anyway, that Tom's complete thought was: *I enjoy hearing your views, I need to hear them actually, because my own father disappeared a long time ago, and Caroline and I both need an older person to advise us, show us the way. We need a dad. There's a lot of stuff about life we don't know.*

It was remarkable that young Tom Colt knew this, the need to be shown the way. Many young people do not.

The Judge became uncharacteristically quiet for five minutes as they sailed down Lincoln Drive toward the Judge's estate. Then the formerly taboo subject was broached, to Tom's surprise.

"Julia still feels awful about the gun accident. She cries quite often, thinking about it. It affected her terribly. You have no idea how much you mean to my daughter."

Tom didn't know how to react to his. The Judge had quickly and with surgical precision re-oriented Tom's perspective so that he now felt guilty that Julia continued to be distressed from having shot him. Carelessly, stupidly shot him, and nearly costing him his golf career and possibly his life.

"Please tell her I'm all healed. I don't want her suffering over this. It's all forgotten." Tom packed two lies between one truth. Tom was the kind of soul who never wanted anyone to suffer.

"I think it will soon be time for you to tell her yourself."

And with that Judge Wilkinson completed his mission for that evening.

"Sir, do you think someone really wants to murder Mr. Boyle?"

The Judge laughed. It sounded mocking to Tom. He frowned.

"That's not the issue for your investigative inquiry. The question is which of the several individuals who want Red Boyle dead is planning to act on that homicidal impulse during the Grand Opening week at Bogey Island. Identify that person is your assignment."

The remainder of the drive home was deathly quiet.

***

Chapter Nine
The Annual Birthday Fracas—A Colt Family Tradition

Tom Continues Our Story:

I was dreading my birthday, as I did every year as January 27th approached. Since I shared that day with my twin sister, it meant Caroline and our mom Laura going at each other with all the rancor they could muster, over a hearty and invariably delicious Italian birthday dinner of 4 courses at least, and dessert, prepared by mom, the best Italian cook in Phoenix.

Mom never served pie for fear Caroline would toss it at her in the midst of arguing. And mom, never one to back down, would toss some retaliatory pie of her own. So for the last several birthdays she went with heavy ceramic ramekins of chocolate mousse, difficult to heave with any accuracy.

This year, 1963, with the two of us turning 28 years old, I hatched a top-secret plan to defuse conflict and maybe, maybe even have a semi-pleasant time. I did become weary of cleaning up chocolate mousse from the carpet at mom's house every year.

I arrived at Mom's first and executed the elements of my Plan.

Laura Colt still lived in the little bungalow-style house in the modest south Scottsdale neighborhood we grew up in. Its most charming features were the colorful flowers Laura Colt planted on nearly every inch of the front yard. Vines twined up the wrought-iron fence that bordered the property. Every time I visited there, I couldn't believe four of us occupied that tiny space. The Guest House where Caroline and l lived now was much larger.

In the driveway was a maroon van with the sign, COLT CATERING on each side panel.

Laura Colt, at 49, was a trim, petite woman with dark red hair worn in the short bob style. She had a warm, reassuring smile. Some days the smile was an effort for Laura, though. Her years of struggling to make a success of her catering business after her husband was lost in the Korean War had left their mark. In unguarded moments you could see how weary Laura was.

She and I greeted each other the same way every time we got together: an almost fierce hug. We had been through so much, since my father disappeared.

Minutes later, Caroline knocked on the door. "Mother, your crummy little daughter has arrived."

That gives you a concise preview of what happens on our birthdays. We sat down and enjoyed a glass of Merlot while dinner was cooking. The conversation started out harmlessly enough...

Have you noticed how our mothers talk about our days as an infant as though it were yesterday. Maybe to them, it was.

The first course was pasta with pancetta, tomatoes and onions. The dish had garlic, red pepper flakes and basil, topped with pecorino Romano cheese.

Delish! Laura gave me a second helping and said, "When you were infants and I was nursing you, the pediatrician suggested I drink a glass of beer each day. The malt in the beer was good for you and it would relax me, said he. Breastfeeding isn't easy. Guess what brand I chose: BLATZ. And then when you reached drinking age, hopefully it was legal drinking age (Laura glanced over at Caroline with a sharp motherly glare)--what brand did you like best: BLATZ. Isn't that strange."

Caroline thought, *Dang I wish Doc had told her to take cocaine.* Her smile of mischief gave her away.

"What are you thinking about?"

"Only that baby Caroline would have needed something stronger than beer to make it through the rigors of infancy."

We all laughed. So far so good, thought I...

Next was the main course, herbed pork chops. The herb mixture was garlic, rosemary, thyme, marjoram, sage and parsley. They key was Mom covering both sides of the pork with the chopped herbs, then refrigerating them overnight. Wow it was yummy! Caroline thought so, too. She ate two chops by herself. She talked enthusiastically about our private investigation business.

Mom listened with great interest land said, "I think this is just wonderful! Both of you are so smart! The crooks won't have a chance."

I poured us each more wine, hoping to keep the positive vibe going. Mom served the next dish, roasted bell peppers in balsamic vinegar. Yum! But you could put balsamic vinegar on my breakfast cereal and I'd be happy.

I was stuffing my face with all this wonderful food like a starving person, but probably because I was nervous about this dinner. That's the excuse I'll go with.

On to the ramekins of chocolate mousse.

I saw Caroline's mood start to unaccountably sink. I had seen this many times before, but I never understood what happens in her head or why...

Caroline tossed her fork down. It clanked pointedly on mom's fine china dinner plate. "Well, aren't we the wonderful little bullshit family. We'll be on the cover of the *Saturday Evening Post* in no time. Norman Rockwell, get out your paints and easel."

Laura was not going to let Caroline get away with this, not tonight. "Do you have to profane everything Caroline, even the beautiful moments in life?"

I shifted in my chair. I knew well the explosion that was to follow.

"Yes, I do. Because one day my dad left, and never came back to me, and no one, none of you, ever explained to me why."

"It's because none of us knows," Laura said.

Caroline's voice rose. "I don't believe that. You always lie to me."

Silence for a few moments. Laura Colt's forehead creased, the sign of fury on the Colt faces. All three of us did this. To an outside observer, it might have looked comical.

"I don't care if you don't believe it. And I'm tired of treating you like a delicate crystal glass that's going to shatter if I say the wrong thing. So grow up, or shut up."

Laura's vehemence startled Caroline and Tom both. May have startled Laura.

I had to pessimistically conclude that those two, Caroline and Laura, should part ways forever. The bitterness ran too deep. I thought tonight was one last chance to salvage our family. Not even because it was that important to me. But it would have been important to our dad. One of his favorite expressions was, "Let's all be nice." HA! The three of us sure failed him there.

I saw I was a fool to even try. I remember something Judge Wilkinson told me, *You're such an amusing little idealist, Tom. I'll have to get you past that if you want to succeed in life in a big way. Idealism inevitably leads to deep disappointment. Life is for tough, hard men.*

But I wasn't quite ready to throw in the towel that evening. We still had birthday presents to give Caroline.

We had decorated Caroline's old room with her accomplishments through her high school years. After the splendid chocolate mousse, which I am pleased to say, we greedily consumed but did not toss, I led Caroline to the back bedrooms.

She had thrown away her high school yearbooks. I had reacquired them. "How did you find these?"

"Tom put advertisements in the newspaper."

Our English teacher, Lisbeth Stirdivant, signed a Happy Birthday poster and penned a rave about Caroline's essays she wrote in American Lit class.

I had looked through copies of the school newspaper for mentions of Caroline's accomplishments, which were numerous.

Caroline was a star on the girls' basketball team. And the drama club.

I found photos of her high school play performances. Her report cards, all straight 'As' until junior year when dad disappeared. A photo of her at Mission Beach in San Diego when she had a wonderful glow of health, before she lost weight from…well, her lifestyle.

Her emotions rose, but Caroline kept a tight rein on them as she toured her old bedroom. She put her hand to her mouth as if to bottle it all in. She examined every framed photo, every memento. "I didn't think the teachers would remember me. It's been more than ten years…"

From clear across the room, with the peculiar wavelength twins share, I could feel the force of Caroline's will to not show tears of joy to our mom. She touched some of the frames as though trying to access the positive energy from each memory they represented.

Caroline then looked at me, attempting but failing to be mocking. She patted the bed. "You sit here, Tom. It must be tiring being as fabulous as you are. I mean, you win golf tournaments, solve crimes that baffle the cops, and come to the aid of wayward women and various other lost souls. You probably rescue lost puppies and kitties in your spare time. And I forgot, delivering hot meals to shut-ins. Yes, maybe you should rest."

Then in fine Caroline fashion, just as quickly the dripping sarcasm dried up and she said, with surprising warmth and sincerity, "This is the best birthday I've ever had. And you didn't even have to buy me a bicycle. To both of you, it's the nicest thing anyone has ever done for me."

Laura motioned to Tom. "It's not over, dear."

He handed Caroline an envelope.

She opened it. Bit her lower lip so hard Tom was afraid blood would spurt out. "I've been accepted to the Boyle Academy of the Performing Arts. And someone has paid my first year's tuition. Who might those someone's be? Are their initials L and T?"

I fibbed and said, "This was Mom's idea. She paid for the whole thing."

Caroline made a sound like that was sort of a cross between a laugh and a lament.

I'd love to tell all of you that we three had a bonding moment, a reconciliation, the dam of poisoned emotions burst and we all shed tears and hugged and said we're sorry and promised to be inseparable and supportive of each other from now on.

But that's not Caroline. Not in 1963, at any rate. My sister would never willingly participate in a storybook ending.

An hour later, as we departed Mom's house, Caroline stood at her car door, paused before opening it like she had something to say.

I came outside. Laura Colt was watching from the large front window. She and I smiled at one another and exchanged the thumbs up signal. I walked to my red T-Bird.

Caroline said, "I saw that, sly boots. You and Mother cooked this up together for months I bet."

I shrugged. Caroline continued, "When you came out of the womb, your tiny little hand flashed the thumbs up sign."

"It's not good to store up bad feelings for years. Not healthy."

"Did you read that in one of your positive thinking books? Here's a news bulletin: Positive Thinking doesn't work for all of us. Some people's lives just suck."

"Maybe I'm here to make sure yours doesn't suck. Even if you want it to."

Caroline shook her head, got in her car and rumbled off, the long out-of-tune engine emitting a remarkable belch of foul smoke. Why, since we lived under the same roof, did Caroline take her own car to our birthday party? In case she needed to make a quick escape.

For all my efforts, Caroline could still not forgive our mother. But then, I asked myself as I drove home, *Forgive her for what?*

I finally figured out what sets Caroline off: merely being back in the home where we grew up. She remembered our dad sitting at the dining room table, where we had fabulous dinners and lively, hopeful conversation. Now she sees the empty chair where he will never sit again.

A thought crossed my mind that great food was going to bring us together again. I can't explain why. Just one of those intuitive notions that come to me sometimes.

I thought, *Let's try dinner at the Guest House next time...yes! Caroline and I will cook for Mom.*

But all in all, a successful birthday dinner this one, for the start of our 28th year. No one was injured from flying plates or glassware.

"You're such an amusing little idealist, Tom"—Judge Roy Wilkinson, 1963

***

Brooks Benton Continues Our Story:

To be precise, mighty Judge Roy Wilkinson, Tom Colt was a romantic idealist. Still is, all these years later, and after the worst he's seen of humanity as a detective.

An hour after her children left the birthday party, Laura Colt, bundled up in a fur-lined jacket against the deepening chill of the winter night in the desert, went for a brisk walk through her neighborhood. Briskly was how Laura attacked every task.

She hoped the exercise might help rid her of the tension from yet another Tom and Caroline birthday.

This one was a vast improvement over last year's. Chocolate mousse is so very difficult to remove from cream-colored carpet.

She sighed, releasing that tension, and considered her children. Tom was so much like her. They shared the spirit she termed 'Romanza'—that persistent optimism that finding all the good things in life was always possible, especially love.

She wondered if Tom was going to fall in love as many times as she had. There was a downside to this 'romanza' spirit: the potential for heartbreak. Sometimes, as she had experienced more than once, a heartbreak that cannot heal.

Laura never perceived that same spirit in Caroline. Perhaps that was a good thing—it would protect her heart from the kind of damage Laura's had sustained, and Tom's was likely to. But of course, without that spirit, how can you make your dreams come true?

Laura's husband, Tom and Caroline's father, was probably not even the love of her life. There was not one, but two candidates for that laurel.

It would have surely shocked her children to learn the identities of either of those two gentlemen.

And to add further complexity to Laura's heartscape, she wished with all of her might that her husband, lost in the war, was still alive and would return to her someday.

The 'romanza' spirit, Laura knew, and Tom was learning every day, did not lead us down straight and easy paths.

Chapter Ten

The Boyle Academy of the Performing Arts (BAPA) was in the heart of downtown Scottsdale, Arizona. It had been a middle school campus that closed because the town was running out of kids, the population slowly but surely aging as retirees moved there from other states. Red Boyle bought the property for a song and renovated it into a beautiful setting to learn the performing arts—theater, music, film.

It was a very expensive proposition to enroll in BAPA. Caroline might not have accepted the gift from Tom and their Mother (she knew it was Tom's idea, not Mother's) if she were aware how much the tuition set them back.

The BAPA campus had been done over in beautiful Boyle Resort Properties colors including turquoise and plum, gardens and trees had been planted, and the facilities featured state-of-the-art audio-visual and recording technology (for 1963!).

Caroline enrolled in the theater course which included acting and voice training. She also did some sleuthing during her first days in the Academy, knowing Red Boyle had asked for their services with, well, keeping him alive.

She had learned from Tom how to be more outgoing and engage with people as a way of finding clues. She quickly charmed the instructors at the Academy and learned quite a bit about Red Boyle, the Founder.

He was married once, had one child, then divorced and had a kid with each of two mistresses, like Ben Cartwright had three children with three different wives on the *Bonanza* TV series. Red could never be described as a devoted family man. He was a notorious woman-chaser. He funded BAPA not because he was a patron of the arts, but because he was a patron of the young female artist.

His current favorite Academy student was Autumn Amber, whom Caroline recognized from several guest shots she had had on television shows, including *Have Gun Will Travel* and *77 Sunset Strip*. She had gone from precocious teen roles to blossoming into a beauty. A glamour photo of Autumn was hung on the wall outside the little theater where acting classes were held at BAPA.

Caroline's instant assessment of Autumn Amber: Big caramel-colored hair piled high on her head (which was coming in style then), big puppy dog eyes that boys love, large boobs that boys really love, and surprisingly tall, perhaps 5'11" in heels. Caroline had to admit that Autumn had a quality of warmth and vulnerability that shone even in the photo; she could see how a camera, or an old fart like Red, would be drawn to her.

Red had pulled some strings with Hollywood friends and managed to get Autumn a three-film acting contract with a major studio. The instructor who provided this information to Caroline made sure she understood Red intended he would be repaid somehow for his generosity.

Caroline also learned that Autumn and her doting, but pushy, parents were working hard on convincing Red to finance an independent film written by her screenwriter father and produced by her mother.

BAPA, because of Red's salacious behavior, got a bad reputation in town. There were whispers of, "What goes on at that place?"

Anything Red Boyle desired to go on.

More gossip: The Board of Directors of BAPA had asked him at the end of '62 to not be involved in the day-to-day operations. They hired new Managing Directors for the Academy. Red remained Chairman of the Board.

Rumors were rife down the thick-carpeted corridors of BAPA that Red was considering selling the whole thing. Without Red's financial backing, the Academy was not profitable, despite the high tuition that was charged.

Between all this sleuthing, Caroline also impressed her theater/voice instructors. They singled her out in class for her gorgeous singing voice and her natural ability to emote onstage.

Caroline Colt, who for her first 27 years failed at, and had been miserable in, every career she tried, now had promising futures in two, theater and private investigation.

Damn that Tom, she thought. *Why does he always have to be right?*

***

At the spacious, beautifully appointed, and heavily-mortgaged Paradise Valley, AZ home of the Ambersons, film folk from Los Angeles, an argument took place between Asst. Producer at Pacific Sunset Pictures, Tracy Amberson, and her 22-year-old daughter Autumn, an actress who went by the stage name Autumn Amber.

Tracy was blonde, trim, glamourous with a bright Hollywood smile, and an aggressively vivacious personality that featured exaggerated hand gestures at key moments in a conversation. She was always wearing the latest, most expensive styles in clothes. She exuded class. She also looked at least ten years younger than her 44 years.

Tracy had worked up the ladder in the film biz from lowly script reader and struggling actress to Asst. Producer. She only acted in one film before moving behind the camera into production. Tracy's psyche bore the scars of each rung of passage up that ladder. Just imagine an entire industry populated with Red Boyles...

The argument was taking place in the walk-in closet of the upstairs bedroom of their tri-level home set against the majestic backdrop of Mummy Mountain. The two women had to navigate around Tracy's huge collection of shoes to continue the argument. Tracy opened two dress boxes and examined her latest purchases.

"We've spent a fortune on your career. We're almost broke. Your young perky tits, at least passable talent and pretty ass are going to make us rich again. Red Boyle has been so good to us all, including you."

Amber frowned. "Do you want me to sleep with Mr. Boyle? He farts, you know. At BAPA the students call him *The Founding Farter* of the school."

Both women giggled at that one.

Tracy put the dresses on hangers. The closet was bulging with clothes.

"You might be surprised that at one time I was a lot prettier than you, and certainly sexier. And much more ambitious. In America, the ones who win are those who want it the most."

Autumn was going to correct Tracy about the ambition part—her mother had her working as a child actress since Autumn was 10—but never got the chance to open her mouth.

Tracy continued, "But looks aren't enough in this business. Everyone is gorgeous. You have to want success so badly that you're willing to do anything to get it--anything."

Tracy looked at her near-perfect daughter, who looked the part of the young dream girl in movies. She remembered when she looked that way, too. But she didn't really admire Autumn for her beauty. She was just jealous of it. And intended to profit from it.

"You have to learn to be a team player. You, me and your dad are the team. You're not a child star anymore. You're a grown woman. And a beautiful one. Take advantage of what you have! I did, let me tell you."

"But he's creepy."

"Creepy men make the decisions in show business, darling. That's just a fact you must accept. We all do things we don't want to, in order to advance in life. How do you think I got all those promotions at the studio? Me, a young female executive…in a man's world."

She glared at her daughter a few moments.

"Maybe you don't want to know."

But Autumn already knew.

"Your dad and I are depending on you to 'close the deal' with Red. Nothing more your father and I can do. Boyle has the script your father wrote—it's brilliant by the way—and the financial plan I put together for the film."

Dick Amberson called their daughter, our Virgin Queen, because Autumn had not yet been with a man, which always made Tracy chuckle because there weren't too many powerful men in Hollywood Tracy hadn't been with.

"Red Boyle wouldn't be an awful choice for your first time. He's certainly experienced."

Autumn registered revulsion. "I have a precious gift. I can wait. I <u>will</u> wait until I find love."

Hells bells, Tracy thought. *I gave birth to a little Republican. How did that happen?*

***

An hour later, Tracy went into Dick Amberson's home office, where he was sitting by his Underwood typewriter, staring blankly at a blank page.

This would be their usual dreary discussion: how their financial fortunes were sinking like the Titanic. The house in Paradise Valley was nearly in foreclosure. Their savings accounts were depleted by Dick's cocaine habit. They were on the verge of bankruptcy.

They still tried valiantly to live the high life in Scottsdale, which included a membership at the extremely expensive Valley Vista Country Club.

Dick tossed a letter to the edge of his desk, for Tracy to read. It was from Red Boyle:

> *Sorry to let you know via letter rather than in-person, but my schedule is not my own these days with the Grand Opening of my resort coming up. I'm putting the film project with you on hold. Indefinitely I'm afraid. But do come to the Grand Opening anyway. My treat. I want to show off my most famous BAPA graduate. And who knows, you may meet some new financial backers there...*

"What will we do?" Dick said listlessly.

"Leave it to me. We'll go to the island and smooth everything over. Boyle just likes to bluff. Maybe he wants us to grovel for the money."

"We'll go under, lose everything. This was supposed to be our financial comeback. I wrote a great script. It's Academy Award material. And Autumn will be a breakout star."

"I've already told Autumn what needs to be done..."

Dick snorted (which he is quite accomplished at). "The Virgin Queen. Great." He tore the page out of the typewriter and flung it into the waste basket.

If only the scenes he wrote could be so dramatic, Tracy thought.

"We'll have to give up our membership at Valley Vista. Only club in town worth belonging too, you know. Much more prestigious than Paradise Valley CC. We can't let Red Boyle do this to our reputation."

***

Tom and Det. Mathers were having cheeseburgers at the downtown Phoenix Bob's Big Boy restaurant, conveniently located near police headquarters for these two burger loving detectives, one professional and one amateur. Tom believed he had solved The Great Bratwurst Mystery and was ready to tell Mathers.

"There is some kind of spice in the sausages that is mind-altering. All you can think about is sex after you've eaten them. Works on both men and women."

"How'd you figure this out?"

"Keen observation as usual. Tom Colt's always on top of the case."

"Maybe the spice is on the list of controlled substances. I could bust Stan Barker on drug charges."

Tom didn't particularly care for Stan Barker but didn't want to wreck the guy's life. Katrina seemed to like him.

"I doubt he's involved in something illegal. Why don't you just pay him a visit. His processing plant is just down the street, 20th Avenue and Thomas."

"Will do. Thanks for the tip, buddy."

***

The following morning at Barker Fine Sausages Inc.

No doubt about it. Stan Barker wanted that girl. And he was one of those hugely optimistic young businessmen of the 1960s who usually got what they wanted—no matter how much work it required. He had taken his family's small sausage making operation and grown it exponentially in the six years since he succeeded his Uncle Gustav as president of the company.

At work in the test kitchen, as he stuffed sausage casings with a rich, wet mixture of spices and various meats, some of which had names you'd recognize, his staff heard him singing to the tune of song from the popular musical *West Side Story*, "Katrina, Katrina, I just met a girl named Katrina…"

Katrina had an intoxicating effect on Stan. If you're an American of German descent, as he was, meeting an authentic, lovely German girl can be incredibly exciting, stirring deep ethnic bonds that reach back the generations.

Or maybe Stan just like Katrina's cute, firm ass.

Yes, Stan Barker wanted that girl. He was as excited about her as when he acquired his company's major competitor in a hostile takeover, a sausage and cheese company in Omaha. Perhaps Kat could be his next great acquisition.

But did the girl want to be acquired?

Stan didn't spend a lot of time considering that question.

Stan's secretary appeared and said there was Phoenix Police Detective who wanted to see him. This news would knock many a businessman off stride, but Stan was unperturbed, still dreaming of Katrina, Katrina…

Stan was happy to give Detective Mathers a tour of the processing plant.

He revealed that, yes, in his Spicy Brazilian Bratwurst, there is an aphrodisiac spice in the mixture, from a source deep within the rain forest. He wasn't aware the spice was on any kind of prohibited drug list.

"I have heard your sausages are causing strange behavior among the country club set. Not that they aren't always strange over there..."

"I see." Barker was the type of businessman who wanted no trouble with the authorities. In his business, he followed every single regulation to the letter, particularly the health codes for food processors.

"Frankly, detective, I was thinking of discontinuing the product. It's really hard to source the supply of this spice. It's outrageously expensive. I have to price the product at retail so only the very rich can afford it. My mission is to make sausage for the masses. It is one of the healthiest foods."

"I was not aware of that." Mathers noticed the bulging middle-aged belly on not yet middle-aged Barker and wondered about that 'healthy stuff' the Kielbasa King was referring to.

"I will go ahead and stop production tomorrow. We only have a few packages left in inventory. Thank you for coming by and letting me know about the side effects."

"Thank you for your cooperation, Mr. Barker. We police always appreciate citizen cooperation. It happens so seldom."

"I must say, detective, it makes me sad to discontinue making this product. Think about all the shy people, the lonely people, out there. Anything that furthers the cause of romance is a good thing."

"Speaking as a divorced guy who lives alone, not a cop, I agree with you."

Mathers took the last 2 packages of Barker Spicy Brazilian Bratwurst with him, as 'evidence'. A bachelor on a cop's salary needed all the help he can get, in search of love in money-oriented Scottsdale, Arizona.

As Mathers strolled to his car with the packages of bratwurst, he thought Barker should have named the sausage links, Horn Dogs.

He chuckled.

When you go to work as a homicide detective every day and face the absolute worst human beings can do to each other, you learn how to entertain yourself.

Or gradually lose your mind.

***

Two days later, Red Boyle's 250 lb.+ bulk plopped down on a wing-backed corduroy upholstered chair at the corner of the little stage in the theater room of the Boyle Academy of the Performing Arts. On a tripod was a camera. A standard 8MM color zoom camera from Kodak, purchased by the rich but frugal Boyle for only $76.

Autumn Amber arrived shortly thereafter and walked through the deserted hallways—it was a Saturday--to the small theater.

"Autumn!" Red bellowed with enthusiasm and joy. "My most talented graduate!"

She looked scrumptious to old Boyle. She was wearing tight white slacks, sandals and a man's light blue and white checked shirt tied at the midriff. She wore light makeup. Amber looked fresh, exciting, new, *like a flower just ready to bloom*, Red thought.

"Where is my acting coach, Miss Stevens?" Autumn inquired, regarding Boyle with justifiable concern.

"She had another engagement, I'm afraid. Come in please, no need to be shy. I am going to handle the audition."

He got up, strode across the stage and held out a motion picture script. She saw there was an 8mm camera.

"Come up on the stage, Autumn. I thought it best that it's just you and me. No distractions. I can focus on evaluating your performance."

She tentatively took the three steps up to the stage.

He walked over to the camera.

"You're going to film this..." she said with trepidation.

"Yes. I need to have something to review after your audition is completed. You and your parents are asking a lot of me. You want me to put up $250,000 for a feature film for you to star in. Which I am cheerfully willing to do. It is entirely likely I will not make a dime on that investment. Most independent films lose money, as you know. And I made you a beneficiary in my Last Will and Testament. So that if something happens to me, you can still move forward with your career."

Amber nodded. Her parents were tapped out financially. They needed this motion picture deal Red had agreed to finance. She had inherited one vital trait from her mother: the will to survive whatever happened in this cruel business called 'show'.

But Amber was very different from her mother. She took up acting because she enjoyed making people smile, not to become rich and famous, not for notoriety. Performing itself was the reward, the joy. She was born with great comedic timing and had blossomed into a beautiful young woman—a combination Hollywood craved.

Amber was far too young to have to carry the burdens of her parents' failures on her shoulders. But that day, she did.

***

An hour later…

"Mr. Boyle. Do we have a deal, then? Can I tell my parents you will fund the picture?"

Red, in his chair, was breathless, his face reddening. The 'audition' with young Autumn had excited him more than he ever thought she would.

For a moment, Autumn was worried he might have a coronary. If so, she hoped he was telling the truth about her being included in his Will.

"Absolutely you may. And you three are invited as my guests to the Grand Opening of my spectacular Boyle International Properties resort in the Bahamas. I want to show you off to my crowd. You are going places in this business Autumn."

Five minutes later, Autumn walked down the hallway to the exit, buttoning her blouse. *Her mom and her coke addict dad damn well better be proud of her,* she thought.

When she turned the key in her car door, she looked back at the BAPA facility, and said with the cold hard voice of a much more worldly woman, a tone that would have shaken old Red for certain:

"See you at the island, Mr. Boyle."

***

When Red Boyle left the BAPA facility, film in hand to take to the developer's shop, he wondered whether he really wanted to finance a movie. Film people seemed like flakes, full of creative nonsense and airy-fairy dreams. He much preferred building things, structures of steel, cement and bricks that would stand the test of time. Movies seem no more substantial than wisps of cotton candy sold in theater lobbies.

No matter what he had told Autumn, it was by no means a done deal that he would advance the funds for her film project. He used money to control those around him, particularly people who really needed his financial help. What he demanded in return was their subservience.

Autumn Amber had a little too much fire inside of her for his liking—she didn't truckle as he wished. Well, Red thought as he got in his big old red Cadillac Eldorado, little bitch has no idea how quickly I can change my Will.

He'd changed it a dozen times before.

***

Tom Colt was glad to see his buddy Det. Ed Mathers practicing his putting stroke on the green by the Valley Vista CC clubhouse late that Saturday afternoon. He thought his crime fighting mentor might have some advice for him and Caroline before they left in two weeks for Bogey Island on their new assignment: to find out who wants to murder Elwood "Red" Boyle.

"You look deep in thought, Ed."

"Working on a case. Had to get out of the office. You know what I always say. Confined spaces lead to confined thinking."

Mathers seemed to flash on an idea. He pulled out a small notebook and pencil from his back pocket and scribbled for a few moments. Then he got back to golf.

Mathers, his once-awful golf game improving rapidly under Tom's tutelage, sank three putts in a row from 20 feet. Mathers' smile was exuberant. Tom had seldom seen anyone who got so much sheer joy out of the game of golf as Mathers did—nearly as much as Tom.

"Your client Boyle seems to have invited a bunch of his enemies to the Grand Opening. I think he wants to force the killer's hand. Stupid move, if you ask me. A private island is a great place to commit a murder. No cops around, watching things."

"I thought you said it might all be in Red's imagination that someone wants to kill him."

"That's what Officer Rudy said after interviewing old Red. I'm not so sure. Rudy's still a little green."

"Are Caroline and I in danger, then?"

"The would-be killer figures out you're detectives working for Boyle, YES."

Tom swallowed hard. His mouth was suddenly dry.

"But hey, have a good time. I've heard the place is beautiful." Mathers grinned, that special cop grin that they use to mask the fact they, too, are scared every day at work.

Mathers pulled two cards out of his side pocket, handed them to Tom. On them were printed a Proverb Mathers liked.

> *Proverbs 20:5: The purposes of a man's heart are deep waters, but a man of understanding draws them out.*

"I give these to all my men. Reminds us of what our job is, drawing out the truth from people who try to conceal it."

Tom studied the Proverb, pocketed it.

"Please give one to your sister."

"Thanks. Wish you were going with us."

"Me, too," Mathers replied, before he sank another putt. "But generally a homicide detective gets called in after a murder. Just so you know." Mathers snickered.

Tom went to locker room to change into his street shoes. He sat down on a bench, took out the Proverb from Mathers and read it again.

Mathers' sobering warning did not completely hit home with Tom. At 28, he thought he was pretty much invincible, and was certain in his youthful self-confidence that if indeed Boyle was in real danger, he and his equally brainy sister Caroline could discover who the assailant was before he acted.

Tom's early track record as a detective had been so stellar that he already came to believe no criminal could outsmart Colt & Colt Confidential Investigations of Scottsdale, Arizona.

Young Tom Colt was wrong, about everything.

***

Part Two

"Sooner or later, everyone sits down to a banquet of consequences."
---Robert Louis Stevenson

Chapter Eleven

Perched like a verdant, enticing dream on a limestone shelf in the azure, crystal waters of the Bahamas was an island whose colorful and at times bloody history dated back to the golden age of piracy in the early 18th century.

The island was an almost perfect square, two miles in diameter. One of the windiest locations in the area, every afternoon in the winter and spring months, the winds were fierce, strong enough to push tall ships off course.

Approached from the sea, the island was guarded by dangerous, rocky shoals.

Since the pirate days, the island has come under control of the French, English, Spanish and then the English again, sharing the island with the Americans. The foreign powers that jockeyed and sometimes battled for control of the tiny island believed a strategic advantage could be secured in the lucrative trade routes that brought goods from South America to Europe and up the coast to the young United States.

In other words, being able to harbor your warships at the island gave your country a prime opportunity to pounce on any treasure-laden ships that might be sailing by. There were several documented battles at sea--and cryptic legends of some others—that recorded vast treasure being sent to the bottom of the sea along with the defeated ships and crews.

In more modern times, gangsters were said to use the island for the storage and transfer of their own kind of treasure—liquor during the time of Prohibition. Legends arose that the gangsters, being urged rather forcefully by Federal authorities to vacate the island, left behind currency, gold and silver of their own. In 1959, Red Boyle bought the island from a French company. The buildings were in disrepair, but Red had a vision that the property could become a world-class resort.

He envisioned a golf course that would run along the coastline, and a hotel in the interior of the island. The second phase of the project was to offer vacation homes for the rich along the craggy coastline. Red's visions always became a reality, and they were invariably successful.

And all very upscale, as Americans in the early '60s were enjoying prosperity and seeking out new travel experiences.

The project was not without its problems. Since Red wanted to use the best quality-materials, the construction costs soared over budget. Getting skilled workers to the remote location proved to be a challenge. Getting reliable employees for the resort operation as well. Red Boyle hired whoever showed up. He believed his superior management skill could overcome any deficiencies in the staff members' experience.

Red originally planned the Grand Opening Golf Tournament for January 1963. But construction delays, and the injuries he suffered from his mysterious tumble down the stairs, forced him to reschedule it for March. Like all real estate developers, Red was eager to start generating revenue from the Resort property. He rushed the final stages of construction.

The resort property consisted of a lodge with 60 luxurious guest rooms, a dining room that overlooked the ocean, a large ballroom for events that accommodated 125 guests, and 10 guest cottages that at night looked like Christmas lights strung on a path to the beach.

The colors used throughout were bright and fun, rose, turquoise, and the obligatory sea foam green. Red Boyle may have been boorish in his personal life, but his design aesthetics were impeccable. The resort looked like a New England seashore summer haven, with some spicy, colorful accents from the desert southwest added.

This may sound like an odd mash-up of styles, but Red made it work, like Red made everything work.

Part of the lodge was the remodel of an old villa that dated back to the 18th Century, adding atmosphere and history to the resort. Remarkable artifacts were found in the renovation, from both pirate days and gangster days.

And the golf course...well, it was stunning. Only nine holes, but three of them ran along the ocean and offered breathtaking views of the roaring surf. Think Pebble Beach Golf Links in Monterey, California and you get the idea of how stunning this golf course was. Because the norm in golf is an 18-hole layout, players would go around the layout twice. The cost-wise Red Boyle wanted to use the prime real estate for the vacation homes, not just the golf course. He still advertised it as "world-class golf" even though golfers expected 18 holes, not 9.

***

At 24,612 feet (to be exact), somewhere above Texas...

Tom, Caroline and Katrina took a flight from Phoenix to Miami, then were to catch a ferry boat to Red Boyle's island by way of Freeport, Grand Bahama Island. Air travel in '63 was quite different than now. The seats were spacious. The passengers dressed up like they were going to a fine restaurant for a special occasion. No slobs in shorts, t-shirts and flip-flops.

Tom Colt was a nervous flier. *Only good part of flying is the sexy stewardesses*, he thought to himself as he gripped the armrests on takeoff. This was the era when the stewardesses began wearing much shorter skirts, to the delight of young gentlemen like Tom.

Caroline sat by the window, Kat took the middle seat and Tom had the aisle seat—as far from the window as possible.

"I never like the aisle seat," Kat commented. "Glad you took it."

"Easier for Tom to chase the stews," Caroline said.

Katrina unfolded the brochure for Red Boyle's Bogey Island Resort, which was part of his Boyle International Properties real estate group.

Kat read aloud: "The origins of the island's name are obscure. 'Bouger' was thought to be the name the French gave the island, who controlled it in the mid-18th century." Kat added, "That means to move, to stir. Maybe the pirates moved from there, to engage in plundering."

Kat frowned, thinking in French. "It could be from the word Bougrement, which means, like, damned or damn. It would be the island of the damned."

Tom said, "Maybe a reference to ships that perished in its waters."

Kat resumed reading aloud, "In 1959, Scottsdale, Arizona, real estate developer Elwood "Red" Boyle bought the island and simplified the name to Bogey Island. Boyle's organization recently completed the construction of a breathtaking 9-hole golf course on the island. He named the course, Coeur de Lion, heart of a lion. The course is designed to be extremely difficult—a true test of golfing skill as well as allowing players to enjoy spectacular oceanside scenery. And Bogey Island it is indeed for players not at the top of their game...""

Caroline, not a fan of marketing hype, said, "Let's face it. Someone named it Booger Island years ago. Later on they wanted to make it fancy for the tourists so they changed it to a French name. They can charge more for the rooms that way. Like when we stayed in La Jolla during the San Diego Open at that 'partial ocean view' room. That means they can charge double and you have to crane your neck like a giraffe to catch a glimpse of the water."

A pocket of turbulence buffeted the airplane. "What keeps this bird in the air?" Caroline asked.

"Our prayers," responded Tom, tight-lipped.

Katrina smiled. She enjoyed listening to Tom and Caroline playfully spar with each other. Her own sibling, her sister Ingrid, was ten years older than Kat and they had little in common to talk about except that both were high achievers, never satisfied.

Kat had the feeling for some time that Ingrid kept secrets from her about their family history in Germany. Kat knew that several of her relatives were lost in the War. Kat was only 8 when they got on a train in the middle of the night, then transferred to a boat until they reached the sea, boarded another boat and left their family home in Germany forever.

The sisters cheered each other on in their respective careers, but seldom had the kind of fun that Tom and Caroline had together—even though the Colts' conversations sometimes turned quarrelsome.

The airline lunch was served, surprisingly delicious roast beef, mashed potatoes and apple crisp for dessert. After lunch, Caroline started to get drowsy and settled back into her seat for a nap, but not before saying:

"I don't want you two to get all lovey-dovey on me. I was hoping not to upchuck that marginally edible lunch."

Tom looked at Kat and said, "There's always the mile-high club. I checked out the rest rooms and it's kind of small for the two of us, though."

Kat said, "If we're determined enough, it's plenty big enough. We're both limber."

Tom looked eagerly at Kat. "Especially you."

Barf, thought Caroline as she rolled her eyes. They settled back to reading the magazines provided by the stewardess. Tom read, *LOOK*, Kat chose *LIFE*. The cabin began to smell of cigarette smoke as the passengers lit up after lunch.

As they sailed across the skies, Kat abandoned her stern sobriety and shared two glasses of champagne with Tom.

They engaged in light and hopeful conversation about how they were going to kick everyone's ass in Boyle's golf tournament. Frugal Kat enquired what first place prize money was.

Caroline dozed off and started to snore.

Tom leaned over and gently cupped Katrina's neck, drawing her closer to him. Kat's heart warmed when she felt his lips on hers. When Kat responded with equal ardor, Tom's arousal talked him into thinking that rest room might be big enough to accommodate their passion after all. Tom's arousals were even more optimistic than he was.

Kat, her heart now glowing with romantic feelings and the soft buzz from champagne at high altitude, leaned over and put her sweet lips again on Tom's.

"I'm glad we came." Kat thought, *I could so love this man. I hope, I hope it works out for us.*

Their kiss lingered and deepened.

"I saw that," Caroline said, one small eye cocked open. Caroline was secretly thrilled for Tom. Katrina wasn't a ditz, a drama queen, a bubblehead or a psycho.

Big improvement on my brother's part, she thought.

As the pilot announced they were beginning their slow descent to the Miami airport, Katrina felt as good as she had for several months about her relationship with Tom. She had started to have reservations after the hot affair they had begun last summer and into the fall began to cool with the seasons.

Sometimes they had the best times she could imagine. Other times she felt like she was just one of the many pretty girls in Tom's orbit. That wasn't good enough for her. Her wish for this trip—besides winning Red Boyle's golf tournament—was to gain clarity about their relationship.

Unfortunately, she would. More clarity than she ever wanted.

***

On Bogey Island…

Caroline and Tom and Katrina had the identical reaction, as seen in their wide eyes, when they walked into the Boyle International Bogey Island Resort: WOW.

The colors were bold, the floors of shining marble tiles with areas of thick rose rugs that looked like no one had walked on them yet. Bright tapestries of seascapes hung from the walls.

They were greeted by Red Boyle himself, who scurried, as fast as a 275 lb. fellow with stubby legs can, across the spacious lobby to greet them. Tom noticed three others in the lobby, along with the desk clerk. One he recognized, Chandler Boyle. He guessed the two were his siblings.

Red pumped Tom's hand enthusiastically. "Welcome! You are the first of my guests to arrive. I am so excited about this week! We've been planning this Grand Opening for three years!"

"Thank you, sir! What a grand place this is for a Grand Opening!" Tom said, aiming to duplicate Red's enthusiasm.

Caroline thought, *A detective doesn't have to suck up to the client, Tom. Does Bob Mitchum suck up? No.*

Red noticed his three children standing in a corner, chatting and said, "Hey, over there! Get to work! We have 80 of the most important people from Phoenix arriving today! And remember, a meeting in my office at 1PM sharp." This last sentence was said with a growl of irritation.

The three looked startled for a moment, then hurried off in separate directions, Chandler coming toward Tom and Caroline and Red.

"Tom, may I speak to you privately for a few moments. My son Chandler will show Miss Stern and your sister to their rooms. Your luggage will be delivered to you."

Chandler led Katrina and Caroline off. The latter looked peeved that she wasn't going to be involved in a conversation about their assignment to protect Red from the apparent danger he was facing. But Caroline remembered her 'cover' was that she was caddying for Tom. They didn't want to alert anyone that they were there in a detective capacity.

Red started off toward the elevator that went up to the 2nd floor, where the resort offices were located. Tom followed him. Tom thought it odd Red chose to castigate his children in front of us, guests of the hotel. He seemed to treat them like they were lower-level and rather incompetent employees rather than his beloved children.

Tom Continues Our Story:

When we arrived on the island, it was apparent that the conflict between Red and his three children would be the central focus of Colt & Colt Confidential's detective efforts. My time as an assistant pro at Valley Vista CC had introduced me to the peculiar animosity between rich fathers and their offspring.

What I had learned before we left Phoenix was that Boyle is a skinflint. The three kids were cash-strapped to the point of cruelty and the boy, Chandler, was over-extended. One rumor was that he gambled at the private gaming clubs in Phoenix.

Jilly Flannery told me a story that when Chandler was a senior in high school, when he met with a career counselor, on the form where it said 'career objective', Chandler wrote 'inheritance'.

The three children came from three different moms. And couldn't be more different in appearance. Boyle was only married once, to the mother of the eldest, Fredonia "Freddy" Boyle, 38. The youngest was Patagonia "Patti" Boyle" 25. Chandler was 34.

Apparently because of Red's laser-focus on real estate acquisition, they were, oddly, named after locations in Arizona. Fredonia was a city in the northern part of the state, Patagonia in the southern region, and Chandler was a sleepy town east of Phoenix, that would be booming with real estate activity by the 1980s. All that was lacking was a fourth kid named after someplace in the Western part of Arizona, near the California border.

Patagonia was the 'Patti' whom you may recall stuffed a topless picture of herself in my back pocket after I won my very first tournament in Las Vegas. I learned that she had a big crush on me.

Yes, this week on Bogey Island could get interesting.

After a few hours on the Island, and comparing notes with Caroline of course, this was our first impression of the Boyles.

Fredonia. Freddie. Striking eyes like cold sapphires. Blonde hair so straight it appeared she ironed it in the morning. Looked at you with a slightly pained expression, her mouth tight, downturned at one corner as though appraising you to see if you were worth her time. She was tall, cool, calculating. A cigarette was always in her fingers or on her lips. I imagined she exhaled smoke that was frosty. The true ice blond. Her low-register voice could have been sexually alluring coming out of another girl's mouth. Any other girl's.

Chandler Boyle. Nervous laugh, jerky, quick movements. Always scanning the room like there was someone important to meet that he was missing out on by talking with you. Red, steel-wool hair like his dad's when a youth. I thought him to be an insecure sort of chap. He called himself the General Manager of the resort even though clearly that was not a title his father had granted him. Chandler made it up and claimed it.

Chandler and Fredonia shared a trait with their father: hard, cold, appraising eyes. The third child, Patti, was very different.

Patagonia. Patti. A petite girl with warm, sincere eyes and a memorable figure. Her smile was sweet. She gathered her light brown hair in a bouncy ponytail. I learned that she loved the hospitality industry. She enjoyed taking care of people and seeing they had a good time. Her brother and sister had such overpowering personalities that she seemed left in the shadows. I thought she was quite pretty and didn't need to pull stunts like leaving the topless picture of herself in my pocket to get attention. If she had just trained those deep ocean-blue eyes on me, I would have noticed her, believe me.

Red Boyle by appearance only was the quintessential genial, funny fat man. Believe it or not, he was a top athlete in college, with a trim physique. He starred on his college (Princeton) golf team and on the swim team. He aspired to be a pro golfer. But his huge appetite for food and fun, women and money, served to kill that dream. He didn't even give the professional golf tour a try. Went into business instead, where he found immediate success.

In his business dealings, he was a major horse's ass. He was as shrewd a businessman as you could ever meet, and one of the toughest. He also had a cruel streak. It only took a few minutes with him for me to decide I really didn't want him as a client for Colt & Colt Confidential Investigations. But at this point we needed clients and couldn't afford to be choosy.

And don't forget the Judge insisted we take the case. I owed it to Judge Wilkinson to help him however I could. Without his financial assistance, I would have still been stuck in a dingy apartment, not enjoying the good life in a guest house at his estate in the most desirable part of North Phoenix.

When we got to Red's office, he beckoned me in and closed the door. A very modern looking room. Light oak furniture, chrome and glass tables. A map of the world dominated one wall with little flags evidently depicting Red's real estate holdings.

Boyle sat down behind his desk. I took a chair angled to one side.

"You come highly recommended Tom. Roy Wilkinson is very high on you as a detective and as a high-character individual."

"Thank you, sir. Have there been any other incidents I should know about?"

He leaned back in his high-backed chair. The springs in the chair groaned. I worried his bulk was going to topple it.

"No, but I feel uneasy about this week. Some of my 'guests' are business rivals who wish me ill. And there are others from Valley Vista that nurse grudges. That's the price of achieving great wealth, Tom. I've collected enemies even faster than I've collected real estate properties."

"I don't know exactly how to ask this sir...but..."

"Speak up, Tom. I have nothing to hide from you. I'm one of the most honest and direct bastards you're ever going to meet."

He laughed at his own jest and lit up a cigar. I tried to gather my words into a diplomatic statement. "Do you think one of your children could be behind these incidents."

Boyle laughed again, this time coughing out cigar smoke.

"No. Not one of them. But I think the three of them are conspiring against me. My children do not love me. They love my money. We have conflict over...well, I am going to deal with that conflict later today so I don't need to belabor you with it."

I could feel Boyle's stare. He was measuring me.

"Truth is, Tom, my children are a disappointment to me. It's not like I've failed them. They've failed me."

Tom thought about how many parents, like Boyle, are disappointed in their children when they become adults. They had kids to create and then shape little miniature versions of the best aspects of themselves, minus the warts. And then are disappointed when the kids turn out to be completely different individuals with their own very individual warts.

***

I strolled the grounds after our meeting ended. It was a stunning property. Pink, orange and purple bougainvillea plants were everywhere, along with Allamanda plants with striking yellow trumpet-shaped flowers and dark red Hibiscus. Coconut palms dotted the property, seemingly spaced at perfect intervals. Beauty surrounded me, but my mind was too occupied with the Boyle family and their conflicts to enjoy it much.

Crushed seashell paths meandered throughout the property, with benches set in the shade of the coconut palms, perfect places for quiet conversations—or I feared, to plot a murder. As I strolled around, I was alone with my thoughts.

I grew up poor, at times terribly poor. My mom, my sister and I were perilously close to being what the rich folks in Scottsdale called poor white trash. My mom Laura did her best to support us. We were just flat broke a lot of the time. Nonetheless Laura Colt was classier than any of the members at Valley Vista.

In my career as a pro golfer giving lessons at the Valley Vista Country Club, I live my life among these rich. I have on occasion given lessons to three generations of a wealthy family, including the patriarch who amassed the original fortune, the second generation that was striving, often unsuccessfully, to maintain it, and their third generation that was most interested in spending it. I learned a lot about the special advantages, and sometimes disadvantages of growing up rich.

It would not be fair to minimize the challenges they face, these offspring of the man who created the family's wealth. On the way up the financial ladder in life, the patriarch takes considerable risks. The poor boy has nothing to lose. If you stumble and fall, you simply get up and start again. No one notices, or cares, that you failed. And each success you have breeds confidence. After all, most people didn't believe you could do it.

The offspring of the rich grow up in a very different world. They live, always, under the scrutiny of the vastly successful parent. Any mistakes they make are magnified. They too, as we all do, must make mistakes, stumble and fall, and learn. But their stumbles are viewed as embarrassments by their wealthy parents, grandparents, or even their friends. The so-called self-made men forget the dark, mean, sometimes dishonest acts required to amass their wealth.

I have found it is often the element of self-confidence that distinguishes the self-made men from their offspring. All the sweaty struggles through which they prevailed gave them the view that they could surmount any obstacles set before them.

The downside to struggle early in life is that many of us don't survive it, financially or emotionally. We become one of the sad thousands trapped in a life of grim toil, any dreams they once had trampled and long forgotten. The flip side to Survival of the Fittest is, what becomes of those that are less fit for the challenges and battles of life?

In my 20s I nearly joined those permanent strugglers when after several years on the golf tour, I barely made enough money to pay for my cheap apartment and gas for my old car. And that was gas at 30 cents a gallon.

For me, things changed immediately when wealthy and powerful Judge Roy Wilkinson took me under his wing, for reasons I still don't fully understand. Doors immediately opened for me. Financial opportunities came my way. Club members cheerfully paid whatever I wanted to charge for golf lessons. Suddenly I could afford to stay in decent hotels at the tournament venues, not some dump on the Interstate 20 miles from the course. I could say, I worked hard for all this to happen. But I had always worked hard. And nothing good seemed to happen.

I recognized that fate had smiled on me.

The offspring of the rich must make do with self-confidence that is borrowed, not earned, and as such is fragile. Their status among their peers comes from uttering the phrases, "my father is..." or "my grandfather was..." rather than being able to declare, "I am..." as both Katrina Stern and I can say, "I am a winner on the professional golf tour." I can even say, "I helped Phoenix PD solve a murder."

A young woman who knows young rich men intimately, and I mean intimately, Julia Wilkinson, the Judge's daughter, once told me that she loved in me the quality of gratitude, which she said I possessed in abundance. I was so grateful for each positive development in my life that lifted me up out of early poverty. I was grateful to everyone who helped me, everyone who cheered for me in golf tournaments, grateful for life, grateful to God.

What she didn't express, but I believe she perceived, was that I was particularly grateful that a beautiful, rich woman like Julia would even pay attention to me. She represented the ultimate gift my new life had granted to me, the unmistakable sign that I had 'made it'.

The sons and daughters of the very rich do not experience this glorious feeling of gratitude. The good things life has to offer were always there. What is to be grateful for?

I've also found that the very rich don't recall how the element of luck, of good fortune, played in their success. Through the fuzzy lens of memory, they pompously come to believe it was a kind of destiny. They were just better than the fellows they competed against--that's all there is too it.

Their children many times do not share in the luck, and do not see success as their destiny. The Scottish proverb comes to mind: *Better be the lucky man than the lucky man's son.*

All in all, I didn't envy these scions of the wealthy.

I do not want to leave the impression that I felt sorry for the three Boyles. I thought it quite possible that they were going to make an attempt on their father's life. Murder is never acceptable, as Det. Mathers has said to me many times. The wild card was Patti. I couldn't see her being part of such a monstrous thing. She was a little sweetheart.

***

After my stroll, I got my room key at the front desk. Other guests were beginning to arrive.

Many of the guests were the usual gang from Valley Vista Country Club. I spotted Carter and Babs Vonessen and a real estate developer I remember reading about who built churches for the various large religious denominations, including the Episcopalian and the Roman Catholic churches. His name was Terrrence Egglesworth, his wife named Judith. I also spotted the towering presence of 6'6" Al Langdon, who I believe owned a property insurance brokerage. Big Al did not have the look of a man on a restful island vacation, more like King Kong ready for a jungle rampage.

Stan Barker, the sausage king, walked through the lobby. He had those purposeful, quick strides many businessmen have—like they're late for an important meeting. He had jet black hair cut short. A fleshy face, kind of red, and wire framed glasses. All I knew about him was that he was a golf fanatic. And that he created that unusual bratwurst everyone in the rich set was talking about...

With room key in hand, I was escorted by an efficient maid/waitress named according to her badge, Carol Thorn. She had dark hair chopped short. Thick glasses and a thickening waist. It appeared she took full advantage of the free meals Red Boyle offered his loyal employees (if they were in good favor with him at that particular moment).

She was one of those hard workers that keeps a fine resort property humming. Clearly, it wasn't the Boyle siblings who did so. I found out from her that my room was on the first floor of the lodge, and Katrina and Caroline were far down toward the beach in one of the cottages. Peculiar arrangements, I thought.

Carol left. I kept the door open and immediately saw the architect of the peculiar room arrangements: Jilly Flannery came out the door from across the hall. She rushed over to me and gave me a hug. She looked great in a short shorts, a thin cotton shirt hugging her full breasts.

"You made it. Isn't this place spectacular. And the two of us next to each other all week!"

"Yes, what a coincidence. I wonder if you didn't help old Red decide the room arrangements..."

"Perhaps. He and I go way back. He thinks I'm in love with him. I can get him to do almost anything. HA! But don't worry about Katrina. She won't be lonely. Stan Barker is in the cottage right next to her."

I could only smile.

Chapter Twelve

Red Boyle's Office   The 1PM Family Meeting

Red and his three children were gathered around a conference table in his office. The contentious meeting had been going on for an hour. It was nearly 2PM. Fredonia sat erect, defiant and cold. Chandler looked angry, his red complected face even redder than normal. Patti sat small and soft and said very little.

"I want you to have nothing to do with treasure hunters. I will not allow them on the island. Word gets out there might be gold hidden here—and I don't believe there is any—and our beautiful new resort property will be overrun with treasure seekers, riff raff of all kinds from the shithole countries around here."

Chandler said, "But we could make a fortune, father."

"I already have a fortune."

"But the three of us don't. We're broke half the time," Fredonia said.

"And you never will be rich as lazy as you three are. Let me put it plainly. If I see any treasure hunters on my island, I will have them shot as trespassers. I brought several key pieces of my gun collection here. The guns are cleaned and ready to use as needed."

Chandler's tone was imploring, nearly begging. "I need seed capital or I'm not going to get anywhere until—"

"Until I'm dead? That's what you were going to say? Well, don't be so cocksure. I can change my will with the stroke of a pen."

Fredonia thought, *like you already have a dozen times.*

Red had placed his entire holdings, every single asset, into a Trust. The percentages of his holdings allocated to beneficiaries in the event of his death was the Addendum to the Trust. All he had to do to change his Will was redo that one page, the Addendum. Simple and clean.

Fredonia said, "We have dreams, too. All we each need is like, an advance on our inheritance."

"I cannot help you. All my free capital is tied up in this resort project."

"That's not true," Fredonia said. She was right: she had seen Red's financial statements when she snuck into his home office at his Arizona manse one night.

Red particularly hated Fredonia, because at the end of their marriage he had particularly hated her mother, Josephine. They were both cold and untrustworthy women, Red thought.

Red had had enough. He wasn't going to have his useless daughter call him a liar.

"In my new Will, each of your shares is going to be drastically reduced. I have a new beneficiary, someone who will be a good steward of my money and help others more worthy than you three."

"That little actress bitch, Autumn Amber?" Chandler spat out.

"No. I am removing her altogether from my Will."

That was greeted with bright smiles of relief.

"You may have to start working for a living, for someone besides me. And let me state again, forget about that treasure. It would belong to me, anyway, not you. Finding treasure would be too easy. I want you to struggle like I did. Struggle reveals character. The answer is, no, I'm not letting anyone poke around on my island. I'll have them shot, I tell you again!"

Red banged his desk with his hammy fist. Only Patti of the three was startled.

***

Later that day, as he scooped dead leaves from the resort swimming pool—one of the menial duties Red assigned to Chandler--Fredonia and Patti sat on nearby lounge chairs.

"Well, guys. Have we had enough?" Fredonia asked.

Patti finally spoke up. "Dad's changed the Will a bunch of times. He can change it back in our favor. We should do more to please him."

"I can't believe you're my sister, you little simpleton."

Patti, stung, looked down.

"What we are going to do is find that treasure, and Red Boyle be damned."

Chandler finished sweeping and tossed the scoop angrily away. "Why can't he just die, already...his health is terrible."

"I don't think we can count on that happening anytime soon," Fredonia said with wistful disappointment.

***

At 3:00 Red Boyle was on the phone with his attorney in Phoenix.

"I've made my decision, Don. I'm selling the Boyle Academy of the Performing Arts to the two guys I brought out to run it. I've wasted too much money on that, anyway. I'm a builder at heart, not a show business guy. We're taking out the share I set aside for Autumn Amber, the young actress. My infatuation with her, and my business relationship with her loathsome parents, is over. And I have a new idea where to leave my money. It'll sound strange to you, perhaps radical, I know. But I'm finally at peace."

***

After settling into their luxurious accommodations—Tom for some reason had the largest suite with the loveliest ocean view—Kat and Tom went out to the golf course to get in a practice round.

It was 3:30PM. The promised afternoon winds had shown up with full fury. Kat estimated that the gusts were 40mph. Tom did not disagree. They quickly saw that Red had designed the course to be brutally difficult. In his youth, Red wanted to be a champion golfer, but failed in a big way. Possibly in retaliation, he set out to build a punishing 9-hole course on the island that featured every hazard except alligators.

Red added 50 yards to each hole for the pros to play in the tournament. Generally, the longer the shot, accuracy is more difficult to achieve. For resort guests toddling along on the course, even poor players, the course is not daunting at 3300 yards for 9 holes. But for the pros, a stiff test of 3,750 yards. And back in '63 the equipment, clubs and golf balls, were not as advanced as they are today. A pro considered a 260 yard drive a long one, now 300 yards+ is the norm.

Tom scored a shaky 6 on the Par-4 first hole. Kat was even worse with a 7. Three of the holes were along the sea. One was a Par-3 that went partially over a chasm—the rocky shoals looming below. Kat hit a strong 5-iron that didn't come close to clearing the water. She tried a 3-iron and the same thing happened.

"What does he want us to do, Tom? Hit a driver on a Par-3?"

Tom, who could barely hear Kat in the fierce wind, selected a four-wood. His ball almost cleared the chasm but joined Kat's first two shots for a swim in the surf.

Kat took out another ball and hit it away from the green, kind of sideways. From there it was a shorter shot to the green. "I've never had to lay up on a Par-3."

Kat didn't notice old Red rolling along the fairway in a golf cart.

Red stopped and chortled, "I forgot, Miss Stern, are you one of the professionals or the amateurs I invited?" He guffawed, then added, "Now you know why I named it Bogey Island!" Red drove off to torment English pro Rodney Burkett, who was playing one hole ahead.

On the next hole, a gust of wind blew Kat as she was starting her backswing. She was pushed so far off balance that she missed the ball completely. Whiffed. A pro golfer never whiffs.

For the nine holes, Kat shot 46 and Tom 44. For a full 18 holes, that meant they would have shot a 92 and 88 respectively. A pro golfer would expect to shoot no higher than 36 for nine holes, 72 for 18. Kat's scoring average for her career as a pro was 71.9, Tom's was 71.7.

When they finished, Kat said ruefully, "Very professional scores. This is Goony Golf, Tom. He should have put in a Clown's Mouth for us to hit a shot through."

Kat, who was always nicely dressed, with perfectly arranged hair, looked a windblown, defeated mess. Her shirt was even untucked and flapping, which Tom had never seen before.

Tom thought she looked beautiful. She would have disagreed.

"Our only hope is drawing an early tee time. The wind is calm until afternoon."

"I do not like Mr. Elwood 'Red' Boyle," Kat announced.

"From what I've observed so far, hardly anyone does. Can I buy you a beer?"

"Several! I was pathetic! I haven't shot anything as lousy as 46 on nine holes since I was 12 years old."

Tom thought Katrina, as usual, was too hard on herself. He thought it was comical attempting to play golf in that wind. He understood that golf, like life, was game of dealing with adversity, and sometimes the adversity wins.

***

At 4PM, Tom felt overwhelmed when he and Caroline walked into the high-ceilinged ballroom where the welcoming reception party for the Grand Opening was taking place. It was another impressive space, decked out in golden opulence with sparkling chandeliers.

The food was buffet style, serve yourself. Cheerful waitresses (who pulled double duty as maids) buzzed about with trays of champagne. Tables were spaced far enough apart that guests could circulate and chat or sit and nosh.

Tom's big idea was that he would overhear bits of conversation that might indicate which one of the guests might be angry enough at Red Boyle to have made three attempts to hurt—or kill—him.

But there were probably 75 people in the room already. It seemed quite impossible the two young detectives could wander round, listen and predict who a future murderer might be. In March of '63, Tom's experience with crime and criminals was still quite limited.

Both Tom and Caroline were blessed with amazingly acute hearing, though. If any auditory clues were available, they would pick up on them.

Tom was dressed in a powder-blue sport coat, navy slacks and a maroon shirt. Caroline had on a red cocktail dress, rather short, and an elegant string of black pearls that had been a gift from Jilly Flannery, who last year had taught Caroline how to dress well or at least dress like a rich girl. She looked great. Every bit as elegant as any of the rich women at the party.

The party was billed as a 'Come as You Are' affair and indeed some of the guests had on shorts and sport shirts, probably with swimming attire underneath. Some had the rumpled look of people who had spent the day in airports and on airplanes.

The first item of interest Tom and Caroline noticed was movie starlet Autumn Amber fairly draped around old Red Boyle, dressed as though she were attending a Hollywood premiere. She was wearing a shimmering light blue, short dress with a plunging back that very nearly revealed her butt cheeks.

"Autumn Amber what? That name sounds incomplete," Caroline inquired.

"Not sure what you mean…"

"Have you ever met anyone with the last name Amber before? Morton Amber? Jessica Amber."

"No, come to think of it, you're right. Amber is a color, right? Wonder why she dropped her last name."

Sterling Gould overheard them and said, "Her name is Amberson. Just shortened it. Her father was a big deal screenwriter ten years ago. Don't know what's happened to him since. I've heard the white powder got him. I think the daughter is the family meal ticket now."

Red put his arm around Autumn. She nuzzled him and whispered in his ear. Tom and Caroline could not overhear.

Red noticed the looks of admiration from the other old men in the room, thinking Autumn was <u>his</u> girl.

Let the old dogs think it. And no harm in stringing her along. "I think you have an amazing career ahead of you."

"You do. That means so much to me, Mr. Boyle."

"Absolutely. And I want to be a part of it."

Good actress she, Amber kissed Red on the cheek. In his excitement he farted slightly. Just a small one. Only noticed by the grimacing Miss Autumn.

Carol Thorn stopped by with a tray of champagne glasses. Caroline grabbed one for Tom and one for herself, then said about Autumn Amber:

"She's a total skank, that girl. The kind of skank that a guy can catch a social disease just from brushing up against her."

"You tend to think every overtly sexual girl is a skank."

"How often am I wrong?"

"Seldom."

Admirers buzzed around Autumn. Old Sterling Gould, who resembled and behaved like a hearty, portly English squire, stared down the back of Autumn's dress. From his blissful expression, the view down there must be lovely.

Tom remarked, "I hope when I'm Red's age, I'm not a ridiculous old fat guy making a fool of himself chasing chicks 35 years younger than he is."

"No worries. I doubt you'll be fat. Our family genetics tend to the thin side."

"I'll still be a fool, though, just a thin fool."

"Nice and trim you'll be, I reckon."

Chandler Boyle drifted over to welcome Tom and Caroline to the party. "Hope you're enjoying yourselves. We've spared no expense."

"It's wonderful," Tom said. "How did you pull all this together with such a small staff?"

Chandler noticed Carol Thorn, the waitress/maid bustling around. He remarked, "Employees like Carol, that's how. I wish we had a hundred on our staff like her. She is such a hard worker. The best on our staff. I hired her, by the way. I'm by far the best manager of us three Boyle kids."

"Is it difficult to get staff members way out here?" Caroline asked.

"Absolutely. But I'm a Boyle. We find a way to get things done."

Like pushing your dad down the stairs in the hopes of getting an inheritance? Caroline thought.

"I'm a people person. I love the meet and greet part of my role. If you need anything, just holler." He resumed his meeting and greeting around the room.

Caroline asked Tom, "What does that even mean?—'I'm a people person'. What else could you be...and aardvark person? A hippopotamus person?"

"Good point. All right, detective, let's split up and mingle. See what secrets we can uncover."

"I'm on it." Caroline finished her glass of champagne, grabbed a fresh one and headed to another part of the ballroom.

She stopped by Red Boyle who was watching the party like a hawk, pretending to enjoy himself. Caroline could feel his dislike for several of his guests; it was palpable. His eyes darkened when he looked at a few of them. *Why invite people you hate, or hate you, to your big Grand Opening shindig?* she thought.

"Bitchin' bash, Mr. Boyle," Caroline said.

Red tried to interpret her words then said, "I hope that means you are having a good time."

She nodded and smiled.

He was sipping a greenish liquid out of a teensy glass. He noticed her looking at it. "La Fee Verte, my dear. The Green Fairy. Absinthe. Banned in the good old USA since 1915. But we aren't in the good old USA, are we. The rules don't apply. Any of them," he added, ominously Caroline thought. An idea popped into her head: was Boyle going to try to kill the killer before the killer killed him?

He held out the glass. "Take a sip. It's 120 proof. Out here, anything goes!"

Caroline thought of responding, *So, Red, we can let 'er rip,* and had to stifle a giggle.

"Thanks, but I think I'll stick to champagne."

He took another sip. It seemed to have a warming quality. His already red face flushed a bit more. "I've found it improves my virility."

"Absinthe makes the heart grow fonder."

Red guffawed. "You're a clever girl, Caroline Colt!"

"At times, not always," she said honestly.

"I'm having dinner with Jillian Flannery tonight, and I was hoping she and I might get together after dinner as well. She has the most exquisite body."

Caroline thought, *I'd have a better chance of being invited to Jilly's bed than you, Red. Word has it Jilly likes the occasional female. Wouldn't that freak out Tom if he found out. Make a note to tell him someday at just the right moment.*

Tom unfortunately had been collared by William Tisdale, a novelist of dreadful golf-themed potboilers, mostly from the 1940s and '50s. His book sales, and reputation had been on the wane for some time. You may have read some of his titles, *The Bloody Back 9. Par for the Corpse. Death Plays Through. Bleeder in the Clubhouse.*

Tisdale was a mousy little man with a lean and aquiline face, wearing a rumpled dark brown suit of clothes that matched his brown hair, and sporting a pugnacious attitude.

He had told Tom that he was at the Grand Opening, "researching his next golf novel" and also covering the tournament for "a major golf magazine". Both claims were later shown to be lies. His publisher had terminated his book contract and there was no magazine article assignment. But Tom and Caroline would learn he had a sound objective for being there.

"You'd make a great character for my next book. Maybe we could team up on..."

Tom said, "I don't think your readers would find a book about a struggling pro golfer to be too interesting."

"But you're here as a detective, right?"

"No, no. Just invited to play in the pro-am."

"Why? You're no big deal on the golf tour. Why would old Boyle pay your way out here? This is a prestigious little tournament. Rodney Burkett's even playing. Cough it up, Colt. What's the case you're on? Some Boyle family intrigue perhaps."

"No, I am here to win a tournament and the $1,500 prize money."

"Why do I not believe you?"

Tom was relieved, sort of, when Dick Amberson, Autumn's dissipated-looking daddy, joined the conversation.

"Don't listen to this gasbag, Tom. I was hired to adapt one of his novels. Couldn't stand the thing. His books should have been adapted into compost."

"Amberson, you haven't written a good screenplay in 10 years."

"And you've never written a good novel, Tisdale. Tom Colt here could write a better book, and I bet he's only read half a dozen."

Tom knew these people looked down on him because they thought he was poor but didn't think they considered him dumb and illiterate. This 'party' was starting to depress him. He made a graceful exit and rejoined Caroline.

Tom told Caroline, "I read a couple of that guy's novels. The plots are implausible. I mean, golfers are peaceful souls, dedicated to our craft. We never get involved in crime, sex or mayhem."

"And of course, they never get shot by femme fatales, either." Caroline grinned.

Red Boyle stepped to the small stage in the back of the ballroom and announced, "In ten minutes we will be selecting the pairings for our inaugural pro-am tournament."

"Selecting? I thought the pairings were all set. I'm playing with Katrina."

Caroline noticed Jilly Flannery stepping up to the stage and setting several golf hats, upside down, on a table. "Think again," she said sardonically.

She noticed a thin, tall man with a grey goatee and short-cropped grey hair enter the room. He strode in with an air of authority, clearly someone who believed he was important and wanted each of the guests to confirm that fact. He also had weird, darting eyes, Caroline thought.

"I need to talk to this guy. I heard he's the Resort Chaplain. Chaplains tend to know what dirty deeds are going on. Confessions from the vacationing sinners and all."

After introducing herself to the Rev. Damien Tucker, she took an instant dislike to him especially when he began lecturing her about evils of money.

"This is where my ministry is so valuable. Saving souls of the rich. All these people dedicated to laying up treasure on earth, neglecting the spiritual aspect of existence."

Caroline thought, *looks like an expensive Swiss watch you're wearing, Rev.*

Caroline perceived there was zero sincerity in what Rev. Tucker said. It was a prepared speech.

The Reverend asked Caroline if she ever goes to church.

"Nope. I read the Bible on my own."

"The Holy Bible is much too complex for laymen such as you to understand. It requires interpretation from the reverend clergy like myself to guide the individual as to what to believe."

"I think I can handle my spiritual journey, a meandering journey at best, I admit, without your help there, Rev. You know Einstein, the scientist guy--he and I constantly argue about which one of us is the smartest."

The condescension in the Reverend's smile grated on Caroline. He said, "In the Middle Ages, only the priesthood was allowed to have a copy of Scripture."

"Until the invention of the printing press. Then we all got an equal shot a reading it. Must've put a few of you gents out of business."

His scowl was positively malevolent.

"What do you think of Red Boyle, our gracious host?"

She could see the mental wheels turning. "A truly fine man striving to be a better man each day."

And you are a truly fine liar, Caroline thought.

"Anyways, it was cool beans to meet you, Rev. I gotta scoot."

"Let's continue this conversation soon." It sounded more of a threat than an invitation.

Caroline hurried off toward the back of the room where the tournament pairings were soon to be announced.

As Caroline walked away, Rev. Tucker thought, *that girl is going to be trouble. They told me Tom Colt was the amateur detective to watch out for. I'm not so sure.*

Tom went to the hors d'oeuvres table and grabbed several wedges of delicious cheese. He overheard a nice tidbit as he ate the tidbits, courtesy of a couple he had not yet met:

"Oh my, there's Mr. Grumpy, Carter Vonessen. He's a jerk and a bore. Have you ever noticed his head is like Fred Flintstone's. A blockhead. I want to yell Yabba Dabba Do! When I see him. His fat sister fell out of a boat and drowned on Roosevelt Lake and he blames Red, who she was seeing at the time."

"I've heard Red's a Patron of the Arts, particularly a patron of the young actresses in his Academy. Some of his favorites receive free tuition. I wonder how they qualify...the sad part is old Red thinks these girls are interested in him."

As Caroline joined Katrina and Tom at the back of the room near the stage, Red Boyle bounded up the stairs to polite applause. You could hear the boards creaking.

"Here we go...the lovely Jillian Flannery will assist me with the drawing." Red consulted a clipboard he was carrying. "Our first Pro is Katrina Stern. Let's see who her partner shall be...Jilly, do the honors."

Jilly drew a folded piece of paper from the golf hat, opened it and read. "Stan Barker."

Stan stepped forward and said to Katrina, "How fun! We're next-door neighbors for a whole week and paired together."

Kat displayed that frowny face she was known for, then tried to smile. "Yes, fun." She looked at Caroline like, "What is This?"

Caroline shrugged.

The pairings drawing continued until there were two more teams to announce out of eight total in the field...Rodney Burkett was paired with Judith Egglesworth, who was reputed to be a pretty fair golfer. Next up was Tom Colt.

The mention of his name drew applause from many in the crowd, mostly the females. There was one boo, from Rodney Burkett.

Jilly pulled out another slip of paper, opened it and exclaimed, "Jillian Flannery!"

She beamed. She waved at Tom. He returned the wave with a confused expression.

"There we have it. The tournament begins Thursday morning at 9AM sharp."

Eight teams in all. One pro and one amateur per team. Tom was surprised, with all of Red's influence, that he couldn't get one or two of rising stars on the golf tour, maybe a Ken Venturi or Gene Littler, to play in the event. Then he realized he had just declared himself to not be a rising star. Tom had been studying the positive thinking books penned by Napoleon Hill. He evidently had a way to go before the philosophy took hold.

The crowd resumed their drinking, snacking and socializing. Red and Jillian stepped down the stairs and joined them.

Caroline's detective curiosity was aroused. She went up the stairs to the table with the golf hat. She looked at it—there were more slips of paper in it. She opened them one by one.

They all said, 'Jillian Flannery'. Under the table was another, identical hat. That one was empty.

Caroline had to smile. *What a bitch! I love her.* She knew it was 'game on': Jilly was not about to give up Tom to any of the younger women.

She sat on a chair on the stage and watched the interactions of the guests. She marveled at the social skills of her brother, Mr. Popularity.

Caroline Continues Our Story:

I was finally beginning to understand Tom. You might think that odd, given we are twins, but from the time I left home when I was 17, until last year when Tom reached out to me to repair our relationship, we had spent hardly any time together. It was my bad, I admit it. It's all on me.

Every positive interaction with an upper-class female, socially or on the golf course (or in the sack) reassured Tom that he wasn't a poor boy anymore—and would never be again. Money was like the scorecard in golf to him. It told the cold hard facts of your progress in life or lack of same. As for me, I never gave a shit about money until lately.

Now, I finally realize how incredible it is to have money— and how shitty it was to be poor. In college, Tom had to work a job, study, go to class, and practice for the university golf team.

He'd see the rich kids on the golf team barely study— because they had jobs in the family business waiting for them after college—never have to work during the school year, and mostly spent their days and nights partying, with a little golf thrown in. At times, Tom got so discouraged, so physically and mentally worn out, it really pissed me off at these spoiled guys.

Katrina has flipped her lid over Tom being a detective. Thinks it's too dangerous. I've gotta get through to her how much Tom and I enjoy it; the thrill of solving puzzles and the joy of nailing the bad guys and helping people. My last job was setting out squash, green peppers and potatoes at the corner market; I didn't get the idea squash helps people in any significant way.

I love being a private eye. I finally have a purpose in life.

It's not fair of Katrina to ask him to give something up that means so much to him—and to me. We helped Det. Mathers solve three murders last year.

The Boyle Party tonight showed me so much. My brother was witty, charming, a great and sympathetic listener, who could make anyone think he was focused only on them as they talked. He was the whole, classy package. All these rich people wanted to be around him, wanted to know him. And to think how poor we started out in life...

The reaction of the ladies to him was also proof of how handsome he was, in a boyish All-American way. Not the sophisticated charm of, say, David Niven in the movies. Tom was the guy all the young women grew up believing they would have someday, and almost none of them did. They ended up having to settle for the Sterling Goulds and Carter Vonessens.

I noticed Katrina noticing the adoring glances from Patti Boyle to Tom. If this were a cartoon, there would be little red hearts floating above Patti's head. Kat better get used to this if she wants to continue to date Tom. And I hope she does.

As the party started to wind down, I already knew that there were people in attendance who were giving serious consideration to murdering Red Boyle. I also knew that when they saw Tom, and recalled his detective exploits, the would-be killers made a mental note to keep an eye on Tom. I would be able to work on preventing the murder without being under any scrutiny whatsoever. They were told I was here as Tom's caddie. None of them knew that I was Tom's equal as a detective—or perhaps even a bit more skilled, if you want my totally honest opinion.

From my perch on the stage, I surveyed the crowd. Good grief, there are a lot of conflicts and intrigues going on, personal, financial and sexual. If they hold golf tournaments in hell, they probably resemble this one, the 1963 Boyle International Bogey Island Pro-Am. Trying to emulate my overly positive brother I cheerfully thought, *Well, at least Julia Wilkinson isn't here. That would really be hell.*

Brooks Benton Continues Our Story:

Katrina, not far from the stage, making small talk with her frightfully enthusiastic pro-am partner Stan Barker, saw Tom's popularity, particularly with Ladies, in a different light than Caroline. She had hoped the island trip would bring the two of them closer together. But she was starting to be pessimistic.

Kat believed popularity could only be rooted in achievement in life, through winning golf tournaments in her case. Though Kat had been an American for less than 15 years, Americans, she knew, loved winners.

The concept of charisma, people being drawn to you because of your winning personality, was completely foreign to her. There was no such thing as personal charisma, she believed. A person's deeds, the great things they accomplished, told the whole story.

The young Katrina Stern could not perceive that she and Tom were pursuing the same objectives. But using completely different methods. They both wanted to please others.

She was pulled out of these serious thoughts by her partner Stan, who said, "Will you have dinner with me Thursday night? We can celebrate leading the tournament after Round One."

"I'd really like that." She wasn't lying and she wasn't telling the truth. Her opinion of Stan Barker at this point was a blank slate.

Patti Boyle, a few paces from Tom, thought, *no time for being subtle, too many pretty chicks here and some of them already have their inheritance.* She approached Tom.

"I'm Patti Boyle. We sort of met after you won the Vegas tournament."

Patti, in short shorts, a clingy, satiny shirt and Roman sandals, was a cutie. A little diffident, a little unsure of herself—which was part of the charm.

Tom said, "Of course. I never forget a...face."

She giggled, he smiled. Katrina nearby, frowned.

Not everyone at the party was a fan of Tom Colt's. Rodney Burkett, a bit too drunk for someone who had to tee off on a brutally difficult golf course in the morning, told Dick Amberson and several others gathered around him: "Colt is no detective. I mean, c'mon. Bogart plays that detective Sam Spade in the movies. They call him Bogie. What does that make Colt, double bogey?"

His attempted humor earned him weak laughter, but mostly scowls from the ladies. They all liked Tom. Burkett said, "Bollocks" and left, but not before adding, "Why am I paired with that old broad? Is this tournament rigged against me?"

One person at the party, a person with possibly the sharpest eyes and ears there, concluded that this Tom Colt person was not telling the complete truth about being there to play in the Pro-Am. Tom was also there as a private detective. Why would he want to fly all the way out here to play in a meaningless Pro-Am when the pro golf tournament season was in full swing? He'd end up missing two pro tournaments at least.

The question for this keen observer was, *what am I going to do about it? There's got to be a way of scaring him off...he's not a real detective anyway.*

Tom had just taken leave from Patti and walked over to the refreshment tables to get a glass of wine, not to drink but to hold, so he looked like he was socializing, not sleuthing. He spotted Marco Greene coming toward him.

Marco was a powerfully built man, almost fearsome looking. His face was rough, pock-marked, either from adolescent acne or very small caliber bullet holes acquired in gun battles. He was half Italian and half Jewish, a combo that all but guaranteed success in business. He was affable, great to work for and incredibly kind to the poor.

And Marco Greene was also one of the most prosperous organized crime figures in the Western US. He was an extremely efficient gangster, succeeding with a minimum of bloodshed. Bless his heart.

His greeting to Tom was a slap on the back so hard that Tom nearly coughed. Tom was relieved to see that Greene's wife, Tom's ex-wife Mandy, had not come on this trip. Mandy always had some personal problem she wanted Tom's help dealing with.

"Hey, it's supersleuth Tom Colt. How 'ya doing!"

"Hey, supergangster Marco. You're looking good. What brings you to the Grand Opening?"

"Boyle wanted me to see his posh new golf resort. He's thinking of franchising the concept, mini-resorts in island locales. He wants me to buy one."

"What a great idea! Each room could have one of your working girls there when the guest checks in. Saves having to pick one up in a bar."

Marco would let Tom needle him, because Mandy still adored Tom, but only so far. Tom supposed he'd know if he ever went too far, because he'd be dead.

"Thomas, remember our discussion about avoiding stereotypes. I run a clean business, as you are well aware."

"Laundering, I think it's called."

Thomas, you so enjoy needling me. And I must say you're the only living person I allow to do so."

"I am honored, kind sir."

Marco snorted.

"Could it be because I have the financial resources to provide my wife, your ex-wife Mandy, a wonderful life, and you did not."

"Spot-on Marco. They must offer excellent psychology courses at your alma mater, the old GU, Gangster University."

Tom's playful, although mortally dangerous, banter with Greene was interrupted by Red Boyle and Terrence Egglesworth passing by. Their conversation was not pleasant.

Boyle said, "This is your last chance to sell that 5-acre parcel to me. My offer is only good for the next week…"

"Go to hell, Boyle. But before you do, stop by that location next year this time and you will see a beautiful new Methodist Church, courtesy of Egglesworth Group Properties, built on that site."

"I assure you I can prevent that from happening."

The two men continued walking. Marco remarked, "Boyle is one of the nastiest bastards in business I've ever seen. We all can learn from him."

Looking on were Carter Vonessen and his wife Babs. Babs was a hard-looking woman with a head of tight black curls and a tightly-wound personality. Her bad temper exceeded that of her husband's. Many of their friends at Valley Vista CC thought it remarkable they hadn't killed each other by now.

She was concerned about the expression on her husband's face. As a younger man, he had a violent temper, but fortunately had learned how to control it as he got older and was successful in business. But Babs had seen that the anniversary of his sister's death, from drowning in Roosevelt Lake, had seemed to bring the Mr. Hyde side of his personality back to the surface. She really wished they had not come on this trip. But Carter, stewing in anger, would not have missed it for the world.

Big Al Langdon, walking alone on the beach, would have agreed with Babs: he wished he hadn't come too. What really galled him was that Boyle didn't even seem to recognize him when he checked into the resort. Maybe he should do something to jog that old bastard's memory!

At the same time, a weird meeting was happening, weirdly in the sauna room at the resort. With their father occupied by the reception, the Boyle kids, who call themselves Team Boyle, thought it would be a good time for a planning meeting. Each of them doubted they could trust the other. The Team concept was laughable.

The sauna was on full blast; dripping with both sweat and resentment, in their bathing suits, they were near the end of their meeting.

"We need money. Either the treasure or our inheritance. I'll be 40 soon. 40!" Fredonia said.

Chandler said, "We're wasting the best years of our lives being at Red's beck and call. We've been waiting all our lives. It's miserable to be in a rich family and each of us is scraping for money. It's humiliating."

Fredonia added, "We need to keep snoopy Tom Colt and that beatnik sister of his occupied while we take care of things so we can get what we deserve."

***

Caroline suffered fitful sleep those first nights on Bogey Island. Her mind was so full of activity, of ideas. Her embryonic detective business with Tom had awakened something in her that had been dormant, numbed by too many days and nights of drugs and aimlessness. Of shitty dead-end jobs and even shittier dead-end relationships.

Her mind was fully engaged on the task of making their PI business a success. She had picked up tons of info and as she termed them, 'vibes', at the pairings party—all of which led her to believe that Red Boyle's life truly was in danger.

She couldn't wait for the sun to come up so she could get to work on stopping the bad guys.

Chapter Thirteen

Early the next morning…

Tom was amped up to be back at the seashore. Not even the practice round disaster with Kat had dampened his spirits. Before they moved to the desert, his family had lived in Florida, his father working at a military installation there.

The white-capped azure surf at Bogey Island reminded Tom of good times when his dad took him fishing. He couldn't recall whether they ever caught anything; it just felt good to be with his dad.

He was strolling contentedly along the shoreline, in bare feet and swim trunks, when who should he see but Jilly Flannery jogging toward him from a secluded inlet known as Lover's Cove.

Tom paused his strolling to watch, because Jilly was naked. Ample-chested Jilly jiggled and smiled happily as she approached Tom.

She ran up and grabbed him. "I was hoping to see you!" she enthusiastically exclaimed.

"I think you misplaced your bikini young lady."

"Don't be such a conservative little Presbyterian boy. I've been thinking about sex on the beach with you ever since I boarded the plane to Miami, you cad."

"We need to focus on golf, Jilly. We have an important tournament to play."

"First let's focus on the magic our bodies can make in the warm sand. It's a beautiful day for sex on the beach. Nothing more wonderful than that, to hear the waves crashing the shore while we--"

"I thought sex on the beach is illegal."

"What fool told you that nonsense?"

"Det. Mathers calls it public indecency."

"Tell your friend Mathers that when it comes to sex, Jillian Flannery is always much better than merely decent."

Tom laughed. "I'll do that, goofy girl."

"Life is much more fun if there's a little danger involved."

She had no way of knowing they'd all have their fill of danger before the island adventure was over.

"We need to get in a practice round this afternoon. This course is brutal."

"Don't worry so much sweetie. We got this. In March the prevailing winds blow like hell in the afternoon here. We are first off the tee, 9AM, in the calm morning."

Tom laughed. "You arranged this, no doubt."

"Nothing wrong with grabbing a competitive advantage when it's available. That's why we have time for some rolling together in the soft sand—"

"Nope. I'm headed to the course." He turned to walk off. She followed.

She feigned looking miffed. "You just don't want me, I guess."

"Jilly, that's ridiculous. Making love with you is better than playing a round at Pine Valley on a warm day in June."

Jilly looked stunned for a moment, then her face was alive with girlish delight. "Sweetie, that's the nicest, most romantic thing you've ever said to me."

She grabbed him. "Hold me tight. I'm going to weep a little now."

Pine Valley is a magnificent course located in an evidently enchanted forest in the wilds of New Jersey, spoken of with reverence, perhaps awe, in men's and women's locker rooms at the best country clubs in America. The odd thing is, you seldom met anyone who had received an invitation to play Pine Valley—that's how exclusive the club was.

The membership of Pine Valley was a closely-guarded secret, and guests of members can play there only if they have low handicaps (excellent players, no duffs).

(Editorial note from Your Narrator: I've been trying to score an invite to play there for 15 years. So far, no luck).

And that's why the Country Club life is not an easy one. Because no matter how proud you are of your Club, how many prestigious tournaments your Club has hosted, there's always a superior club out there that won't let you in to play. That makes you even more desirous of being a member there.

Jilly was entitled to joyful weeping. Tom had in effect told her she was the personification of desire.

But young Tom's analogy was shaky at best. For as we know, many gentlemen have enjoyed the rolling hills, the peaks and valleys, of Jilly Flannery's soft and supple body. They usually didn't even need to book a tee time in advance.

Tom and Jilly released each other.

"Go find your clothes and we'll get out there and prepare to win this tournament. I have no idea why they decided we are playing alternate shot matches. That's like, you and your partner have to totally be in sync, like merging two people into one golfer, be bonded like lovers."

Jilly grinned. "That's exactly what I have in mind here on the beach this morning."

"It was you! Again."

"I may have whispered a few words into Red Boyle's ears. Never stand behind him, though, the farty old thing, while you're whispering. Whew."

"And Katrina is paired with Stan Barker. Your doing?"

"I can neither confirm nor deny. Isn't it wonderful we're playing as a team!"

She pulled Tom as close as possible without squeezing the air out of the poor guy. "Okay, you win. We'll do it your way, Coach. I'm going to give up sex for the next three hours."

"You can do it, kid." Tom thought a moment. "And give up thinking about sex?"

"Now you're asking too much of me, Coach."

***

Caroline had lately developed an interest in bird watching. She purchased several illustrated volumes of the birds of the Northern Hemisphere. And bought an expensive pair of binoculars, $79.95, to take to the island. The motivation for her newfound avian fascination was unclear, except there were times when Caroline wished she could spread her wings like the bold beautiful American eagle and fly far, far away from everyone and everything. She also wished she had talons like an eagle.

But it wasn't a pelican Caroline spied that morning as she trained her binoculars on the surf, looking for interesting foul, it was naked Jilly bird talking to Tom. Katrina was seated next to her on the patio of their cottage. They were finishing their morning coffee and chocolate croissants.

"I can't believe that woman," Kat said when Caroline told her what was transpiring.

Caroline reported: "She has pulled Tom in so tight she can feel his throbbing manhood against the soft moist fleece at the gates to the paradise she so fervently wished for him to enter. Or maybe that glorious, moist welcoming harbor within her she where so fervently wished him to dock."

"You read those romance novels from the 5 and dime."

"Not unless there's nothing else available. I like books with murder and mayhem. The more mayhem, the better."

"You are weird, Caroline." Kat was starting to get a headache that morning.

"Right back at you, Kitty Kat. You're the one who thinks the highest purpose of human existence is to whack a little white ball toward a tiny hole in the ground, a long distance away."

"Not all human existence, just mine."

"Jilly does have an amazing body for an older woman."

Katrina said with a note of indignation, "I know. We tried on clothes together at a department store and she took everything off in the dressing room so she could show me her fabulous body. She told me Tom only likes curvy girls."

"On some level we girls must admire Jilly. She has enough money to do whatever the hell she wants. I've only had enough money to do about ten percent of the hell I want. It's hard to be an authentic rebel on such a limited budget."

"I never wanted to be a rebel..."

This did not come as news to Caroline.

"I used to think Jilly was cool. But I'm not sure she does Tom any good. She's like the huntress and Tom is the unsuspecting prey. I'm firmly in Katrina Stern's corner."

Kat smiled. "What about you? You never talk about your own romances."

"Nothing interesting to report at this time. But check back in maybe 5 years or so. Tom is the hopeless romantic. I'm hopeless at romance. Guys say I talk too much. The 1960s male wants a girl who's great in bed, good at keeping house, has large breasts—thanks Mr. Hefner—and is a wonderful cook."

"I can only attest to having one of those four."

"Tom told me you're a good little homemaker."

Caroline smirked. Kat frowned.

"Tom always believes the best about people and it really aggravates me. Look at today. Jillian Flannery does not love Tom. She just wants him for sex because she knows she won't be desirable much longer, and young studs won't want to be with her, no matter how much money she has. You, on the other hand, could love him. But you're too classy or maybe too stubborn to get in there and battle Jilly for him."

"Or maybe too scared."

"Good grief. Don't be scared of my brother. But here's something I need to share with you. He's not ready to settle down. He's not ready for monotony."

"You mean monogamy, don't you?"

"Same thing. He won't be marriage material for a long time. He's having a blast being known, being popular. He grooves to the notoriety he gets from golf. When we were in school, he was a shy kid, I was the extrovert."

Caroline resumed looking through the binoculars.

"What's going on now?"

"Jilly is pulling on Tom's swim trunks like she wants him to take them off and roll around in the sand with her. He seems to be resisting. Good for him."

Caroline noticed Katrina looked dejected.

"Cheer up, Kitty Kat, here's what you do. Leave a note for Tom to join you at Lover's Cove. Go down there, before he arrives, take everything off and lie down on a beach towel waiting for him."

Kat's face displayed extreme disgust with that idea. "It would seem like I just want to act desperate. That's not me."

"Your competition is bold. You be bold, too."

"Ach. Not this again."

"Worked in golf, didn't it? You won. Give Tom some credit."

"I give him tons of credit!"

Caroline liked how fiercely Kat declared her admiration for Tom. This was going to work out fine. *With a little help from me*, she thought, with a note of conceit.

"Work with me here. At least take your top off when you get to the beach. It'll show Tom you can be the sexy, playful girl Jilly is, and you're younger and a much better golfer."

Caroline resumed looking through the binoculars. "I wish our mother could be here to see Tom, whom she thinks is so wonderful, so perfect that she has a museum room dedicated to his career in her house, frolicking on the beach with a naked lady just slightly younger than she is."

"You have mommy issues."

"How psychologically perceptive of you. But then again, Freud was a German, so I shouldn't be surprised."

"Austrian. And please don't call me Kitty Kat."

***

The team of Jilly and Tom teed off for their practice round at 11AM. The wind was totally calm. It seemed like a different, much more benign course than the one Tom and Kat faced just the day before.

It still had fangs, though. Narrow fairways and tricky, tiny greens surrounded by deep sand traps. The ocean ready to gobble up errant shots. "This course is a bigger bitch than I am," Jilly cheerfully observed.

And amazingly, Jilly switched her focus exclusively to golf. "I really want to win this," She told Tom as they teed off. In all aspects of life Jilly was a voracious competitor, never fully satisfied.

Tom had seen her spending extra time on the driving range at Valley Vista. He had no idea it was to practice hitting the ball lower so her shots would bore through the wind on the island. *Always planning ahead, that girl.*

"I will give our team everything I've got, Tom. I won't let you down, I promise. You mean too much to me. I've been practicing like mad for the last two weeks."

"So you knew you and I would be paired together before you ever got here."

"You are correct, Detective. Sheesh. This is like dating Lord Peter Wimsey. You're starting to irritate me. Don't you want us to win? Don't you want me?"

She took out a sheet of paper. "Before you got here, I even stepped off the yardages on the course and made a chart for us to use." She kind of chucked the paper at him, indignantly. He picked it up off the turf.

Tom was continually amazed how Jilly could go from a slightly goofy party girl to become a dead-serious, determined friend in a matter of seconds. Tom almost felt guilty for not having sex on the beach with her before they golfed that afternoon. Or perhaps guilt was not the precise emotion.

They sailed along the first 5 holes, shooting a team score of two under par. All was serene.

Until a gun was fired at them from a grove of trees behind the 6th hole.

The bullet struck a palm tree ten feet from Tom's head. Recalling being shot last year, Tom jumped two feet back. Then he instinctively drew Jilly to him and placed himself between her and the direction the bullet appeared to come from.

They waited, both expelling frightened breaths, their hearts pounding, but not from passion.

"Told you Red has lots of enemies. Someone knows you're here to keep him safe, so now you have an enemy too."

"How do you know why I'm here..."

"People tell me things."

"Why do they think they could scare me off?"

"Because you seem like a harmless young golfer boy. The would-be killer doesn't know you took a bullet from your true love."

"Julia is not my true love!"

A sly grin from savvy Jilly. "Glad I ferreted out who shot you. We've been speculating about that for months in the ladies' locker room. My money was on Julia all along."

"But you think Julia and I will end up together?"

"Only in the sense that every Private Eye worth his salt needs a femme fatale to make his life a living hell. Julia fills that role so well for aspiring Private Investigator Tom Colt."

"Cheered me right up. Let's play some golf."

That day, Jilly and Tom realized something about their normally playful, even silly friendship: the moment that shot rang out they felt safer together than they would have alone. They were friends willing to protect each other from trouble. For both, it was an awakening moment. They had each other's back. Their friendship had acquired a complex new dimension.

He told Jilly, "The would-be killer was at the Grand Opening Reception. It was brought up that I am a private detective. The assailant must be an amateur. Taking a potshot at me to scare me off is the stuff of B-grade detective movies. All it did was put me on alert. Kinda stupid."

"Dang, Tom. You really are a sleuth. As long as you're in my bed, I'm safe."

"But I'm not!"

"That's for sure! And never forget that." They laughed until the tension of the afternoon subsided.

When they finished their practice round, Tom asked Jilly, "Please don't tell Katrina we were shot at. She worries too much."

"You can count on my discretion, detective. And please don't tell anyone how scared I was. I'm supposed to be a fearless broad from the south side of Chicago."

And it occurred to Jilly Flannery the only man whose opinion of her mattered was that of Thomas J. Colt. *How strange life can be,* she thought. Could Jilly be falling in love? *NO. I, Jillian Marie Flannery do not fall in love. EVER.* She couldn't believe the thought even crossed her mind.

***

Later that afternoon, beautiful sunshine sprinkling diamonds on the serene cobalt blue waves, Katrina was indeed at Lover's Cove, on a towel, her bikini in sections lying a few feet away.

A bikini then was a 2-piece swimsuit, to be sure, but the bottom was more like short shorts, not the miniscule swatches of cloth we see today, roughly the size of a pirate's eyepatch. And a thong bikini? The local constable would immediately be summoned to the beach. And several middle-aged ladies would likely faint at the sight of glistening, taut, uncovered buns.

Lying naked and alone in Lover's Cove, listening to the soft whispering breezes and the rhythm of the pounding surf, Kat felt relaxed. Really. She had to admit it felt nice to take a break from her obsession to be the greatest female golfer on the planet.

She also had to admit to herself she felt great anticipation. Maybe sex on the beach was going to be as good as advertised. She was glad she took Caroline's advice.

She lay back and watched the lithe palm trees swaying to the sweet rhythm of their own romantic song. Romantic feelings swept over her. Tom would be there any minute...

Kat heard a slight wheezing sound, but she was half-dozing in the glorious sunshine and seduced by the sound of the ocean swells, in a half-dream of feeling Tom deep inside her.

Then she saw old Red Boyle coming around the thick curtain of vegetation that sheltered Lover's Cove. He was huffing from the exertion of walking. She was of course horrified.

She stood up and tried to cover herself, like the Venus statue by Botticelli. But it was too late. Red had spied all the fine goods.

Red ran his eyes up and down Kat's naked frame, smiled. "You are lovely, Katrina, but too thin for my taste. Your chest is...well, not quite developed. I heard a rumor that Jillian was sunbathing down here au natural. I like those curvy little gals. They're my weakness."

He drew out his handkerchief, mopped his brow on the hot afternoon. "But no more dalliances with young women, actresses and such, who just want me for my money. The Autumn Ambers were very nearly costing me a fortune. My future lovers will be women who have amassed capital of their own, like Jilly Flannery."

Katrina had no idea what he meant, or why he was telling her these things.

"I was...waiting for someone," Kat offered as a needless explanation for her lack of clothes.

"Perhaps for a spirited young Colt to gallop in? Although from the sounds you were making when I approached, you were doing quite well without him."

Suddenly, Kat felt very naked.

Red huffed off down the beach in search of Jilly's curves and capital.

Kat, humiliated, sat down, put her head in her hands and cried. *How dare he call her undeveloped.* The primary emotion she felt, though, was anger at Caroline for talking her into such a daffy stunt. Rising anger quickly dried her tears.

"Caroline!" Kat yelled to the silently swaying, disinterested coconut palms. Kat thought they were mocking her. "I'm never listening to you again!"

She didn't even notice Tom walking up until he was almost in front of her.

"Kat, what happened?" Tom asked after pausing a few moments to admire her unclothed form, dappled with sunshine. Katrina shone with athletic health as well as feminine beauty. He loved how her bikini tan lines highlighted her beautiful alabaster breasts, those "little beauties" as he called them. He loved those strong legs of hers that seemed to go on forever.

She had no idea how beautiful she was. If only she could have seen herself through Tom's eyes that afternoon.

"With her new bird-watching binoculars, Caroline was watching you and a bird named Jilly and your throbbing manhood at the gates to Jilly's paradise."

Tom sat down in the sand, perplexed. "Throbbing manhood? Paradise? What are you talking about? And why is my sister spying on me? All that happened today with Jilly was that we got in a practice round for the tournament."

"She was naked, Tom."

"That had nothing to do with me. She's proud of her body. Likes to show it off every chance she gets."

Kat slumped back on the towel and emitted a groan. "I am such a dummkopf. Caroline put me up to this. I don't normally parade around--"

"I've always loved a good parade..."

Tom slipped out of his swim trunks. Kat rallied after she saw the manhood was indeed throbbing.

They made love on the beach towel, wide enough so neither got covered with sand as they twined. At the peak moment, Kat cried out something in either German, French, Italian or Portuguese. Tom wasn't sure. She was sexually fluent.

Tom learned a new vocabulary word every time they made love, which was a nice bonus.

Jilly was right, there was something magical about making love on the beach, under the endless blue sky, surrounded by the powerful beauty of the timeless sea. It was a primal feeling, but also a feeling of being connected to forever, a feeling they would never die.

Kat lay contentedly next to Tom. A few quiet moments passed. These were among the glorious moments Tom and Katrina always were able to summon, throughout their lives. For that brief time, there were no issues between them, no obstacles they couldn't overcome.

Bliss is never the prevailing condition in life, but at Lover's Cove, for those few moments, Tom made bliss a reality for Katrina, and she for him.

The hell of it was, those special feelings could never be sustained for those two best friends. Life always found a way to interfere.

***

Chapter Fourteen

On the patio, ever-present and super-efficient waitress Carol Thorn had just refilled the iced tea glasses of Rev. Damien Tucker and Red Boyle, seated at a corner table by themselves.

"We call it 'radical giving'," said the Reverend, stroking his grey goatee. "Think of all the good your money will do after you are gone. I'm sure it warms your heart thinking about it. My foundation has a worldwide reach."

Red swirled his iced tea glass, contemplating. "Yes. I can see it. You can't take it with you, as they say."

"Selling your performing arts academy is a wise move, Mr. Boyle. It will remove temptation…"

"I should never have stooped to dalliances with those young actresses like Autumn Amber. But they are so beautiful, so young. Her breasts are like ripe fruit. I just want to grab them. And those full lips of hers. But I must not think these things. Help me, Rev. Tucker."

"Proverbs 11:22, sir. 'Like a gold ring in a pig's snout is a beautiful woman who shows no discretion'."

His quote was not quite on the mark: In this instance, the only Pig in question was Red Boyle.

"Your counsel has been so valuable to me, Rev. Tucker. I wish I had met you years before."

"I wish the same."

"And won't that shock a few people when my Will is read. Wish I could be here to see it!" Red bellowed.

The Reverend formed a thin smile and nodded, in that serious, pious way Reverends often do.

***

Chandler Boyle was steamed, and not from the frequent secret meetings with his siblings in the sauna room. Around sunset, he walked the mile to an old stone cottage, now nicely refurbished, that dated back to pirate days, near the beach that was purported to be where pirates used to land. The cottage now served as the Resort Chapel, which Rev. Tucker convinced Red to have renovated. For the privacy of those who wish to worship, he said. Chandler heard two voices as he approached. *Good*, he thought, *everyone's together.*

He opened the old wooden door, and its rusty hinges announced his arrival. Seated at one of the four pews were Rev. Damien Tucker and novelist William Tisdale.

"Are you in need of spiritual guidance, my son," Rev. Tucker asked Chandler.

"No, I'm in need of treasure, gold and jewels preferably."

The three conspirators smiled. Treasure was such a lovely word.

Tisdale asked, "How is Team Boyle doing with getting daddy to go along with the treasure hunt."

Chandler paced nervously. "Not well. He's threatening to shoot any trespassers searching for treasure. That would be you."

The Rev. said, "My good man, I am Red Boyle's spiritual advisor. He trusts me implicitly."

"And I am one of America's most beloved mystery writers."

Chandler. "One of you has never been to church and the other's books stink like Limburger cheese."

The Rev. laughed. He could afford to: Chandler had no idea that the Rev. would shortly be the major beneficiary of Red's estate. The treasure was just icing on the cake.

"I say we ignore my dear father and proceed full speed to find that treasure. He's so occupied with his guests that he won't care what we're doing out here."

Chandler stopped pacing and glared at the other two.

"You guys getting anywhere?"

"We're about to crack the code on that map you found," Tisdale remarked.

That was merely a hope on Tisdale's part. The map was fragmentary, found in a box of records the Boyles inherited after they bought the old villa and the island. Key parts of the map were missing.

Chandler even speculated that the map might just be someone's idea of a practical joke. Perhaps his father's.

"Can you get it done in a week?"

"We'll have to, won't we. But what if we don't…"

"My sister Fredonia has a Plan B."

***

Carter and Babs Vonessen asked for a tour of the resort kitchen before they retired to their room that night. Carter owned a small restaurant chain that served Italian food in a fast-food format—not very edible food according to Italian food expert and renowned caterer Laura Colt.

Carter announced in his loud, grating voice (amplified by alcohol), "Brings me back the days when I worked as a cook at the Biltmore Resort. Now I walk in there and they call me Mr. Vonessen, Sir!—almost with a salute."

He picked up one of the carving knives on a butcher block cart in the middle of the kitchen. It was a beautiful pearl-handled tool. "Boyle spares no expense. These knives are better than the ones we have at home, Babs."

He twirled the knife in the kitchen light and then put it back. "Remember what I said," he told the kitchen staff, "You can be as great as me someday if you keep working hard. Anything's possible in America."

Babs thought, shaking her head, *none of them believes that, Carter, most of them wouldn't want to be like you, and we're not in America.*

Babs led Carter out of the kitchen and up to their room.

***

Round One of the 1963 Boyle International Properties Bogey Island Pro-AM began at 9AM the next morning. Four of the teams were to play in the morning round, four more in the afternoon when the wind was predicted to be particularly brutal, gusts up to 50mph. Thanks to Jilly's influence with Red Boyle, she and Tom were first off the tee in the morning. The wind was absolutely calm. Perfect conditions for golf. Temperature about 70.

Next off was Tom's nemesis Rodney Burkett, paired with Judith Egglesworth. Rodney was despondent that he was paired with a "dog" partner but when he saw her warmup on the practice range, he was pleasantly surprised. She was strong, had a solid swing and was much younger than expected. He wondered why she typically dressed to look so dowdy.

Burkett, one of Tom's least favorite pros on tour, was a stocky but short Englishman with a prominent aquiline nose—one of the biggest beaks ever seen on a non-avian face--cold eyes, a cruel mouth with a cocky expression. He even walked like he thought he was hot shit, a kind of petulant strut.

Tom had seldom seen Jilly so determined. While warming up, she had a Katrina-like frown of determination on her face, which normally had the sunbeamy smile of those who are blissfully rich.

Katrina and Stan unfortunately drew the worst tee time, last off in the afternoon. Tom felt bad for Kat because he had invited her to play in the event as his partner.

Since this was a 9-hole layout, the round would consist of two trips around the course to play the regulation 18 holes. The Burkett-Egglesworth team shot a brilliant 31, 5 under par, on the front nine in the morning. Tom and Jilly shot a solid 33. On the second loop around the course, Rodney and partner shot a 36, Tom and Jilly a 37. After the first round, Rodney and Judith led with a 67, Tom and Jilly came in with 70.

They finished at 12:30. And then the wind started to blow in from the East. By the time Kat and Stan teed off, the wind was blowing in gusts of 30-50mph.

Wind is perhaps the golfer's worst weather obstacle. You can play in cold, even in rain, but wind makes it difficult if not impossible to hit your shots as planned. One the 4th hole, Kat aimed her shot over the beach, thinking the howling wind would push it back toward the green. But the wind suddenly becalmed and her ball plopped into the surf. A double-bogey six was their score on one of the easier holes on the course.

Their first nine score was a shaky 39, their second trip around a dreadful seven-over-par 43. Their score of 82 put them a full 15 strokes behind Rodney and Judith, the leading team from the morning round.

Tom watched them finish up on the ninth hole. Being in the wind all day had worn them both out. Kat looked crestfallen. They both had red, wind-burned faces.

Kat saw Tom and walked over to him. "This was miserable. Why did Red want us to play in these conditions?"

"Red hates pro golfers. He wanted to be one of us and wasn't good enough."

She shook her head and added with sarcasm, "Thank you so much for inviting me to this tournament. Please keep me in mind for future events." She stalked off.

Tom knew better than to follow her. When Kat played poorly, the wise move was to leave her alone. Fortunately, she usually played brilliantly.

Tom saw Red Boyle, their genial host, sitting in a golf cart under the shade of a palm tree, sipping a glass of beer. He gave Tom the 'thumbs up' and laughed. Tom had a different finger in mind.

Tom saw Caroline strolling over. He knew she was going to give him the needle over a dreadful shot he hit on the 8th hole, a "shank" as it is called. He had struck the ball not on the clubface but on the hosel, the segment of a golf club just above the clubface.

She broke into song, doing her own rendition of Bob Hope's signature tune, *Thanks for the Memories.*

"Shanks for the memories," she crooned, and grinned.

"Do you have to dwell on the one bad shot I made all day?"

"You gotta admit, it was a doozy. A cold shank with a 5-iron, went straight off the cliff into the deep blue sea."

"The wind threw me off balance."

"Strange how the wind never blows Jack Nicklaus off balance, just Tom Colt. And yes, as a matter of fact, I do have to dwell on it. My mission is to temper your nauseatingly sunny outlook on life. I bet on your deathbed, you'll be making a note to book a tee time at Pebble Beach for the following summer."

"Your philosophy is groundbreaking stuff. Why don't you write a book, Caroline Colt's *Unleashing the Power of Negative Thinking.* It might outsell Napoleon Hill."

"How do you know I'm not already working on it? I have a lot of time on my hands waiting for my brother to win another tournament. Do you know Arnie's already won 38 events! Now that's what I call a golf career. I guess you could write a book, *Winning Isn't Everything.*"

"How about *Caroline Colt's Guide to Abusing Legal and Illegal Drugs.*"

"How 'bout *Tom Colt's Guide to Always Dating the Wrong Woman.*"

"On your deathbed, you'll just keep talking nonstop until the Grim Reaper gets bored, gives up and walks away."

She chuckled at that one. She agreed.

"Want to go on?" Tom asked.

"No. That's Enough. I feel better."

"Me, too. Love you, Caroline."

"Love you, Tom. Nice round today. See you at dinner."

The Stern-Barker team was walking back to their cottages, disconsolate. Kat, in typical Kat style, blamed herself for their poor score, even though Stan was pretty much dreadful and useless the whole afternoon. He had a fusspot personality: when things didn't go his way—such as golfing in 45mph winds—he let frustration compound the difficulty. Powerful men who run corporations and bark orders at 1000 cowering employees are often shocked to learn they can't control little things like the weather.

To Stan's credit, he never lost his temper, such as heaving a golf club after a bad shot. He bolstered Kat several times during the round, even encircling his arm around her and telling her how much he loved having her as a partner. They began to bond.

Katrina thought, *Stan is a cool guy. Endearing, earnest. Rigid, though. More German than I am.*

He was something of a neat freak, clean freak. He supplied hot dogs for the concession stand and made sure the servers wore plastic gloves. He wiped a smudge of mustard off Kat's cheek. He also wiped the steering wheel on the golf cart with disinfectant when they started. He carried cloth towels and alcohol in his golf bag for the task.

"In the food industry we're always focused on cleanliness," he explained. Kat, who washed her hands approximately 25 times a day, appreciated this.

Their stroll back to their cottages allowed Stan to learn more about this lovely girl he was so enamored of. He was clearly looking at Kat as a potential life partner.

"When do you golf tour gals retire and have a family?"

"Depends how much we love the competition. And whether we're still winning. I'm just entering my best years."

"Just don't wait too long, until it's too late. You're a beautiful woman. Your children would be beautiful, too."

Stan's words touched Katrina's heart, and for the first time she considered she might want a child someday. Just one, though. A girl. With long, straight black hair. A serious outlook on life. And excellent posture.

Stan also took the opportunity to diss Tom as a scatterbrain. "He lacks focus. I mean, does he want to be a detective, or a golfer. Seems strange if you ask me. It takes total commitment, total focus, to succeed in life. I'm a big follower of Napoleon Hill's success philosophy. Have you read, *Think and Grow Rich*?"

Kat shook her head. She wasn't a big reader. Playing and practicing golf 20 hours a day doesn't leave you much leisure time.

"I've known since I was a teenager that I wanted to own my own business. And I always had a passion for sausage. Wonderful food, sausage is, and so good for you. I'm always experimenting with new blends of meat and spices to squeeze into those animal intestine casings."

Kat couldn't come up with anything to say. She hadn't thought a lot about sausage during her life.

"Don't get me wrong, Colt seems like a descent fellow. But I doubt he'll ever amount to much financially. He likes being the drifting golf bum. You see those guys at a lot of the country clubs, schmoozing the ladies. They work in the south and west in the winter and then head north to a club in summertime. One long party, their lives are. Someday all the pretty girls won't want him anymore and the party will be over."

Katrina disagreed with Stan's assessment of course, but even she wasn't aware that Judge Wilkinson was teaching Tom how to become wealthy.

"You have to think long-term, Katrina—40 years from now, where do you want to be? Tom will be giving lessons at a dilapidated driving range off the Interstate. I have goals, big goals. I want to acquire more companies and have a Global Sausage Empire."

Although she admired Stan's ambition, his goal gave her the mental image of *Stan Barker, King Weiner.* She stifled a chuckle.

"And I also don't like that woman Tom is pals with, Jillian Flannery. She's trash as far as I'm concerned. Her only talent is getting old rich men to marry her. That's where you and I are alike, Katrina, we both prefer to earn everything ourselves. You earn it out of the ground with your golf clubs. I mold ground meat into cylindrical casings to create little culinary masterpieces."

Stan seemed to forget the small detail that he inherited the sausage business from his Uncle Gus. And by 2005, Stan was long dead from heart disease and emphysema, and Tom owned Valley Vista Country Club. Stan could not perceive, or perhaps didn't care, that Tom had a long-range plan for his life, too. The upper classes like to think the lower classes are content with, or perhaps doomed to, their current situation.

"It's my mission to get people to eat more sausage. It's an extremely healthy food, you know," he repeated. "Packed with protein."

Stan had, two years ago, opened a processing plant in non-unionized Phoenix. Thanks to the supply of workers from south of the border, labor costs were much lower than in the Midwest. Stan also saved on distribution costs to the Western states. The result was his net profit margin went from 8% to 23%.

With his financial future assured, it was time for Stan to turn his attention to finding a bride. He was turning 40 the following year. His own biological clock was ticking. He decided to be bold. Kat was 26.

"I've had a crush on you since we met. I even named my Barker Spicy Brazilian Bratwurst after you, since you lived there."

This was a big fib. But give Stan credit for thinking on his feet.

Kat was taken aback...what German/Brazilian girl wouldn't be flattered to have a wurst named after her.

"I don't know what to say..."

And truly, she didn't.

***

Red Boyle thanked Doris, the resort's pastry chef, and Marquita, a member of the maid staff, for joining him in his office. They took seats in front of his desk, understandably puzzled looks on their faces. He sat down and gave each of them a pen, black ink.

Doris was a hefty lady of 52, whose red nose gave evidence of 10,000 nights guzzling gin. Marquita was a slight, nervous girl of 21. She had left her little hometown, Magdelena de Kino, in Sonora, Mexico, to see the world. After two years of cleaning toilets for 8 hours a day for Boyle International Properties, she had seen enough of the world and was ready to return home. She saved every penny she could to finance her trip back.

Doris had worked for the Boyle Organization for 20 years. She was a damn good pastry chef, when sober. She was from England and still spoke with a Cockney accent.

From a folder on his desk, Boyle took out two copies of a one-page document. "I am going to sign these, and then you are going to sign them as witnesses and date the document."

They nodded submissively. He passed a copy to each of them, which they read. It was Amendment #12 of the Elwood Brinton Boyle Trust. On it were listed 4 names, each with a percentage next to them. They were:

Desert Light Charitable Mission 75%

Fredonia M. Boyle 8.33%

Chandler A. Boyle 8.33%

Patagonia N. Boyle 8.34%

Total   100%

"Do you understand what you are signing?"

They nodded somberly, honored to be chosen for such an important task. They slid the documents back across the desk to him.

Red Boyle signed them with his flourishing script. He gave them back to the two ladies who, with serious faces, affixed their signatures and dated them. Boyle took the documents back, placed them in an envelope and put them in the top left drawer of the desk.

From the middle drawer he took out another envelope, stuffed with cash. He counted out ten $50 bills and gave five to each of them.

The ladies' eyes lit up. $250 was a lot of money for 10 minutes work in 1963. But if Red Boyle liked you, he was incredibly generous. If he didn't, well…your life was gonna be hell.

Boyle made his kids, or anyone for that matter, plead their case like starving peasants before including them in his Will. He loved to torment them with, "Your share will be reduced to 5%." He frequently changed the percentages, hence this was the 12th Amendment. It was his way of controlling them. Each person's share increased or decreased depending on whether they were in his good graces or not.

The previous Amendment read as follows:

Fredonia M. Boyle	25%
Chandler A. Boyle	25%
Patagonia N. Boyle	25%
Autumn L. Amberson	20%
Desert Light Charitable Mission	5%
Total	100%

It would be a mistake to conclude these changes in percentages were insignificant. Boyle's Estate would conservatively be valued at $25 million in 1963.

***

Red Boyle, alternating stinginess with generosity to keep his employees on edge, paid for a lunch buffet for them, served on the patio by the swimming pool every day at 2PM, after the guests had been fed of course.

Doris tossed down her first glass of gin of the day and told everyone within earshot all about how Red had entrusted her with such an important task as witnessing the Will. Everyone wanted to know what, or who, the Desert Light Charitable Mission was.

"Maybe it's that Reverend guy who's always hanging around," speculated Louis, the Head Chef.

Doris, $250 ahead of where she started the day and just finished making the desserts for that night, didn't really care. She poured herself another gin from the flask she carried in her uniform.

Dick Amberson, who cared dearly, heard everything from his lounge chair by the pool. He felt like jumping in and drowning himself. He, and Tracy, were finished. The mistake Dick had made was not recognizing that reneging on promises was another way Red Boyle jerked people around, to Red's great amusement.

***

Chapter Fifteen

The following day, while all of this palace intrigue was going on, **Round 2 of the 1963 Bogey Island Pro-Am Tournament** was being played. For the second round, the teams with the worst scores from Day 1 teed off first, in the calm morning, and the leaders teed off in the fierce afternoon winds.

Before Tom and partner Jilly even arrived at the first tee, Tom's fan Patti Boyle was waiting there to watch them play.

Tom told Jilly the story of Patti's topless photo ending up in his pocket in Vegas. "The brazen little hussy," Jilly said.

Tom smiled at the irony.

Tom and Jilly started the round three strokes behind the team of Rodney Burkett and Judith Egglesworth, who was the surprise of the tournament, a fine athletic young woman with a strong swing. She was more of a Judy than a Judith.

By the time Tom and Jilly teed off, Kat and Stan Barker, who teed off first after their horrible 82, in the first round, took advantage of the calm winds and shot an incredible seven under par 65—mostly due to Kat's outstanding play. Stan was still sorta worthless. His golf swing was a choppy, ugly thing. Even though this was a rinky-dink tournament, Katrina gave it her all—as she did in everything.

Stan was so excited about their fine score he gave Kat a passionate kiss on the mouth when they finished. She was startled, then smiled. She was reluctant to admit it to herself, but the kiss felt good. She was starting to have real feelings for Stan.

He was way ahead of her in that regard. Watching her walk over to the scorer's table to sign their scorecard, admiring her sturdy hips and firm backside, he was thinking, "She will pop out such wonderful babies for us!" Stan was ready and willing to get the project underway that night...

The little crowd of hotel guests watching the action on the 9th green cheered enthusiastically for Kat and Stan's great round when they finished. Their two-day total was 147. There was still a chance they could win. The leaders were playing in the teeth of the afternoon gale; their scores were bound to be much higher than the previous day.

Stan was thrilled by the applause to the point of blushing. Businessmen never get that thrill, the crowd applauding, until their retirement banquet.

For Tom and Jilly, things didn't get off to a great start that day. The wind was indeed ferocious. Tom's long, strong swing was not designed for windy conditions. He tended to get off balance and hit the ball every direction but straight. By the third hole, the Colt-Flannery duo was three more strokes behind steady Burkett and Egglesworth, or six strokes in total.

When Tom three-putted the fourth hole to blow a chance to gain a stroke, Burkett smirked at Tom in his typically condescending manner. Almost no one on the golf tour liked Burkett. Caroline did not like what she had just seen. *Time for me to step in*, she thought.

She took Tom aside before they teed off on the 5th hole. "Rodney Burkett is European royalty. He psyches you out because he swaggers up to the tee like he owns the country club, which he could if his dad, The Viscount de Manures or whatever he is, bought it for him. He makes you feel like a po' boy who doesn't belong inside the club gates. And that's why, good brother, you miss the point of the game you supposedly love as much as you love anything."

"And the point would be..."

"It's not about who you are or where you came from. It's simply and authentically about who can hit the ball the farthest, the straightest, the truest. And that's where you, Thomas J. Colt, leave Rodney Burkett in the dust."

Tom smiled. "Thank you."

"Here endeth the lesson. For today. Now let's get out there and play some golf. You and Jilly make a great team. Strange team, somewhat revolting team, but great."

Caroline's pep talk worked wonders. By the time the first 9 holes of play ended, Tom and Jilly were only 2 strokes behind. By the time they reached the last hole of the second trip around the course—the last hole of the tournament--they were tied.

This was an alternate shot match. The ninth hole was a long Par-5 with the ocean on the left side. It was Jilly's turn to hit the first shot for their team.

Jilly, trying to maximize distance on her tee shot, swung way too hard and hit a big hooking ball, right to left, that sailed all the way down over the cliff and onto the beach.

She was crushed. She thought she'd blown their chances to win. Tom gave her a little hug. "Don't worry, partner."

Her attempted smile masked the true emotion: she was furious with herself, dogged competitor that she was in business, love, and golf.

When they reached the ball, they found they had caught a break. It was nested atop a tuft of weeds—a much easier shot for Tom than picking the ball clean off the fluffy beach sand.

Tom had brought three clubs with him down to the beach: an 8-iron, a 4-iron and a 3-wood. The worse the lie, the more likely he would have to hit a short recovery shot with an 8-iron, back up the cliff and onto the fairway, leaving Jilly with a long third shot to the green.

Jilly commented, "I think you could hit the 4-iron. The lie isn't awful. We lay up. I hit a 3-wood maybe for our third shot. You sink the putt for a birdie 4 and the worst that can happen is we tie for 1st place."

The surprisingly athletic and youthful Judith Egglesworth had hit a terrific drive that left their team in great shape for the 2nd shot. Her partner, long-hitting Rodney, might very well hit the green in 2.

Tom took a few long moments to decide. He checked the breeze by tossing up a few blades of weeds. But that didn't tell him what the breeze was like up above them on the fairway.

"I'm not a layup kind of guy. If I had played it safe, I'd still be living in a cruddy apartment that smelled like cat piss and old-man sweat. Instead, I'm at a ritzy resort in the Bahamas playing in a tournament with an incredibly lovely, make that drop dead gorgeous, woman, who I think the world of. We're going with the 3-wood. We're going for the green in 2. We're going for the outright victory."

Jilly smiled. "Gosh!" she exclaimed. She felt surprisingly warm inside. "Gosh!" she repeated.

Tom tossed away the 8 and 4-irons, gripped the 3-wood with authority. The little crowd watching from above on the cliffside applauded. Tom hadn't watched Arnold Palmer all those years in competition without learning that golfers were, in the end, performers.

"Can we make it up and over the cliff side? You hit your 3-wood so low."

"Why don't we find out?"

Jilly stepped back as Tom took three practice swings, imagining the flight of the ball, imagining the perfect shot. He took his stance.

Against the spectacular backdrop of the sparkling pale blue sea riddled with whitecaps from the stiff breeze, Tom swung. Perhaps swung isn't the best descriptive verb. It was more of a detonation. He put every mighty muscle, and all the competitive juice of his iron will to win, into the shot.

His long blond hair blown by the stiff wind, his teeth gritted, his proud chin, his powerful shoulders on a 6'2" frame—to Jilly, Tom was the very picture of male strength and vitality, and of that peculiar American zeal to rise above whatever difficulties life throws at us. He took her breath away with that majestic stroke. Not an easy thing to do with cynical Ms Flannery.

She almost blurted out, "I love you," but painful life experience had trained Jilly to never use those words again.

You might think that moment of sheer athletic excellence was the lasting image Jilly would have kept of Tom Colt rather than the one when he was standing naked by her bedroom window that sunny morning in January. But she was Jilly Flannery after all, so she went with the window image.

The ball soared toward the cliff face. It looked to Jilly like it wouldn't clear the cliff, but instead bounce off and back down to the sand, dooming their match.

But, barely, it did clear the cliff and bored into the stiff breeze. The ball bounced 15 feet in front of the green and came to rest on the edge, but not quite on, the putting surface.

Tom's shot rendered Jilly speechless, which as you know happens even more seldom than Caroline Colt being rendered speechless. Her face felt flushed, she felt aroused. Golf and sex were similar things to her.

"C'mon, partner. Let's win this!" Tom said. She took his hand and they walked up the path back up the cliff face to the fairway.

Jilly immediately decided to putt the ball rather than hit a chip shot with, say, a 7-iron. Jilly was extremely confident putting the ball.

She would be putting for an eagle-3 to win the match. Unfortunately, it was from more than 60 feet away from the hole, a massively long putt. And it was the most treacherous green on the course, slick as glass, twisty and mean as a diamondback rattlesnake back in Phoenix, and all downhill.

Rodney had hit their 2nd shot to the right and short of the green. Judith then hit a nice pitch shot 10 feet from the hole, where Rodney would be putting for a birdie 4.

Jilly was an excellent putter to be sure, but Tom wished the ball could have rolled 20 feet or more closer to the hole to make a more reasonable putt for her.

Burkett-Egglesworth were on the green in three strokes, 10 feet from the hole, putting for a birdie 4. Jilly needed to cozy her putt up close enough for them to make a matching birdie 4.

This was the kind of difficult putt that can embarrass a pro, let alone an amateur like Jilly. Anything up to a 4-putt was possible. And Jilly, after all, was an amateur (at golf).

Jilly chose to leave the flagstick in the cup, in the hopes that if she hit the putt too hard, the flagstick would stop the ball from sailing off the green.

Jilly surveyed the putt from several angles. She shook her head, recognizing the difficulty.

She stood behind the ball and gave it one more look before taking her stance.

Tom standing nearby, said to her, "Pine Valley, Jilly. That's who you are to me."

"Pine Valley, really..."

"Absolutely."

She beamed a smile, then she got the most sublime, quiet, determined, look of concentration Tom had ever seen. She gave the ball a solid knock with her putter; it started down the hill.

Slowly, slowly, the ball went, then gained speed. It twisted and turned and turned direction again.

Tom had the sudden, strange thought, that the putt was like the path our lives take. All we can do is set things in motion and then see what happens. If Tom Colt had fewer stray thoughts, he would have won more tournaments. But Tom enjoyed thinking more than he enjoyed competing.

Fifteen feet from the hole, Tom saw the ball was going much too fast. Jilly, in her excitement, had stroked the putt too firmly. The green was so slick, Tom thought her ball might roll off the edge of the green and down into a little valley below. End of match.

The putt struck the flagstick, was knocked back two inches by the impact, then spun forward into the hole. EAGLE 3 FOR COLT-FLANNERY, AND THE VICTORY!

The little crowd cheered. Autumn Amber, seeing the magic of golf for the first time, resolved to take up the game. It seemed like the most exciting sport she had ever seen. And people cheer for you, like in showbiz. Ten years later she was

Ladies' Club Champion at Riviera Country Club in LA, where the movie stars play.

Jilly fell to her knees with ecstasy, saying, "Yes! Yes! Oh, Tom, yes! Yes, Tom, yes!"

She clutched the firm shaft of her putter.

Tom thought, *I get the $1,500 First Prize, Jilly gets a near-orgasm. It's all good.*

He rushed forward and embraced his oddly wonderful partner.

Good sport Rodney Burkett yelled "Bollocks!" then angrily tossed his ball toward the ocean. He added: "What is that ditzy broad babbling about? Is she mental?"

Caroline responded, "I think it's the sound of victory, Rodney baby."

What Caroline was thinking was, *I don't think the ancient Scots invented golf with this scene in mind.*

The top three finishers were, Colt-Flannery with a two-day total of 142, two under par. Burkett-Egglesworth at 143, and the Stern-Barker duo at 147 after their incredible 2nd round 65.

And the first annual Boyle International Properties Bogey Island Pro-Am was concluded by a smiling Red Boyle waddling onto the green and giving Tom and Jilly their trophy, and Tom the first-place check. The official Rules of Golf prohibit an amateur like Jilly from accepting prize money in an event. Although Jilly would have taken offense at being called 'an amateur' at anything.

Tom said to Jilly, "This trophy is kind of puny. I was expecting something bigger."

"Me, too, but we girls are used to disappointments like that."

Tom feigned a frown at his wonderful but goofy partner.

Jilly planted a kiss on Tom's lips as a photographer memorialized the moment. "Told you I'd never let you down."

"If I could putt as good as you, I'd win The Masters."

"There aren't 5 men on planet earth who could execute that 3-wood shot on the final hole, with the game on the line, and one of those is Tom Colt, my partner, my sweetie, my coach, my best friend."

She beamed.

Kat and Caroline were watching from the other side of the green. Caroline commented, "Don't be jealous, Kat. Smooching between male and female team members after winning a golf event is permitted, particularly when it was unexpected. And my brother winning any kind of tournament is always unexpected."

Caroline pulled a slender volume from her back pocket, showed it to Kat. It was *The Rules of Golf.* "See. It says right here, rule 71-B, section 4."

Kat chuckled, but the island adventure had caused her to re-evaluate her hot romance with Tom.

Red, surveying the happy throng that cheered for golf's Mr. Popularity, Tom Colt, thought that he may have overreacted to think he was in danger. The Grand Opening of his resort had been an even bigger success than he imagined. *Why was I so worried? Everybody loves it here. Everybody loves me!*

Jilly took off her golf shoes and socks and sort of skipped up the soft sandy path to her guest cottage. *Jilly Flannery,* Tom thought, *45 years old going on 19.*"

She turned back to Tom and exclaimed, "Can life get any better than this?"

Tom ran several snappy sex-related replies through his head before he settled on, "The best is yet to come."

Jilly had to fly back that night to Phoenix, to attend a grand opening of her own, her latest shopping center project. She took the little trophy with her. Not as good as taking Tom home, which is what she fervently hoped to do.

***

Tom, Katrina and Caroline were scheduled to have dinner that night. Stan Barker was having dinner in his cottage and tending to some financial reports from his company he had neglected. Knackwurst sales had unexpected slowed; he needed to find out why.

At 6:30, Kat walked down the corridor of the resort's main building toward Tom's room. The door to his room was open. She heard conversation. She recognized, Tom, Caroline and Autumn Amber, the young actress and protégé of Red Boyle's.

Kat stopped outside the door and listened.

She heard the sound of unzipping.

"Let me show you my equipment," Tom said happily.

Autumn exclaimed, "Look at that! You've got a Big One!" Then she giggled with excitement. "It's huge!!!"

Caroline said, "Bigger isn't always better. I can attest to that. Sometimes I think golfers just want to use it to show off to their adoring fans."

"It's so smooth," Amber purred. "Can I rub it?"

Tom said, "I polish it once a month. It can get rough from being handled too much. Go ahead."

Kat thought, an expression of horror seizing her face, *I can't take this. This is way too weird. We're losing their minds from being on this remote island.* Kat recalled her own escapade of stripping naked at Lover's Cove. *It's making us all crazy. I need to get Tom and me back to civilization.*

Autumn said, "Look, it even has your name stenciled on it. You must be proud."

Kat had to stifle a shriek. In their intimate adventures together, she had never noticed...

"I guess I'll put it away now. Let me zip up."

Kat heard more sound of zipping.

"Thanks for showing it to me, Tom."

"The pleasure was all mine. Hope you want to try it yourself someday soon."

That was quite enough for Kat. She took a deep breath for courage and stepped into Tom's room. She saw Tom standing next to...his golf bag. She recalled his superstition about keeping his clubs with him at all times, not leaving them in the trunk of his car or at the course.

"Kat, we've been waiting for you. Let's get down to the restaurant. I'm starved. Have you met Autumn Amber? She's interested in learning more about our great game. I showed her my equipment. It's a good way to get started. Maybe you could teach her."

Now Kat stifled an embarrassed laugh.

"Sure," she sort of croaked out.

"Nice to meet you Katrina," Autumn said, politely extending her hand to Kat, who took it for a brief, weak shake.

Kat had a foolish, forced grin on her face. "A pleasure meeting you Amber Autumn."

"It's Autumn Amber."

"Of course it is." Kat's face was very red. Like most Germans, she never handled embarrassment well.

Tom, the observant detective said, "Everything okay, Kat? You look a little..."

"All is well. Let's go. I'm hungry too."

***

Caroline went to her cottage to change clothes before dinner; Tom and Kat had a beer on Tom's patio while waiting to meet her.

Walking back to the lodge, Caroline almost felt like singing she was so joyful that night. She helped Tom beat Rodney Burkett, they so far had seen no signs of anyone trying to murder Red Boyle, though she thought he might deserve it, and she was really liking this Resort Life. *I was meant for a life like this. And I'm a real, professional detective. Nothing more exciting than finding your true calling!* She suddenly felt a warm, sweet surge of un-Caroline-like optimism.

But as often happens in life, when we feel on top of the world, Life slaps us back down.

She walked around the corner of the hallway, past the ballroom and saw an easel with a placard on it. She was frozen in place, like a chick in a horror film when the monster is finally revealed.

The placard said *'TONIGHT! Grand Ballroom, a special performance by recording star Julia Renee and her band, The Loose Impediments'.* There was a photo of a record album with a beautiful blonde singer, with rose-gold hair that tumbled down to her shoulders, and a voluptuous figure.

Julia Renee was Julia Renee Wilkinson. Yes indeed, the Judge's daughter Julia was there.

On a table next to the poster was a stack of record albums. The album was titled *A Swinging Time*, with *Julia and The Loose Impediments* band. The album was published by Red Dog Music, a well-known label. The logo on the album was a lovely Irish Setter named Rose.

Caroline thought, *OH CRAP! No, this is even more calamitous. It qualifies as DOUBLE CRAP! I wonder how that slut got a recording contract. Wait...I answered my own question.*

Chandler Boyle stopped by, in affable host mode. "My old flame from High School. We were Homecoming King and Queen. She's a recording star now, you know, with Red Dog Music—a big label. If all goes well, I'm going to get back together with my high school sweetheart this week."

Caroline had heard that Julia was in New York at a renowned mental health clinic, getting her medications adjusted. Julia suffered from what we now term bi-polar disorder, fortunately a mild case.

Caroline thought she would be a lame detective indeed if she didn't piece together: Red is stingy with money. Keeping his children basically broke and threatening to disown them for any petty issue. Cash-strapped Chandler would need money to pursue Julia.

It is cruel, she thought, to hold out that someday they might get part of the money—if they are perfect in his eyes, which of course is impossible.

A soft bell went off in her head: MOTIVE!

Chandler kissed two of his fingers then tapped the poster of Julia. Chandler wandered off, visions of Julia's enormous breasts dancing in his head, no doubt. Presumably the visions were dancing, not the breasts.

***

"Put Autumn on the phone," Dick Amberson heard his wife Tracy's voice demand. He complied, as he did with any request from his overbearing spouse.

"Mom! The connection's so clear!"

"How are you doing, honey?"

"I'm making progress for us, mom. Mr. Boyle says he's still very interested in financing our movie…"

"That's great news! I'll be there in two days. We're wrapping up production on the TV series. I had no idea we'd be on location for so long. Can't wait to see you, darling. Now put your father back on."

She did. Dick said to Autumn, "Could you fetch us so more ice, sweetheart?"

"Sure, dad." Autumn picked up the ice bucket and left. Dick waited until he heard the door click.

"Bad news, Tracy. Boyle already changed the Will. I heard it directly from two of the staff members who witnessed him execute a new one. Autumn is out, some Reverend guy is in."

"Oh, no, oh no," Tracy said with fury.

"Autumn's done great. Practically threw herself at creepy Boyle. But you know how that bastard like to string people along. We're all his puppets on a chain. You wouldn't believe how many people at this Grand Opening hate the guy."

There was a long, thoughtful pause on the other end.

"Well, maybe we can still salvage this ugly situation. We'll talk strategy when I get there."

Tracy thought, *Maybe I'll seduce Old Red Boyle myself and close the deal. I've still got it.*

***

On the other side of the island, Rev. Tucker was hot, sweaty and dirty. He had spent three hours exploring a series of caves near the south shoreline, likely spots for pirates to have stashed their loot 250 years ago.

For his trouble, he'd gotten soaked feet, bruises and scratches from climbing into narrow crevices. He uttered more than a few oaths and was starting to conclude this whole treasure hunt idea was a waste of time. It may not be worth the risk of Red finding out his real identity and booting him out of the Will.

All this changed when he found a shelf in a cavern that happened to have chest placed on it. Oddly, it wasn't a treasure chest from the 1720s; it was a metal chest that looked at most 30 years old, he estimated.

Rev. Tucker picked up a stone and smashed the rusty hinges on the strong box, then pulled open the top.

No pirate loot—no rubies, no gold, no emeralds.

Just piles of US currency, neatly bound in paper wrappers, profits from the liquor smuggling trade. He had found the money the gangsters left behind in the 1930s!

Rev. Tucker's reaction at this good fortune, this discovery surprised him: his emotion was disappointment. With greedy people, particularly those who resort to crime, the loot in hand is never enough. Tucker wanted the pirate treasure.

He had no idea that he had walked right past the place the 18th century pirates had left their treasure for safekeeping, to retrieve when they returned to the island from further plunder. They never made it back.

He instantly made several decisions: he would not tell his partner, novelist Tisdale, or Chandler and Fredonia Boyle, his other partners. They, after all, didn't even keep their kid sister Patti in the loop.

The little strong box was light enough for the Reverend to carry. He knew the perfect place to bury it, in a sandy grove of trees near the shallows a half mile closer to the resort. After everyone departed the Grand Opening celebration, it would be easy for him to land a motorboat there and retrieve his find unseen.

Toting a strong box up the steps to the lodge that night might draw attention, even from clueless sleuth Tom Colt and his daffy sister.

When he arrived at the grove, he heard the sound of digging. A hooded figure—he couldn't make out whether it was male or female--was shoveling the soft sandy earth, a very dead body lying face up nearby. He thought the body looked familiar: it was one of the kitchen staff, Doris he thought her name was.

Fearing for his safety if the digger, evidently a murderer, saw him, Tucker faded back into the shadows, returning an hour later when the digger, and probably a killer, had departed. He buried the gangsters' strong box next to the body. The Rev. was unsettled by what he had seen, wondering if the murder had to do with Boyle's *Last Will and Testament*, a subject of keen interest to Rev. Damien Tucker.

He knew he easily could find the spot where he left the box, and by marking where the body was buried for later discovery, there might be an opportunity for blackmail as well.

***

The late afternoon sunshine made the azure sea so sparkly that it almost hurt the eyes of the guests enjoying cocktails on the veranda of the lodge, waiting for the concert to begin inside in the ballroom.

Carter and Babs Vonessen had snagged the table with the best view. They were enjoying a fascinating conversation with a vivacious red-haired woman, late thirties perhaps, fashionably dressed in a dark blue blouse and dress with stars, the constellations of the sky, patterned on them. She had frizzy red hair, a shocking amount of it.

Her name was Yuma Boyle. She had arrived at Bogey Island just that afternoon, the Vonessens learned. Yuma was Red Boyle's first child she told the fascinated and shocked Vonessens. She said she and her father had been estranged since he took off from Los Angeles one morning when she was 6, leaving Yuma and her mother nearly penniless. They were essentially homeless people for 2 years, until her mother died of pneumonia. Little Yuma was placed in foster care.

She had no idea her father was the vastly wealthy Red Boyle until she saw him on a TV ad for one of his golf resorts two years ago.

She told Carter and Babs she was there to press her claim to be recognized as a proper member of the Boyle family—and of course share in the estate.

Carter was thrilled: he was in favor of anything that could cause the hated Red Boyle embarrassment, legal trouble and hopefully, financial harm.

Babs said, "What a unique, beautiful outfit, Yuma. Are those the constellations? I thought I recognized Orion's belt."

"Yes, who doesn't want to be a star?"

"If you need an attorney to represent you in obtaining your rightful share, just let me know. Here's my business card. I'd even be willing to pay the attorney's retainer, if that would help you."

"I take it you don't like my father, Carter."

"That would be an understatement, Miss Boyle."

A waitstaff member stopped by the table. "Would you like a Polaroid to remember your vacation here?" she asked.

Yuma considered that a few moments. "Certainly."

Babs and Carter moved closer to Yuma and leaned in so all three could be in the photo. The staff member snapped the photo. In a few moments, a picture emerged from the instant print camera.

"I'll take that," Yuma said.

***

Back in his room at the main lodge, Rev. Tucker wrote down the precise directions to where he had hidden his new-found loot, along with the rather vague treasure map, addressed it to his sister and sometimes partner in confidence games in Las Vegas, and left the envelope in his room in the back of a picture frame. He was afraid his former partner William Tisdale might search his room, drawers and luggage, while he was out.

He would post the letter as soon as he got a chance. Like all successful criminals, Rev. Tucker was realistic enough to know that he might not get off the island alive—especially if the money hungry Boyle kids found out he double-crossed them on the treasure and was now the major beneficiary of his father's will. The inheritance and the piles of currency were the elusive double-dip that all con men dream of.

He got a bottle and a glass from the dresser, poured a celebratory whiskey, sat on the bed and mused about whether he might still have time to locate the fortune the pirates left behind two hundred years ago.

What would that be, The Trifecta?

Chapter Sixteen

Tom, strolling down the long hallway of the lodge with Kat, on the way to join Caroline for cocktail hour and then dinner, pondered what he had learned so far about the Boyle family dramas and discontents. The kids were the obvious suspects; everything he had observed reinforced that impression. Although he had heard a lot of gossip at the resort about others who resented or despised Red, would any of these affluent guests risk everything to have their revenge? The motive just wasn't there.

Det. Mathers always coached, Motive, Motive, Motive. A suspect could be standing over a body, holding a still-smoking revolver, and unless Mathers saw a reason for the person's action, he might believe their innocence.

Tom and Kat arrived in the lobby. Caroline noted his stunned expression when he saw the poster of Julia. He picked up one of the 45 rpm albums. Caroline walked over to him. Kat excused herself to visit the ladies room.

He chuckled when he saw what his sister was wearing. Known for putting together funky outfits, she had chosen a mannish black shirt with the collar buttoned up. Black stretch pants like Mary Tyler Moore made famous on *The Dick Van Dyke Show* on TV in the early '60s. Flat black shoes and a black beret.

"I just felt '50s tonight," she commented.

Tom thought she looked like she was performing at a coffee house, maybe in 1955 or so, in Greenwich Village, that was mercifully slated for closing. Caroline looked over his shoulder as he studied the back of the album.

"Look at those songs Julia wrote. They're all about you two. *My short walk to paradise. A shot in the dark. My lover's the longest on tour. One cup of sugar is never enough. My heart can't find the fairway. Love in the rough.*"

One of Julia's compositions was getting some play by the DJs on AM radio. It was titled *High Temps*, a sultry ballad about how falling in love can raise your temperature, in the vein of *Tropical Heat Wave* and Peggy Lee's *Fever*.

Caroline's instincts, detective and feminine, told her the island was going to be hit with rough emotional weather. And back in '63, they couldn't get away with blaming it on climate change.

If Julia Wilkinson was here, could disaster be far behind?

Caroline noticed Kat wandering around in a mopey fashion. She joined her.

"Are you still worried about our Private Eye biz?"

She nodded.

"It gives us both a purpose. It's brought us closer—I used to not even see Tom for six months at a time."

"But it's dangerous...he got shot!"

"That had nothing to do with our detective biz. It was crazy Julia Wilkinson who shot him."

"Really?" This news almost knocked Kat over.

"Yes. So don't try to take this away from him, Katrina. Det. Mathers says Tom is a great private detective. I know I can be, too. Please, think about this."

Kat mulled that over and nodded in a non-committal fashion.

Caroline, fretting about her conversation with Kat, rejoined Tom and saw that familiar reverie on his face that only Julia Wilkinson could cause. She thought, *if there were golf tournaments in hell, they would pretty much be like this one.*

Tom, Kat and Caroline joined the other guests gathered in the ballroom, mingling and enjoying cocktails and snacks. Their dinner together would be delayed by an hour for the upcoming concert.

Soon it was time for the concert to start. A crowd of about 100 filled the ballroom and sat on comfortably upholstered chairs facing the small stage.

Five minutes later, Julia and her band took the stage. She was wearing a strapless red glittering gown, her breasts ready to burst out of the dress any moment, like tropical flowers about to bloom. The lovely gown was slit up the left side. Any of the men in the audience who weren't entranced by her bountiful breasts, or her tumbling rose-gold hair, would have been by her shapely, tan legs. And they hadn't even heard her amazing voice.

Julia's smile, which reached all the way to her large, deep blue eyes, was almost aggressive in its brightness.

Her vocal talent was considerable: she had great range and her expressive face told the story of the songs brilliantly. Even budding performer Caroline, seeing Julia in concert for the first time, was impressed.

She sang a few of her new songs from the album. The golf theme of the songs went over well with the Valley Vista CC crowd.

After she finished one tune, she stopped and said, "I heard there was a fabulous golf tournament played on this very island this week, won by Phoenix' own Tom Colt!!! Tom, take a bow."

Tom stood up and waved to the crowd, who applauded enthusiastically. Tom and Julia exchanged warm smiles, like nothing negative had ever come between them. Caroline's face was a dark grimace.

Everyone in the room could tell there was something strong between Tom and Julia. They just couldn't tell what. Of course, neither could Tom. Only Julia knew.

Julia almost looked like she was starting to cry. "I'm sorry to get emotional, but Tom is just…quite wonderful."

Oh barf! Thought Caroline, quite reasonably. But Caroline had to give Julia credit. She had effectively laid claim to Tom in front of their whole little golf-y community from Phoenix. Julia might as well have stuck a harpoon in the floundering fish.

Caroline looked to the row in front of her, where Kat was sitting. Her head was down. Kat had to compete with Jilly on Bogey Island, and now the incredibly beautiful Julia shows up. Caroline crudely once referred to Julia as 'sex on a stick'. She still thought that description was accurate.

The band struck up the opening notes for *High Temps*.

Julia started singing, with overpowering sexuality.

"This song is hot! I'm feeling a bit feverish," Tom remarked to Caroline.

Caroline thought, *Shit, I've got to do something.* Caroline noticed the hypnotic effect the song was having on her hopeless twin brother. He had that look in his eyes that he's falling for her again. She considered what to do.

She rose, walked up the aisle and climbed the three steps to the little stage. Julia cast a questioning glance her way then kept on singing like all show business troopers do.

Caroline proceeded to interpret the song with avant-garde and spastic dance moves that caused the audience to break out in laughter, many wondering whether these were indeed dance steps or some kind of ineffective karate demonstration.

Her dancing featured thrusting arms, leg kicks, jerky head movements. If she were trying to depict a romantic fever, it appeared more like the onset of malaria.

Caroline danced close to Julia, whose little band was playing a few jazzy riffs between stanzas of the song.

"I thought we were friends."

"We were until you shot my brother."

"That was an accident!"

"I don't believe in accidents. You are no damn good. You don't respect anyone, and you have too much money coupled with zero common sense and maximum selfishness."

"You can't talk to me that way. You're a nobody. And you live rent-free in my family's guest house."

"You're not putting Tom under your evil spell again Julia."

"Butt out little sister. He's a big boy, he can take care of himself."

"If that were true, I wouldn't have followed him out of the womb fifteen minutes later."

"Why'd it take you that long?"

"I was debating whether it would be worthwhile to come out or not."

"So, was it?"

"Only at times, like now." Caroline grinned wickedly.

The band's section of the song ended and Caroline returned to her wildly interpretive dance steps. She also broke into song, butchering the lyrics of *High Temps*. Her pretty voice combined with the weird dance moves caused the crowd to roar with laughter and applause.

Julia tried to resume her seductive singing, but the "Fever" had broken. The audience was giggling. She finished, flashed a fake smile at the crowed and stalked off the stage. As far as the audience was concerned, they seemed to prefer Caroline's performance.

Caroline of course stayed on stage for a bow and a round of applause.

Caroline looked over at Tom. He was laughing and talking to the guests seated next to him. He hadn't been gorgonized by Julia's sexuality.

Caroline breathed a hard-earned sigh of relief. All was well.

***

Not so fast, Caroline…

The evening stroll was probably inevitable. Julia was the luminous moon and Tom the mutable tide. They had both changed into t-shirts and shorts. The setting could not have been more romantic. They were walking barefoot down the shoreline by the softly lapping sea, just after sunset.

Tom Continues Our Story:

What a lovely night to stroll down the shoreline with your sweetheart. If only that was what Julia Wilkinson was to me. That's the question of the evening: who was she?

She touched my hand. I am sorry to report I felt the same crackle of sexual electricity I always did.

"Tom, how do I even begin to say how grateful I am to you for saving me that night. What if Derrick had been carrying a gun? I could have been killed. Or I could have faced a murder charge. Think of the scandal for my family."

Note she did not mention, 'think of the guy who would be lying in his grave'.

"When you took that bullet, you saved me. I knew that night that our love would last forever."

This of course was bullshit. But it was good bullshit, really good.

I said, "Why did you disappear that night? I never told the police that you shot me. Mathers suspected, but I made up a story about a prowler."

She looked away. I knew she was a fabricating a brand new, beautiful lie.

"For a long time, I was too ashamed to face you. I almost killed the most wonderful man in my world."

Like I said, beautiful bullshit.

She told me about her doctor prescribing a new drug for the depression pole of her bi-polar disorder.

"It's given me so much positive energy. And I've lost weight, which is a bonus. I feel so pumped up each day. It's taken away those horrible lows I had. The other two meds they gave me are terribly strong. Have to be careful with the dosage—it can make you black out."

Some days Julia was so depressed, she confessed to me, that she didn't go anywhere. She stayed home with her vast collection of stuffed toys and unfinished musical compositions. She described the feeling as being down in a pit, or frozen, unable to move. And her brain was so foggy. Her thoughts were sluggish as well. She got out of bed and felt stiff in her joints, like a mild case of the flu.

Then that passed and she became energetic, almost hyper, and super joyful. Those were the times I remembered, when she was the most alive person I ever met.

"I've so missed being close to you. It seems like ages ago when I walked up your path and we made love on that couch in my father's guest house."

Please note she didn't refer to it as my house.

I thought, *so sorry I wasn't available, Julia, but I spent a lot of time at Doctors Hospital in physical therapy—after you shot me.*

Reaching inside my shirt, she found the scar from the bullet would on my shoulder--and wept or seemed to at least. I could feel the moisture of authentic tears, or what seemed like authentic tears. I couldn't tell for sure.

She said, "I would kiss it 1,000 times if the scar would go away, if I could take away the pain you suffered from our accident."

Pulling up my shirt, she pressed her lips lightly to the scar. It made me shudder with mixed emotions of warmth and warning and hope and fear. Spinning thick webs of confusion was her greatest skill.

We hugged and held onto each other for what seemed like the entire heart of the evening, but probably was only a few moments. It was my way of forgiving her. Which she of course realized.

Then her eyes sharpened and shifted their gaze to the resort lodge. She seemed to remember she had to get back. She kissed me again, this time on the lips.

Julia smiled. It was a neutral smile, neither warm nor wicked. "You still love me, don't you."

"Yes," I said bitterly. *How does Raymond B. Lasalle's song go...Doctor says, There's No Cure for Love.*

She put her sandals on and strolled back toward the lodge to continue the serious business of being Julia, conqueror of all men, the weak and the strong. I stayed and watched the waves. I don't know why I stayed. Maybe to do some long-overdue pondering.

If you realize you're a fool for love, the love of a particular girl, and you are fully aware of it, are you still a fool? Or does being a fool require a kind of sensory numbness, an inability to process what is right in front of you, and an absence of that awareness we all need to protect ourselves from harm. Maybe instead of fool, a better term for me would be, willing participant in your own destruction.

Being with Julia was like living in a dangerous dream. Your conscious mind tells you to get the hell out of there, but the dream won't let go of you. That's what I have such a hard time explaining to dear sister Caroline.

***

Brooks Benton Continues Our Story:

A two-person team of maid service staff was preparing Julia's suite for the evening. New towels. The bed turned down. The sheets primped. And snooping, as maids are occasionally known to do.

The first maid noticed the medicine bottles on the table by Julia's bed. She examined the bottles.

Her colleague commented, "Rich people, always taking drugs to solve life's problems."

"My experience is, they cause more problems than they solve."

"Which…rich people or drugs?"

"Both."

They paused for lower-class derisive mirth at the expense of the upscale resort guests.

***

Team Boyle was having another contentious meeting, in one of the small conference rooms at the resort lodge. The tension was evident in Fredonia's face, frozen in anger, Chandler's proud chin jutting out at his older sister as they argued over what to do, and Patti's usual look of a confused outcast.

Fredonia finally said, "Don't you two want to be rich? I can't believe I'm half-related to you two wimpy simps. Do I have to do this all alone?"

Chandler: "What's <u>this</u>?"

"I guess I got my answer."

Fredonia puffed on a cigarette and considered her options. Her primary thought was, as far as partners, these two are the worst.

"Patti darling, could you please keep Red occupied for an hour or so tonight?"

Patti had a puzzled expression." I guess so. But a whole hour? Why?"

"Chandler and I need to attend to something. Just babble on like you do about your happy life and how much you love working for your Dear Old Dad, being his servant girl and all."

Patti bristled, but she always feared Fredonia. They were not warm and fuzzy, affectionate siblings by any means. Patti feared that if she ever hugged Fredonia, she might get frostbite.

Patti felt very real fear rise in her throat. Had Fredonia just admitted she wanted to kill their father—over money? Patti wasn't sure. She felt like fleeing. *Shall I confide in Tom?*

***

Patti sat in the library room with her father later that night. They each took a high-backed buttery-soft oxblood leather chair. Patti was so petite the chair seemed to engulf her. She asked him if he could recommend some books on business management. She told him she loved working in his company and wanted to acquire more skills.

He swirled his tiny, fluted glass of absinthe.

"You don't learn how to succeed in business through reading books, my dear. Business is hand-to-hand combat. Getting you boxing or fencing lessons would be more beneficial than my recommending books. Survival of the fittest, and the meanest, is the best way to describe the businessman's life, particularly in real estate. The only man tougher than myself is my old friend Judge Roy Wilkinson. Even I am afraid of that reprobate."

When Patti left the library after the hour-and-ten-minute visit with him, Red thought, *That soft, sweet girl has no chance to make it in the business world. She'll be eaten alive.*

Speaking of eating, two years later, Patti enrolled in culinary school and after graduating with honors, created her own signature line of grilled sandwiches, which she trademarked as *Patti Melts.*

Her concept was franchised into 100 restaurants around the Western US.

Take that, Elwood 'Red' Boyle.

***

Chandler watched the hallway outside of Red's office while Fredonia investigated inside, in search of the purported new Amendment to Red's Last Will and Testament.

It only took her 5 minutes. Desperation can fuel inspiration. The document was in the unlocked top left drawer in Red's desk. Her face turned to a stony block of ice when she saw that Rev. Damien Tucker was now the major beneficiary. *That double-crossing, phony sonofabitch.*

It took her less than 5 minutes to plan a course of action. She carefully replaced the document and joined Chandler in the hallway.

"What did you learn," Chandler asked, puffing on a stinky cigar, the same brand his dad smoked.

"We're fucked, totally fucked, is what I learned. But what a fool our father is. I'd have kept the desk drawer locked."

***

Patti Boyle walked through the lobby, saw her siblings coming, both with dark, angry looks on their faces. She wondered what horrible thing could have happened. Or might be happening later...

They stalked past her without even noticing her.

"You keep an eye on Tom Colt. I'll take care of everyone else. I can't believe our partner double-crossed us. He was supposed to work with us!"

"Greed is a disease with people like him."

"Time for him to exit the stage," Fredonia said, sending a chill down Patti's spine.

Patti concluded that her siblings intended to kill their father. Why? For changing the Will again? What did that mean about greed being a disease? And the double-cross? Nothing made sense to Patti that night.

Patti was afraid, very afraid.

***

Tom sat out on the patio of his first-floor room, enjoying a cold beer. Thoughtful innkeeper Red Boyle had stocked Tom's favorite brand, Blatz.

He'd barely had time to enjoy winning the pro-am tournament, a little event to be sure but victory of all kinds is satisfying, especially to someone who had struggled as much as Tom to achieve success on the pro golf tour.

He was looking forward to winning again on the actual golf tour this year. He knew he could, he was ready. But first there was the issue of their private detective assignment on the island. Unless they watched Boyle 24/7, like bodyguards more than detectives, it was impossible to keep a determined foe from harming him or killing him. They needed to unravel the malevolent motives before the killer acted on them.

He decided to spend more time talking with each of the three Boyle children.

***

Patti Boyle, her mind swirling with a mixture of worries, walked disconsolately outside the lodge through the dappled shadows cast by the trees and the porch lights from the guest rooms. It was kind of how she felt. Seeking the light, but mostly in the dark about what was going on.

She saw Tom Colt sitting on his porch, by himself for once. Mr. Popularity was seldom alone, she noted. She hurried to his patio gate and opened it.

"Tom, I need to talk to you."

"Sure, come in." He rose from his chair. He saw the light of anguish, or perhaps confusion, on her face.

She was too agitated to sit down. She paced in the small space and chewed nervously on her lower lip. Tom, patient listener and detective, was now on full alert.

"I think my brother and sister are planning to do something very bad."

Tom agreed with her but said nothing for a few moments, thinking she would add details. She didn't.

"They'd be foolish to try something with Caroline and me watching. They're smart enough to know that."

Patti shook her head. "You don't know how angry they are, how much they love money. Our father can be at times…stingy and cruel. Other times he's the most generous man."

"I won't let anything happen to your father. I guarantee I will keep him safe."

Patti turned to Tom and he saw her eyes were watery. She reached out and hugged him tightly. She was trembling with currents of deep emotion. Tom saw that she was nothing like her conniving siblings. She was a fragile, warm girl. He thought, *she really loves her father.*

And then she said it, "I love my father. He's a rough man but he's treated me well. He didn't have to take me in. He and my mother were just acquaintances. I was, as they say, unexpected, a mistake."

"A beautiful soul like you being born is not a mistake. God does not make mistakes."

Tom held her in his arms until she calmed at least a bit.

Tom said, "If you want to see me, no more stunts like the photo in my pocket." He smiled. "I'm in the Phoenix metro phone book. Look under Knights for Hire."

She finally laughed. "I wish I had your self-confidence."

"I wish I did, too."

She paused a few moments, then, "I believe you, Tom. I know you will protect my dad."

She smiled with evident relief from having told Tom her concerns. "I'm going to kiss you now. Not just because you want to help me, but because I _want_ to kiss you. I've been trying to be bolder. I'm learning positive thinking from this book by Napoleon Hill. My godfather gave it to me for my birthday. I really want to succeed in the business world, Tom, and my godfather's been so helpful to me."

She kissed Tom. Kisses were a sweet surprise, an awakening moment. This one was no different. Tom thought that the positive thinking author might be amazed to see how Patti was applying his teachings.

"I got a mad crush on you after seeing you win that Vegas event. What I've seen is that you're a better man than the athlete I got the crush on."

She went to the gate and left, with a soft, though bold, wave of thanks.

Kat, walking back to her cottage, saw Patti leaving. She witnessed the kiss. She had also seen Tom strolling down the beach with Julia. At that moment her emotions boiled over. She decided to leave the island the next night. She also decided to put her romantic relationship with Tom on hold, perhaps even end it.

She couldn't articulate the one single reason for this decision; it was a combination of things. She had hoped that the time together on the island would have been idyllic, but conniving Jilly Flannery scuttled that. And she still could not deal with Tom being in a dangerous profession like private detective, even part-time.

But the larger reason was simply that a possessive streak reared up that Kat didn't even realize she had. In her mind, she and Tom would both work tirelessly on their golf careers, win tournaments, and then spend glorious evenings together. She adored Tom, when they were together. But she could see that to Tom, she would not be enough. _There would always be_ *a Jilly, a Julia, a Patti, or even an Autumn Amber. He was Mr. Popularity,* she thought—not considering it a compliment. *That's never going to change. It's time I faced reality.*

When she stepped onto the patio and told him of her decision, she explained it to him as, "I went into this with my eyes wide open. I know how much you like attention from women. That's fine."

Kat's green eyes burned with intensity.

"I could fall for you, Tom. Maybe in some ways I already have. But I want to give my heart to someone forever. Just once. Only once. You don't want that. I don't think you believe in that one love, forever."

"You don't know that…"

"And you're reckless in golf, you take too many chances. You'll be the same way with your detective career. But the consequences are much worse. You think you're immortal, but you're not. You can't dance so close to the flames and never get burned. I couldn't bear to lose you."

"Is it Julia? You saw us walking on the beach?"

Kat shook her head with frustration. "Is she some kind of sorceress? She <u>shot</u> you and you still look at her with adoration."

"She didn't kill me. It was just a flesh wound."

Kat could only half-laugh at that, it was so absurd.

Tom nodded. In a strange way, he fully understood what she had said, and could not argue with her. He was not even surprised.

"I want to live in the world of golf, where the worst that happens is, you lose a tournament. And as you've taught me, it doesn't matter because there's another one next week. No one has ever died from losing a golf tournament."

"I can't give up helping Det. Mathers, helping the police. Caroline can't either. Mathers needs us."

"Okay. If that's the way it is."

"For now, it is. I'm sorry."

Katrina backed out of the gate and onto the path and concluded with these words, "We're both wonderful people. We should have been able to make this work. Scheisse, I hate this island." Kat disappeared into the darkness.

This was an inflection point in both of their lives. Two people who were most likely soul mates, driven apart by random circumstance, by life. They were more alike than Kat realized. Their lives, in their twenties, were a quest for love— but for very different reasons. Tom thought if enough classy, wealthy girls liked him he would never be a poor boy again. He would be admitted to The Club of the Successful. Kat thought if she achieved enough in golf, she would be loved by one and all in the community of golf fans. She would feel like she really belonged in her adopted country, the USA. She would be admitted to the Club of The Greatest Golfers.

For Kat and Tom, when she left Bogey Island the next night, the moment had passed. Ironically, she would be the one who eventually decided what she really wanted was to be free.

Caroline, who had walked up silently on the path, heard Kat's words and saw how downcast both she and Tom looked when Kat opened the gate and departed. *That's why I will never let myself fall in love*, Caroline thought. *Love is far too complicated, and just a trick to make us miserable.*

Caroline observed that this breakup was typical of Tom and Katrina's emotional transactions: it was absent of rancor and full of respect. She concluded at that moment that Tom and Katrina were meant for each other.

Caroline approached Tom. "Well, you two kids messed that one up but good, bro."

"What did we do?" Tom asked in a softly pleading tone.

"You were just being you, she was being Kat. Nothin' you can do about that."

She gave Tom a small but significant hug.

"The Great Boyle himself, our esteemed client, has summoned you. He has some stag event going on in the 'Gentlemen's Lounge' in 20 minutes. He sent me to 'come git' you as we say back in the Arizona frontier."

At that moment, Tom and Caroline independently felt the exact same emotion: a kind of rising tension, a sense that something evil was going to happen on Bogey Island that night and nights to come. Neither twin claimed to be psychic; it was as though they, together, could pick up on the emotional currents, emotional storms, that were swirling around the lodge that night. It wasn't the first time this happened.

They looked at each other and nodded, with understanding and solidarity—and perhaps a note of fear.

***

Chapter Seventeen
Red Boyle Raises the Stakes

Tom walked into the lounge and saw nearly every seat was filled. The atmosphere was filled with cigar and cigarette smoke and the conversation loud and ribald. The scene resembled an Old West Saloon in the 1880s.

Red Boyle was setting up a portable projection screen and an 8MM projector with a slender reel of film.

Tom walked further into the room and saw Marco Greene sitting by himself at a small table.

Tom sat down there. "Didn't know movie night was on the Grand Opening Agenda."

"Knowing old Red, there's more to it than entertaining us."

How right Marco was, as usual. Everything about Marco Greene conveyed power. His massive hands, his square granite jaw, even his neatly trimmed and permed hair. But in contrast, his face could break out in the brightest, merriest smile.

Red turned to the assembly and said, "Good evening, gents. Glad you could join me. I have a couple of short films that I'm certain you will find enjoyable. Flicks of an adult nature."

Now he had the gentlemen's attention.

He signaled to the bartender, who turned down the house lights. Red switched on the projector.

The picture was grainy, but the scene was clearly filmed at a strip club. A young blonde woman with her back to the camera was gripping a pole on a small stage and doing a shimmery dance to the cheers of the men gathered around the stage. Her backside had a splendid little wiggle, Tom thought.

Her only clothing was what we now term a thong. Back in '63 men just termed it a miracle.

The woman slowly turned toward the camera, revealing enormous, full, fabulous breasts. Now the cheers at the strip club were echoed by cheers from the men gathered at Red's lounge.

The lovely dancer licked her lips seductively and then began peeling the thong down, first one side, then the other. The sight men dream of was shortly revealed.

On the film, a jarring emcee's voice barked out, "You asked for her, and we got her—Presenting Miss Bambi Bazooms straight from Las Vegas!"

The cheers got louder at the strip club, and strangely curious murmurs, then laughter erupted at Red's lounge. The men recognized the dancer as Judith Egglesworth, real estate developer Terrence Egglesworth's much younger, and amazingly limber, wife.

Rodney Burkett, in a burst of horniness, blurted out, "That's my partner! If Colt hadn't hit that lucky shot, we'd have won! Pure luck, it was."

Marco asked Tom, "You want me to get one of my boys to take Burkett out? My boy could go for the knees."

Not thinking, Tom exclaimed, "Yes." Then he reconsidered. "I mean, no. That's not the way."

Marco grinned. *Hell yes, it was the way.*

Terrence looked stricken, which greatly amused Red Boyle. Terrence's fleshy face, already reddened from a lifetime of lunchtime martinis as he closed real estate deals, was mottled with rage.

On the film, now-naked 'Bambi' moved toward the edge of the stage and put her hands up above her head, so the men could admire every inch of her. The Boyle Lounge crowd was roaring.

Boyle said to Terrence, "Guess you won't be needing that 19th Avenue Property now. My last offer is $175,000. Take it or leave it. And give our regards to the lovely Bambi."

Egglesworth stood up and clumsily knocked his chair over. He stormed out of the room. As he passed Tom and Marco he muttered. "I will make Boyle pay!"

"Impressive," Tom remarked to Marco, re: The Bazooms.

"You didn't know Judy started out as a stripper? That's how he met old Terrence, at a club in LA by the airport. He had a layover."

"Evidently quite a nice one."

Tom and Marco both smiled.

"You seem to know everything, Marco Greene."

"Pretty much."

"What'll this do to Egglesworth's church construction biz."

"He's finished. Done. Kaput."

The film clip ended. The second one began, a more recent one, in living Kodachrome. It was another stage, where a sign in the back said Boyle Academy of the Performing Arts. A card on the stage read: 'Audition. Autumn Amber Jan. 1963'. The film jumped to Autumn Amber reading from a motion picture script. The Bambi-stimulated men did not seem impressed. For one thing, Amber was fully dressed.

"This lovely girl is the most celebrated graduate of my Academy for the Performing Arts," Red said, swelling with evident pride. The film cut to the next scene. Autumn removing her top and continuing, like a trooper, to read her lines.

Now it was Dick Amberson's turn to be embarrassed and enraged. The clip jumped to Autumn stepping out of her jeans. *There was something so fresh, so youthful about Autumn Amber*, Tom thought. She had a face that could 'sell" even a poorly written scene like the one she was performing.

"Turn that off!" Amberson hollered as he stood up. Red gave him a dismissive wave.

"Sit down, Dickie," Red bellowed back. "What do you think, guys," Red asked. "Should I put the money up for her next movie?"

The question was met with a uniformly positive response. Red could have taken up a collection and funded the picture right there.

The last clip showed Autumn, now nude, still rather defiantly it seemed to Tom, reading her lines for the audition. Dick Amberson fled to the door and exited.

The film ended. The men applauded. The house lights went back up and the animated drinking and smoking resumed.

After Bambi's robust, professional strip club performance, Tom thought Autumn's performance was almost sweet. The camera, even Red's 8mm, loved her.

He also knew Boyle had filmed her that day at BAPA for the sole purpose of humiliating her and her family tonight at the party. But why? Was Boyle trying to smoke out who wanted to kill him? *If so, that was idiotic*, Tom thought.

Red exited the lounge into the lobby. He didn't see the 6'6" angry hulk, Al Langdon, come up behind him. "You don't even remember me, Boyle," Langdon spat out.

Red continued walking, unperturbed, through his lobby. "I invited you here, you big clod."

"You stole my idea! You ruined my company! I never recovered!"

"You were a hopeless case. No business sense at all."

All Big Al could do was sputter as Red, probably a foot shorter than he, continued:

"Early in the race to market, the field is crowded. Some of the jockeys get knocked off their horse. Just the way it goes, old man. I got the idea we came up with—simultaneously as I recall-- to market first."

Red strolled off, leaving Al Langdon stunned. He thought Boyle would have some remorse about promising to financially back his venture 10 years earlier, then backing out of the deal and marketing Al's idea himself. At this point, Al had been reduced to little more than an insurance salesman. He coulda been a tycoon, he maintained to that day.

Remorse from Red Boyle? Not likely, foolish Mr. Langdon.

Red walked over to Patti who was standing by the check-in desk. He hugged her with true affection. Patti, it seemed, was Red's favorite—for whatever that's worth.

"This is great fun! What a fabulous Grand Opening I'm having!"

Caroline, waiting for Tom to leave the stag party, saw all this unfold. She had snuck through the kitchen to the back of the Lounge and seen the stag films as well. *Mr. Elwood Boyle, you do like to make things happen, don't you...great fun you're having...but what happens when one of these guys snaps?*

***

Back in his room, Dick Amberson tossed down three shots of whiskey in rapid succession. They did little to calm him down. Autumn, unaware of the humiliation she had just suffered, was sitting on the beach enjoying the pretty evening, dreaming of her bright future as a film actress, and excited about taking up the great game of golf. At Valley Vista CC, she had heard Tom Colt was a fabulous instructor.

Kind of a cute guy, too, she thought.

The phone rang, Dick picked it up. He filled in the events of the evening for his wife Tracy back in Los Angeles.

"Our daughter was naked! All those old men leering at her! I can't let Boyle get away with this! He's a dead man!"

Tracy said, "Don't do anything rash. We'll figure this out when I get there."

She wasn't too concerned that her mild-manner screenwriter hubby would do something violent. She did not know that in 1948, he had beaten an *LA Times* movie critic half to death at a party after the guy panned one of Dick's screenwriting efforts in the newspaper. The studio got the whole episode hushed up, the critic paid off. The head of the studio frankly thought the critic deserved the beating.

***

In the lobby, just outside the door to the gentlemen's lounge, Judith Egglesworth was standing with a small, eager crowd gathered around her. She was signing autographs as 'Bambi Bazooms' and then a series of x's and o's.

She had unfastened three buttons of her white chiffon blouse, liberating those famous bazooms, which evidently had been under wraps for far too long.

"Could you sign this, Miss Bazooms?" Sterling Gould asked, almost bashfully. He noticed that Judith was at least 25 years younger than her husband Terrence. Sterling wondered if she might enjoy a dalliance with him the following afternoon while his wife Missy was enjoying the resort spa...

Like an angry tempest, Terrence marched over to the little crowd. "Don't ask her for an autograph! She was a sinner until she met me. I rescued her!"

"Oh, shut the hell up, Terrence, you pompous fraud," Bambi replied, penning two more autographs. "I was never half the sinner you are. I would think cheating the sub-contractors on your construction projects would count as a sin."

"You stop this! It's an outrage!"

"Well, I'm leaving you. You act all ashamed of me and I'm the one who should be ashamed of you. I thought I'd follow the pro golf tour for a while. Maybe I'll meet a handsome golf pro."

***

Chapter Eighteen
The Simmering Conflict Finally Boyles Over:
Elwood's Final Fart

A private island is a great place to commit a murder, as Det. Mathers had told Tom. You don't face the risk of nosy neighbors observing the comings and goings in a neighborhood. The guests are expected to roam the property freely. Revelers make noise, under the influence of alcohol. Nothing seems particularly suspicious to anyone's eyes or ears.

And there are no cops around.

At 8:35PM, Elwood "Red" Boyle was stabbed in the back while in his office standing by the map of the world that depicted his far-flung real estate holdings.

The last thing he did was rip one last fart. The killer exclaimed, "Ewwww" about the stink.

Boyle turned around, still alive enough to see who stabbed him. He said, "You. But why?"

Red expired, falling face down. The killer removed Boyle's watch, wound it back one hour, smashed it to fix the time earlier than the murder happened, and then cooly put the watch back on the dead man's left wrist.

At 9:01, Chandler Boyle found Julia Wilkinson passed out on her bed in her room, a wicked kitchen knife on the floor near her. He saw a bottle of prescription pills on the nightstand. He checked her pulse. She was still alive.

At 9:45, Fredonia and Chandler Boyle knocked on the door to their father's office. They had not been able to find him anywhere in the lodge. The door was locked.

They ran into Big Al Langdon walking down the hallway toward his suite. They asked for his help in breaking the lock to Red Boyle's office. Chandler and Langdon teamed up to kick in the door; after several attempts the lock gave way.

Patti Boyle heard the noise of the door being kicked in. She came out of her room and rushed down the hall to see what happened.

Fredonia, Patti and Chandler all saw their father lying on the floor, blood pooled around him. Patti screamed and ran out to find Tom Colt.

Chandler and Fredonia walked into the room and confirmed Red Boyle was deceased.

"Why am I not surprised?" Chandler said, looking at his half-sister, who had a half-smile on her face.

"Why are you looking at me?" she said.

***

Tom was outside on the patio, watching the moon over the ocean, when Patti Boyle rushed to him.

"They killed my father!" she exclaimed.

"Who?"

She was again trembling with currents of deep emotion, but Tom could not read them, and could not tell whether that emotion was real grief or faked.

Was her reaction because she knew one of the siblings was the killer? Tom wondered. He got his answer immediately.

"I think it was Fredonia and Chandler," she said, with the tears starting to flow. Tom could feel now, they were real.

Tom winced, remembering his conceited, empty words from earlier that day in his head: *I won't let anything happen to your father. I guarantee I will keep him safe.*

"Take me to him," Tom said. She grabbed his hand and quickly led him upstairs to the crime scene.

"The Great Detective!" Chandler said with all the bitter sarcasm and flaring anger he could muster. "You were really on the job. Why the hell did my father hire you?"

Fredonia said, "I'm the eldest. I'll oversee summoning the police. Chandler, you—"

Tom said, in a voice of authority the Boyles had not heard before: "I will do that. And we will gather everyone in the ballroom and tell them what happened. They'll be safer together. We don't know the killer is finished tonight."

Caroline appeared in the doorway. "Tom's right. And we can't let anyone leave the island."

Fredonia's stare at Tom and Caroline was pure frost. He didn't blink. Neither did his sister. Oddly, it seemed to Tom, Fredonia left the room as though she were late for a scheduled appointment.

Tom called the nearest authorities, on Grand Bahama Island, and reported the murder. He was told Inspector Archie Weatherford would be sent to the island immediately along with two other investigators and would be there within the hour.

Caroline left to knock on doors and round everyone up to go to the ballroom. She could hear a rising tide of noise and confusion as word spread that Red Boyle was dead. She didn't hear any noticeable sounds of grief, however. *Shouldn't there be at least mild wailing?* She wondered. *The guy who threw this cool party for y'all is dead.*

***

THE INVESTIGATION BEGINS...

Twenty minutes later, Tom walked into the ballroom of the resort, picked up a spoon, clinked a water tumbler to get everyone's attention and said, "I assume by now you know that there was a murder committed here tonight. I will invoke the old cliché from mystery novels and B-movie detective stories, NOBODY LEAVES HERE without permission from the police—who are on their way."

The room was alive with speculative conversation.

Tom was peppered with questions. He deferred to the Inspector who was to arrive shortly. Chandler Boyle instructed the kitchen staff to prepare snacks and open the bar to free alcoholic refreshments. The latter seemed to calm the antsy crowd.

Almost exactly an hour since he had been summoned, Inspector Archie Weatherford arrived with two young cops in tow. Was the Scotland Yard Inspector an old, weathered guy with pipe and deerstalker hat? NO. Young guy, maybe 35, in a beige linen suit, blue silk shirt and Italian loafers. Classy. Slicked back dark hair. A guy who evidently spent more time at the beaches of St. Tropez than looking for that big ol' Hound at Baskerville Hall.

Though Weatherford had the cheerful first name of Archie, he was far from a pleasant fellow. He seemed irritated to be there, like he had more important corpses and cases to worry about than the murder of an American on an American-owned island. In truth it was majority-owned by the Brits. Boyle got much of the financing for the project from an investment group in London. Therein lies the secret to the rapid growth of Boyle's real estate empire: Use Other People's Money whenever possible.

The two cops with him were rookies, a male named Rupert James and a female, Phoebe Clybourne-Chambers. Phoebe was petite for a woman with such as long name. She had a long face and large nose. A bit horsy, Caroline thought. Rupert was a fussy looking, arrogant gent with bushy eyebrows that moved like black beetles when he expressed himself. The two of them were wide-eyed and Caroline quickly concluded, clueless. Evidently a murder on a private island owned by an American didn't merit dispatching the top crime investigators from the British Empire.

After brief introductions, Weatherford hurried, with great authority, to the crime scene, escorted by Tom and Caroline.

Weatherford asked of Tom and Caroline, "Who might you be?"

"Sort of, well, private detectives," Tom said bashfully. "Tom Colt and Caroline Colt from Scottsdale, Arizona, USA."

"I see," Weatherford said, his nose wrinkling like he just smelled something foul. "Thank you for securing the crime scene, but from now on, I'm in charge of the investigation. Don't have use for amateur sleuths in London. No use here either."

Seeing Weatherford in action, Caroline whispered to Tom, "Do you mean Colt & Colt Confidential is matching wits with Scotland Yard?"

Tom whispered back: "That's why we need Mathers out here, ASAP!"

"You're right!"

Weatherford turned to Tom, "Tom Colt...you're a golfer..."

"Yes..."

Tom then learned that Inspector Weatherford came from a wealthy family, his father a member of the House of Lords. And that Inspector Weatherford belonged to two famous country clubs, one in England and one in Scotland. To Tom's chagrin, the Inspector was a Big Fan of Rodney Burkett.

"I've always wanted to meet Rodney. Brilliant player, don't you think? One of the best young players around. I followed him in The Open last year."

For Brits, their national championship, The British Open, was simply The Open, as though there were none other.

"We're you in the field, Tom?"

"No. Didn't make it over there." A trip to Britain to play in The Open was far too expensive for Tom at that time in his life. Very few American pros, only the top ones, made the trip in the early '60s.

"I see."

And just like that, Weatherford had made Tom admit he was not a top player--or was too broke to make the trip across the pond.

***

A mile away from the lodge, at the Little Chapel, Rev. Damien Tucker and novelist William Tisdale were coming to blows.

"You found the fucking treasure, didn't you? And you're thinking of cutting me out. Gonna cut out the Boyle kids, too."

"I haven't even found so much as one gold doubloon. And we're partners. I'd never cheat you, or the Boyle kids. We're all in this together."

"Maybe I should tell old Red what you're up to."

"Do that and I'll—"

"You'll what?" Tisdale, who had been drinking rum all evening, made the mistake of shoving the good Reverend.

The Rev. hit Tisdale in the face with a vicious right hook. The crunching sound was terrible. Tisdale's nose, not a thing of beauty before except perhaps to a female bald eagle, now was a bloody mess. The smallish writer staggered backwards, holding his hand up to his smashed nose.

The novelist retreated out the door of the Chapel and hurried back to the lodge, yelling "This isn't over!" as he went.

Rev. Tucker sat down and considered his options. He wished he hadn't punched the guy. But in truth, he hadn't lied, and it pissed him off to be accused of doing so. He hadn't found so much as one gold doubloon.

***

Caroline, outside the lodge on the patio, saw Tisdale coming up the path with a handkerchief to his face. She walked down the stone stairs to intercept him.

"What happened to you?"

"Nothing. I fell. Shouldn't walk at night after drinking." His laugh was nervous and fake.

Caroline didn't need to be a detective to see through that lie. She wondered what was going on that night on the beach. *Who would beat up a writer? All they do is type.*

Just then she heard the unmistakable sound of Julia Wilkinson's voice, hysterical, from the open window above her:

"Tom, you have to help me! I didn't kill anyone! I took my medication and passed out! I don't know what happened! Tom, I need you."

"I know it wasn't you. You were set up."

"What can I do? Oh, Tom, help me!"

With Julia, there was always an element of fine acting in her performances. Her mobile, beautiful face was made for drama. But this time Tom knew she was genuinely terrified.

"I would never let anything happen to you. I love you, Julia."

Down below, Caroline shook her head. *Could this night get any worse?*

Indeed, it could.

Caroline noticed a figure leaving the lodge, hurrying down the same path that novelist Tisdale had taken up to the lodge from the beach on the south shore. "The action seems like it's down at the beach," she said aloud. "Strange time for an evening walk, wouldn't you say. Meeting treasure hunters perhaps? Treasure hunters that just committed a murder, perhaps?"

She went into Tom's room from the patio side and grabbed a box of a dozen Titleist golf balls from the dresser. She took a sheet of lodge stationery from a desk drawer and scrawled 'I'M AT THE SOUTH SHORE BEACH' and rushed out.

The beach and the caves are about one mile from the lodge. There are 1760 yards in a mile. I have 12 balls, so if I put one out every 150 yards to mark my path, Tom should be able to track me. Like breadcrumbs.

Caroline's calculations were slightly off. The caves were 1.25 miles from the lodge. She ran out of golf balls before she got there.

***

Inspector Weatherford had deployed the guest room nearest the ballroom to interview everyone there, guests and staff, that night.

His two investigators had fanned out looking for clues. They found a set of weird footprints, like the letter "G", in the soft earth on the east side of the lodge, on a path that led to the dock used by boats ferrying in passengers. They noted the prints, which were washed away in a rain shower early the next morning.

Weatherford quickly ascertained (British detectives ascertain, not merely find out) that the haughty, wealthy guests, most of whom were members of the same country club in Phoenix, Valley Vista, and therefore the same social set, were not going to give up any information without a fight. Weatherford learned:

Chandler Boyle was to meet Julia Wilkinson in her room—for a celebration that included champagne that had been ordered the day before. Why did Chandler arrive late? Did he commit the murder and try to frame her? Chandler did cough up that Rev. Tucker and novelist Tisdale were on the island looking for treasure, which, Chandler said, the entire Boyle family was adamantly opposed to.

Novelist William Tisdale would not reveal who his treasure hunting partner is. From Dick Amberson, Weatherford learned that the novelist is a drunk who lost this publishing contract due to lousy sales. People heard him arguing with Chandler about the treasure hunt on the island. Tisdale would not reveal how he came to have an injured face. He said he had fallen while exploring the island...

Three staff members had disappeared.

When Weatherford returned to the ballroom to invite the next interviewee to come with him, he saw Tracy Amberson arrive dramatically thorough the double doors like she was horrified by the news of Red's demise. Her face shone with anguish.

She tightly embraced her daughter Autumn. "Are you OK, sweetheart? I knew how much Mr. Boyle meant to you. He was your greatest booster, he wanted so much for you to succeed."

Tracy was in Hollywood working on a TV production, she told Weatherford later in the evening when he got a chance to talk to her. She's an assistant producer of some kind, he wrote down.

Weatherford noticed the daughter, Autumn Amber, did not look particularly upset that Red Boyle, her apparent benefactor, was dead. Was that because she was the killer? Or because she benefited from his death?

***

The interviews with the guests featured one peculiar aspect: Each of them was asked, "Are you glad Elwood Boyle is dead?"

At least half of them answered, Yes, with very little hesitation.

Weatherford, on his 50th murder investigation in a 14-year career, had never seen anything like that reaction. "Extraordinary," he remarked to himself.

***

Upstairs, Tom was prepping Julia for her upcoming interview with Weatherford.

For many years afterward, Tom wondered why he had blurted out a declaration of love to Julia at that critical moment. Because it wasn't truly love that he felt for her. It was a kind of fevered excitement accompanied by youthful lust.

If this sounds confusing, it was for Tom as well. He had come to the island believing he was falling in love with Katrina Stern.

At 28, Tom Colt, when Julia took the time to pay attention to him, could convince himself that what he felt for Julia was the best feeling that could ever be. He had no way of knowing that he would truly, deeply fall in love several times in his life. Old-er Tom's advice to Tom at 28 would have been: Run, kid, run.

Julia's reaction to Tom's declaration was simply relief. She knew Tom would do anything she asked, as always. She had a genuine worry: She didn't remember much of what happened that evening after she finished dinner with her band *The Loose Impediments* and walked back to her room.

"Let's sit down, and tell me what happened tonight, from dinnertime, on until you woke up here. I'll write it down and we'll give it to Weatherford."

Julia squeezed his hand, lovingly it seemed to ever-hopeful Tom.

As if that weren't enough on young Tom Colt's mind for one night, he began getting this strange vibe that Caroline was in trouble. Tom, throughout his life, was on the same frequency as she.

Tom felt agitated. His mind wandered from Julia's predicament to wondering where Caroline was...

Chapter Nineteen

Caroline reached a path that led to the Little Chapel and then branched off toward an opening on the cliff face. She chose the latter to investigate first.

Inside the opening in the rock wall, she saw something that looked like a well, like a wishing well, either carved by nature or dug down into the rock.

She walked carefully around the edge. A rock ledge nearby looked like a good place to ensconce treasure. It flashed in her mind that the legend of the pirate gold may have set events into motion that led to Red Boyle's death.

She felt a blow to her shoulder that knocked her forward, right down into the deep dark waters of the well.

She screamed as she hit the water. She had bounced off the rock wall and landed feet up in the water—fortunately her legs were not injured on impact. Her shoulder hurt like it was on fire.

She was up to her waist in water.

She heard something like a valve opening. Above her head, water began pouring into the well. She looked around her. She could climb out, she believed, but when she tried, she got only a few feet up the wall before her shoulder pain was so severe she fell back in.

The water was dirty and oily. This was not a well to fetch fresh water, or toss coins in and dream, it was an 18th century pirate torture chamber, she realized. She could almost hear the ghostly voices of long-dead pirates: *Tell us where you hid the gold or you will die.*

Caroline had not panicked—yet. But she estimated that within the hour the water would be over her head.

"Who pushed me?" she screamed, but of course got no answer. Caroline figured it had to be the good Reverend Tucker, who she instantly knew was not a Reverend at all, but a treasure hunter. It all added up: Tucker posed as a clergyman to gain access to the island.

She struggled several more times to gain purchase on the wall, but it was no use. She slumped back down, leaned against the wall and looked up.

"This can't be how it all ends."

***

"I have to go!" Tom suddenly said, startling Julia who was trying to write down everything that had happened that day for her interview with Weatherford.

"You can't leave me, Tom! I need you. What if I'm arrested tonight? What if they put me in handcuffs?"

"I have to go to Caroline. I'll be back. Don't you worry. I won't let anything happen to you."

Tom bit his lip, remembering the short time ago he had made the same idiotic boastful promise to Patti Boyle. He rushed out the door.

He looked around the resort property for some sign of where Caroline went. He never saw the note she left. The crushed seashell path usually showed prints, but it was dark. He saw something unusual on one of the branching paths ahead. He ran to it: A Titleist brand golf ball, the brand he played. He picked up the ball and pocketed it—he was still a frugal young man—and started down the path.

Caroline listened to the water running into the well for a few minutes, her spirits fading.

 Finally, she laughed and said aloud: "Caroline Colt, born January 27, 1935. Died March 21, 1963. She never fell in love. She only found her calling as a detective in the last 6 months of her life. Her mother hated her. Her father left her to fight in some stupid foreign war and never returned. Yes, her life was mostly a disappointment."

She stopped to massage her injured shoulder. It hurt like hell.

"What will Tom do without me? He'll goof up even more than he does now."

She heard a voice: "Oh, just drown already, if that's what you think. And thanks for the vote of confidence."

"What took you so long? Did you stop to bang Julia?"

"No. To comfort her. She's scared they think she killed Boyle."

"Just 'cause the knife was in her room and she has a history of violent behavior? Silly coppers. How'd you find me?"

"I listened for the sound of nonstop chattering."

Tom tossed down a rope ladder he found in a corner of the cavern. The ladder reached the surface of the water. He climbed down. Holding onto the ladder with one arm, he motioned for Caroline to put her good arm around him. He clasped her with his other arm and began climbing.

They got to the top of the ladder. Tom set her gently on solid ground. She was shivering from the cold water. He climbed out, took off his shirt, tossed it over to her. "Go over to the Chapel and change out of your wet shirt."

Caroline stood up, walked to the chapel and went inside. A few seconds later, Caroline yelled…"TOM!!!"

He sprinted to the door of the chapel and looked in. Caroline had not changed shirts and was shivering even more. The body of the very dead Rev. Damien Tucker was sprawled across a wooden chair. He had a gunshot wound in the middle of his forehead. The gun was lying on the floor just below his right hand.

Caroline felt his dead hand. "Still warm. This happened the same time I was pushed. The Rev. probably didn't do the pushing…"

Tom shook his head. Identical frowns creased their foreheads. There was more to this situation, this danger, than either of them thought. Tom and Caroline often reasoned alike, and their like thoughts at that moment were: *We need Det. Ed Mathers.*

Tom and Caroline rushed back to the resort. On the way back, Caroline stopped a moment to retch, never having seen a murder before and almost having drowned that night.

The phrase, 'at sea' came into Tom's head. He remembered it meant, confused, lost, clueless. It accurately described how he currently felt. He went to the wireless operator's room at the resort and sent a telegram to Det. Ed Mathers at the Phoenix Police Department. **Junior Detectives at sea. Situation perilous. A murder to solve. Come soonest.**

He sent a second telegram to Judge Wilkinson: **Boyle murdered tonight.**

***

A Dr. Richard Levy from Tucson, Arizona, was one of the guests at the Grand Opening. He examined Caroline's injured left shoulder and determined that nothing was broken, just a deep bruise and mild sprain. He opened his black case and took out a bottle of pills. "Take these for pain, Ms Colt."

She examined the bottle. "Kinda strong, Doc. I'll tough it out. We have a crime to solve. I need my wits about me."

She handed the bottle back to the doctor. "Good pills, though. I used to carry these in my purse."

Dr. Levy looked quizzically at Tom.

Tom said, "Her purse is better stocked then many pharmacies.'

Chapter Twenty

Judge Roy Wilkinson Kicks Ass Downtown
(As Only The Judge Can Do)

At Phoenix PD headquarters, the Next Morning at 8AM…

Det. Ed Mathers meeting with Chief Flannery.

"We need you here, Ed."

"Understood, Chief. Just thought I'd ask." Mathers sent a return telegram to Tom. **Sorry Buddy. Chief says no go.**

Tom relayed this immediately via Telegram to The Judge, who got in his car and headed downtown 10 minutes later.

***

It was a bright clear morning in the young vibrant city of Phoenix, the streets glistening from an overnight rain. At 9AM, The Judge, who always saw his path forward with clarity, strode into downtown police headquarters. "I'm going in to see the Chief," he stated with authority. None of the cops in the room raised an objection.

Cops in big, dangerous cities learn how to sense Evil and how to team up and combat it. This is why police officers form such a tight brotherhood. To protect all of us, they must also protect themselves.

They also learn how to sense Good. Which will help us understand why, when The Judge walked in, they had the confused look of animals that couldn't decide which category the Judge fit into.

Chief Flannery was at his desk. The Judge didn't bother to knock. He opened the door and stepped inside.

"Might have made an appointment, Roy, like the other private citizens do."

The Judge ignored him. "Red Boyle was a great businessman and one of our prominent citizens."

"So you say. We've had three murders in the last two weeks. I can't spare my best detective to go island hopping for you."

"Red Boyle was an important person. He deserves better."

The Chief says, "That's where you and I differ. I think all crime victims are equally important."

The Judge, Flannery knew, was measuring his next words very carefully.

"Jimmy, I plucked you out of a corrupt ward in Chicago and installed you as Chief of Police in the fastest growing, most dynamic city in America."

"I don't report to you, Judge."

"You are like all the bureaucrats. You burrow into your jobs and think you don't have to listen to 'We The People'. Well, you report to We The People whether you like it or not. And for the purposes of this conversation, <u>I am</u> We The People."

Flannery said nothing. He pushed his chair back and folded his fleshy but still muscular arms—he was an amateur boxer before going into law enforcement. He tried to stare down Judge Roy Wilkinson, a tactic which never worked.

Finally, Chief Flannery said, "Did you not hear me, Roy? I said I cannot spare any of my detectives."

"In Phoenix, Arizona in 1963 there is no one higher than Roy Wilkinson. One word from me and you'll be back on the streets of the South Side of Chicago chasing down petty thieves through the slushy streets in February. Remember those, dirty, slushy frigid streets, Jimmy? And the shabby little criminals."

The Judge had gravitas. The Judge had Mana, the very force of nature itself. The Judge had the Mayor and City Council under his control. The Chief of Police had no choice. It was not lost on Flannery that the Judge called him 'Jimmy', not 'Chief'.

Softly, Roy Wilkinson said, "And your sister Jillian is on the island with a killer on the loose."

Flannery snorted. "Half-sister. And Jillian can take care of herself. She's tougher than I am."

"Tom and Caroline are there, too. They asked for our help. They are my—"

"Your <u>what</u>, Roy?"

"They are important to me. More than I can say."

"We have no jurisdiction there. My detective couldn't do squat."

"We're Americans. When any of us are threatened, our jurisdiction is the world."

"Someday, Roy, you won't run this city anymore."

"Someday is a long way off."

The Chief tapped his pencil nervously on his green desk blotter.

The Chief buzzed his intercom. "Send Ed Mathers in here, please."

A few seconds later, Ed Mathers stepped into the tense office. He was surprised how red the Judge's face was. The animosity between the two men hung in the air like stale cigarette smoke. Only for once, the Judge wasn't smoking.

"Ed. Your expense request is approved. You may go to that island—for one week."

"I haven't made a request yet."

"You have now. Get out there to that damned island and solve a murder."

Mathers, uncharacteristically grim, said, "Yes sir." He wasn't sure what to say to Roy Wilkinson. As much as he wanted to help Tom and Caroline, Mathers had correctly read that Judge Roy Wilkinson had bullied his boss, which angered a veteran cop like Mathers to the edge of rage.

The Judge lit a cigarette, puffed a few times, looked at the Chief of Police and said, "Thank you." Then walked out.

The Chief exhaled, letting go of tension.

"Coming from Chicago, I can tell you Ed, at the end of the day, Phoenix in 1963 is just the wild frontier with linoleum floors instead of dirt. We still need that old sheriff."

Mathers nodded in grudging agreement.

***

The next day on Bogey Island, Elwood "Red" Boyle's Last Will and Testament was read to a small group gathered in a conference room near the ballroom at the lodge. The attorney was a young nervous fellow name Devin Mulroney, with a British accent, a pencil thin moustache, and a wrinkled suit of clothes that hung loose on his thin frame. He had been sent over from Freeport, Grand Bahama Island where his law firm was located. Tom found out that firm had a relationship with Red's law firm in Phoenix.

Tom studied the reaction of the gathered group. He was certain something important would be revealed.

The lawyer disclosed:

Autumn Amber was still a near-equal beneficiary with each of the Boyle children. Chandler Boyle was all smiles: he apparently believed the rumor that Red had made a big change to the Will, cutting the kids mostly out.

Tom thought something was off about Fredonia's reaction: she looked almost stricken for a moment, noticed that Tom noticed her, then quickly returned to looking completely unfazed, as though she already knew this information.

Tom knew the Will was big news to her...but why?

Autumn Amber, for her part, looked completely serene, using her acting training to the fullest. Tom thought she was straining to not look overjoyed that she hadn't been cut out.

His ability to read beneath the surface expressions, the masks people use, came in particularly handy that day. Amber had seemed under the impression that she may be on 'the outs' with Red...but why? Had Red Boyle told her? Told her parents?

Tom's mind was reeling with all these contradictions. At the party, it sure appeared that Boyle will still going to be Autumn Amber's financial backer.

Tom had heard rumors that a new Will had recently been executed. Were the rumors false? Or had the new Will been misplaced—or stolen? Or was the document a myth?

***

Weatherford's search of Boyle's desk yielded a major break in the case. There were two letters between Red Boyle and Yuma Boyle, who claimed in the first letter that she was his...daughter. His first child. The letter was written in a friendly happy tone of a woman who believed she had found her long-lost father. The letter did, though, make a firm request to be included in Boyle's estate. It closed with excitement about finally meeting him on Bogey Island at the Grand Opening celebration.

The response from Boyle, on Bogey Island Resort stationery, was terse and cold. Boyle denied having fathered her and denied her claim absolutely, saying his lawyers would be happy to deal with her if she persisted in this "foolishness" of demanding a share of his estate. He signed the letter EBB for (Elwood Brinton Boyle).

Weatherford showed the letters to each of the Boyle siblings. They denied knowing anything about a Yuma Boyle or her claim on the estate.

He showed the letter to Tom, who remarked, "Why did he sign the letter with just initials? It's an important document. He threatened legal action, after all."

Weatherford was momentarily impressed with the young golfer/detective.

The initials were indeed curious. Was Boyle just trying to be dismissive?

Weatherford inquired of the guests and staff if anyone had met this Yuma Boyle. She was not listed as a hotel guest on the guest ledger.

Only the Vonessens had met Yuma Boyle. They verified the information in the letter: she believed herself to be Red Boyle's daughter and intended to assert her claim to share in the inheritance.

Babs Vonessen contributed an odd little clue: Yuma Boyle wore a very distinctive perfume, attar of roses, she called it. This didn't mean a whole lot to Weatherford or Tom, and Caroline never wore perfume. Weatherford wrote in his notebook, 'smelled like tar and roses'.

Tom asked the Vonessens, "Did the girl seem nervous? Like she had something dangerous planned?"

Carter said, "Not at all. A cool and charming young woman. We were both taken with her. I offered to help her get her rightful share of the estate through proper legal channels. She seemed receptive to my idea."

Tom thought, *You're all heart, Carter Vonessen.*

***

The two cops Weatherford had brought with him were very young, and Tom quickly decided, not competent. Tom observed they were inept at interviewing the suspects. They were brusque, bumptious, almost like they thought they could browbeat these rich, savvy Americans, many of whom were lifelong friends, into ratting on each other. No chance of that. The suspects quickly clammed up and the interviews were pretty much worthless.

Weatherford, of course, thought his young minions were doing outstanding work. Tom and Caroline were gradually being sidelined from the investigation—in a polite, British way. Weatherford told them little to nothing about what he and his team were learning.

Mathers had taught Tom to engage suspects in relaxed, friendly conversations, get them talking, don't interrupt them, to coax info out of them. And he fared much better with his interviews with the resort guests. He was seen as the harmless golfer boy, so people let down their guard when talking to him. Caroline, not as smooth as Tom, was nonetheless effective because she had a knack for phrasing questions that that threw them off stride.

Tom and Caroline identified several inconsistencies in the guests' and staff members' statements.

But what should they do with them? They decided to keep detailed notes and hope that...they weren't sure what to hope for. They continued talking with everyone they could.

When they finished the morning's interviews and broke for lunch, Tom told Caroline, "The thing about rich people I've learned is that they aren't smarter or cleverer than the rest of us. They are much better at surviving anything life throws at them, including being interrogated by law enforcement. They are hard-shelled and stick together no matter what."

She said, "To Det. Mathers, that's why it's so much fun to catch one of them..."

As the day wore on, the investigation was a muddle. The British cops were wandering around as if in a maze. Tom and Caroline were on the outside looking in.

***

In the afternoon, Marco Greene asked to see the body of the Reverend Damien Tucker. Marco was always keenly interested in crime, being highly skilled at it himself and all. Weatherford agreed to Marco's request.

He chuckled when he saw the face.

Marco knew the guy. He was no Reverend, probably had never attended church. His name was Bruno Belk, a top-flight grifter who works—worked—out of Vegas.

Marco pulled on the Rev's goatee; it came off.

"Do you know this man?" Weatherford asked.

Marco never assisted the cops unless there was something in it for him. He quickly analyzed all the angles in this situation and saw no practical benefit to Marco Greene Enterprises Inc.

"Nope. The goatee just looked fake."

"Who are you, sir?"

"Businessman from Phoenix. I run lodging establishments and entertainment venues."

Caroline smirked at that one, thinking, *I guess you could call them that...*

***

Patti Boyle tracked down Tom as he was walking through the lobby to meet with Weatherford. "I don't know if this is important, but the morning after my dad was killed, I got to the front desk for my shift and I, well, smelled an unusual perfume."

"Thank you," Tom said. "Every scrap of information helps at this point."

And scraps were a good description of what the British cops were able to gather. Tom was learning that some police are just plain stupid, or at least incompetent. Tom was used to working with the brilliant Det. Ed Mathers. The mess these cops on the island were making of the investigation surprised Tom. But it was also useful information for him going forward in his private detective career. There were times upcoming, he knew, when he would be considered an adversary by the police.

***

The young Brit investigators got around to checking through the staff quarters, tiny cottages located on the back side of the resort property. The missing maid, Carol Thorn, had taken her uniform with her, which they thought was odd.

"It had the Boyle Properties logo on it. She couldn't wear it at her next job."

"Souvenir?" said the other one.

"I think she's dead. Saw too much. Heard too much."

***

Two days later, hope arrived. Mathers arrived. To both Tom and Caroline's mild shock, he was wearing a stereotypical American island tourist outfit. Flowered shirt. Bermuda shorts that revealed pale legs. Sandals with socks. Black socks! Panama hat with the widest brim available.

Mathers was a casual guy when it came to dress, they both knew. Comfortable in his own skin. The colors often clashed in the outfits he wore. He didn't care about clothes. He cared about justice. And golf. And was dedicated to both. Mathers saw no need to impress anyone—until he made an arrest.

Even so, Tom and Caroline both thought his choice of outfit that day was...strange.

Tom and Caroline beamed when they saw him, though. Outside the lodge, strolling toward the outside patio, they filled him in on the lack of progress in the investigation and the animosity between them and Weatherford.

"Not sure what good I can do here. We have no jurisdiction. I looked the island up. Controlled by The Brits. I couldn't even bring my gun."

Marco Greene, relaxing in a white wicker chair under a palm tree, sipping a colorful rum drink said, "Don't worry, Ed, I can loan you one of mine."

Caroline and Tom got a chuckle out of that one. "Thanks a bunch," Mathers replied, testily.

Inspector Weatherford appeared. Mathers and Weatherford sized each other up. Without introduction, Mathers knew he was a cop. Weatherford didn't know quite what to make of Mathers. Weatherford scrutinized Mathers' outfit with disdain: the floral print shirt particularly appalled him—the flower an odd, ugly looking one that was hopefully extinct. And sandals with socks! and Bermuda shorts.

"And who might you be, sir?"

Caroline said, "He's John Wayne, and he brought the Cavalry."

Mathers smiled and puffed up. He loved Westerns. He loved Duke Wayne. He handed Weatherford his business card.

Weatherford scoffed, "Doubtful a movie hero would wear those dreadful shorts. Even an American one."

Weatherford thought it amusing that Tom and Caroline frowned at him in an identical way. He deduced they were twins—one of the only successful deductions he had made on the island thus far.

Weatherford said, "Unless you're here to relax on the beach, you've made a wasted trip, Det. Mathers."

Mathers was undeterred. "I understand your concerns. Turf and all that. We won't interfere. Time is of the essence, a few days the suspects will all scatter, rabbit out of here. I call it the 72-hour rule. That's about the time you have after a body is discovered, to discover the murderer."

"Americans...always in such a rush. I've solved homicides three years after the crime."

Tom said, "We can help. We know these people—all the suspects. They belong to Valley Vista Country Club, where I give golf lessons. Det. Mathers is a member of the Club."

Weatherford's perfectly trimmed left eyebrow twitched at that. *This rustic fellow is a member of a fine golf Club? The admission standards in American Clubs must be low...*

Caroline sensed what he was thinking. "Besides being an excellent golfer, Det. Mathers is the premier homicide detective in Phoenix, the fastest growing city in the United States. Or as you say, the Colonies."

Weatherford half-smiled. Caroline, encouraged by that, added, "Tom knows what makes these people tick. And which ones have ticks."

That earned a half-chuckle from Inspector Weatherford. But he replied frigidly, "Phoenix isn't quite the size of London, now is it, Miss Colt."

Mathers noticed the young Brits lurking behind Weatherford.

"You have quite a young investigative team, Inspector."

"How old were you when you solved your first murder?"

"27"

"There you go."

Mathers said, "You'd be surprised how many murders Tom and Caroline helped me solve last year."

"With the terrible murder rate in America, I expect you get more opportunities."

Weatherford scanned the azure sea and matching sky, as though for direction. He expelled a frustrated breath. "All right. I see your point. I'm understaffed here. Too many people to interview in a short time. You Yanks are a particularly pushy species, aren't you?"

"We're just helpful sorts of folks," Caroline said with a sweet smile that she almost never displayed.

Reluctantly Weatherford said, "Okay, but it's my lead. And you share every shred of information, no matter how seemingly inconsequential, with me."

"Deal," Mathers said without hesitation.

Mathers again cautioned Weatherford that these people all knew each other, were part of the same 'Club' in more ways than one and would lie to protect each other.

Weatherford arched that eyebrow again and replied, "I always appreciate it when Americans come along and explain police work to me."

Mathers was undeterred. "We can't make the guests stay here indefinitely. They're already calling their lawyers in Phoenix, I guran-damn-tee it. We have to hustle, people."

"And not surprisingly, the American detective endeavors to take over the investigation already," Weatherford said wearily.

"You'll find I'm quite the little endeavoror, Inspector," Mathers said with a toothy smile.

Caroline flashed on why Mathers arrived in that ridiculous tourist outfit. To make Weatherford think he had nothing to fear from his involvement in the case. Mathers knew he and Weatherford would have an adversarial relationship. Mathers was trying to appear less formidable to his adversary than he really was. Smart!

Caroline marveled at how adept Mathers was at the strategic aspect of investigation and crime solving. She got an unexpectedly, warm, energized feeling. It was going to be a sweet ride working with Det. Ed Mathers!

***

Terrence Egglesworth and his wife Judith were having a tense stroll on the beach. Judy was back to her normal 'Bambi' self. Her too-small bikini top barely restrained, but excitingly displayed, the famous bazooms.

"You told Weatherford that you were with me that entire evening in our room, correct?'

"Absolutely. I said I had a touch of stomach upset and you were keeping an eye on me, so much in love you are."

Terrence expelled the breath of deep relief. "No need for sarcasm, Judy. I couldn't tell them I went upstairs that night to Boyle's office to confront him. They'd think I did it. I wish I could tell them I saw someone hurrying down the hallway, from the direction of Boyle's office, but that would implicate me, too. And anyway, I have no idea who it was. A woman, I think, but I'm not even sure about that."

He gave her hand a little squeeze. "Anyway, I'm in your debt."

"When we get back to Phoenix, we can settle the debt. I want a divorce."

"I can't give you a divorce…that will scuttle my reputation with the Bishops. The final nail in my business' coffin. You know that!"

"I don't care."

***

Chapter Twenty-One
More Questions than Answers

The American Investigative Team, Tom, Mathers and Caroline, decided to use Tom's room as a headquarters for their investigation. It was centrally located, a vantage point to easily observe what the other guests were doing and saying in the hallways. Mathers would be staying in the room across the hall vacated by Jilly Flannery's departure.

With 6 investigators, 3 Brits and 3 Americans, they were able to fan out and complete interviews with everyone at the resort, guests and staff, in 24 hours.

When they were working on the Lisa Luck murder in '62, Caroline had designed a clever way to keep track of the suspects. She called it THE LEADERBOARD, like you would see at a golf tournament.

Names were listed in the rows, with the top suspect at the top, the "leader". There were four columns across, labeled motive, opportunity, and an upward arrow for why the suspect was likely to have committed the crime, and a negative arrow for why they weren't.

Even Mathers, who didn't like gimmicks, admitted her idea was 'cool'.

Since they didn't think they'd be investigating a murder—their assignment was to prevent one—Tom didn't bring his 'Leaderboard' with him.

Mathers found a chalkboard in the kitchen, used to post the day's recipes, which he brought to Tom's room, to serve the same purpose as the Leaderboard, keeping track of the suspects.

"Okay, Junior Detectives, why do rich people have so many enemies? I'll give you a hint. Most people want to be rich, but only a few figure out how to get there."

Caroline remarked, "So if they can't make it, they wanna take it."

Mathers patted Caroline on the head. "Very good!"

"I know. But don't pat me on the head. And Tom's the Junior Detective. I'm legit." She smiled brightly.

"Oh, you're well beyond legit, Caroline. Anyways, maybe it'd be easier if we worked backwards. Make a list of people who didn't want to kill old Boyle. Be a shorter, more manageable list for us."

Mathers wrote names and motives on the chalkboard. "I get so tired of these amateur criminals thinking they can get away with murder. They can't. Even the pros seldom do."

Tom and Caroline were already of the opinion the killer was not the kind of amateur Mathers was referring to.

"One thing I had to learn early on is to not read too much into everything a suspect, a person, says. People sometimes just fill dead air with chatter, meaningless words, because they're nervous. As you grow as a detective, that skill will come. The great detective, he learns how to pick out the key information, the info most relevant to advancing a case toward solution. That's what he does so well."

"Or she," Caroline said, with the hint of a scowl.

"Of course. Or she," Mathers said. "Anyways, your interviewing skills will come in handy. We need to take turns talking to each of our possible suspects several times, until their stories start to change, and we shake loose some contradictions. And my friends, we will."

Tom and Caroline felt better already: Mathers' confidence was contagious.

But Mathers was a cop the suspects all knew from Valley Vista CC. His presence on the island only served to put the suspects further on guard.

***

Later that afternoon, Inspector Weatherford popped his head into Tom's room as the three Americans were going over their suspect list on the chalkboard.

Weatherford said, "Hullo, team. Let's go for a stroll by the sea, led by your commander, me, and exchange notes on our suspect interviews. I've found getting outside is often the ticket. Small narrow spaces lead to small narrow thinking, I always say."

Mathers expression was a slow burn. Tom smiled: That was Mathers' favorite investigative axiom. He was sure he invented it.

The stroll down the beach looked more like an army platoon in formation: Weatherford and his two minions were in the front row, behind them followed Mathers, Tom and Caroline.

The six discussed the case as they walked along the margin of gentle incoming waves. Each had a theory of who the killer was—already.

By late afternoon, they had their first 'Leaderboard' nailed down, so they thought. They returned to Tom's room and to the chalkboard.

***

Yuma Boyle was the name at the top of The Leaderboard. "Our first step is to find Miss Yuma Boyle," Weatherford said with almost smug assurance.

"I'm all in for Fredonia and Chandler Boyle," Mathers said. "Chandler said he and Fredonia were playing cards in the game room at the time of the murder. Plenty of time for either of them to go up to Boyle's office. No one else came into the card room except a waitress bringing them drinks. But a staff member could be paid to lie…"

Tom said, "Patti Boyle, not so much. She loved her father and expressed concern to me about what her siblings were up to. Her remorse at his death seemed genuine."

Caroline added, "Each of the 3 Boyle kids receives the father's favor, his good graces, but on a rotation. One in, two out. Maybe he feared they would conspire to get rid of him, so he tried to divide them and pit them against each other. But it backfired: his cruel action brought them together."

Mathers, "After talking to young Master Boyle, I gotta say, if he was any more full of bullshit, he'd explode."

Weatherford agreed. "When I talked to him he broke down crying, saying 'I can't believe you British cops think we would kill our beloved father. We were devoted to him. We all willingly chose to work in the family business, to help him'." Weatherford looked up at the ceiling. "What tosh! He should indeed explode."

Caroline made the sound of an explosion.

Weatherford said, "Sister Fredonia took another tack. When I was with my associates, she stormed over and said, with acid dripping in her voice, 'Do you really think you can divide us? We'll you can't. You're wasting our time and the time of our guests. Either make an arrest or get off my island'."

"My island," Caroline immediately caught.

Weatherford smiled. Briefly. "And let me tell you what happened when I asked her if she knew of the existence of this half-sister, Yuma. She said, without even blinking, 'Not surprised. Old Red plowed a lot of fertile fields'."

Mathers pointed at a name on the chalkboard and said, "Big Al Langdon. Positive: No other reason for him to be at the

Grand Opening other than revenge. He had no alibi for the time of the murder. Said he was walking on the beach. Negative: Entry angle for the knife all wrong. So tall, he'd have to be on his knees."

One of the young British cops said, "We should consider Terrence Egglesworth. Motive: Humiliation of his wife at the stag party and the ruination of his business by Boyle. Said he and his wife were in their room packing to leave at the time of the murder. Bags were indeed packed when we went in the room the night of the murder."

Tom nominated Carter Vonessen. "Back in Phoenix he confessed to me how much he hated Boyle, blaming him for the death of his sister. He is known to have a bad temper. Was seen in the kitchen admiring the murder weapon. Negative: Would a smart businessman like him be so obvious as to admire the knife in front of witnesses?"

Caroline tossed in Nick Amberson. "Boyle threatened to renege on the movie deal for Autumn. He was enraged by Boyle showing a nudie movie of his daughter. The Will reading revealed Boyle did in fact leave money to Amber. Negative: Amber swears she was with her dad all evening, after dinner to bedtime, in their suite. They read movie scripts together. Ain't that sweet..."

Mathers nodded his head then said, "Rev. Damien Tucker: Stood to make a good pile of money when Red kicked off. Did he hurry things along? Also, Red tried to kibosh the treasure hunters. Rev. was posing as a Rev. He was looking for the treasure. Negative: He's dead. One of the suspects killed him as well. Why?"

Weatherford said, "If Tucker were dead, his share reverts to the remaining beneficiaries, the children. Was there a 2nd Will? That has somehow disappeared?"

The group went quiet for a few moments as they considered this. More and more, this seemed likely.

"Weatherford said, "And then we have William Tisdale, the novelist. Had solid alibis for both the night of the murder—he was in the conservatory with a hotel guest who was a horticulturist, and for Rev. Tucker's murder."

Tom asked, "What exactly is a conservatory?"

Caroline replied, "Where they store old conservatives."

"Got it. Thanks, Caroline."

"Quite a few copper-bottomed alibis here on Bogey Island," Weatherford commented.

Caroline was thrilled. She was waiting for Weatherford to use an authentic British detective expression, just like in the detective novels.

Mathers re-re-iterated, "We can't forget these people all belong to the same club, literally and figuratively. They close ranks. Their statements are many times useless. We gotta keep hammering them until someone cracks."

"What about the missing staff members?" Tom asked. He pointed at the chalk board:

<u>Missing Staff Members</u>
Doris
Carol
Marquita

Weatherford commented. "You wouldn't know this, but out here in the islands finding reliable help is quite difficult. They are transient, come and go on a whim. Always looking for a better set-up, pay and working conditions. Not a good lot, those. Their disappearance doesn't indicate guilt."

The notion that the maid, waitress or other staff did the crime was also rejected by Mathers. "Nothing of any value was taken. No motive for a robbery. Those employees probably didn't want to be involved and bolted. Maybe they were afraid. I've seen rich people try to pin a crime on the hired help."

Mathers stopped to take a sip of iced tea. The thrill of the chase always left him thirsty. "And then we have Julia Wilkinson: Had no motive to kill Boyle. He had treated her very well. Selected her to perform at the Grand Opening. The knife was clearly a plant. Pretty lame frame, as frames go."

Weatherford disagreed with a dour shake of the head. "I heard from three of the guests that she had a history of mental instability. I heard a rumor that she even shot your very own Tom Colt last year."

Weatherford was pleased to present this thorny tidbit.

"That rumor is a lie, sir," Tom said. "A prowler shot me at the Wilkinsons' property."

Caroline was impressed at how well Tom had lied. As much as she would like to get Julia out of Tom's life, even she couldn't picture her plunging a knife into Red Boyle's back. She knew the 'three guests' Weatherford referenced were all females. They tended to not like Julia because their husbands lusted after her.

Tom stood up and walked over to the chalkboard, picked up an eraser and eliminated Julia's name. "I can vouch for Julia, on my honor. She had nothing to do with this."

Weatherford, surprisingly, said," I am inclined to agree with you." The question becomes why the killer overdosed Julia Wilkinson to pin the crime on her. And further, how would the killer know when Julia was likely to take her pills each evening?"

Weatherford walked over to the window and looked out at the sea, wishing he were playing golf on the lovely links on Bogey Island rather than working on this tedious case with these tedious Americans.

"Only the maid staff would enter the rooms each day," he continued. "And now we're back to…the staff members had no motive. I will submit to you that Yuma Boyle is smart. Really smart. She must have gathered enough information about Julia Wilkinson and her prescription drug use, to know she could be framed."

The meeting continued a half hour longer, until Weatherford abruptly concluded, "Miss Yuma Boyle did the crime. She had no reason to bolt out of here if she thought she still had a chance to insinuate herself into Mr. Boyle's estate. She's undoubtedly back in America. Your job is to find her. My job is thankfully about completed here."

Caroline had this nagging little feeling that the good Inspector was hasty with this conclusion. But she had nothing solid to back her little feeling up, so she remained quiet. As unlikely as that sounds.

Weatherford turned his attention to the Second Murder, the demise of Reverend Damien Tucker via gunshot wound.

The clues there were even more scanty. The novelist would be the prime suspect, except for that pesky alibi.

Caroline said she had probably followed the murderer out to the chapel, but couldn't identify who it was, or even whether it was a male or female. The figure disappeared into the shadows of the path too quickly.

The group of detectives elected to break for dinner at 7PM.

Caroline turned to Weatherford and said, "Inspector, every conversation we've had, every idea I've come up with, ends up with you saying, 'No, Miss Colt'. Or, 'that's incorrect Miss Colt'. Let's try something different. Would you like to have dinner with me this evening? I've never met a real British detective before. I've only read about your heroics in stories."

"Yes, Miss Colt," he surprisingly answered. He gallantly offered his arm and escorted her into the dining room.

Mathers said to Tom, "You're buying dinner. I heard you just won 1,500 bucks. With a helluva shot on the last hole, I might add. I didn't know Jillian Flannery had game."

"You have no idea."

They wisely took a mental break from the complicated case they were working on and chatted mostly about their other favorite subject...golf. Mathers had shot his best 18-hole score ever the previous week at Papago Park, a long and difficult public course in Tempe, a college town near Phoenix. Mathers went over every shot in the round, all 82 of them.

At the corner of the dining room opposite where Weatherford and Caroline were dining, Mathers and Tom dined on their usual fare: enormous medium-rare porterhouse steaks and potatoes swimming in butter, the latter they termed the healthy vegetable portion of the meal.

Caroline wasn't having a good time with Inspector Weatherford. Dinner with him turned out not to be one of her better ideas. As they discussed the case, it became clear to Caroline that Weatherford wasn't as certain as he had let on earlier that Yuma Boyle had committed the murder. He mostly wanted to get this case off his desk and get on to other ones that might better advance his career in London.

"And Scotland Yard is baffled by this murder," Caroline said with high drama in her voice.

"We're never baffled, Miss Colt. That's a fiction of bad American cinema."

"No need to get all crabby, Inspector. That was just good American humor."

The great Inspector irritated her with his frequent snide remarks about America and Americans. As the dinner progressed, she had the urge to smack him, cop or no cop. Caroline seldom loved herself, but she dearly loved the USA. *What a pompous bore this guy is. I'll be glad when this dinner was over.*

Real-life British detectives aren't at all like the ones in detective stories, Caroline thought. She briefly felt disillusioned.

As they were finishing their after-dinner coffee, Julia Wilkinson swept into the room, ran over to Tom and Mathers' table and dramatically hugged Tom from behind. He turned and got out of his chair.

She spoke loudly enough everyone in the dining room could hear.

"Inspector Weatherford says I'm free to go! You saved me Tom!" She grabbed him and planted a kiss on his lips.

Tom said, "No one seriously thought you could have done it…"

"My wonderful, fabulous Tom. How could I be such a fool to not realize that you're the best man for me?"

He had no idea what to say to that obvious lie, so he said nothing. He'd learned long ago that Julia created her own reality as she went along. And yesterday's reality seldom resembled today's.

She looked over at Weatherford and Caroline, blew a kiss at the Inspector. "Thank you!"

Weatherford nodded, looking stolid and serious and veddy British. To Caroline, he said, "Nice bit of goods, that girl."

"You have no idea," Caroline said.

At Tom and Mathers' table, Julia said, "I am going to my room and pack and get out of here tonight! See y'all back in Phoenix."

She swept out of the room with the same sexual magnetism she entered it. All male eyes were on her.

Mathers noticed for the first time how Julia's big luminous eyes could turn Tom to mush, or perhaps stone, or maybe mushy stone. Like auto headlights, she had a bright setting that she used only on Tom.

"I'll say it again, pretty lame frame," Mathers commented. "Almost seems like the killer is laughing at us. I never like that. Although the arrogant killers are the easiest to catch. They always slip up."

He indicated the departing Julia.

"Not sure I did you a favor, though." *Are they back together?* Mathers wondered. He looked at Tom speculatively. *I certainly hope not. She is trouble with a capital T.*

***

After dinner, Tom and Mathers went strolling through the lobby. A staff member came over and told Tom a telegram had arrived for him. Mathers said he'd be on the patio and Tom should join him there.

Tom knew it was a response from the Judge to a telegram he sent thanking him for getting Mathers out there to help.

Tom read the response:

Tom, thank you! Julia is on her way home because of your great work.

Red Boyle was one of the most dynamic business leaders we ever had in Arizona. We can't let the killer of an American citizen go unpunished because of the incompetence of island cops. Stay on the job. Roy.

***

On the patio, Mathers was seated at a table. He had ordered a pitcher of beer and three glasses. He took his Proverb for Detectives, as he called it, out of his wallet and read it, for probably the thousandth time:

> *The purposes of a man's heart are deep waters,*
> *but a man of understanding draws them out.*

"That's our job, to be the man of understanding," Mathers said out loud.

"Or woman," Caroline remarked, coming up behind him and taking a seat.

Mathers laughed. Tom joined them and sat down. Mathers poured each of them a beer.

Mathers began, "This case is a doozy. So many people hated Boyle. But yet they all seem to have solid alibis, with a few exceptions. Everyone wanted to kill Red, but evidently no one actually did. I guess he stuck the knife in his own back."

Caroline tried to mime sticking a knife in her own back. Mathers smiled.

"Kinda difficult, isn't it," Tom commented.

Mathers said, "Weatherford is off in left field with this Yuma business. This illegitimate daughter Yuma wasn't in the Will before, and Red says she won't ever be in a letter to her. So Yuma doesn't lose anything. She comes all the way out here to off the guy. What's the motive? Wouldn't she keep working on him until he cuts her in on a share? If you sucked up to him, Boyle was a generous guy, we've heard."

Tom said, "Boyle was a horrible person, we all agree. Maybe the daughter Yuma thought he'd gone too far."

Mathers' face was skeptical. "Doesn't that sound weak to your keen detective ears?"

Tom nodded. "Weak, yes. I think I'm just tired."

Caroline said, "Maybe she felt rejected all her life. Her dad didn't want her. Now, she hoped for some kind of reconciliation—and he cruelly rejected her again. Emotionally and financially."

"Good sound reasoning, Miss C, but it still feels like we're missing a key piece."

Tom: "We don't have enough info about this Yuma Boyle girl for her to seem real to us."

Mathers nodded his agreement. They sipped beers and pondered a few moments. Detectives couldn't ask for a more beautiful setting for a meeting. The surf was pounding, white waves sparkling in the surprisingly bright light from a half-moon.

"Okay, say she off'd the guy. So she leaves in plain sight, with the Vonessens and Kat as witnesses? Makes no sense. If she had come here to murder Boyle, she would have used an alias."

Caroline thought, *Deus Ex Machina.* But she couldn't articulate what her thought meant, so she stayed silent. Her mind turned and turned, but it was like a car engine that wouldn't turn over, her thoughts too convoluted for her to unravel. Yet.

Mathers sipped his beer then said, "This whole business of Yuma's distinctive perfume seems fake, too. Why would a killer be that stupid as to leave a scent behind?"

"You're saying: It doesn't pass the sniff test."

"Good one, Caroline."

She grinned.

When they called it a night, Caroline, exhausted from the tiresome dinner conversation with Weatherford, returned to her cottage. Caroline never suffered fools very well.

Tom and Mathers walked to their rooms. Mathers paused in the hallway and reversed course, going back to the card room. He beckoned Tom with a flick of his wrist. Tom followed.

Mathers walked to the back of the room where he noticed an indentation in the woodwork. He pulled on the raised portion. A door opened. To the hallway that led to the kitchen or out to the stairs.

"So much for the kids' alibi."

"Except Patti's," Tom hastily added.

***

Weatherford, the next morning, with the group of 6 investigators gathered at a breakfast table on the patio, abruptly announced that he and his team were leaving the island that afternoon.

"Yuma Boyle killed her father. She is undoubtedly back in the US. I learned that an airline ticket from Miami to Los Angeles was purchased for cash by Yuma Boyle. We couldn't confirm an identification of her from the airline staff, but I think it's clear she went home thinking we did not suspect her because she had already left the island before the time of the murder. As confirmed by the broken watch we found on Red Boyle's body."

Mathers shook his head in disagreement. "We, my team and I, are not as sure as you are about this."

Weatherford had that smug look again. "All you Yanks have to do is track down Yuma Boyle and she's...how do you put it...toast. I am returning to Grand Bahama, and then back to London next week. And I have told the guests they are free to leave."

Weatherford gulped down his orange juice, got up from the table and said, "It was a pleasure working with you."

The three Americans each mumbled an insincerely positive reply about how they enjoyed it, too. Caroline's insincere reply was obvious to Weatherford. He chuckled as he strode away, the two young cops following him like little ducks.

So just like that, without fanfare, the Investigation simply petered out. One by one the guests trotted out the doors of Boyle International's Bogey Island Resort—many vowed never to come back there.

Mathers noted how despondent his young and still green team looked, particularly Caroline. "We can't win them all," he said, philosophically.

"You don't really believe that," Caroline said.

"No. I get paid to win 'em all. But this isn't over."

We've all read detective stories where the super-sleuth seemingly bumbles around talking to the wide array of suspects, gathers clues and then calls them together into a room and dramatically points out the killer.

Then he/she explains it so clearly that we, the readers, think, I should have thought of that!

That scene did not unfold at Bogey Island. Not in the least. Scotland Yard, Colt & Colt Confidential Investigations and the premier homicide investigator in Phoenix, Ed Mathers, had struggled in vain until they simply ran out of time.

Mathers knew there wasn't much they could have done differently. He had arrived too late to do any good. All the key players in the crime had time to circle the wagons, come up with a story to exonerate themselves and practice the story enough that they couldn't be shaken.

Weatherford didn't seem too concerned with the results of the investigation. The failure to apprehend the killer hit the three Americans much harder. The boat ride back to Grand Bahama and then Miami was a dispirited one for Tom, Caroline and Det. Mathers.

Caroline was especially disconsolate. "We were supposed to prevent a murder. We didn't. We can't solve that one and then another murder, at least one, maybe more, happened right under our noses."

She sat back in her seat with a sullen expression. She thought, *I don't want to go back to Phoenix.* Defeat was especially hard for her to accept. She loved the detective work. Insecure as she was then, she worried the Judge might not be their patron anymore. Mathers might not ask them to assist the Phoenix PD. She'd quickly be back at her old job: produce clerk at an Italian market on Third Avenue.

And she couldn't reconcile what happened in the last three days: The suspects were captive on an island. The clues were all right there. The American investigators left Bogey Island with three notebooks full of jumbled notes from the interviews they conducted. Nothing made sense.

As they walked through the Miami airport to catch their plane to Phoenix, Caroline walked slowly behind Tom, thinking, *First case I team up with Tom to solve, and it's all screwed up. Typical of me. I'm called upon for derring-do and I turn it into derring doo-doo.*

Part Three
"It is much easier to catch a murderer than it is to prevent a murder."
--Detective Hercule Poirot, from *The Labors of Hercules*

Chapter Twenty-Two
The Dejected Detectives Return to Phoenix

On the flight back to Phoenix, Caroline and Tom vowed to avoid discussing the Boyle murder investigation. They needed a break from the feelings of failure they shared. If not failure, then confusion. They knew all the 'suspects'. They should have been able to put the pieces together. There was an unspoken sense between them that perhaps they weren't cut out to be private detectives after all. For Tom's part, he didn't want to let Judge Wilkinson down.

Tom, Caroline and Mathers mutually decided to go over all the evidence they had found on the island a week after they got back home. "Let the details percolate through our minds," was the way Mathers put it.

Tom thought Caroline was almost too cheerful on the plane ride back home, given how badly the trip had turned out. He anticipated she would have a meltdown. They were twins, alike in many ways, but she was by far the most hyper-sensitive of the two.

Tom could content himself with his own interests—golf, girls, and now being a private investigator—and ignore all the noisy nonsense we are confronted with by life. She couldn't. To her the noise was deafening, overwhelming at times. This was one of the reasons she had the ongoing battle with drugs, for most of her days. She wanted the noise to stop.

On the plane flight, family was on her mind, perhaps because when she saw how horrible the Boyle family was, it had caused her to re-evaluate her relationship with their mother.

She said, "Our family isn't so bad. At least we don't kill each other. We never even consider it."

"The most hostile action I've ever contemplated was temporarily placing duct tape over your mouth."

"Sadly, you're not the only man who's considered that. Remember I used to have that slight line of dark hair on my upper lip? Why do you think it's no longer there?"

"Your big-ass mustache? Sure, I remember. I'd guess...a boyfriend?"

"Yep. I retaliated by getting three other girls together and duct-taping his sorry ass to a stop sign on 7th and Van Buren. Took two of his chums a half-hour to cut him loose."

"Dates with you should come with a hazard warning."

Caroline liked the idea. "Could prevent misunderstandings."

"So, brother, when we get home, lets invite Mother*** over for dinner. I'll cook one of her signature recipes. Make it like a reconciliation."

Tom looked stunned, then that familiar Look of the Rascal appeared on his face. He said, in a dramatic voice, "And the dark clouds parted and beams of golden sunshine bathed Caroline's lovely face. The Angels joined in a heavenly chorus so impassioned that it shook the crystalline celestial sphere."

"I really hate you sometimes."

"As well you should. It's richly deserved."

"In any case, I'm sure our dinner party will be a debacle as usual, featuring lots of mayhem and shouting. Anchovy pasta served with a side dish of acrimony."

"I look forward to it. You and Mom are both great cooks. And pretty good at chucking plates at each other. Your accuracy has really improved."

Caroline motioned for the stewardess to come over. "'scuze me, Miss, but could you please open that emergency door so we can toss my annoying brother out the plane?"

"My name's not Miss, it's Sherry. See, Western Airlines gives us these spiffy name badges for you passengers to refer to." She had a sweet smile and a Southern accent.

Caroline made a sour face. She never liked passive-aggressive women.

Sherry continued, "And there are much more fun things I'd do with Tom Colt, if I got the chance."

She wrote that something on a cocktail napkin and handed it to Tom. "Here's my number. I'm based in Phoenix. Maybe we could go out sometime. I saw you win that tourney in Vegas. You were amazing!"

Caroline thought, *Tom Colt, the only golfer in history to win one tournament and become an American legend.*

Sherry left. Tom said, "Sherry is a pretty name, don't you think?"

She gently banged her head on the seat back. "I quit. I just quit."

**Caroline always said 'Mother' as though it was a mild cuss word.

***

Tom had coping mechanisms to accept life's ups and downs and could brush off failure. Perhaps that's what being a pro golfer taught him. It's an occupation with drastic ups and downs from week to week or even day to day.

Caroline, in general, could not. Their failure as detectives on Bogey Island—both in keeping Red Boyle out of harm's way and in figuring out who killed him—hit each of them hard, but Caroline by far the hardest.

Tom mailed the check for the prize money he won at the Boyle Pro-Am back to the attorney handling Boyle's estate. It didn't seem right keeping the money after what happened.

The meltdown Tom anticipated occurred several days after they had returned home. Caroline split to her favorite escape from reality, the beaches at Puerto Penasco, Sonora, Mexico.

Tom resumed a full schedule of lessons at Valley Vista—hoping he might shake loose some clues from the garrulous Club members now that they were back on home turf and relaxed. Mathers had two new murders in the Phoenix metro area to occupy his mind.

***

Puerto Penasco, Sonora, Mexico...On a Sunny Mid-April Afternoon

Caroline passed two weeks drinking tequila and smoking weed, sleeping on the beach at this sleepy little fishing village, waking up and then throwing up, eating much too little, and repeating the same program the next day. During her sober periods, she enjoyed arguing about any and all subjects with other American ex-pats who were there. Remember, in those days we didn't have Social Media and the Internet. We had to argue with random strangers in person.

Caroline was sinking fast. She was losing weight, something she clearly didn't need to do on her slender frame. She seldom bathed down there except to dip into the sea to cool off. She began to resemble a once-civilized person returning to the wild state.

She had one friend there, quite a loyal one, a young, sinewy, bronzed fisherman. We can only speculate what he saw in this strange girl from Phoenix. Half the time she called him Paco, half the time Pablo. He never seemed to mind. Perhaps he was accustomed to the eccentricities of the American tourist or had given up trying to understand them.

For his part, he called her Karen half the time, not Caroline. Can two people who botch each other's name remain friends? Apparently so. She'd been coming down there to visit him for 6 years. The language barrier proved to be a boon to their friendship. They never argued about anything.

That afternoon, Caroline was in particularly bad shape. She'd already thrown up twice on the beach. She was lying face down on a towel and groaning occasionally from her stubborn hangover.

"Please rub some of that suntan oil on my back, Paco," she mumbled to him. He grabbed the bottle and obliged. The suntan oil we applied back then was not the 50+SPF-efficient sun blocker that we use today. It was basically coconut-scented grease. But it made us feel like we were protected. He considered using it to fry up some fresh-caught shrimp that evening.

Caroline liked the feeling of her friend's strong hands on her back. She started to come back to life.

A young boy from the shack-like hotel where Caroline was staying walked over to them. In Spanish, he said, "This note came for Miss Caroline Colt." Since Caroline appeared to be passed out, he handed the note to Paco/Pablo, who gently nudged her.

She stirred and sat up. He handed her the note. She read it, then read it again. Her eyes lit up with a hopeful brightness her friend had never seen before. Caroline generally showed up on his beach only when she wanted to be morose.

Caroline...I just wanted to send you a special note of thanks for your work on Bogey Island, which was exemplary. I know how disappointed you were to not keep Red Boyle safe. I was perhaps remiss in assigning that near-impossible task to you. Please accept my apology. I have every confidence that you will be able to solve his murder. Please remember what the great

detective Hercule Poirot said, "It is much easier to catch a murderer than to prevent a murder."
Your friend, Roy Wilkinson, Phoenix, Arizona, 14 April 1963

Judge Wilkinson's note may have saved Caroline's life that afternoon. She was spiraling down day by day at Puerto Penasco. Sometimes all a troubled person needs is to have a successful person treat them as successful too, or at least as having the potential to succeed.

While reading Tom's adventures, you may read things about The Judge that make you question whether he was a good man. Fair enough. At times Tom questioned it, too. But we should always remember what he did for Tom's sister, at a desperate time in her life. He reached her, when her own family couldn't.

He saw potential for greatness in her, whether she did or not. He was the shrewdest man Tom ever met. He tried to profit from every waking moment on this earth. He sought out only those people who could help him profit. Who knows, he may even have consummated business deals in his sleep. He didn't waste time on anyone who didn't have potential to be a winner.

Caroline carried the Judge's note with her, in a compartment in her wallet, for years, until the paper literally disintegrated.

In a surprisingly revitalized voice, Caroline said to her companion, "I came down here so bummed out, but you know, my brother always says there's no such thing as defeat, because there's always another tournament next week. He's right! And we're not defeated. We're just missing something. We can still figure out who killed Red Boyle. We just need a fresh start. Like the start of a new tournament. You get this, what I'm saying, Paco?"

He responded with something like "Ummmmmm."

"Thanks for talking me through this. I so enjoy our conversations. You're a wonderful friend, Paco, the best. But I gotta go. Gotta catch a murderer!"

She got up and half-ran back to her hotel. She was not up to running. She was out of breath by the time she got there. She threw up one last time as she reached the front door, one last time for that trip to Mexico at least.

He knew she would return to him and to the sea. She always did. And he understood more English than he admitted to Caroline.

"Eeet ees Pablo," he said, then muttered to himself in Spanish, "Karen, why cannot you remember my name?"

Caroline, packing her small duffel bag, wondered, why does silly Paco call me Karen? *But I think sometimes it might be great fun to be someone else.*

As she drove back to Phoenix—much too fast, singing merrily with the car radio, she considered this question?

How did the Judge know I was in Mexico?

The answer was, if you were in Judge Roy Wilkinson's sphere of influence, he knew everything important, for good or bad, that was going on in your life. He always kept a watchful eye on you. This wasn't simply altruism on his part, it served his own interests well.

***

Tom Colt Continues Our Story:

The Curious Case of the Too-Convenient Condom

Our failures on Bogey Island bled into my golf game when we got back to Phoenix. I played horribly in the two tournaments after we returned, in Texas, finishing nearly last in the field of players. I didn't even win enough money to cover my travel expenses.

I felt especially bad for Caroline, though. She was so excited about our detective agency. Our first big case together, the man we were hired to protect is murdered right in front of us and we have no clue (literally!) about who did it.

When we landed at Sky Harbor Airport, Caroline split for Mexico. She liked to hang out on the beach near Rocky Point (Puerto Penasco) when she got fed up with her life in Phoenix. I was concerned she was going to lapse into her gloomy little word of self-loathing.

My golf got so bad I even shot poor scores in the practice rounds, when there was no competitive pressure. I began to think I should quit tournament play for a few months until my game improved. Sometimes a break from the stress of competition can help a golf pro. There's a golfer's lament that goes, spoken as he hurries away from the site of a tournament where he failed miserably, "See 'ya in the fall if I see 'ya at all."

But as life often does, mine turned up quickly. Det. Mathers asked me to help him solve a murder that had taken place in a mid-town hotel frequented by business travelers. An executive, Dale Bing, 58 years of age, employed by an electronics firm in LA, was found in his room with his throat slashed. Blood was everywhere. It was a sickening sight.

The man was naked, lying on the bed with the covers askew. In the bathroom was an unopened box of condoms. He was balding, overweight, didn't seem like the lothario type.

By the bedside was a glass with his dentures soaking in a bluish solution. Next to it was the Holy Bible, not the one provided in hotel rooms but a personal Bible. The police officer who had arrived at the scene had formed an opinion that the guy had picked up a woman, the wrong woman, in a bar and she killed and robbed him. No money was found in his wallet, suitcase or briefcase.

Mathers and I weren't so sure about the officer's swift conclusion. Why does a guy don his jammies and soak his dentures, take out his Bible to read, then admit a woman to his room who proceeds to kill him?

What struck me was the image of the woman, probably a young one, looking over to the nightstand during intercourse and seeing the guy's teeth in a jar.

The next morning, I drove down to the downtown Phoenix public library to do a little research. I always loved that place. After my father disappeared in the War, the library became my refuge, books my release from the despair and loneliness that I felt from being a teenage boy losing my dad. I probably read 10 books a month for several years after his disappearance—and a lot of them were not about golf.

This was the same period Caroline found solace in drugs, prescription and illegal. The Public Library may have saved my life.

The library had the back issues of the *LA Times* newspaper on microfilm. You placed the film in this clunky viewing machine and tried your best to get the image of the newspaper page in focus.

After two hours of fruitless searching, I found an article about the murder victim from two years earlier. It was a profile on his career in the business section of the paper. His father had lost everything in the Great Depression, when the bank that held his savings had failed. Our murder victim had grown up with a healthy distrust of banks.

I wondered if he kept a lot of money on his person, a kind of insurance—and a strong motive for murder. In the afternoon I met Mathers back at the scene of the crime. I talked about my idea and Mathers contacted the man's widow, confirming that he did indeed keep $5,000 in large bills in his briefcase, which never left his sight.

Mathers interviewed the hotel General Manager and found out the victim had inquired whether the hotel had safety deposit boxes, which it did not.

After looking around the room again, I didn't think sexual intercourse took place there that night.

The unopened box of condoms decided that for me.

I asked the hotel GM for the keys to a room across the hall from the murder scene. I got the feeling the solution to the crime was in the building somewhere, and I was moving in for a few days to find it.

Next, I walked down to the Western Union office and sent a telegram to Caroline in Puerto Penasco, Mexico. I needed my sister's help. I had no idea she was already on her way back, raring to go back to work at Colt & Colt Confidential Investigations.

Back at the crime scene, I had noticed the man kept his hotel room extremely cold. He wouldn't have slept naked. If he were there for a tryst, where were the nightclothes he discarded when his paramour arrived that night?

I surmised he had been killed, then the killer removed his bloody nightclothes. It was obvious to me that the crime scene was staged to look like his female visitor killed him. There were no pajamas in the room, anywhere.

And the bedside Bible was also key. Prostitutes and clients seldom read The Good Book together in bed.

Someone gained admittance to the room when the guy was sleeping, cut his throat, removed the bloody pajamas and robbed him.

Creative speculation, but of course I had zero proof.

If a night of passion were planned, he would have opened the box of condoms, and had one or more at his bedside, probably in the drawer in the bedside table. A careful guy has the protection ready to go when needed, not off in the bathroom, had this been an authentic murder of a client by a hooker, let's say.

The crime scene investigation team reported no signs of semen stains in the bed. We found a receipt from a nearby pharmacy. All he bought was anta-acid tablets, the newspaper, and some chocolate chip cookies. No condoms. That brand of condom was sold at the little store in the hotel, however.

When Caroline returned from Mexico, she was upbeat again, which surprised me. "Paco always cheers me up," she told me simply. Her eyes were bright and clear, like her beach vacation agreed with her. *Must be the healthy salt air*, I thought.

The next morning, I told Mathers to meet us in the hotel lobby, which as usual was bustling with activity.

Crime solving involves imagination. You must see the criminal and the victim's interactions in your mind, hear their conversations even. I always believed having Caroline and I both working on a case gave us an advantage. Like training two strong flashlights on a dark mystery. The two lights could explore a wider area than just one. Also, being twins, we thought a lot alike, but also quite differently, if that makes any sense.

We quickly hatched a plan to catch the killer. We told Mathers, who said it sounded a bit too *Hardy Boys* for his taste, but reluctantly agreed to give it a try.

Mathers wore his police uniform that day, which he seldom did. I walked up to him in the lobby. "Det. Mathers," I said in a loud voice, to get his attention but mostly the others in the lobby. I told him that I was staying across the hall from the crime scene and had heard what happened that night.

Mathers hurried over to me.

"I can identify the man who came out of the room, he had some distinctive features," I said.

Mathers did his best to look excited, "Outstanding. Come on down to the station tomorrow at 9AM and make a statement. We have sketch artists. Maybe we can get a good idea what the guy looks like."

Notice we both said, the man and the guy. Our guess was that there was no angry girlfriend or psychotic hooker involved.

Using the back stairs rather than the elevator, the two of us went up to my room and waited.

Caroline sat in the lobby looking at the people coming and going, hoping the killer had heard the conversation.

Mathers and I waited, nothing happened. We repeated the scene in the lobby at 2-hour intervals. Finally, at 11PM the door lock clicked and in stepped the Night Desk Clerk. He padded softly toward the bed.

Mathers and I were waiting in the dark in chairs in the corner of the room. Mathers switched on the light like Bogart in a film noir. I thought it was very cool.

"Looking for something, slick?" Mathers asked, with his .38 revolver in his hand.

Our vicious murder suspect was a non-descript, skinny fellow with a terrible pock-marked complexion and the darting eyes of a frightened rat.

The man dashed for the door, then thought better of it. "I...ah..." he stuttered with futility at coming up with a plausible explanation of why he was in the room at night. Finally he said, "Sorry, sir. Came to the wrong room."

Mathers got up from the chair, made his revolver more visible. The perp gave up.

Cuffed and searched, the man had a wickedly sharp straightedge razor, the murder weapon. He was fully prepared to cut my throat that night, too. Katrina's point about the dangers inherent in my PI business finally hit home. I had trouble breathing when I saw the gleaming blade.

The Chief of Police, James Flannery, was astounded that Mathers (and Colt & Colt) had solved the crime in less than 48 hours. He offered to get us both fast-tracked into the police academy. I politely declined. Caroline thought about it awhile before she declined.

Two nights later, Mathers took us out for a celebratory prime rib dinner at the famed Red Dog Restaurant in Scottsdale. With the first of many glasses of beer, he offered a toast to us, "From now on, I'll bring you to the crime scene, you work the case, and I'll be at the Club playing golf if you need me to consult. How's that sound?"

A news story about our solving the crime had appeared in the *Arizona Republic* newspaper. Caroline and I were treated like minor celebrities. We didn't even have to wait for a table on this busy Friday night.

Life is good again, I was thinking.

Caroline interrupted my reverie, as usual. "Couple of questions, Sherlock. You addressed Ed in the lobby by name, Det. Mathers. How would a hotel guest already know his name, without being introduced?"

"Good question." I smiled. "Said hotel guest would not know his name."

"And then you announced the suspect had distinctive features? How did you know that?"

"Because we all have distinctive features."

"The suspect had a scar just above his left eye," Mathers contributed.

Mathers smiled at me with what looked like the tremendous pride a teacher has with his best student.

Caroline reluctantly ceased her cross-examination of me.

Mathers contributed, "As soon as we figured out it had to be someone with a key to the room, like an employee's passkey, this was an easy one to solve."

***

Brooks Benton Continues Our Story:

Mathers hoped his private detective buddies had their confidence back after solving this relatively simple hotel room murder. The real challenge lay ahead, and he would need their help.

Red Boyle's killer was much smarter than the average criminal. The guy they had just nailed was as amateurish as they come.

In Boyle's case, the crime had been meticulously planned and flawlessly executed.

Chapter Twenty-Three

Tom Continues Our Story:

Our good work with Mathers pumped me up. My golf game, from tee to green, immediately returned to fine form. My putting continued to be dismal, though, but good enough for me to earn a 4th place finish in the Heartland Celebrity Pro-Am in Des Moines, Iowa. They had to import the celebrities to the event from California of course.

I was hitting my tee shots long and straight, surprisingly straight for me, who relied more on power than accuracy. My iron shots were also on target. If I could just solve the mystery of the putting stroke.

So much of success stems from belief in yourself. Our dismal failure on Bogey Island shook the confidence of all of us. Caroline and I particularly, but I'm sure Mathers, too. That shouldn't have been a difficult puzzle to solve. We just missed something…

Independently, each of believed we would put the puzzle together, sooner than later, and certainly yet in 1963.

The Summer of '63 was just around the corner. I was excited about my pro golf career again. My game was razor-sharp heading into the important events coming up on the tour schedule. I was certain I was going to win another tournament—and soon.

Unfortunately, I missed the US Open, our National Championship, this year at Brookline, Massachusetts. Because I got so involved in detective work with Mathers, I forgot to send my entry form in on time.

I explained to my caddie Sheboygan, who was looking forward to the East Coast seafood on our trip to Massachusetts: "Even the greatest detectives miss the occasional detail."

"And Tom Colt does, too, evidently."

Sheboygan looked away and grinned. I regretted my efforts to build up my once-forlorn caddy's self-confidence. May have created a monster.

The US Open winner at Brookline was Julius Boros, at 43 one of the oldest winners of the event. The golfers had to cope with extremely high winds, gusts up to 50mph, and as a result the winning score was 9 over par, the highest (worst) winning score in many years. After the fourth round, Boros was tied with Jacky Cupit and Arnold Palmer. In the playoff for the title the next day, Boros shot a smooth 70 and won easily.

Perhaps my not sending in the entry form was a blessing. I hit the ball very high with my iron shots and as a result do not cope with windy conditions very well.

With that timely rationalization I feel much better about being such a bonehead I forgot to send in my entry form.

***

Autumn Amber decided to sign up for golf lessons. She requested me to be her instructor.

In just the few months since we returned from Bogey Island, Autumn returning as a wealthy young woman, she had acquired a star quality, a presence. All the males on the practice range cocked an eye at her as she walked over to where I was waiting with her brand-new bag of First Flight golf clubs. The bag was a pretty rose color, and was as large as the professionals use.

Strange stuff, money is, especially Big Money. Her inheritance from sugar daddy Red Boyle had funded her starring role in a movie—which was rumored to be excellent, a breakout performance from a new Star. I noticed she had started to carry herself with great confidence, not simply an awareness of her arresting beauty, but an awareness that she was somebody important now. She seemed to greet me with a touch of superiority. She was no longer a young girl in the shadow of her show-biz parents. She was a grown woman ready to take on the world.

On Bogey Island, Autumn was this nice, almost shy girl. Now she acted like I should call her Your Highness.

I wondered how having Big Money might affect Tom Colt. Damn, I wished I could find out, and soon.

Red Boyle had given her another inheritance, it turned out. Several years later, when her movie career sputtered as they often do, the 8MM 'audition film' he shot of Autumn found its way to the desk of the head of production at a Hollywood studio, Sandstorm Films (the studio's capital came from a Middle Eastern investor). Autumn had a 3-picture deal with the studio a month later.

While Autumn was warming up for the golf lesson with some stretching exercises her instructor suggested, Kat Stern walked up to us. I hadn't seen much of Kat since we got back from Bogey Island. She was playing nearly every event on the ladies' tour, and surprisingly had found herself in a slump, a period of bad play that every pro golfer experiences from time to time, but Kat never had before.

The three of us exchanged greetings and then Kat said, "I think I'm the one who needs a lesson," she said glumly. "But I hear you are headed out of town on Tuesday.

"I got a last-minute invite to the Western Open in Chicago. Two guys withdrew."

That seemed to make her even more glum. Did she miss me? I certainly missed her.

"Good luck up there," Kat said. "I'll let you get back to your pupil." She drifted off.

My approach to teaching beginners was to get them comfortable with making contact with the golf ball—positive reinforcement. I had them make short, ¼ length swings rather than a full backswing, which could lead to missing the ball—negative reinforcement.

"I didn't know what to wear for this," she said.

She had on a short turquoise skirt, black top and a visor that looked very golf pro-like on her head, with all the tumbling waves of caramel-colored hair.

"You look great," I said. "Wear loose fitting shirts, sweaters and jackets in the colder months. Tight clothes restrict your backswing."

She had just purchased a full membership at The Club and seemed desperate to fit in. "Thanks for the fashion advice--"

From the dreamy looks of the guys watching her, she had nothing to worry about.

"—but from what I've heard in the locker room, you're more well-known for undressing women."

"Malicious gossip, that. Not too long ago a young lady described me as The Perfect Gentleman."

Autumn took a few more swings. She was batting about .300 so far. We would not have to return to the pro shop for more practice balls anytime soon.

"Who said that?"

"MoniQue Jones."

"Oh, gad, Miss Goody Two-Shoes. I should have guessed. We dated the same football player senior year. He told me they were on a date at the drive-in by the Salt River. Things got romantic, a little back seat bingo. He reached inside her blouse for a quick feel and she slapped him--hard. I mean, what did she expect. That's what boys want. What a Goody Two-Shoes that chick is."

I got the mental image of MoniQue tearing open her shirt that day at her house, the lovely breasts tumbling into full view. I softly chuckled.

"What's so funny?"

"Nothin'. What was the movie?"

"*The High and the Mighty* with John Wayne and Robert Stack. I liked that one."

"Me too." I whistled the catchy theme song from the movie. She joined in. We laughed. Our whistling was not in tune with the tune. Maybe Autumn Amber wasn't really a self-centered rich-bitch actress. Someone just told her to act that way. Her agent or her mom, I guessed.

"Can I take a full swing yet? This is like training wheels...I'm a grown woman."

"Just get used to the swing..."

"Fine," she said glumly. This was my day for making pretty girls glum. I didn't mean to.

I may have mentioned that the Club Members often felt compelled to share their most intimate secrets with me, their golf instructor. I never understood why. It's not like the Club made me sign a non-disclosure agreement.

"I shouldn't tell you this, Tom, but you are such a good listener all the girls say...my parents still think I'm a virgin. Can you believe that? Maybe I am a good actress."

Autumn Amber grinned. I smiled back. This lesson was possibly going to be fun.

I let her graduate to ½ swings.

She stopped for a moment and said, "I've already forgiven Mr. Boyle for taking that nudie movie of me. He was right, my body is part of my Art."

"Yes, Art," I readily agreed.

"Wait...did you see that film when he showed it at Bogey Island?"

"Yes, I did," I replied perhaps too enthusiastically.

"Now I feel sooooo embarrassed."

"Don't be. In college I majored in Art Appreciation. I certainly appreciated you."

She laughed.

"If he hadn't left me that money, I don't know what my family would have done. Mom lost her job with that production company in LA, you know."

"No, I didn't. Sorry to hear that. Where did she work?"

"Pacific Sunset Pictures."

"I heard Red kept threatening to cut you out of the Will, not fund your movie."

"I was kinda surprised when they read Mr. Boyle's Will that day. I guess Mr. Boyle really did love me."

I reflected that the word Love has so many different meanings.

"It's funny. My mom is jealous of me. She was an actress a long time ago. Was in exactly one movie. Not much of a career. You know, I already have 17 acting credits."

She hit several little shots with her 5-iron. I noticed her sunny attitude was turning dark after her mention of Red and The Money. I couldn't tell you why.

"Enough of these boring little swings. I'm a movie star now. I can do what I want. I don't have to listen to you."

At least she didn't say, I don't have to listen to You, Boy, the Hired Help.

She swung the club as far back as it could go—and she was quite flexible. But she lost her balance and fell on her sweet little turquoise tush.

I reached over and helped her back up. "That's your First Lesson: the little white golf ball doesn't give a shit that you're a movie star."

"You are so mean to me!" she said. Then a wicked smile appeared. "I think you're just grouchy because you and your squeeze Katrina broke up on Bogey Island and you're still in love with each other."

I found myself struck silent for a moment. "How can you know that?"

"It was written all over your faces when she stopped by to say hello."

Many times in these sessions on the practice range at Valley Vista CC, I wondered exactly who was giving lessons to whom.

She turned and I saw there was mud on her backside. She noticed it too. "If you laugh at me, I will never take a lesson from you again!" She raised her voice to a perfect pitch for a movie scene.

"Very dramatic. And the Academy Award goes to—"

"Just shut up. I have had quite enough of you." She started back toward the clubhouse.

"See you back here next Wednesday," I casually replied.

"Fine," she announced to the entire practice range. "I like this stupid game! You...not so much. Not at all, really. Don't get any ideas about dating me."

Darlin', you have absolutely no worries there, I thought.

I carried her golf bag back to the clubhouse. I was certain that down the years many young men would be doing the heavy lifting for Autumn Amber, lovely, tempestuous, stuck-up and irresistible movie star.

So, is Big Money good stuff, or bad stuff? In my 28th year, I wasn't sure.

Chapter Twenty-Four

The '63 Western Open was played at Beverly Country Club in Chicago, Illinois. It was a club that had hosted many premier golf events. The Western was one of the prestigious tournaments on the summer swing of the pro golf tour. The best players usually included that event on their playing schedule.

And this year, so did Tom Colt.

I flew into Chicago on the Monday before the tournament, which began on Thursday. I was so confident in my game I thought I had a chance to win—yes, win—and I wanted to familiarize myself with the course and the place I would be staying.

Fans don't realize that it is difficult for a traveling golf pro to stay in a new hotel every week. We all get used to the comforts of home, the familiar sights and sounds and our familiar comfortable bed. But on the golf tour, your environment is completely different each week. Some pros have trouble sleeping. Some get stomach upset from the unfamiliar--or bad--food. And frequent travelers are of course susceptible to the viruses that other travelers bring with them.

On the morning of my Tuesday practice round I warmed up on the practice range and was next to the newly-crowned US Open Champion, Julius Boros. He was 43 years old, and his golf swing certainly stood the test of time.

I could have watched Julius Boros swing all day. One of his nicknames among his fellow pros was, The Old Smoothie. His motto was *Swing Easy, Hit Hard.* Seems like a simple enough concept to implement. It is, when I'm teaching amateurs on a quiet driving range. Different though, for a pro golfer in the heat of tournament battle, with his livelihood on the line and thousands of spectators watching.

I was never referred to as The Young Smoothie.

Brooks Benton Continues Our Story:

Tom played well that week, but not great. He was hovering at 20th place as the third round began when who should appear as Tom warmed up on the practice range but Katrina Stern.

He was thrilled to see her. She was thrilled to see how thrilled he was. He walked over to the gallery rope that separated competitors from spectators, stepped under it and they gave each other an enthusiastic hug.

"I missed this," she said happily. "I missed us."

She told him she was on her way to a tournament in Milwaukee, 90 miles north of Chicago. She flew into Chicago and rented a car to drive up there.

They shared something that neither of them at the time could identify. We know it now as a bond that stood the test of time, 40+ years, and was sustained through all the changes, challenges and tribulations that occur in a person's life over that time.

But then, in the summer of '63, it was just a strong feeling of being happy to be together, doing anything together.

"I found myself thinking about you when I'm playing. You're my rock.   I wanted to talk to you about something...it's important."

"Fire away..."

Tom was not one of those players who needed absolute concentration during the pre-round warmup. Truth was, he thought practicing was a bore. The joy of golf for him was the challenge you face when you get out on the course. He looked at his watch.

"Can we talk after the round? I tee off in 5 minutes."

"Yes. It'll be fun to see you play a tournament."

Tom had a wry grin. "Hope it's fun for both of us. This is a tough course and the wind is supposed to be up today."

Tom shot a splendid 70, two under par. Kat was impressed with how long and straight he was hitting his tee shots. And perhaps inspired by Kat, he made some key putts for birdies. His good play attracted lots of fans—spectators can hear the cheers for players who did something spectacular.

Tom finished his round and signed his scorecard. Walking back to where the spectators were, including Katrina, Tom was mobbed by fans wanting an autograph. Kat knew that the fans, particularly females, were drawn to Tom, but it startled her just how popular he was on the golf circuit. Kat got at most 5 requests for autographs when she finished a tournament round. Even when she won the tournament.

The leaders after round three were legendary Sam Snead, at 51 trying to be the oldest golfer to win a PGA tournament, and legend-to-be Arnold Palmer, tied at 207 strokes for three rounds. Tom was tied for 16th. In the third round, Snead shot a fine 68 and Palmer bettered him by one with a 67, capped off with sinking an 18-ft. birdie putt on the 18th hole, which got the crowd buzzing with excitement.

Kat waited patiently to get Tom by himself so she could ask the important question: *If she gave up her objections about his dangerous detective work, did he think they still had a chance to be couple?*

Out the corner of her ever-sharp eyes, Kat saw a glimpse of a woman with frizzy red hair. The woman looked oddly familiar. As unlikely as it was, she could have sworn the woman was Yuma Boyle. The phantom from Bogey Island.

Kat left Tom to his admirers and started to follow the woman, but she had disappeared into the throng of spectators. Katrina shook it off, thinking she was seeing things. She returned to Tom, still signing autographs for a crowd of about 20.

Three young women, perhaps late 20s, were next in line for his autograph. They crowded Katrina out of the way.

One of the girls pulled up her shirt, revealing a tight, firm belly.

"Please sign here," she said with the giggle of a younger girl than she was. He complied with her request, just above her belly button.

"Sorry," Tom said to Katrina. "It's part of my job."

"I know. I have to get up to Milwaukee. See you back in Phoenix."

Katrina shook her head, both irritated and amused. *At least he didn't autograph her tits,* she thought.

She didn't get an answer to her question, but then maybe that was an answer in itself.

Later, walking to his car, Tom noticed something in his back pocket. He pulled it out. It was a Polaroid picture of the Vonessens with a red-haired woman. It looked to have been taken on the patio at the Bogey Island resort. Who was the woman? Tom wondered. Yuma Boyle? He scanned the spectators around him. No one resembling her. Was she here? Why? What is going on?

Katrina didn't tell Tom she was on her way to Lake Geneva, Wisconsin to stay with Stan Barker and his family for a week—and play in a tournament in Milwaukee. Why did Kat stop to see Tom? She had no idea. She hadn't lied when she said, "I missed us." She just wasn't sure what 'US' was.

Her confusion grew when she had a lovely time with Stan and his friendly, fun, huge, welcoming German family. Each one of them was a golf fanatic. Having a real pro golfer, a tournament winner, visit them was akin to royalty arriving. She was showered with so much attention and love it wore her out. The Barkers were the kind of large family she had always dreamed of having. But World War II and all its horrors crushed that dream. She had no idea where most of her family members were.

One afternoon she walked by herself down the pebbly path to the shoreline of the lake, to contemplate her complex romantic life. She saw her reflection in the water. The reflection had that familiar Katrina Stern frowny face.

***

In the fourth round of the Western Open, both Snead and Palmer struggled, shooting 75 and 73 respectively. Young Jack Nicklaus with a fine 66 and US Open champ Boros with a 67, tied Palmer at 280 strokes. Snead finished fourth after 4 rounds.

Kat's unexpected visit inspired Tom to more good play. He shot another 70 and finished in 12th place for four rounds.

In the playoff for the title the next day, Palmer took the lead with a 3 under 33 on the front nine, then held off Nicklaus and Boros to win, finishing with a 70. Boros shot 71 and Nicklaus 73. Matters were settled when Boros and Nicklaus both double-bogied the 17th hole.

Tom Colt's confidence in his golf game continued to build. And it was a blast for him to have Katrina there to see him play well in competition. He played that third round for her, only for her.

***

Meanwhile, back in Scottsdale, Arizona, Julia Wilkinson continued to tell her father, The Judge, the story of how Tom saved her from being arrested by 'inept little pipsqueak island cops'. And their romance might have been rekindled. Judge Wilkinson was delighted. His persistent hope was that Tom and his daughter could be together. Tom was incredibly good for her, he thought. He was the kind of solid, determined young man the Judge himself was when he was starting out.

But was Julia good for Tom? The Judge didn't particularly care. He was of the age, 64, when you start to worry about what happens to your family after you're gone. Julia's welfare was paramount in his thinking. Tom, after all, recovered just fine from the night she shot him.

The Judge's admiration for his daughter was such that he thought any young man would be privileged to have Julia make his life miserable.

But why was Julia declaring them a couple? Tom certainly would have been surprised had he known.

***

In Wisconsin, Katrina and Stan were getting closer. His company was the sponsor of a small tournament, the Catholic Charities Ladies Pro-AM, a two-day affair at his beloved Blue Mound Golf and CC. Katrina played in it and won easily. First prize was only $800, but the winner also received a year's worth of the sausage of her choice.

For Kat, victory in golf was more than achievement, it was a portent. She wondered if, indeed, she and Stan were destined to be together. To Kat, golf was life.

On the drive back to his family's estate, Stan, calculating fellow that he was, got in a few more digs, indirectly, about Tom.

"I don't like Valley Vista Country Club. I only joined it because right now it's THE CLUB to belong to. The golf course is much too hard for business networking. For people like me, golf is about making contacts, building relationships during the round. Valley Vista is so damned hard it interrupts the flow of commerce. One round I hit three shots into the water on that long par-3 on the back nine, number 13. I got so mad I couldn't close the deal I was trying to make with my playing partners. Blue Mound is superior, a fine, relaxed place to conduct dignified business. Way more beautiful—an exquisite venue, really--and it has history, tradition. The 1933 PGA Championship was played here."

Kat tended to not fall in love with individual golf courses. They were after all the primary obstacle to her goal—victory.

The jab at Tom was on target because Tom adored everything about Valley Vista. He was the one who arranged for Katrina to represent Valley Vista on the ladies tour.

Katrina thought about the last time she and Tom played there: he drilled a 5-iron shot within two feet of the hole on that 13th hole--hitting into a 25mph wind.

When she and Tom (and Stan) returned to Phoenix, Kat and Tom seamlessly resumed their friendship, playing golf frequently and practicing together on the driving range. This should have tipped both off that they would stay friends forever. They had forged an incredibly strong bond.

In the midsummer of 1963 Katrina was wavering between Tom and Stan. She had lots of fun with Tom, including their great connection on the golf course. But with Stan, there seemed to be something deeper. Maybe. Possibly. Perhaps. Katrina, who was so resolute, so determined with her golf career, when it came to matters of the heart became a bundle of confusion.

***

When Tom returned to Phoenix, he called Mathers to let him know about the Yuma Boyle photo at the Western Open. He sent a courier over to Mathers' office with the Polaroid that Yuma apparently put in his pocket.

Neither Tom, Mathers nor Caroline thought it made any sense for Yuma to take that chance, of coming to the tournament and obviously trying to be spotted. *What did she gain by that?* was the question each of them asked and could not answer. Was she so confident that it was a 'Catch Me If You Can' kind of taunt?

Caroline tossed an interesting idea out, that Yuma wanted us to make sure we know she existed. She wasn't some kind of phantom.

"I can see that," Mathers responded. "But why?"

***

Tom quietly continued the investigation into Red Boyle's murder by talking to everyone he could at Valley Vista CC, in the hope that something, anything might be revealed in the relaxed atmosphere of the Club. He knew the guests at Bogey Island had withheld information from Weatherford and his two cops—a polite way of saying, they lied. It was chilling, though, to realize that one of the people he gave lessons to at the Club could well be a murderer.

Tom Continues Our Story:

I was giving a golf lesson to my Aunt Felicity on the practice range at Valley Vista. She was a terrible player. One of her problems was she would talk nonstop throughout the process of selecting a club and all the way up to hitting the ball.

That day she wore a super low cut frilly blue blouse that barely constrained her ample cleavage. She was justifiably proud of that cleavage: it was after all the main reason she got so many choice movie roles.

Felicity had been a busy and popular B-movie star in her 20s and 30s, usually playing beautiful and well-endowed Indian maidens in Westerns. She took advantage of what was evidently a critical shortage of authentic Indians to play those roles.

After her career waned, she kept the Indian image. She wore enough Indian jewelry to keep several families of silversmiths in Navaho County, Arizona, prospering. Her skin was a burnt copper color, like those pre-mummified ladies you see lounging by the pools in Palm Springs. Felicity wore her long dark hair braided in the back.

At least I got her to wear proper golf shoes with spikes instead of moccasins.

Felicity had lots of social contacts and heard lots of chatter. She maintains that she is 'psychic'. Her psychic powers somehow seem to work.

I can't help needling her, though. Some say I'm a bit of a rascal.

I asked her, "Are you a real person or a movie character?"

"Scoff as you will, nephew, but this character made me a millionaire before I was 35. I knew early on I didn't want to be Florence Plotnik, I wanted to be Felicity Greyhawk. I created her, just like a kid from Iowa named Duke Morrison created mighty John Wayne. Archie Leach from England became known to you as Cary Grant. Any more questions?"

"You are a font of cinema knowledge, Aunt Felicity."

"I read in *Variety* that young Autumn Amber is starring in a film. What a hoot. She was in one of my westerns when she was a little kid. Her mother had a bit part in a movie I starred in later on, a crime show." She added with an affected accent, "Or Film Noir as we say in the BIZ."

"There was an Indian maiden with a large bust in a film noir?"

"NOOOO, funny boy, I'm a versatile actress who can play any part."

"Play any part," I repeated to myself. This seemed significant, but I had no idea why.

Felicity took another chop at the poor golf ball. "Dammit all…how much longer until I get good at this game?"

No comment, was the expression on my face. Reading that perfectly, Felicity's mean streak surfaced.

"I heard your mattress pal Katrina is going at it hot and heavy with bratwurst baron Stan Barker."

I took stock of how I felt about that news, which I had already suspected. I wasn't certain. And when I was in doubt, my fallback position was: "Perhaps that's for the best."

I didn't really believe that, in this instance.

"So, my headstrong young nephew, are going to listen to me now, when I get a vision. Remember I said you were in danger and would not play in the US Open last year. I have a gift."

Two of them, actually, I thought, staring at her jiggly breasts as she chopped away at the golf balls I set on the practice tee for her. "Absolutely, I'll listen."

She hit about a foot behind the next ball. The divot went 10 yards, the ball only five. "Shit, shit, shit. This game is too hard. Am I always going to be a hopeless hacker?"

I had no appreciable psychic abilities I was aware of but could predict a big "Yes" to that question. But my job was to encourage the unfortunate, hopeless amateurs, so I said, "Hang in there, kid, you'll get there. And there's no cussing at Valley Vista Country Club. Golf is a game for ladies and gentlemen."

"Mostly bitchy ladies. In the locker room, one of the 'ladies' was joking about the absurd names the late Red Boyle gave his kids, Fredonia, Patagonia, Chandler. She wondered if he'd had another kid, would she be named Yuma."

I stopped daydreaming about the 2" thick porterhouse steak in my refrigerator I was going to grill that night and snapped to attention. "What was the lady's name? This is important. Older lady? Younger?"

"I didn't recognize her voice. Sorry."

"If you think of it, please tell me."

"Don't worry. It will come to me…" She put her golf club down and pointed to her skull. "Everything is in here."

I wanted to say, "Oh, good grief." But didn't. On the Boyle Murder Case, I needed all the help I could get, from wherever or whomever I could get it.

Chapter Twenty-Five

As the summer of 1963 rolled on, Caroline got very involved in her classes as Boyle Academy of the Performing Arts. I heard through the grapevine that Caroline was the star of the theater section at the Academy and was thriving being around other creative people. She didn't talk about it much at home, though. That would've required admitting that our mom had chosen the perfect birthday gift for her, though being a great detective, she suspected I was the one who came up with the idea.

I split my time between giving lessons at Valley Vista CC and playing in several more tournaments. I settled back into my usual routine of hitting the ball great from tee to green but putting poorly. The geniuses at *Gentleman Golfer Monthly* said my putting woes were all in my head. Dang, I would have never figured that out on my own.

Det. Mathers found himself without a lot to do that summer. For some reason, the number of homicides had dropped off. We had a blistering heat wave that sent the temperatures soaring past 115 degrees most days. It was too hot for the bad guys to get motivated to go out and kill someone. They stayed inside, sat on the couch in their underwear and sucked down cold beer, dreaming of being criminals in a cooler climate, Oregon perhaps.

The lack of a summer crime wave was not sufficient for Mathers to be concerned about his job security. He knew the crime rate in Phoenix would return to normal sooner than later.

We hadn't given up our efforts to solve Red Boyle's murder, by any means. We met once a week, on Friday afternoons, at the Colt & Colt Confidential offices at Valley Vista CC, spread out all the sheets of notes with clues and tried to come up with a solution. Or at least a working hypothesis.

One afternoon Mathers even took us to the Phoenix Zoo to walk around and discuss the case while looking at all the animals, as they looked at us.

Caroline remarked as we strolled through the primate house, "I get it, it's like Inspector Weatherford always says, Small narrow spaces lead to small narrow thinking'."

"Ha! Ha!, Caroline," Mathers remarked tersely, still smarting from his British counterpart thinking he had invented that axiom.

By August, the Boyle Murder was starting to look like it would be a Cold Case, an unsolved mystery that is eventually forgotten, the evidence stored in a musty, dusty warehouse.

If our meetings and investigative work regarding the murder seem incoherent, rambling and ineffective to you— well, they did to us, too.

But one of those Fridays in our offices, we began to form a workable idea...

We all agreed that Fredonia Boyle seemed the likeliest suspect. She was nasty enough to do the crime, and crafty enough to plan it so she wouldn't be implicated. We thought how she did it was to be seen going into the card room with her brother the night of the murder, then slipping out the service door that the staff used to bring food and drinks to the card players.

No one saw Fredonia leave the card room through the main door until well after the murder. Fredonia had the strongest motive(s), her desperate need for money coupled with her hatred of her father.

But we also had the obvious suspect, the elusive Yuma Boyle. The authorities had no luck whatsoever locating her, in California or Arizona. Why she taunted us by flying to Chicago and appearing at the Western Open, was the mystery within the mystery. How would she even know I was playing in the event? I received a last-minute invite.

We sat in silence for a good ten minutes, each of us trying to envision how the crime might have been done. Finally, Caroline stood up and said, "Guys...Fredonia is a cold bitch, but also an arrogant one. She taunted us at the Western Open because Yuma Boyle doesn't exist...Fredonia created the Yuma Boyle persona, killed her father, and made it appear Yuma did it."

More silence in the room...Mathers' mind was whirring like the overhead fan in our office on this hot day.

Mathers stood up. "Bless you, Caroline Colt. I think you have solved this."

I'd like to tell you we were so excited, we all jumped up and down with joy. But we knew there was the matter of proving Caroline's theory...no easy task. Mathers went back to the station house and convened a small team of detectives to pursue Caroline's idea.

Brooks Benton Continues Our Story:

In May, Officer Rudy W. had transferred out of the homicide division, still having trouble dealing with the tragedy of the Lisa Luck Murder. The evil on display with every homicide was more than he could deal with. But he asked to transfer back in after Red Boyle was killed. He regretted not taking Boyle's concerns for his safety more seriously.

Rudy suggested to Mathers that he enlist the aid of none other than local 'crime figure' Marco Greene to gather more information on the Boyles. Greene had done business with them--and also had the best network of informants in the Southwest—far better than Phoenix PD.

Though Mathers loathed Greene, he saw the merits of Rudy's suggestion. He asked Greene to join him for a friendly game of golf at Valley Vista CC.

Greene, The Merry Mobster, was an enigma to Mathers, who did not like enigmas—his job being to seek clarity. At Easter season, Marco bought toys for poor children in south Phoenix, and on the west side in the impoverished neighborhoods, dropping them off at churches. He did this under an anonymous name. Greene said, "Everybody makes a show of giving at Christmas. Poor kids need things all year-round."

He also ran a kind of consumer protection agency aimed at small businesses in lower-class neighborhoods, particularly small grocers, that rip-off poor people. Kind of the inverse of protection money. He "suggested" to them that they lower their prices.

He even took a page from Al Capone's book in Chicago during the Depression and set up a soup kitchen type place in downtown Phoenix (never publicized it, though).

On the other hand, Tom told Mathers that on a visit to Greene's office, he found a framed quote from Al Capone on the wall:

> *Do not mistake my kindness for weakness. I am*
> *kind to everyone, but when someone is unkind to*
> *me, weak is not what you are going to remember*
> *about me.*

Mathers reminded himself of something he learned in church: God often uses imperfect people, flawed people, King David for example, to accomplish good in the world. But

Mathers thought using Marco Greene was a bit of a reach, even for The Almighty.

They say an individual's behavior on the golf course reveals character. Or perhaps reveals that many golfers are strange characters indeed.

Det. Ed Mathers was learning about Marco Greene as they teed off at Valley Vista on a hot, humid August morning. Marco's assaults on the golf ball were not what you would term a 'swing'. More like a fearsome clobbering. There was an element of viciousness in his golf game. Marco had massive hands and well-developed arms. Good hands for strangling, Mathers observed.

But the odd thing that was revealed to Mathers, given that his playing partner was an organized crime figure, was how courteous Greene was on the golf course. A fine gentleman, was the Joyful Gee, a pleasure to play with. Mathers chided himself for having such fun that morning on the links.

Cops weren't supposed to enjoy the company of gangsters. But Greene was one of the most polite, considerate players he had ever seen. He never lost his temper, even when his crude golf swing sent the ball hooking two fairways over. He never cursed either, when the little white ball failed to cooperate, which it often does. He was, surprisingly, always cheerful no matter the results of his golf shots.

Mathers' purpose that day was to pump the well-connected Greene for info about the Boyle murder. Marco had attended the Grand Opening event on Bogey Island. A guy as sharp as Greene must have observed something, Mathers reasoned. Mathers' research had uncovered that Greene and Red Boyle had invested together in several retail development projects. They knew each other well.

On the first tee, Marco sprayed a wild slice off into the trees on the right side of the hole. Mathers hit a crisp 240-yard drive down the middle. Greene remarked: "Heard you took lessons from Tom Colt. He must be a good coach."

Mathers thought, *Greene really does know everything that goes on...*

"I've always been an athlete. Tom just fine tuned my game."

If Tom had been present, he would have rolled his eyes at that one. Det. Mathers was an atrocious duffer when Tom started teaching him. Even tough cops fall prey to vanity.

"So, Mathers, you asked me here to help you solve the Boyle murder. That's rich—you're always trying to put me in the slammer."

"I do indeed. You run prostitutes here like they ran cattle in Arizona 100 years ago."

"My girls combat the terrible loneliness so many men experience and provide physical relief from the stress of everyday living in our complex, urban world. You make me out to be some kind of crude Mafioso. You must realize that some business enterprises are not deemed socially acceptable by the dolts who run the gov-a-mint."

"They're illegal, you mean." Mathers mused that Marco sounded just like Judge Wilkinson on that point.

"I provide a safe working environment. My girls are cleaner than a lot of the country club wives here at Valley Vista."

"That is quite possibly true."

Marco said with soft exasperation, "Why is it so hard for a businessman to gain respect in this town?"

"Back to today's topic. Think of this as your civic duty. Giving back to the community."

Marco, just as ruthless in business as Red Boyle, understood Red Boyle. Marco had some ideas about who might have murdered him. But he faced a moral dilemma: he was reluctant to help the police, ever. *I'll think of it as helping Tom Colt...Mandy would like that, right?*

Mathers then filled in Marco Greene on how they were stymied with the case. He did not share their creative idea of how Fredonia might have committed the murder. Mathers' method was to always acquire far more information than he gave.

Green informed Mathers that one of the Boyle kids had borrowed money from a loan shark on the west side (the shady side) of Phoenix.

"Which kid?"

"The boy, Chandler Boyle."

"I'd heard old Red Boyle clamped down on the kids' spending. They were not happy with that. Chandler got used to a certain lifestyle."

"You can take the boy out of the Country Club, but you can't take the Country Club out of the boy."

"Good way of putting it."

Marco pondered all this for a few minutes as they played their second shots. Marco hit a miracle recovery and got his ball on the green in two. Mathers hit another nice straight shot but found himself 40 feet from the hole.

Marco putted within a foot of the hole. Then tapped the ball into the cup. "The Boyle kids wouldn't have done it. Other than the girl, Fredonia, they're spineless like most rich kids. Look outside the family. One of the many people Red screwed over in business."

"Their alibis check out."

"You and I both know, they told the British Cops a bunch of lies and flimsy stories. I was there. Those coppers were easy to dupe. And they were just going through the motions anyway."

"Agreed…but…"

"Someone who worked for him then. I heard he treated them like shit, too."

"Why off the guy because he's a bear to work for? Seems weak. And Boyle supposedly paid well. Maybe paid them well to shut them up. Employees would come and go. He had high staff turnover. We can't find three of them. They took off to parts unknown."

On the next tee, a Par-3, Greene drilled a 5-iron straight at the flag. It nearly dropped into the cup on the fly. As Mathers prepared to hit his shot, Greene said, "Maybe consider a hybrid motive. Something business, something personal. Taken together, the motive could be strong to send someone over the edge and kill."

"Does this person have a name?"

"That night Red showed us the stag films, I've never seen an angrier individual than Terrence Egglesworth, when the boys in the room all laughed finding out his wife was a stripper. His whole life fell apart that night. The wife, Judy, AKA Bambi Bazooms, just filed for divorce by the way. I know Judy from way back. Smart as hell. The bazooms are used to distract you. I'll bet she got old Terrence to give her a quick out of the marriage because she knows where Terrence was the night of the murder, and it wasn't in her bed."

Mathers lost focus on his swing as he considered what Green said—a damn good suggestion he thought. He hit behind the ball and it only made it halfway to the green.

By the time they reached the 18th hole, a long, uphill difficult Par 5, Mathers was only one shot ahead in the match. Greene decided to try to reach the green in two to catch up. He swung so hard that he lost his balance and hit a sweeping hook that soared over the trees and landed two fairways over. He heard a metallic "smack" sound as the ball hit something solid.

Mathers hit another straight drive, turned to Marco and said, "Any other insight you want to share?"

"The Reverend who was killed was not a man of the cloth. Except the green cloth on the tables at the casinos."

"What?"

"I recognized him from when I worked in Vegas. His name is Bruno Belk. Con man extraordinaire, a brilliant grifter who works—worked—out of Vegas."

Mathers couldn't believe what he just heard—another complex layer to this case had just been revealed. He lost concentration on his second shot and hit it into a stand of eucalyptus trees on the right.

"I guess old Red Boyle was The Pidge this time."

Mathers' eyes sought further explanation.

"His mark, his pigeon for the con. Bruno conned me to the tune of 50k ten years ago."

"So, did you kill him?" Mathers reasonably asked.

"Kill someone over 50k? Detective, you've got to be kidding. A lot more money would have to be involved for me to take lethal action."

From the mix of emotions on Mathers' face, Marco's answer both satisfied and appalled him.

"He played old Boyle like a violin. Bruno ran some of the best confidence games in the good ol' USA over the last ten years. He is—was—to con games what Larry Olivier is to acting. He even ran a good con on me—Marco Greene. I admired his artistry."

Mathers nodded, taking all this in.

Greene said, "I heard Boyle was going to name 'The Rev.' in his Will."

"We heard that too, from one of the Boyle kids. But a new Will was never executed."

"Never found, you mean."

Greene is so smart, Mathers thought. *Shame he's not on our side.*

They saw a Cushman golf cart steaming their way, going at least 7mph. The cart came to a halt at the tee. An irate Carter Vonessen, well-known hothead, held up a golf ball. "You almost hit me in the head. Who's the rude asshole who did this?"

Vonessen saw the menacing figure of Marco Greene walking toward him. Carter suddenly swallowed. Hard.

"That would be me," Marco said.

"Oh. Okay. No problem. Here's your ball, Mr. Greene. Sorry to bother you. Enjoy your round, sir."

Carter hurriedly tossed the ball to Greene, who grabbed it out of the air. Vonessen steamed away in the Cushman, at a speed that seemed faster than the cart could actually go. A change in underwear after he finished golfing that afternoon might be in order for Mr. Carter Vonessen.

Greene dropped his golf ball in the middle of the fairway. "Vonessen interfered with my lie. I get to place the ball here."

Mathers sputtered at this clear rules violation but said nothing. He hit a nice third shot but was still short of the putting surface. Marco hit a shaky second shot but hit a good 7-iron on the green in three. Mathers hit his fourth shot to within 30 feet of the hole. Greene was 23 feet away.

Mathers said, "You are skilled at deduction, Greene. Maybe you should have been a cop."

"Funny you should say that, Ed. Cop was my second career choice. But I've got my dream job."

Mathers chuckled and lined up his putt.

Marco asked Mathers, "How does a low-paid copper get in this posh club."

"Graft and corruption."

"Good man." Marco grinned.

Mathers missed his putt, tapped the ball into the hole for a bogey 6.

"Tom convinced his mentor Judge Wilkinson to give me a dues-free membership, after he and I solved the Lisa Luck murder case."

"What does the Judge expect from you in return?"

"Good question. It's what he expects of Tom that concerns me. Got one for you. Any idea where the Judge's money came from?"

"Sure do," Greene said affably.

"Gonna tell me?"

"Nope."

"Any idea where the Judge came from?"

"Nope. He was just...here."

Mathers filed that away under, 'Bears Further Investigation'.

"Do you trust the Judge?"

"No," Marco replied with strong emphasis.

"Finally something we can agree on."

Greene missed his putt, tapped the ball in for a par 5. The match ended in a tie.

Mathers drove back to the station house in good spirits, reflecting on the valuable information he had obtained from

Greene. He had that heightened, anticipatory feeling he often got when a case was ready to crack open. Rudy W. asked to see him when he got to his office.

Rudy said excitedly, "I was able to track down Fredonia Boyle's itinerary.

"Great!"

"During the Western Open golf tournament, she was attending a hospitality industry convention in Denver."

"Check the flight logs for Denver to Chicago. She could have taken a break—"

Mathers didn't care for the sheepish look on Rudy W.'s face.

"At the time Tom said they saw Yuma Boyle at the golf tournament, Fredonia Boyle was delivering the keynote address at the convention in front of 652 people."

"Golly." Mathers leaned back in his chair. "You ever been on the roller coaster during the Arizona State Fair?"

"Sure."

"This case is like that, but they never let us off the ride. We just get dizzier and dizzier." Mathers smiled. "Thanks Rudy. Good police work. As usual."

***

From the 'Greens Clippings' column in *Gentleman Golfer Monthly* magazine, June 7th edition. The magazine was published in Scottsdale, so it often included gossip about the local golf scene.

Just Call Him 'The Visitor'
Yes, we had a visitor to the tour events the last 2 weeks of the Texas swing. None other than Tom Colt. As you devoted readers know he disappears from the golf circuit for months at a time. Gentleman Golfer has learned that he moonlights as some kind of private detective. Talented though Tom surely is, he just can't focus on his golf long enough to achieve anything meaningful.

This writer wishes he could ask Colt, "Lad, are you a golfer or a gumshoe? Because clearly you can't be both. Or in your case, perhaps either, competently."

At the Texas tourneys, he finished a dismal 57th and 62nd. We wonder why he bothered to show up to play at all.

We also learned while he was absent from the Big Tour he won a teeny, tiny team tourney somewhere in the Bahamas.

Colt has apparently never learned that the goal is to win the BIG EVENTS, THE MAJORS, not the teeny, tiny tourneys.

His partner in the Bahamas by the way was none other than aging Scottsdale socialite and pro tour gadfly, Jillian Flannery.

And finally, Colt forgot to send in his entry form for the US Open, so we won't see him competing at Brookline this month. Methinks young Thomas Colt needs a nanny to keep him organized.

***

At a lavish home in fashionable north central Phoenix, the sound of a crystal glass shattering against a patio block wall was heard. Moments later, a magazine was flung into a nearby koi pond.

"Aging Scottsdale socialite!!! Gadfly!!! How 'bout, fuck you *Gentleman Golfer magazine*," Jillian Flannery exclaimed.

She stood up, and declared as she mixed another drink, "Maybe I'll buy that rag and shut it down."

***

Tom got home later than usual that night, having stopped at his favorite clothing store downtown to pick up a tux for an upcoming event he had been invited to.

When he opened the patio door of the guest house, he saw a note taped to it. It looked like Judge Wilkinson's confident handwriting.

He read the note:

Tom, just something I wanted you to think about…

Many people are afraid to stand alone, to stand apart from the crowd, all by themselves in the spotlight. I've never been that way. I was never afraid to seek out my own individual path.

Since I was a very young man, your age in fact, I refused to cower in the shadows cast by men who thought themselves superior to me, just so that I could feel part of the group. I've never felt alone. Not once. And neither should you. God is there, with us, always. The spotlight is the light he shines on each of us.

I am certain this accounts for my success, against the odds.

Best,

Roy Wilkinson 1 August 1963

Tom reflected on what the Judge had written, struggling to understand as usual. He folded the note, walked inside and placed it in the top drawer of the nightstand by his bed, along with the other two dozen notes the Judge had sent.

***

The Friday afternoon meeting regarding the Red Boyle Murder was in progress at the Colt & Colt Confidential offices on the third floor of Valley Vista CC...

Based on the tired, gray expressions on our three detectives' faces, not to mention the empty cups of coffee and plates of snacks strewn on the desks, they were again struggling to piece together the evidence into any kind of pattern.

Mathers got up to visit the rest room. He opened the door to the hallway just as Judge Wilkinson walked by.

"Nice to see you again, Detective," the Judge said without any real feeling of "nice" in the tone.

"Swell offices you got here. Caroline said you set this up for them. Much better than what we have at Police Headquarters."

The Judge couldn't resist: "It's called the private sector, Detective. We do things first class."

Mathers and the Judge exchanged appropriate scowls. The Judge walked away. When Mathers returned, he said, with two fingers spaced an inch apart, "We're this close! I can almost see the solution..."

Tom and Caroline were not so sure.

"I re-interviewed Chandler Boyle about the employees that disappeared, Carol Thorn and Marquita Vasquez. He said Carol arrived a week before the grand opening. He hired her on the spot. She looked 'classy and efficient', not like one of the 'lazy islanders'," he said.

"She didn't have to provide references?" Caroline asked.

"Chandler said he didn't bother with that because he's an excellent judge of character."

Caroline groaned at that one. "Let's run with my theory that the maid posed as Yuma Boyle. Marquita was dark-skinned. Yuma Boyle we know was white."

"Motive..." Mathers said skeptically.

Caroline said, "It could have been another enemy Boyle made along the way. We don't know anything about this Carol Thorn's background."

Mathers said, "Suppose she killed Boyle, as herself, the maid, then made a show of becoming Yuma Boyle to leave the island that night."

"Seeing the maid in the corridors pushing her cart would not have been memorable enough for anyone to remember," Tom added. "Who could pass down the hallways completely unnoticed…The Maid. Who would know when Julia was taking her medication…only someone with access to the room…The Maid."

Now all three were starting to become more animated—like they could sniff the solution.

"Yes, absolutely," said Mathers. Mathers paced over to The Leaderboard, studied the long list of names and possible motives. "One thing, guys, we might be latching onto this theory because it's like the murder we solved at the hotel in Phoenix—a staff member did it."

That unfortunate truth seemed to let the air back out of their collective balloons.

"Could we talk about that perfume angle?" Tom inquired. "Patti remembers the fragrance Yuma was wearing. It was distinctive. She swore she detected it in the lobby the next day—after 'Yuma Boyle' had left the night before."

Mathers puffed the air of frustration through his lips.

"I still don't understand why Red rejected Yuma—in writing with that cold note. But he embraced Patti, whose background as the same, a child born out of wedlock by a woman Red had already broken up with, or was at least not seeing."

Mathers said, "I remember in our interview with Patti that she said how generous Red had been with her, when he wasn't required to. Remember that, she broke down in tears. They seemed like real tears, not the faked grief we got from Fredonia and Chandler."

Tom repeated something he told Inspector Weatherford: "Who signs an important document with just their initials, anyway. If Red intended to close out the matter and send Yuma on her way."

"The more we seek answers, the more questions we stir up. I gotta get back downtown for a meeting with the Chief. Let's keep at it. I know we're going to nail the killer. And I gotta tell you, my gut still says Fredonia was in the middle of this. She is one frosty, nasty woman. Money is everything to her. In my book, that always spells motive."

The detectives went their separate ways with their minds churning.

***

August 15, 1963, 9PM

The Best of Times, The Wurst of Times

She is a beautiful bride, Tom Colt thought as he stood in the doorway watching the wedding reception for Katrina Stern and Stan Barker unfold at Arizona Country Club. The simple, but elegant affair was set up on the beautifully manicured grounds outside the club.

About 60 guests were in attendance, Tom estimated, including several stars of the ladies' golf tour in the '60s, whom he was thrilled to meet. He always learned something about the simple but infinitely complex game of golf from talking to the best players, male or female. And Tom fully understood he was, alas, not yet one of the best.

Talking golf took his mind off what was going on there: farewell to a portion of Tom and Katrina's friendship.

The wedding ceremony and the reception that followed had been crisp, neat, efficient—and frugal—just as Katrina and Stan would have planned it, Tom thought. Stan's brother was a member there, at Arizona CC, and got a good deal on the price of the reception.

The weather had cooperated. The night was unseasonably cool for that time of year in the desert.

Tom brought his sister Caroline as his 'date' that night.

At the first chance to exit the reception, Tom walked out by himself onto the Arizona Country Club course. Never let 'em know you're hurting, was a phrase from his dad that came into his mind as he strolled from the 18th green down the back 9 holes, walking the course in reverse.

He mused how Arizona CC was significant in his year of 1963. Just a few short months ago he was playing in the Phoenix Open there. He played well at times that week, encouraging him. But, as things had a way of going in his life, his tournament playing schedule faced lots of interruptions and he didn't really get into a good rhythm.

This, he admitted, was his own fault. He loved the private investigating work, and assisting the Phoenix PD, as much or perhaps more than he loved competing in tournaments. And the interruptions caused by well, matters of the heart, those couldn't be avoided. That was just how he was. *Romanza*, his mom Laura calls it.

And now he was at Arizona CC to attend the union of Katrina Stern to Stan Barker. Once upon a time, that now seemed long ago, Tom and Katrina had both thought they might be married someday...

Stan had popped the question one night when he and Kat were having dinner at the Islands Restaurant, a popular Polynesian-themed eatery on 7th Street. She shocked herself by saying, yes.

She had sipped just a half glass of wine, so alcohol could not be blamed. In matters of the heart, Kat was uncertain, often lost. That night, her proud heart told her, for reasons she couldn't fully explain, Go For It. It's Time.

For those of us who find irony interesting, The Islands Restaurant was the place where Tom first saw Julia Wilkinson perform as a singer. And probably fell in love with her that night, in early 1962.

On the tee box for the 18th hole, Tom didn't notice bride Katrina walking up behind him.

"You OK?" she asked.

"I'm great!" Tom said with that fake affability that Tom was so skilled at. "And you're a lovely bride."

Katrina made her famous frowny face. "I guess." She sat down on the bench by the tee. "I don't know why I did this."

Tom took a seat next to her.

"Stan seems like a super guy. And anyone can see how much he loves you. He'll be a good provider."

"Yes, a good provider." She laughed, with a hint of bitterness. "Provider," she repeated, shaking her head. "What happens to us?"

"I don't know." Tom looked out at the lovely quiet golf course and pondered that. "We'll remain friends. We'll both have wonderful lives. You will win many more tournaments than I will."

That made her smile. "That's a given..."

"And you'll have a couple, make that three, kids."

"Yes, Stan talks about that incessantly."

She leaned in and put her head on Tom's shoulder. "I think we both screwed up."

"Have to agree with you there. But don't beat yourself up— not on this special day. A wedding is the best of times."

Tom gently moved Katrina's head off his shoulder, turned and kissed her on the cheek. He got up and walked back toward the clubhouse. Tom was emotionally strong, but he couldn't say more to Katrina at that moment, not that night.

Caroline passed him on the way and walked over to Katrina, took his place on the bench next to her.

"Tom did better than I thought he would. I was afraid he'd cry when you said 'I do'."

"Don't tell me that, Caroline, I feel like a dummkopf already."

"Life is designed to make dummkopfs of us all." Caroline got up and tugged Katrina to her feet. "Let's go back to the party. Tom's driving home. I got a ride with one of the bridesmaids. I am in desperate need of more champagne." Caroline paused a moment, then added, "Tom told me over and over how beautiful you looked tonight. He'll love you, always and forever."

"You're sure."

"I'm his twin. I know all. Tom will be your devoted friend for the rest of your lives. He'll be there for you, whenever you need him. No questions asked. Forever. I mean this. Forever."

Kat was reassured by Caroline's unusually serious tone of voice.

And so that night a rocky, and doomed, marriage began between Stan and Katrina. His possessiveness would quickly drive Katrina batty. He in turn was peeved by her many attempts at asserting what he viewed as needless independence. He believed in the 'lock' part in the word wedlock. And that a man's home was his castle. And that the woman's role was to obey her husband. Stan was eager to start a family. Katrina wanted to postpone it, to pursue her golf career for 5 more years at least. She was not yet even 27.

She had worked so hard to get where she was in golf. She couldn't quit now. *How unfair to ask a person to give up a career they love,* she thought, as ironic as that may seem.

A reasonable question to ask was, why did Stan Barker want to marry Katrina Stern?

And the irony of ironies was that because Tom and Katrina never again tried to possess each other, but instead encouraged each other to pursue their dreams, they would stay together, in a fashion, all their lives.

***

The Sexual Metaphysics of the Putting Stroke
August 31, 1963
At the Guest House on the Wilkinsons' Estate

His performance in tournaments over the summer had brought Tom's frustration with his putting stroke to a head. The other elements of his golf game had progressed tremendously—he was now able to hit his tee shots consistently straight, not just consistently long. It was driving Tom nuts that he couldn't master, or even be reasonably competent at, putting—which involves rolling a ball on a nicely manicured green grass surface for no more than 40 feet. *Why is it so hard?*

Tom Colt Continues Our Story:

It was a hot, humid evening, the kind of night in the Arizona desert when it never cools off. We get what are termed 'monsoon' storms starting in July and sometimes going on all the way to Labor Day. Heat and humidity combine to make it miserable to be outside, day or night.

Caroline was at BAPA that evening for her course on 'Building Dramatic Tension'. When she was leaving, I asked her if she was attending the course, or teaching it. She saluted me with one finger.

I put on my swimsuit and went outside to the small pool we have in the back of the Guest House, intending to take a swim and cool off.

The yellow porch light illuminated the putting green that stood next to the pool. I decided to forego the swim and work on my putting stroke. It was maddening to hit perfect drives off the tee, crisp iron shots to set up an easy birdie putt—and then not being able to get the ball into the hole from 10 feet. I had a nagging fear that if I didn't fix this problem, it was going to drive me off the professional golf tour. To win out there, you *must* be a good putter. Putting skill is the difference maker in many tournaments.

I drew my putter out of the golf bag, took 3 golf balls and padded out to the green in bare feet. The practice green had 9 little 12" red flagsticks and cups set in the ground, so you could practice putts of various length and speed and slope. I brought a bottle of Blatz beer with me and set it down on the green.

I fiddled with my grip on the club. I fiddled with my stance, turning my left toe more outward. My first few putts were scattershot—long, short, wide left, wide right. I lacked that subtle element golfers call 'touch' or 'feel'.

I kept at it though. All my life, that method had served me well. The only way to fail is to quit.

But then, something clicked. I made a tiny adjustment of the position of my left hand on the grip. I relaxed my shoulders and turned my left toe out a bit more in my stance. I began sinking putts from 15 feet. One after the other.

I aimed at the variously spaced targets and sank putt after putt. I had no idea why I was improving. But it felt great!

Everything slowed down. Even my breathing. My putting stroke was smooth. The tension left my hands—for just about the first time. The putter felt incredibly light in my hands. I could almost see the individual blades of grass on the green.

I sank ten straight putts!

What was going on? I stopped for a moment to take a slug of beer. I had earned it.

And then I saw Julia Wilkinson standing by the pool. She was wearing a long, loose white cotton dress, was in bare feet and carrying a bottle of Jack Daniels. The fabric of her dress was swaying in the soft breeze. I hadn't noticed there was any kind of breeze that stifling night until that moment. She brought the refreshing breeze with her.

On that breeze was the scent of her lovely perfume. I knew little about perfume, but loved the one she wore. It was like the essence of roses.

I hadn't heard her walk down the path from the Main House, high up on the hill above me. Her voice sounded like she had tossed down a few glasses of Jack Daniels before she came over. She looked soft and vulnerable. Her rose-gold hair swayed in the breeze and shimmered in the light from the porch.

"Don't let me interrupt. You're doing wonderfully!"

Now that you're here, was the thought that came to my mind.

She flashed that special smile that I had convinced myself was reserved only for me—it contained warmth and lust and expectations of great things to come.

"How long have you been there?"

"I counted you made nine putts in a row. I enjoy watching you play golf. You love the game so much. It brings you the same kind of joy that singing brings me."

"And congratulations on your hit single."

Her composition *HIGH TEMPS*, the featured song in her first album, had cracked the Top 20 in the *Billboard* rankings.

She took a bow, a bit unsteadily. "Let's celebrate! Could you please get me a tall glass and 4 ice cubes."

I set the putter down and went inside to get her 4 ice cubes, not 3, not 5. I walked across the green to give her the glass. She had set the bottle of Jack Daniels down on the pool deck and was standing by the pool steps. I poured the Jack Daniels into the glass and set it down.

"Maybe a swim first."

She pulled the loose dress over her head and turned toward me.

She was naked. All I could do is gasp. That's all I could ever do when glimpsing Julia unclothed. She had a body that a Greek Goddess would have to work out at the best gymnasia in Athens every day for 5 years to acquire.

Her body was exquisite, starting with the soft rose-gold waves that tumbled down her shoulders—strong shoulders, she was a very healthy, all-natural, all-American girl, one of a kind. Her huge breasts were perfectly proportioned on her strong frame. And there was that beckoning triangle of rose gold fleece between her legs.

"You won't need swim trunks," she said in the happy melody of her voice. "Join me..." She held out her hand.

I stayed composed enough to set the glass down, not drop it to shatter on the pool deck, and peeled out of my trunks.

I took her hand and we walked down the steps into the water, which was cool, refreshing, but not cold.

We embraced.

"This feels wonderful, Tom! I've wanted to be with you so much, but my travel schedule is horrendous with the album being released. "We feel so good together, like we belong."

Still not quite believing that a naked Julia was again in my arms, all I could do is stammer, "Y...yes."

Somewhere in my brain, which unaccountably seemed to shrink when Julia was around, I realized that this night was a kind of make-up date for the deep humiliation I suffered when I came home that night a year and a half ago to find this same naked, gorgeous woman in this same pool—making love to her boyfriend Derrick. Rich boyfriend, of course.

But I didn't care. Her smile, the fragrance of her, and her amazing body so close to mine, made all the colors of the world brighter, brought my dreams of her back to life, and wiped out all unpleasant history.

She giggled, softly, another wonderful melody. "What a lovely evening. What a lovely man."

She led me back to the pool steps. She grabbed my beach towel from the patio table and spread it out on the putting green.

And that is where we made love. I turned the porch light out so we were bathed in quiet moonlight as Julia lay down on the towel.

I joined her for a series of warm, soft but urgent kisses. I hungered for her and convinced myself she felt the same hunger. Even after being in the cool water, the hot night combined with our passion made me think we might melt together.

Our lovemaking was not a tender reunion of long-lost lovers, not a reprise of the playful exploration of our bodies last year when we met. Now there was history between us, some of it unfortunately dark. Julia was my equal physically. We wanted to say to each other that all was forgiven, all accounts were again square. Giving each other all the pleasure in the world was the means of communication we chose that incredible night.

Our passion was fierce. We quickly became soaked with sweat, a sheen visible on our bodies in the moonlight. I brushed back the rose-gold curls from her damp forehead. The look in her eyes was something I had not seen before, a calm satisfaction, a kind of peace.

I had to believe after that night that I was more to her than an available and quick cure for the loneliness she so often felt.

Yes, I _had_ to believe.

Later, we moved to the cool grass of the lawn—which had been watered late that afternoon--and I retrieved our drinks. We sipped and chatted. Totally together, totally in sync. And this night, unlike at Bogey Island, there was no mention of the bullet scar on my shoulder. I wouldn't at all have been surprised if it wasn't there anymore.

"You and Katrina bit the dust I heard. Sorry." But Julia said that like the outcome was inevitable and I had finally realized it, gotten rid of the problem.

After an hour or so she stood up and said, "I better be going. Travel day tomorrow. You know how that is..."

She slipped her dress back on, I retrieved my trunks. Then I switched the porch light back on.

"Let me walk you home," I said.

"Afraid one of my evil ex-boyfriends is lurking in the shadows to accost me?"

"No, more like mountain lions. We think we've tamed the desert, but it's still wild out here."

She smiled doubtfully, took my hand and we strolled up the path to the enormous Main House looming above us. More precisely, I strolled and she prowled. What was I thinking being worried about her? The local tribe of mountain lions would have knelt at Julia's feet and declared her their Queen.

We got to the top of the hill and the edge of her own patio/pool area.

"Please tell your baby sister to quit hating me. I'm not going anywhere. She has no say in the matter." She smiled, but it seemed a cold smile, of finality.

She leaned forward and kissed me. I felt that jolt of Julia-generated electricity again.

"And do hurry and get rich, Tom. Father would never permit me to marry a poor boy."

My forehead creased with Colt confusion. "Was she saying she wanted to marry me? Or was she secure in her knowledge that I could never get rich, so it was a joke?"

"I have the best time with you..." She kissed me again and then walked the remaining 20 yards to the back door.

"Goodnight," was all I could say.

I could have asked her when I would see her again. But I already knew the answer: whenever Julia Wilkinson decided I would see her again. Turned out, I didn't see her again in 1963 until December. But I thought about her daily.

I had the feeling Julia had planned and choreographed every detail of this evening. She might have considered handing me an itinerary before we began.

I got back to the Guest House and went inside. I saw my reflection in the hallway mirror. Did I just waste another night of my life being a fool over Julia Wilkinson? I saw myself shaking my head 'no' in the mirror.

The night was not a waste at all. My putting stroke was much improved.

***

Caroline came home about an hour later, her cheerful expression telling me she had a great time at her acting class. She fetched us two Blatz beers and we sat on the patio. She chattered merrily about how much she was learning at the Academy.

Eventually she calmed down and took a few sips of her beer. She said, "How was sex with Julia on the putting green?"

"What???" I exclaimed, Mr. Innocent.

"There's a rumpled beach towel and a bottle of Jack Daniels on the green. You don't drink hard liquor, and golf isn't Julia's game."

"Good detective work."

"Thank you."

***

The next week, on Tuesday, I drove to Albuquerque, New Mexico to play in the Land of Enchantment Charity Classic. The course the tournament was played on was less than enchanting, dry and dusty with hard narrow fairways. As I may have mentioned, I struggle with accuracy with my driver at times.

And I won.

Yes, I won a pro tournament for the 2nd time in my 5-year career. Incredibly, I made nearly every putt I looked at, from 5-footers to 35-footers, all four days of the tournament.

My caddie, Sheboygan, looked on with amazement. Hell, I amazed myself.

It didn't even matter that the event was played on such a narrow course, and I sprayed my tee shots all over the place--- in the trees, in the rough. I visited some spots that the Spanish explorers never got around to.

I shot rounds of 71-64-70-68, for a 15-under-par total of 273.

On the drive home, I decided that it must have been my scorching, fierce evening with Julia on the putting green that caused the sudden, miraculous improvement in my putting stroke. There was no other explanation. Putting must have a metaphysical aspect.

I sustained my good play for the next three events, finishing 7th, 3rd and 4th.

I wish someone would explain this crazy game of golf to me. And then explain love. And then if time allows explain life. Or perhaps they were all the same thing for me in my 28th year.

When I got back home from the four-tournament swing, I thought about that hot August night with Julia every time I practiced on the putting green in the back of the Guest House. My putting stroke continued to be smooth and steady.

I recall in high school American Lit class our teacher, Miss Stirdivant, tried in vain to explain the concept of metaphor in literature to us. I finally understood.

Julia was a metaphor for the maddeningly elusive trophies I sought to win in golf. There was a strong possibility, I was well aware, that I will never win these trophies. There is an equally strong possibility that Julia will never be mine. Did I have to win Julia's heart before I can win The Masters?

Perhaps deep down I didn't believe I deserved the trophies. The true winners in life always believe.

My 10th class reunion is coming up. Miss Stirdivant's bound to be at the party. Maybe I should tell her I finally 'get' it, though how do I explain the circumstances of acquiring this wisdom? As I recall, Miss Stirdivant was rather prim and proper.

Chapter Twenty-Six
Det. Mathers Goes Camping
The Mystery of the Third Face

September 24, 1963

Brooks Benton Continues Our Story:

Det. Ed Mathers had that rarest of quality for law enforcement officers, and Judge Wilkinson would argue, government employees in general—imagination. He could close his eyes and see a crime taking place. He could even hear the conversations among the criminals as they made their dark plans. The quality Tom Colt had in abundance was being able to coax people into blabbing their secrets. And Caroline? Well, Mathers had already seen that she was simply brilliant at seeing the possible relationships between seemingly unrelated clues.

One afternoon in September, Mathers paced his tiny downtown office with more frustration than usual. The confined spaces were getting to him. His thought process was sluggish.

He drove out to the uninhabited desert north and west of downtown Phoenix, not far from the little town of Wickenburg—and camped out for the night.

As evening approached, he built a campfire and cooked a simple dinner of hamburgers and cowboy-style beans with bacon and jalapeno peppers.

He spread a sleeping bag out under the stars and tried yet again to sort out the Boyle murder case.

He imagined he was the great John Wayne in a Western, ready to face any danger that arose. He was not aware that when filming on location, John Wayne slept in a comfortable motor home.

Mathers slept fitfully, awakened periodically by the mournful sound of the coyotes, and once the shrill cry of two bobcats fighting. Clues bubbled and floated through his head but solutions eluded him.

At 5AM he got up and made coffee. He sipped the strong brew and watched a gorgeous red-orange sunrise peeking over Wickenburg Mountain.

Mathers, since he was a young boy, had felt a spiritual connection to the desert, to The West. Though he didn't talk of it much, he considered himself the successor to the great lawmen of Arizona's past, like Wyatt Earp.

As the coffee got him going that morning, the questions, the questions, and more questions buzzed around him like annoying insects. Was the maid Carol Storm posing as Yuma Boyle or was Yuma Boyle posing as the maid? Does Yuma Boyle even exist? Does Carol Storm exist?

What did either one accomplish by killing Red Boyle?

Mathers thought, there must be a completely different motive than the ones we've considered, but what?

Suppose Boyle had drawn up a new Will, one with the kids cut out. Was he going to sign it but died before he could? Who was this new beneficiary we heard rumors about?

Mathers thought, suppose it was the Reverend Tucker? If he's dead, his share reverts to the Boyle kids. Neither Carol Storm nor Yuma Boyle were named in the Will, everyone agrees.

He closed his eyes and concentrated. He saw something, a face in the shadows. The dark silhouette of a face.

A Third Face. A third suspect, Mathers thought.

***

Mathers had accrued a bunch of vacation days. He took three of them and flew on his own nickel back to Bogey Island via Freeport on Grand Bahama Island. He retraced the steps he thought the murderer of Red Boyle might have taken.

The Bogey Island Resort was closed for the summer, but Mathers got a set of keys from the Boyle estate lawyer. Walking through the silent, deserted resort proved beneficial: Mathers could let his imagination run as his mind's eye saw the possible actions of a killer. He scoured every inch of the property.

He picked up fresh clues in surprising places: a tourist bar in Freeport, a homeless camp on the beach, and a ferry boat service to Bogey Island.

He was exhausted when his return plane landed in Phoenix. He was an unshaven, rumpled, sweat-stained mess.

Plenty of time to sleep when you're dead, Mathers thought. *And I'm not dead yet.*

Mathers didn't tell Tom and Caroline he was going back to the island. He was not at all sure the trip would generate any tangible results. He truly enjoyed teaming up with Tom and Caroline whose zeal for justice surprisingly equaled his own.

He was concerned if they failed to find Boyle's killer, Tom and Caroline would get discouraged about their private investigation work, particularly because Judge Wilkinson had asked Tom and Caroline to go to Bogey Island and investigate whether Boyle was in danger. He was worried that Tom thought he had let the Judge down.

Mathers didn't understand why the Judge was so important to them. Tom and Caroline were so resourceful, why did they need Judge Wilkinson? Mathers was not entirely certain the Judge was a good person to associate with.

Tom and Caroline had skills that were rare and could not be taught. He didn't know anyone on Phoenix PD apart from himself who possessed those skills.

Police are a remarkable brotherhood but get worn down by the grinding pressure of their jobs and the constant exposure to the dregs of humanity. The outsider, the private investigator, can on occasion add great value and fresh perspective to an investigation, Mathers believed.

Early in Mathers' career as a homicide detective he occasionally worked with another PI, a classic, old-style, seedy gumshoe right out of a film noir, but that fellow was killed one night when trying to apprehend a suspect.

Katrina Stern's concerns for Tom's safety were entirely justified.

Mathers was certain that the three of them, Tom, Caroline and himself, were going to accomplish great things in crime solving.

He was also concerned that Judge Wilkinson was working hard to turn Tom into a rich young snob—and a possible suitor for his crazy daughter. *What a waste of talent*, Mathers thought. *There are more than enough rich men in the world. Not enough seekers of justice.*

***

October 15, 1963

Budding movie star Autumn Amber was at her parents' house, waiting for them to come back from a shopping trip to pick up their costumes for a Halloween party in two weeks. She wandered into her mom's cavernous closet. She and Tracy were identical sizes and often shared clothes. Autumn was going on a press tour for her upcoming feature film debut and wanted to borrow a few outfits from her mom, who spent lavishly on clothes and had fantastic fashion sense.

Autumn had already selected a costume for the upcoming party, Cinderella. Her mother was going as a Witch, and her father as a Circus Clown.

In the equally outsized bathroom, Autumn looked through a cabinet and sampled some of her mom's perfumes. She found one that was different from the ones her mom usually wore. The scent was 'attar of roses' She spritzed the air and took a sniff.

She liked it and popped the tiny bottle into her purse. The scent was named *Mischief.*

Chapter Twenty-Seven
The Kiss of the Vampire

The Annual Halloween Party Dinner/Dance at Valley Vista Country Club was a big and popular event on the Club social calendar.

In the 1960s, Halloween became more popular for adults to participate in with dress-up parties. It wasn't just for kids trick or treating. In those days the neighborhoods were safe enough that youngsters could walk through the streets of Phoenix after dark, without supervision, and knock on doors without fear.

Everyone knew who their neighbors were, for one thing. A lot of families lived in the same houses for generations. Were there some weird residents? Sure. But everyone knew who they were an avoided them. The weird ones were generally just eccentric and harmless, anyway. Tom said he couldn't recall a single axe murderer living in his neighborhood growing up.

At 5PM on Halloween, the ladies' locker room at Valley Vista CC was full of happy, chirping party goers primping their costumes and checking their makeup.

Patti Boyle was going as a very cute Minnie Mouse, complete with big ears. She was trying to decide whether she needed darker eye shadow. But elected to go with what she had. Too much makeup and a fun-loving mouse could look more like a sinister rat.

Autumn Amber arrived, creating an instant buzz amongst the women, as she so hoped she would.

She strolled past Patti and said, gushingly, "Oh, Patti, so nice to see you. It's been so long since we were on the island. I missed you. We're almost like sisters, now…"

The hell we are, Patti thought darkly. And Patti rarely had dark thoughts.

Autumn checked herself out in the mirror, pronounced herself perfect, took a tiny bottle from her purse and gave herself a light mist of perfume.

"Have fun," Autumn said cheerily to her 'sister' as she left.

Patti finished applying her cute mouse makeup. The scent of Amber's perfume lingered. There was something unusual about it…

The Valley Vista Halloween Party was in full swing when Tom Colt arrived at 5:30. The main dining room had been converted into a dinner/dance setup, the tables moved against the walls and a wooden dance floor placed in the middle of the large room.

That year, Tom went as a Medieval Knight. He enjoyed a glass of generously spiked rum punch and watched the colorfully and in some cases absurdly clad Club members dancing and socializing.

The first person to come up to Mr. Popularity was MoniQue Jones, dressed as a very sexy vampire. She wore a black cape over a black gown with stunning cleavage, and the gown slit far up the side. Ruby red lipstick, her long shiny black hair unbound and flowing behind her, exotic purple eye shadow, and very realistic vampire fangs completed the costume. Tom took time to admire the long legs that flashed through the skirt.

Tom noticed as she walked over that she was a bit tipsy and sloshed champagne out of her glass as she walked over.

She put an affectionate arm around Tom. "Cool party, isn't it! Even the old fuds got into the spirit of the thing. Carter Vonessen came as Frankenstein!"

"He has the blocky head for it," Tom observed.

"His wife Babs told me it would take more than electricity to bring him back to life in bed."

She giggled.

Tom took a sip of his own drink and admired her chest as the cape fell open for a moment.

"If all the vampires were as cute as you, I could be convinced to stay up later at night."

"It's time I initiate you into the undead." She brushed the fangs lightly over his neck and slipped her hand lightly over his crotch. "Would you mind if I drained a little fluid from you..."

"I'd be honored."

MoniQue was so into her Vampirella role Tom felt himself getting aroused.

She abruptly pulled away and laughed. "I'm not really like this. I don't even talk like this. I've always gotten carried away when I dress up for All Hallows Eve."

"This is the real MoniQue. Our costumes free us up to be our true selves."

"Nope. Nope. Nope. My dad is a bank president. I am his darling, good daughter. I went to Catholic school with your sister Caroline."

Tom thought, but did not say, *Yes, and look how Caroline turned out.* He said, "The tenets of Roman Catholicism didn't exactly take with my sister. I hope you fared better."

"Truthfully, no. I wish there were a church where you could dance and laugh and sing and be gay."

A slow-danceable tune started up from the small band in the corner. The pretty vampire took Tom's hand and led him to the center of the dance floor.

They make a lovely couple, thought Missy Gould, who was dancing a few feet away from them with her portly husband Sterling. Dancing with him was more like a tugboat dragging a trans-oceanic liner, but Missy was a woman who gave everything her best effort. Spending her life with a philanderer like Sterling required a great effort. Her daily regimen of Yoga helped, along with alcohol.

Also looking on was Jilly Flannery, dancing with the ancient Irv Fortman, a retired investment banker (or so he claims). Investment banker is one of those professions you can simply declare yourself to be, like the profession of politician. Irv looked every bit of his 70 years.

Jilly watched Tom and MoniQue swaying sweetly to the music, practically glued to each other, and seethed. *I just got Katrina Stern set up with Stan the Bratwurst man, and now MoniQue Jones gets her hooks into Tom. And she isn't even attractive! Those bushy eyebrows of hers look like shrubbery. Am I doomed to spend the rest of my days of youth dancing with limp dicks like little Irv Fortman?*

She sighed, heavily. *I want me some young Tom Colt, and I want it now.* Jilly was not used to not getting what she wanted—immediately when she wanted it.

Irv, whose dance steps were mere shuffles spaced inches apart, noticed the deep sigh. "What are you thinking about, my Jilly girl?"

She grimaced. She hated it when he called her his Jilly girl. In her mind, she was Tom's girl. Irv coughed one of those typical old man hacks. She hoped none of it the thick, nasty spittle got on her.

"Oh, Irving darling, I'm all yours! It feels like heaven to be in your arms. Tell me more about your new shopping mall project in Glendale."

Jilly saw Tom and MoniQue dance their way to the door. They each grabbed a fresh glass of punch as they went.

Jilly made a noise like a small shriek, *this is not good!*

Tom led his lovely vampire out to the golf course. They passed through the bright light cast by the clubhouse windows into the dark, cool grass and sheltering trees.

They stopped by the tee to Tom's favorite hole, the short par-4 third, which he had birdied at least 100 times and eagled seven times.

"What's more romantic than a golf course at night?" He inquired.

The vampire girl laughed. "Lotsa things. You're kinda weird, but strangely appealing to me tonight. You must be a blood type-O. Always been my favorite."

She led Tom over to a bench lit by a nearby lamp, sat down. He joined her. "Let's not go back to the party just yet." She took off her shoes. He noticed there was a letter 'G' on the bottom of the soles.

"These are both uncomfortable and hugely expensive. Birthday present from my Stepmother. Always trying to buy my affection. Not going to happen. Anyway, Grenville brand shoes, they're called. All the rage with the Hollywood set, I've been told. I may toss them. I could donate them to the poor, but then I'd be giving the poor folks sore feet, which isn't nice. They have so many other things to worry about."

"Always thinking of others. See, you really are a good girl."

She leaned back and sighed. "I don't know who I am, or what I want to be. Daddy says 'come to work at the bank'. What a disaster that would be. First time I made a mistake the other employees would say, 'she only got the job because of her father'. I want to find something of my very own. I do know I don't want to get married, not for a long time. Does that make any sense?"

"Absolutely. I don't want to get married either."

"And tonight, maybe I just want to be a girl spending the evening with a wonderful guy, at least one night and perhaps more. That would be splendid."

"For me, too." He leaned toward her and stroked the soft thigh that revealed itself through the slit skirt.

She almost purred, which confused Tom. In the horror films, the vampires never softly purr.

"May I ask where you do your banking?"

Tom chuckled. "Valley National Bank."

"What could I do to get you to move your money to my father's bank?"

"Several things, and they'd all be wonderful I imagine."

MoniQue took another shot at kissing him on the neck. He was beginning to understand why erotically themed vampire films were becoming so popular at that time.

"See, you're already working for your dad. And a good job you're doing. I'll open an account on Monday. First thing when the bank opens."

"The good news for you is, I tend to fall in love with golfers. I had this major crush on Doug Sanders for several years until I found out he had a bigger, more colorful, more expensive wardrobe than I did. So you're in the running for my next big crush. Don't screw it up, kiddo."

"Given my track record lately, that might be hard."

She grinned. "I heard Katrina Stern dumped you for the Bratwurst Baron, Stan Barker."

"I wouldn't say dumped. And don't you gals have anything better to do than gossip about me in the locker room?"

"No, not really. And we gossip about you in the dining room, too. Also in the parking lot sometimes, while we're waiting for that geriatric valet Hans to bring our cars."

Tom couldn't resist again putting a hand on the shapely thigh revealed by the drifting gown.

"Do you think I talk too much?" she asked.

"For a vampire, you are kinda chatty."

"Well, we spend a lot of time alone, in the dark. In deserted castles. When we get out...we thirst for lively conversation as well as blood."

Tom felt a surge of glorious warmth. Snappy romantic banter always turned him on.

"So, what do you really like to do? The best careers come from the activities we love. Look at me and golf. And detective work."

The dark and lovely vampire eyes shot open with excitement. "I know! I've heard about you solving crimes with the Phoenix PD. That is beyond cool! The danger of it all. How brave you are! Could I come work at your PI firm?"

Tom deftly deflected that question.

"Not everyone agrees with you, I'm afraid. Some think I'm taking unnecessary, even stupid, risks. But I love solving puzzles."

"At the Club I heard some gossip that Julia Wilkinson was the one who shot you last year. Was it an accident or did you deserve it? I'm leaning toward deserved it."

"That question remains open. Sharp little fangs ya' got there, by the way."

"Just so you know, I don't own a gun. That should reassure you in case we ever have a lovers' quarrel."

Tom like the sound of that: Lovers.

She looked in the distance and became thoughtful. "I love to cook. My grandma taught me all the family recipes from the old country—Ohio, not Lebanon—I used to spend my summers with her."

"How'd you like to join my mom's catering business? She's expanding so fast she needs to train an assistant catering director."

"That sounds like work, real work, something I've been able to avoid. I wouldn't mind being a screenwriter, though. How hard could it be to write a movie? That's what I'm going to pursue—for now."

"Probably not hard at all to write a bad movie."

"Your caddie Sheboygan is a fabulous writer. He's working on a screenplay that takes place in a prison. It's so realistic. I wonder how he knows so much?"

"Probably just born with a vivid imagination."

"MMMMM," she said contentedly. She took his hand. She noticed how strong and calloused a golfer's hands are, like a working man's. They each had 'a moment'.

"At my house that day during the Phoenix Open in February—remember! I'm still embarrassed about that. I don't know what came over me. I think I flashed my breasts at you."

Tom feigns a puzzled expression. "I can't really recall."

"Don't believe that for a minute. I bet you could accurately sketch my boobs from memory."

"Dang, I forgot my sketch pad. And I always bring it with me…"

They laughed. MoniQue knew Tom really liked her. She was thrilled.

"Don't be embarrassed. You were under the influence of a controlled sausage substance."

"So the rumors about that Barker Bratwurst are true. I heard he had to take those off the market. They were more like an out-of-control substance. Some kind of Brazilian spice in them that drove people wild."

"Yes, they were so potent, even Episcopalian women wanted to have sex."

"You wouldn't think that would be possible." She laughed softly and then grabbed his arm affectionately. "This is fun, this night. You're fun. I'm fun, too. And that doesn't happen very often these days."

They turned at the same moment and looked into each other's eyes. Each liked what they saw.

"MoniQue, Queen of the Vampires, it wasn't the bratwurst that got into you. It was us. We share a powerful attraction. I can feel it in my heart—and other places."

"Me, too. I would like...to see you again."

"I would really like that."

And so beneath an unusually bright autumn crescent moon, the golfer/detective boy and the lovely vampire girl walked back to the clubhouse porch. They paused under a yellow light that illuminated them in a soft glow like a shot from a romantic movie.

"What happens next?"

"If you take out your vampire fangs, we could share a kiss."

"That would be lovely."

And so she did, and it was.

***

Chapter Twenty-Eight

Det. Mathers, at home, was dressing for the Valley Vista party—he was coming as a cowboy, kind of a fancy cowboy, *The Lone Ranger*, complete with mask.

Mathers seldom went to the Club social events, though he played golf there every chance he got.   Since he believed at least 70% of rich people are probably crooks, he was afraid he couldn't resist the urge to arrest one of these rich clowns in front of their stuck-up friends in their beloved Club. No way to earn that much dough honestly. They're bound to be guilty of something...

At the last minute, he decided to go that night. His cop instinct told him the killer would likely be there. But he knew it might not do him any good because confusion about this case, the Boyle Murder, still reigned in his head.

His mind was again swimming in clues and suppositions about who killed Red Boyle.

"Something business, something personal." Marco Greene's cryptic words echoed in his head. Boyle humiliated Amber with the 8MM nudie movie he showed at the Grand Opening event—with her father in the room.

Mathers grabbed his car keys off the dresser and hustled out to his car.

Mathers only got as far as a pay phone outside Bob's Big Boy restaurant in Scottsdale. He dialed police headquarters and asked for Rudy W.

"I need you to call Pacific Sunset Pictures in Los Angeles..." he began.

***

Tom and MoniQue were on their way to their respective locker rooms at the Club. They saw Autumn Amber in the hallway—signing autographs!

This caused MoniQue to growl, not purr: "I can't stand that girl. She thinks she is God's Gift to the Movies. At the BAPA school, there was a rumor old Boyle was all set to finance a movie starring none other than Phoenix's own Autumn Amber. Can you believe that? She's a terrible actress. He came to his senses and decided against the deal."

"You're sure of that?" Tom asked.

"Got it from Red's own personal secretary. She would know." Tom gave himself a small mental kick for not thinking of interviewing the secretary about the murder. But then again, Mathers didn't think of it either.

Tom left MoniQue and went into the Men's Locker Room. He walked by his locker and found a small note from Kat in an envelope taped to it. He was surprised. He hadn't seen or heard much from Kat lately. Tom wasn't sure married life was agreeing with her. She hadn't earned a Top-5 finish in a tournament since her wedding day. Before that time, she had already won twice in '63. This was the first real slump of her brilliant golf career.

> *Hi, I don't know if this will help you, but I remember something from the night I left Bogey Island. I was in a boat on the way back to the main island, with the Vonessens and a woman named Yuma. I must have looked glum because Yuma said, "Boy trouble can be rough. Don't worry, it will all work out." Or maybe she said, "everything will be fine". Something like that.*
> *The odd part is, I'd never seen her before. How did she even know who I was?*
> *Hope that helps.*
> *And Tom, I love you, forever.*
> *Katrina*

Tom left the locker room. He needed to find Caroline. *Maybe she was upstairs in their office...*

He headed for the stairs, saw Felicity Greyhawk arriving through the rear entrance to the Club. She came to the party dressed as Felicity Greyhawk, Indian maiden and sexy movie starlet from the '40s. He had never heard of anyone coming to a Halloween Party dressed as a younger version of themselves. *But that's my Auntie...*

She rushed over to Tom. "I sense evil here tonight, nephew. You must be cautious. I felt an aura of danger when I passed by Autumn Amber."

"You're absolutely right, Aunt Felicity."

She looked stunned. "I am?"

"Aunt Felicity, I need your help with a case..."

"You do???" She cleared her throat. "I knew you would say that eventually."

"Of course you knew, you're psychic."

Felicity was too vain to perceive Tom was poking fun at her.

"How may I help you, Thomas?"

"You said during one of your golf lessons with me that you were in a movie, a film noir, with Tracy, Autumn's mother. What was her name then?"

"Tracy Colter, I think. Yes, that's it."

"What was the movie?"

"*Double Blind*," she said proudly. "I had the most wonderful seduction scene—my character had to distract a cop so the bad guy could get away. I wanted to play the scene in the nude but back then they had these silly production codes...Imagine if we were doing that movie today. I still work out regularly in the gym, you know."

"Yes, well." Tom worked hard to completely erase the image of a nude middle-aged Aunt Felicity from his brain. "What else can you tell me about Tracy the actress?"

"Tracy? Nothing. She played a hotel maid, I think. On screen for maybe a minute. I had this marvelous starring role—involving mistaken identity. I posed as two different women and as my real character. Of course, the project was handicapped by the dreadful script we had; that hack Dick Amberson wrote it."

Tom exclaimed, "You are the most wonderful Aunt any nephew ever had! Thank you, thank you!"

She indicated her cheek. Tom went ahead and kissed it. She indicated the other cheek. He obliged again. Her skin was a tad leathery; it felt like a cowboy kissing his saddle.

"Let me know if you need further psychic assistance."

"Yes. And thank you for helping solve a murder. You are amazing."

Tom hurried up the stairs. Felicity, still stunned that Tom no longer thought of her a quack psychic, made her way to the rum punch bowl, with a satisfied smile and her proud head held even higher than usual, the 20 or so bracelets she wore jingling merrily.

***

Mathers arrived at the Club. He went straight for a bank of pay phones in the rear of the building near the golf shop. After making a call, he gave one of the busboys a $5 bill to tell him what costumes one of the couples at the dance were wearing. If he went into the party and was obvious about poking around the ballroom himself, he knew he would spook them.

***

Tom was almost never afflicted by headaches, but he was getting one that night at the party. There was so much information they had uncovered about the Boyle murder, but none of it fit together, at least in his mind. He wished Mathers were there, but knew the Detective seldom attended social events at the Club. Mathers didn't think he fit in, a conclusion shared by nearly all of the members.

Tom went outside to his favorite place—the golf course— and tried to relax and organize his thoughts. He was mad at himself for not being able to unravel this mystery.

***

Caroline opened the door to the Colt & Colt offices on the third floor, went over to her desk, sat down and put her feet up on the desk like a real private dick. Which is what her costume was for the party, a '40s style detective like Humphrey Bogart, complete with a well-worn dark suit and tie, a rakish fedora on her head. She leaned back in the chair. She looked over at the Sherlock Holmes motto on the wall in a picture frame, a gift from Judge Wilkinson:

> *Once you eliminate the **impossible**, whatever remains, no matter how **improbable**, must be the truth."*

She shook her head. Her bright ideas about this case had all seemed impossible.

Caroline got more frustrated the more she looked at page after page of notes they had made during the investigation. She felt herself slipping into despondency—something she had trouble climbing out of.

She threw the file off her desk, the papers scattering.

"I hate this! I hate failure! I am not a loser like everyone thinks, except for Tom! Damn, I know we can solve this crime." She didn't realize she was screaming.

She didn't see Judge Roy Wilkinson standing in the doorway. He wasn't in a costume, other than the one he wore every day in battle, his black wool trousers, white shirt starched to formidable stiffness, sleeves rolled up his forearms and ready for action, and red and silver striped tie.

Caroline finally saw his shadow and looked over. "I'm sorry. I didn't mean to make all this noise."

"Caroline," he said, and then walked slowly toward her. "I couldn't be prouder of you. Not even if you were my own daughter."

Caroline's explosive meltdown turned into Caroline melting into sort of a warm liquid chocolate state. She choked back a few tears as he walked toward her. She got out of her chair and came around the desk.

"Thank you...sir," she said. She had never called him sir before. Tom always called this mighty man sir.

"Do you need a hug?"

"Yes, sir, I do." She threw her arms around him. He felt as solid as granite to her, and probably just as immortal.

She let go and leaned back on her desk. Snuffled.

"Why aren't you at the party?"

"Just had a little work to clean up here for next week's Board Meeting. I'm not one for partying."

Caroline nodded. "Me, either."

"I'll let you get back to solving the tragic, horrible murder of my great and dear friend Red Boyle. The rotten sonofabitch."

Caroline and the Judge smiled at each other, and he walked out to the hallway and back to his office.

Caroline picked up the case notes off the floor, re-organized them and got back to work at her desk.

***

Tom walked back to the patio that overlooked the 9th green. He sat down by himself. Out of the darkness he saw Minnie Mouse rushing toward him as though to report an emergency. *Odd evening, this,* he thought.

"Tom!" Patti Boyle said breathlessly.

Tom stood up, "Patti, Hi, what's—"

"That perfume I remembered at the Island, the one Yuma Boyle was wearing. I smelled that fragrance again tonight. Autumn Amber was wearing it."

"Are you certain..." Tom knew that Patti and her siblings deeply resented Autumn sharing in the huge family inheritance.

"I am. What are you going to do?"

"I..." Truthfully, Tom had no idea. He adored the game of golf because it was a solitary sport, just you against the course. But crime solving, he had already learned, was a team effort. He needed his teammates desperately. He had the awful feeling the tiny threads that were finally coming together were going to unravel before he and his colleagues secured them, tightly and irrevocably.

"And Tom, I don't blame you for anything. My father pissed off too many people, it finally caught up to him. You are brave and sweet."

"Thank you. That means a lot to me."

***

Caroline stared at the LEADERBOARD. Thought some more...

She flashed on something Mathers said when they were at dinner after solving the hotel room murder in Phoenix: "As soon as we figured out it had to be someone with a key to the room, like an employee's passkey, this was an easy one to figure out."

Caroline had never understood why Tracy wasn't at the island with hubby Dick and Autumn until after the murder. Her story was that she was at work in California. But if closing the deal on the financing for the movie was so critically important to them...

The gossip at the Academy was that Autumn's mom Tracy was an actress.

Caroline remembered her own words in Puerto Penasco: *Sometimes it might be great fun to be someone else.*

"I'VE GOT IT!!!"

It would be wonderful to report that Caroline, seizing on the solution, leapt out of her chair, grabbed her .32 official private detective handgun from the drawer of her desk, the same one Julia shot Tom with, straightened her tie, adjusted her fedora, and stormed downstairs to make the "collar" of the criminal.

But in her excitement, she fell backwards in her desk chair and noisily crashed to the ground, letting out a yelp when her elbow slammed the floor. She was so glad Judge Wilkinson was not around to see that.

She had crushed her rakish fedora in the fall. *Damn!* she thought. *A detective could lose her PI license for crushing her fedora. Especially a girl. We're held to higher standards.*

She knocked her hat back into proper shape. Her elbow stung. She raced downstairs, just slightly slower than her heart was racing.

***

Patti Boyle returned to the party. Tom was contemplating what to do when he saw the lovely vampire MoniQue come back outside. She smiled warmly when she saw Tom. He briefly put his murder and mayhem concerns away and returned the smile.

"Where have you been? I'm getting thirsty without you."

"This will sound weird, but could you take off one of your shoes…"

"That does sound weird. Hope you don't have some sort of fetish…my last boyfriend was into--"

"No, nothing like that."

MoniQue took off her right shoe and handed it to Tom. He went over to the flower bed, pulled up a row of red petunias, smoothed over the soil and then imprinted the sole on the soft earth.

A "G".

Tom smiled. He beckoned MoniQue over. "You said these shoes were all the rage with the Hollywood set. This was the same imprint the British detectives found on Bogey Island in the flower bed outside the maid's quarters—the maid that disappeared."

Tom was reciting this to MoniQue as though he had told her about the case, but he hadn't. She nodded attentively anyway, excited to be part of the action.

The door to the patio opened and Det. Ed Mathers stepped outside, saw Tom and hurried over to him.

"Det. Ed Mathers, please say hello to Miss MoniQue Jones, who just may have helped us solve the murder of Mr. Red Boyle."

"Howdy," Mathers said, in character with his costume.

Tom showed Mathers the imprint of the "G" in the flower bed. "MoniQue told me these very expensive shoes, Grenville footwear, are popular with the movie set. A hotel maid would not be able to afford these shoes."

Mathers smiled. "Officer Rudy found out that Tracy Amberson lost her job with the studio in January. She was not working in Los Angeles the weeks up to the murder."

The patio door opened yet again. Caroline Colt came outside, saw the gathering at the flower bed and rushed over.

She was breathless: "Tracy Amberson was an actress, for a while. Her one and only movie appearance was in a film titled *Double Blind*."

"Yes," Tom exclaimed. "Aunt Felicity was the star of the film. About a killer using mistaken identity to get away with it. Tracy played <u>a maid</u>."

"Bitch couldn't even come up with something original."

Caroline shrieked with excitement. So did MoniQue, just to be part of the group.

Tom said, "Patti found out tonight that Autumn Amber is wearing the famous Yuma Boyle fragrance."

Mathers said, "I got a kid sister. She and our mom share perfume, clothes." He hurried toward the clubhouse door. "You guys stay here. I'll be right back. It was nice to meet you MoniQue."

MoniQue blushed. She's never talked to a real homicide detective before. *This night is so cool!*

***

A Police search at the Amberson residence the next day revealed, on a check register, that Tracy Amberson had purchased an airline ticket from Phoenix to Chicago—during the week the Western Open was played there.

Officer Rudy had already obtained phone records that showed there had been no calls placed to Bogey Island during the Grand Opening week from any phone exchange in Hollywood.

***

Mathers went to the pay phone and again phoned Officer Rudy downtown. "Please get out here to Valley Vista Country Club ASAP. I need you to watch the main parking lot, the comings and goings."

Mathers told him specifically whom to look for, a witch and a circus clown. Rudy was in his squad car and on his way in two minutes.

Now, we wait, Mathers thought.

***

Twenty minutes later, at the party in the ballroom, Tracy Amberson, in a witch costume, and her hubby Dick, dressed as a circus clown, were enjoying a dance. They were once again members in good standing at Valley Vista CC, having paid their long past due restaurant and bar bills there.

When the music ended, Tracy excused herself to visit the ladies' room. She saw her daughter, surrounded by admirers somewhat to Tracy's chagrin. *I'm the one who caused her career to happen!*

She was a few feet from Autumn when she detected the perfume she was wearing. A jolt of bad electricity shot through Tracy's nervous system. The electricity that tells you, you're hosed. She motioned for Autumn to join her in a corner of the hallway.

"Hi, mom! Great party, isn't it."

Tracy was livid. "You stupid little bitch! Why are you wearing that fragrance?"

Autumn was thoroughly confused. "I borrowed the bottle from your bathroom. I borrow your things all the time!"

"You should have borrowed some of my smarts."

Tracy rushed off, leaving Autumn standing there dumfounded.

***

Rudy W. arrived, without lights or siren. He pulled into a parking spot and got out. Mathers, by the door, saw him and walked over.

Rudy commented: "Nice costume, sir. Rather 'on the nose' don't you think?"

Mathers saw someone coming out the door. He turned, "It's her."

Tracy saw them and hurried back into the clubhouse. Mathers ran toward the door.

Tracy exited one of the back doors and hurried out onto the golf course. At the far end of the golf course was a gate that led out to a highway. Across the highway was a hotel with a cab stand.

Mathers came outside and joined Tom, Caroline and MoniQue on the patio.

"She gets to the cab stand we're screwed, she'll rabbit," Mathers said as he began running—well, lightly jogging—toward Tracy.

All four struggled to keep up with the surprisingly fleet-footed Tracy Amberson. MoniQue unzipped her skirt, stepped out of it, and kicked off the famous Grenville shoes.

"I was a track star at Scottsdale High," she said as she took off running, flashing past the other three.

Mathers stopped and pulled off his cowboy boots and followed MoniQue. Tom, trapped in a heavy knight costume, did his best to follow, helped by his natural athleticism.

In last place was Caroline wheezing from the exertion. "I <u>have to</u> get in better shape if I'm going to be a successful detective," she observed as the others quickly got far ahead of her.

MoniQue caught up to and jumped Tracy, who screamed, thinking for a moment that her assailant was a real vampire until she saw MoniQue was wearing pink polka dot panties.

Tracy flailed at MoniQue, landing a punch in her left eye. MoniQue punched back--CRUNCH!--and bloodied Tracy's nose as Mathers finally got there. Tom noted that MoniQue had a solid left hook.

"That's enough, Mrs. Amberson. It's over."

Tom got there, limping in his heavy boots.

Tracy gave up the fight. Got to her feet. And laughed as Caroline arrived.

"I am being apprehended by a vampire in her underwear, a cowboy without boots, a golfer boy doofus pretending to be a knight, and his annoying little sister. Helluva night."

"Tom is not a doofus," Caroline declared. "But yes, I am annoying."

Tom put his arm around Monique. "You were awesome! You collared a suspect..."

"I was!" she exclaimed, with a beamy smile. "I still hold the state high school record in the 400 meters."

Mathers, for inexplicable reasons, had handcuffs in his Lone Ranger jeans. He really did believe that crime could break out at any time wherever the rich were gathered, Tom observed.

He cuffed Tracy Amberson, who said nothing, just sent him a fierce stare. He escorted her back to the clubhouse.

She could stare all the daggers she wanted to at Det. Ed Mathers. After his 15 years on the force, he was pretty much dagger-proof. He responded with a bland smile.

He said, "You almost made it. Turning the watch back and shattering it was something that bothered me. You wanted to show the murder took place before you, as Tracy, got to the island. But you ended up focusing us on who arrived at the island that night. Just you. Over-thinking, that's what you did."

Tracy made a bitter face. "You can't prove any of this. My lawyers will eat you alive."

"And your daughter Autumn even chipped in a key clue: in the interviews on Bogey Island she said you called her several times before you came out from LA. There is no record of any calls to Bogey Island from Los Angeles that week. You were calling her from right there in the resort lodge."

Tracy absurdly tried to wriggle out of the handcuffs.

"You got trapped by the trappings of success. When it all falls away, you got nothing left but anger."

"Very philosophical. Aren't you clever, for some flatfoot underpaid cop."

"I like to think so, yes."

Tom and Monique followed, arm in arm, as though arresting Tracy was just a typical activity on a first date.

Caroline said, "I'll be along in a few. Just need to catch my breath."

"Take your time, detective. You earned it," Mathers said.

The word thrilled her. *Detective.*

Caroline, a devotee of PG Wodehouse stories, sat down on a bench near one of the tee boxes and said, *So it goes, Jeeves, and so it goes. No matter what danger we encounter, no matter what mayhem ensues, Tom Colt walks off with a beautiful woman, usually she's partially unclothed and always has a cute round ass.*

She said aloud, "Hurray for Caroline, who put the pieces together and solved the crime." She gazed at the silent, disinterested eucalyptus trees above her. "Maybe some applause? Anyone? Please…"

Mathers perp-walked Tracy through the crowd of aghast partygoers. *Rich people are quite skilled at looking aghast,* Mathers thought. *Or maybe it's appalled. I'm not sure.*

Part of being successful in the wealthy social scene is learning how to appear suitably aghast at any unpleasantness that arises.

"Do you have to humiliate me in front of my friends?" Tracy spat out.

"Yes, I do. Maybe It'll keep one of them from attempting something as reprehensible, as killing another human being—for stupid money."

"What a bastard you are," Tracy Amberson hissed.

"Lady, I'm not nearly the bastard I wish I were."

He led the suspected murderer to Rudy's squad car.

Seeing her mom being led away in handcuffs, Autumn Amber's big and bright eyes were wide with alarm. She was so shocked that not a single thought was traveling through her head. But as you well know, for a motion picture actress, that isn't necessarily unusual.

Dick Amberson did not register shock. His mind was fully alive, thinking, *Daaamm, this story will make a great screenplay! What should the title be??? 'House of Cards'. That's it! I'm brilliant!"*

When Dick got home, he rushed to his home office, eager to start on the script. He had the opening scene already planned…

He opened the desk drawer where he kept his typing paper. He saw a small envelope, his stash of cocaine.

"Aaaah," he sighed, "This has been such a stressful night."

He reached for the envelope.

Dick finally noticed he was still wearing his clown costume.

***

Tom went into the ballroom, made a beeline for the beverage tables and drank two glasses of water. The events of the evening had left him as dehydrated as when they play 36 holes the last round of the US Open.

The Club members buzzed over in groups of twos and threes and asked him to recount what happened that night. He obliged them, as he always did. There was a kind of morbid excitement in the air. It began to get on Tom's nerves.

He left the ballroom and went to the storage room where the members' golf bags were kept. His own clubs were at home. He picked out a driver, a #1 wood, from one bag—Carter Vonessens—and took 6 Titleist balls and three wooden tee-pegs from Sterling Gould's.

He walked out to the 10th tee of the course, which was not as visible from the clubhouse as the 1st tee.

He warmed up with several practice swings. For the first time that night, he relaxed.

He set a ball on a tee-peg. He swung. Hard. He hit a perfect long, straight shot that sailed through the dark night and bounded down the fairway. He set another ball on the tee-peg and continued until all 6 balls were gone.

Killing another human being to get money for a fucking movie isn't my reality, he thought. *This is. Hitting a golf ball with a perfect swing on this magnificent course.*

He stared into the darkness. He couldn't see where the balls ended up, but he knew he hit every shot perfectly. A great golfer can feel it.

Caroline walked up behind him. "Hey, Tom. Didn't know where you went. Thinking Deep Thoughts or recalling MoniQue sprinting down the fairway in her underwear?"

He chuckled, but when he turned, she could see a kind of anguish on his face. She knew what he was feeling, because her feelings were identical.

"I had enough of those people in there for one night. The whole lot of them. I don't belong…"

"We've found out the bad guys are badder than we thought. We may get ourselves killed doing this PI stuff, Tom."

"We may well."

"We don't have to do the detective thing. Let someone else chase the bad guys."

"No," he said firmly. "Justice is worth it. Our friendship with Ed Mathers is worth it. And we're damn good at this."

She walked over closer to him.

"I am so damn glad to hear you say that."

She indicated the bright lights of the clubhouse.

"Let's go back in. We're the Guests of Honor at the best country club in the Southwest. They're liable to applaud when we walk in. Let's enjoy our triumph."

"All right, partner."

Tom left Carter Vonessen's golf club sitting on the tee. Let Vonessen solve the mystery of how it got there.

"You know, we spend so much time at this place we should build a condo along one of the fairways. We could walk to work."

"That is a brilliant idea," Tom responded.

***

Five minutes later, Tom and Caroline were back at the party, still in full swing, and each had a glass of champagne. They were chatting with MoniQue, who seemed to be several glasses ahead of them.

Caroline asked him to dance.

"Won't people think that's a bit weird?" he replied.

"Tom, they already think we're weird. We live together. We work together. What Country Club in America has a detective agency on the third floor? Only a weird country club. What other pro golfer would rather solve crimes than win tournaments? Only a weird pro golfer."

"All valid points."

Tom turned to MoniQue. "I'll be right back. My sister wants me to have a celebratory dance with her."

"No worries. We have all eternity, darling." She had put the vampire teeth back in.

"Now you're starting to scare me."

"'bout time someone did, Mr. Popularity. You get away with way too much…"

Caroline had a big grin on her face. "I like this undead chick."

So Colt & Colt Confidential danced…

"You and I are brilliant detectives, Tom. We're better than Nick and Nora Charles!"

"Yes. For one thing, they're fictional and we are real. It's more fun being real."

"Although memorable fictional characters outlive their authors."

The song ended. Caroline and Tom went over to one of the food tables and piled two plates high with roast beef. Young Colts need their strength.

Caroline asked between big bites, "Do you think there's a chance Tracy's lawyer can get her off?"

"Yes, more than just a chance. I still don't have all the details of the night of the murder sorted out in my mind."

"Me either, I'm sorry to say. Do you think Mathers has it sorted out?"

Tom did not hesitate. "Mathers is the smartest man I've ever met—besides…our dad."

Caroline nodded, the pride on her face evident. She tried hard to make certain that the tears did not flow.

Chapter Twenty-Nine
Yes, Det. Ed Mathers Did Have It All Sorted Out...
What Really Happened The Night of Elwood "Red" Boyle's Final Fart

It comes as a shock to many of us to learn that one or more persons on this earth wish us dead. We tend to assume we are universally loved and admired. For most of us, there is at least one individual who harbors this dark wish of bringing about our demise.

Red Boyle, who as you know believed his life was in danger, still registered shock when the knife stolen from the resort kitchen plunged through his back and breached his heart.

He was standing in his office by a huge wall map that depicted his global real estate holdings. Each property was shown as a tiny golf flagstick. Red loved looking at that map. Even better than a ledger book showing his net worth, it was a visual representation that the empire he built now spanned the globe.

As he felt the knife slash into his flesh, he turned to see Carol Thorn, faithful employee, standing there with a frightened look on her face. The act of murder, no matter how carefully thought out or rationally justified, leaves the amateur criminal in a state of shock. Not as shocked as the victim, mind you.

"You?" Boyle croaked out as he felt his body shutting down like a tall building that was quickly losing electrical power, penthouse to basement.

He reached out to grab her with his hammy right hand, but she backed away as he fell to the carpet, face down, and emitted that one final fart.

"EWWWWW," Carol Thorn exclaimed. She was trembling from head to toe. When the gas smell cleared, she took a series of deep breaths to calm herself. I was 8:36.

She had been waiting in the dark recesses of Boyle's office since 8PM, the time, she knew from her careful observations, that Boyle always came up to his office to look at the ledger book that listed his holdings, and then admire them in pictorial form on the wall.

Carol was briefly immobilized from recognizing the enormity of what she had done. The man was dead. But she was roused to action when she thought again of her motivation: poverty and disgrace were not an option.

Carol went to work. She took Red's watch band off, adjusted the time to 7:36, then smashed the watch face with a paperweight from Red's desk, freezing the time forever at that moment.

She placed the watchband back on his wrist, watch face down. She took the murder weapon, the striking pearl-handled carving knife from the kitchen, and placed it in a paper sack. She was wearing the same rubber gloves she had worn to clean the Boyle International Properties toilets earlier that day.

She opened the drawers to Boyle's desk. In the upper left one, which she was pleasantly surprised to find was left unlocked, she found two business envelopes. One was addressed to an attorney in Phoenix, one was left blank. She examined the contents of each one. They were identical: executed and witnessed copies of the 12th Amendment to the Boyle Family Trust.

Now her rapid breathing was from excitement, not fright: she had both copies of the new Will, which strangely Carol thought, left the bulk of the estate to Rev. Damien Tucker.

She removed two envelopes of her own from her pocket and placed them in another desk drawer. One envelope was addressed simply to My Dad.

Carol hurried to the door, opened it, scanned the empty hallway, shut the office door and walked to where she had left the maid cart. She had to coach herself not to run. Someone was bound to see her. She took slow, patient steps, those of a bored lower-level employee tending to routine at work at a job she hated.

She wheeled her cart to room 217. She knew what she would find inside: Julia Wilkinson passed out on the floor from an overdose of the medicine she took to modulate her bi-polar condition.

Carol knocked. "Maid service," she said.

No answer. She turned her pass key, opened the door and went inside.

There lay Julia, on the bed. Carol retrieved the paper sack from her cart and placed the murder weapon next to Julia on the bed. *No, a drama queen like Julia would have flung the knife across the room when she came in, then taken the overdose in a fit of remorse for what she had done.* Carol tossed the knife. *There, that's better.*

How did Carol the maid know that Julia took her meds precisely at 7:30 each night? Carol Thorn saw all. Just as her weak adversary, private detective Tom Colt, was a great listener, Carol Thorn was a great watcher.

Carol knew Chandler Boyle would be arriving at 9PM because he had placed an order for celebratory champagne and caviar to be delivered to Julia's room. *What, Carol wondered, did Chandler Boyle have to celebrate? He had just been all but eliminated from sharing in his father's estate. Well, there was this rumor of treasure on the island. Could he have found it? Carol doubted it. Chandler seemed like a big blowhard not capable of finding his own ass in the dark.*

From Carol's standpoint, this was perfect: the celebration would be construed by the dopey cops as the Boyle children having killed their father and claiming their long-awaited inheritance. Carol knew Chandler was hot for Julia, and knew she would have fun with him, then dump him. Her ability to manipulate men was an aspect of Julia that Carol admired.

Carol Thorn opened the door and scanned the hallway yet again. She took the paper bag, rolled her maid cart to the end of the hallway, near the back exit, where it was stored. She removed her gloves, put them in the bag and exited the building down one flight of stairs, and walked to the staff quarters, spartan tiny cottages, 15' by 20', with just the basics for the hired help, at the far southern end of the lodge. No one had yet seen her—as far as she knew.

She found her door, went inside, closed the door with relief. She sat down on the one couch in the room, a tacky and fading brown one, noticed she was still trembling. She thought about having a scotch, but she needed to be as sharp as possible the rest of the night. Her plan had many tricky steps yet to execute. She recalled a saying of her late father's, who worked as a sound man in the early days of talking pictures in Hollywood: There's many a slip twixt cup and lip.

Carol tried to calm herself with positive thoughts of how much she'd already accomplished that evening. Nothing doing: she was too keyed up.

She took off her shoes, stepped out of her maid uniform, took off the midriff padding she used to appear chunky. She removed her glasses and the dark, short wig.

These items she placed in her small suitcase on the bed. She thought about leaving the maid uniform behind, to show she had departed quickly. But couldn't risk it: there might be minute traces of blood on the light grey cloth with the Boyle International Properties logo on the front.

From the closet she removed a large paper sack containing clothing. Using a mirror in the hallway, she put on the dark blue outfit with the constellation pattern, and red wig, to become Yuma Boyle. She slipped back on the gloriously comfortable shoes she loved, knowing she would be doing a lot of walking that night. She applied a light coat of pale pink lipstick. Finally, she did a spritz of Yuma Boyle's favorite perfume 'attar of roses' behind her left ear.

Taking one last look around the cottage, a look of deep contempt for the dumpy little place, she picked up her suitcase—*why do people want to live this way*, she thought-- and walked out the back patio door, which led to a dark, overgrown part of the island. She stepped carefully on the soft, wet earth, trying not to get her shoes muddy. Carol left multiple impressions of the letter 'G'.

Ten minutes later, she arrived at one of the island's three docks. She knew a charter boat was leaving at in a few minutes to the main island. When she got to the dock she was surprised to see Carter and Babs Vonessen there, as well as Tom Colt's golfer chick, Katrina Stern. This was perfect. Carol Thorn needed witnesses that Yuma left the island that night. She got them.

Her spirits buoyed, Carol/Yuma boarded the modest 17-ft motorboat. The three passengers greeted each other. Not a friendly group. Carter Vonessen looked pissed off, and Katrina had a pensive frown.

Carol/Yuma settled in as the boat left the dock, reflecting on her fellow passengers: *Don't leave now, guys, the party's just starting.*

As time dragged on, Carol/Yuma thought it might look suspicious if she didn't say anything the whole time they were traveling. She turned to morose Katrina, "Boy trouble, I bet. Don't worry. It's all going to work out."

Carol/Yuma thought the look Katrina gave her was odd, but she patted Kat on the hand and resumed watching the waves.

They docked at 10:08. Carol/Yuma was 15 minutes behind her carefully timed schedule. She would have to hustle. The passengers bid each other goodnight. Vonessen gave the boat captain a generous tip, and the passengers, the Vonessens, Kat and Yuma, took separate directions.

Carol/Yuma walked into a busy tourist bar, packed well beyond the fire code regulations. She was noticed by many gentlemen there. You don't see a shapely redhead in a star-themed tight blouse and skirt. She went into the ladies' room, took off her wig, her shoes and her Yuma outfit, unpinned her hair, which tumbled down blonde and bouncy, put on a bland traveler outfit, tan blouse and slacks, put on her trusty shoes and became Tracy Amberson, Hollywood production executive.

She examined herself in the bathroom mirror to make sure no traces of Yuma/Carol remained, saw that she had left on Yuma's pale pink lipstick, removed it with a paper towel and exited the bathroom. This time no one noticed her. The guys were still thinking about the unusual redhead, no doubt.

She needed to discard the Carol/Yuma identities. She walked toward another dock, where a second boat was scheduled to depart. She saw a family of homeless people gathered around a fire burning in an old oil drum, probably from WWII. The night was cold. Not all folks in the Grand Bahamas were having a grand time on this March night in 1963.

She took the sacks of Yuma garb and Carol garb and placed them in the dumpster. She watched a few reflective moments as the wigs and clothes burned. "Some trash from dinner," she commented to the little family.

Tracy pulled out $20 bills and gave them to the startled homeless people. She made sure each one got a good look at the well-coiffed, smartly dressed blonde lady with the confident smile.

She made it to her boat just in time. The grizzled captain, smelling of sweat and the sea, said, "Three more minutes and I'd a left without you."

She flashed another calm, confident, show business smile. Shedding the costumes had caused her to shed some of the apprehension she had been gripped with all evening. "Thank you so much for waiting. My husband and daughter are waiting for me on Bogey Island."

Tracy was charming, for sure. The old gent smiled back and saluted her as he cranked the engine.

Tracy stepped off the boat and onto the island at 11PM. If the authorities ever checked, Tracy Amberson did have a ticket on a flight from Phoenix to Miami that morning. But the woman occupying the seat was Tracy's sister Janine. The ticket was a kind of gift. Janine always wanted to visit Miami.

She knew she would be asked by the cops, "Your plane landed at 2PM. Why not get on a boat and get to the island right away?" *Well, officer, I'm happy to answer your question. I wanted some time by myself to think about my marriage to my husband Dick. We've been having some problems lately.*

As the boat neared the island dock, Tracy couldn't help expelling a cackle of relief.

I am brilliant. The disguises. The broken watch. The timing. No one can tie me to this murder.

I still say I could have been a brilliant actress. But I was never given a chance. I have the flair, the beauty, the drive—much more than my silly daughter with the big brown cow eyes.

And to think that no-talent twit Felicity Greyhawk made millions playing the same character over and over.

The boat reached the dock.

Well, I saved us. I saved my family from financial ruin and social embarrassment. That old bastard Red Boyle thought he could fuck with me. And I stood up to him—like someone should have done a long time ago.

The captain secured the boat to the dock. Tracy stepped out and thanked him for the smooth ride.

Everything would be a smooth ride from now on. She would take the money and start her own company, *Tracy Amberson Productions.*

Chapter Thirty

The morning after the memorable Halloween Party, at breakfast, Caroline asked Tom, "So now you're seeing MoniQue Jones. What's your dating technique—open the metropolitan telephone directory and point?"

"We happened to connect at the party. Maybe I have a thing for vampire girls."

"Your relationships do seem to drain a lot of blood out of you." She poured herself a cup of coffee. "Another rich girl. I don't think they're going to make you happy. Although a bad date with a rich girl is probably better than a bad date with a poor one. The rich girl can at least pick up the dinner tab."

"Yes. You see, I'm just being practical."

"I've said this before, I'll say it again, you need to go to Wickenburg and find a nice hard-working rancher girl to be with. She'll treat you right."

***

At 10AM Tom and Caroline drove downtown to police headquarters for the Chief of Police's press conference regarding the arrest of Tracy Amberson for the murder of Elwood "Red" Boyle.

Chief James Flannery was a great leader of men, a cop from the old school. He was quick to praise the members of his force for doing a great job, rather than taking the credit himself to curry favor with politicians. The result was that his men loved working for him, would do anything for him.

That day, he passed out high praise to Det. Mathers, seated in the front row of the conference room, next to Tom and Caroline. "Please stand up, Ed, and be recognized."

Mathers did. The cops in attendance applauded.

"The people of Phoenix also have several civilians to thank. Tom and Caroline Colt foremost. As you know they are Private Investigators. Tom is also a professional golfer. Busy fellow. Please stand up."

Tom and Caroline did as requested. Caroline was thrilled by the applause. Just a few months ago she had concluded that Colt & Colt Confidential Investigations was a failure, she was a failure.

The Chief then got a strange, pained look on his face. "I also need to thank," he paused, took a deep breath, "Miss Felicity

Greyhawk, a former Hollywood actress who is now renowned for her...psychic abilities...which...helped us solve the crime." The Chief could barely spit those words out.

Felicity popped up to drink in the applause before the Chief even asked her to. She waved her fluttery fingers and smiled proudly.

Caroline said to Tom: "I still think Fredonia and Chandler are mixed up in the murder of fake Rev. Tucker. We'll never be able to prove it though."

Mathers overheard this and said to Caroline, "Never is a long time, Miss C. We'll get 'em."

"Damn straight," Caroline said.

When the press conference ended, Mathers went to his office to check his phone messages. Tom went out to get takeout cheeseburgers at Bob's Big Boy. Caroline took a tour of the police station.

A reporter for the *Arizona Republic* newspaper, Bonnie Blunt, stopped Caroline and asked her if she would be willing to be interviewed about how they solved the murder of Red Boyle.

Caroline looked startled, "Me?"

"Yes, you. It will make for an interesting angle. I don't know of too many female private investigators."

"Sure," Caroline said. The reporter gave Caroline her business card and they set up a time to chat.

A few minutes later, Caroline saw Mathers walking down the corridor. She hustled over and caught up to him.

"Hey, Caroline."

He saw she had a serious expression.

"Ed, I have a question. Is solving a murder always frenzied, scattered, frustrating, hopeless, a muddled mess, and then we somehow pull the solution out of our ass?"

Mathers gave her question thoughtful consideration for several moments. Then smiled.

"Yes."

He gave Caroline a little squeeze on the shoulders, then put his hands in his pockets and continued on his way, whistling the catchy theme tune from the film, *The High and the Mighty.*

"Cool dude," said Caroline Colt, Private Investigator.

Caroline, Det. Mathers thought, *is a beautiful woman, a very beautiful woman. Inside and out."*

***

A radical faction at Valley Vista Country Club tried to have Det. Mathers expelled from the Club because he had arrested a member, but they were outnumbered by the members who tended to look down on murder, even when committed by one of their own. The vote was surprisingly close, though.

***

Back at his tiny office, Mathers saw there was a telegram on his desk. He read it:

> *Greetings, Chief Detective Mathers. Glad to see you ran with the lead I gave you that the killer was 'Yuma Boyle'. If you need further assistance in the future, don't hesitate to contact me.*
> *Cheers, Inspector Archie Weatherford, London, England, The British Empire*
> *2 November, 1963*

Mathers expelled an irritated breath. He popped his head out the door and called Officer Rudy W. into his office.

"Sir?"

"Read this." He handed Rudy the telegram.

Rudy made a sour face.

Mathers said, "Officer Blandings over in Vice grew up in London, correct?"

"I think so, yes."

"Could you please ask him what is a respectful, proper British, upper-class way of saying 'fuck off'?"

Rudy smiled.

"I'll get right on it, sir."

***

Tom, driving home, tried to make sense of the Red Boyle Murder and its aftermath.

Red Boyle collected enemies as eagerly as he amassed his real estate holdings. They gave him equal joy. He reveled in tormenting his foes, even his family. But it finally caught up to him.

Business Axiom #1 that Judge Wilkinson taught me: Enemies who find a way to make big money by working together are less likely to kill each other.

Red couldn't work with his rivals, his enemies. He wanted to destroy them. Inevitably, he was destroyed. What I could not understand was why he treated his own children so deplorably, why he tormented them with money. He had so much money, so much more than he needed. Why be such a miser?

Our mother worked three jobs so Caroline and I could attend a university, at least until Caroline dropped out junior year.

Red Boyle's dream was to be a golf champion—one of the greats. His life showed the toxic effects of your dream not coming true.

He spent his business life, and his family life, making sure no one else's dream came true.

If I am fortunate enough to have the financial resources someday, I'm going to be generous, like Judge Wilkinson has been with me.

Red Boyle's actions made no sense. But one of Ed Mathers' Axioms was: It's not our job to understand these people, just to discover what happened and why.

***

The following day, Tom was alone in the quiet offices of Colt & Colt Confidential Investigations (no sultry dames needing a PI in sight) when Judge Roy Wilkinson walked in. The Judge noted Tom's thoughtful, maybe troubled expression. Tom was leaning against his desk, looking out the window.

"Boyle was a horrible person, sir. He didn't respect golfers. He didn't respect our game."

The Judge smiled to himself. To Tom Colt, that was the unpardonable sin.

"I think you'll find, Tom, that many of the men who achieve great wealth are Red Boyles."

"I couldn't be that way. I guess I'll never be rich."

The Judge chuckled in his patented condescending way. "You won't need to be like Boyle to make your fortune because everyone loves Tom Colt. It's quite extraordinary, really. I've never met anyone quite like you."

Tom wasn't sure what to say to that enormous compliment, so he said nothing.

"If I could find your secret, I'd be twice as rich as I already am. Wouldn't that be fabulous!"

"I guess."

"Tom, never be reluctant to pursue your own self-interest with all your might. That's how our society creates wealth. And that benefits everyone."

Tom's wrinkled forehead indicated he didn't fully understand.

"Has my wealth benefited you and Caroline?"

"Absolutely, sir. Your help has made all the difference."

"Now do you understand?"

"Yes."

"All you lack are social contacts. There is a very short list of people in Phoenix who know how to create wealth. I will make sure you meet every one of them."

The Judge reached inside his suit coat and pulled out an envelope. He handed it to Tom.

"A small bonus for solving the murder of my lifelong friend Red Boyle. Please share with your sister. I reward merit. You and Caroline are individuals of merit."

The Judge lit an unfiltered Pall Mall cigarette.

"Thank you, sir."

"Thank you and Caroline—and I suppose, Mathers." He walked toward the door, stood in the doorway and turned.

"Patti Boyle is my goddaughter, you see."

Tom was surprised, but the Judge was adept at springing surprises.

"She's grown up to be a lovely, smart young woman. If you and Julia weren't going to be together *someday*, Patti would make an excellent wife. A fine head for business she has."

The Judge walked out of Tom's office. Tom opened the envelope. A check for $25,000. How much money was that in 1963? The winner's share at that year's US Open Golf Championship in Brookline, Mass. was $17,500.

Young Tom struggled to understand the Judge's philosophy. When Tom was a much older, and possibly wiser, man, he would even coin a term for it: Romantic Individualism. It was the idea that any achievement was possible if you had absolute belief in your abilities—in your uniqueness, in your separation and differentiation from all the other people on this earth.

Why was it Romantic? Because the Judge was willing and able to help others identify their own uniqueness, their own differentiation, their own special place on this earth, like young Tom Colt and Caroline Colt.

How different their lives would have been if they had never met him. Tom shuddered to think about it.

Chapter Thirty-One
--We return to 2005
And Revisit the Night Carmen Announced Her Engagement

Tom Colt's Condo at Valley Vista CC

Carmen arrived at Tom's door looking nervous. It was 7:59PM.

He welcomed her inside. And tried to read what her emotions were, without success.

She breathed a big sigh and began:

"I want to tell you something."

Tom braced himself. He had a strong feeling this was bad news.

"I'm getting engaged," she said. Those words, together, were one of the worst blows Tom had ever sustained, far worse than the three times he had been shot when he was a private detective.

Wanting to scream out NO! Tom instead remained stoic.

"Who's the lucky guy?" he asked, smiling but with a breaking voice.

Carmen sighed again. Her anguish was evident.

Tom thought, *it flashed in my mind that my life was over. Not the physical, sentient part perhaps, but the joyful, expectant, wondrous part. The part where dreams can still come true.*

Carmen took a deep, deep breath, as though starved for oxygen.

"The lucky guy is you. I want us to be engaged. I went out and bought these rings," which she retrieved from her purse. She set Tom's down on a coffee table.

She continued: "I've thought it through. I want to be more a part of your life than the girl you steal a kiss from when you think none of the Club members are looking."

She studied Tom's reaction, which was an unreadable, level gaze, then continued:

"And...who knows how long any of us has? My mom's best friend died of ovarian cancer when she was 49. I'm not as young as you think, Tom. I've had three disappointing relationships and an expensive disaster of a marriage that I still wake up with nightmares from."

A pause for needed oxygen.

"I know what I feel. And when we're together, I feel something like I've never felt before. You love me the way I want to be loved. Everything else is secondary, including what other people think."

Except she had no idea what Tom was thinking…

"I grew up on a ranch, caring for livestock. You learn about the cycle of life, birth and death. What's important and what's not. You and I have what's important."

She paused again, to breathe in additional vital oxygen, possibly just before passing out.

Carmen turned and walked over to the green couch, sat down. Tom remained standing. "I thought we could have a six-month engagement. And then decide. If it doesn't work out, I'll find a new job so it won't be awkward for the two of us here at the Club."

Tom expression was intense, his face hard. To Carmen, this was devastating.

She sprang back up from the couch and looked away. "I knew it. You don't feel the same way. Well, I just ruined a beautiful friendship. And embarrassed both of us." She dabbed at the corner of her eye with a finger.

She turned around and faced him. He saw the beautiful light in her eyes had dimmed. "I am so sorry, Tom."

He held up his left hand, on which was displayed the gold ring—gleaming it seemed to her.

The warm light of expectation returned to her lovely brown eyes.

"Yes?"

"Yes."

This was now one of the best nights of Tom Colt's life. And surely of Carmen's.

They embraced. She said, "We shouldn't be so afraid of us."

"Grab a blanket from the hall closet. I'll fetch a bottle of wine from the fridge."

Ten minutes later, on the right side of the 12th fairway at Valley Vista CC, where only the boldest players dare to go, Tom and Carmen sat on that blanket and sipped from the shared bottle of wine. The waterfall behind the green was brightly lit with multi-colored lights.

"I wanted with all my heart for you to put the ring on, and now that you have, we can continue just as we are. I had to know if you were serious enough about me to say yes. Let's spend the next six months getting to know each other as more than two kids who struggled their way through life and now have everything we've ever dreamed of. And then, if all goes well, get engaged. She gently removed the ring from his hand, and then hers.

They lay back on the blanket and looked up at the stars.

She smiled. "There's something romantic about a golf course at night."

He laughed, "I agree. I so agree."

"You were right, what you said in your book, Tom. 'Life is all about golf and love'."

"Maybe the correct order would be love and golf."

She took the wine bottle from him and sipped. "MMMM. Yes, that's it." She turned, sat up and looked into his eyes. "I was so afraid you'd say this was madness."

"We have six months to find out just how mad it is. Why did you pick 6 months?"

"I couldn't wait any longer than that to find out we can make a go of this, of us."

Tom and Carmen shared a kiss. Just one. No need to rush. They had 6 months to get to know each other.

That single kiss gently electrified them both.

At that moment, if you had held up a mirror to Tom's face, he would have seen the image from the photograph displayed on the south wall of the Gentlemen's Lounge at the Club, that enduring moment of triumph when he was 28. But he would have seen a vibrant living image, eager for the triumphs to come, not a nearly forgotten record of the distant past.

As for Carmen, like all romantic idealists she carried the lingering scars of hurts she never revealed, hurts that never healed. But the kiss in the dark, that hopeful exploration of the future, changed her. Somehow, all the scars were gone.

She felt as though her life had begun again. After they had sealed the bargain of their courtship, Carmen gained a blazing insight that took her breath away: There was a chance her ideal really did exist. The ideal was not a myth and not just a young girl's dream. And more than just exist: he had fallen in love with her.

***

The Four Horrids Part II

The next week, the golfing abomination known as the Four Horrids had a surprise in store when they trudged in for their Wednesday afternoon lunch at Valley Vista CC.

They had just finished their lunch plates—they ordered the beef in red wine special—like these little old lushes needed more alcohol in their food. Then they started their traditional grousing about all aspects of the meal.

Ginny Bland said, "The place settings were particularly sloppy today, don't you think. It's like they just toss the silverware down and walk away. Part of a genteel luncheon is having everything in its proper place."

"Well," said Daphne Hedgerow conspiratorially, "You can take the girl out of the barrio, but you can't take the barrio out of the girl."

Since Basil's widow was partially deaf, she spoke loudly enough for Carmen, wheeling the dessert cart into the room, to overhear. She left her cart and walked over to the Four Horrids' table, stormed over, to be precise.

No need for a deep breath: Carmen was cranked up.

"Good afternoon, ladies. I wouldn't know how to find a barrio if I were looking for one. My family owns a 1,000-acre cattle ranch in New Mexico. Sometimes we run as many as 800 head to the finest beef cattle in the Southwest. My mother is Irish, named Coneghy, she's descended from a pioneer woman who built that cattle ranch with three other women in the 1880's. They forged the famous cattle trail to Kansas, the Connelly-Douglass Trail. You might have read about those women in the history books in school. And one more thing: Tom Colt, the guy, no, the fabulous guy, who owns this place, and works night and day to make you fussy, spoiled people happy--he thinks I'm wonderful. So wonderful that he believes I'm too good for him. So what do you have to say to that, Ladies?"

Carmen shocked herself with how her voice rose in volume. Being stoic in the face of insults, veiled or obvious, from Club members is part of the job description for the employees at any private club, where the snide remarks, the cutting comments and the all-out insults are frequent. In the era when Tom's mother was a waitress there, she even had to put up with the occasional barroom grope from a geriatric drunk.

The Four Horrids, with their combined more than 300 years of life experience, were seldom taken aback by anything. They smiled at each other, cooly, placidly, and then at Carmen.

Ginny said, "I must tell you, my dear, the vichyssoise was delicious today. Please tell the Chef."

Daphne added, "You are always so attentive, Carmen. We can't thank you enough for your wonderful service to our Club!"

Felicity said, "And the beef was perfectly seasoned! What a heavenly sauce."

They waited for Carmen to say something.

"It's been a pleasure serving you ladies today, as always." She smiled. A kind of fierce smile, but a smile nonetheless.

Felicity said, "Let's do a toast to Tom, our wonderful host."

The always competitive Jilly Flannery lifted her glass first.

"To my sweetie, Tom." She took a slug of vodka. She sighed like a contented puppy when she felt the alcohol warm her all the way down to her soul. Yes, Jilly did have a soul.

Felicity pointed to an empty chair at the table and said, with that serious, deep psychic-reader voice of hers, "I have a vision that it shan't be long before you are seated at one of these tables, Carmen, as our equal, not serving us, my dear."

Jilly said, "Shit, Felicity, you don't have to be psychic to predict that." She took another swig of vodka. In her mind, especially after two vodka tonics, Jilly was still young enough to be Tom's lover—and by that she meant the 28-year-old Tom from 1963.

Carmen bit her lip, hard, so a loud, triumphant giggle would not burst out of her, turned and walked to the kitchen.

In the Evening...

Guest Narrator Brian Hill Continues Our Story (Because Brooks Benton is too inebriated this evening to craft fluid, memorable prose):

Carmen Lopez was the substitute bartender that night in the Gentlemen's Lounge (barroom) at Valley Vista CC.

By 9:45 only a half-dozen gentlemen (drunks) remained, seated at tables by the window. At the bar, only Brooks Benton was there, working on his third glass of scotch. He and Carmen were discussing one of their favorite mutual subjects: Tom Colt.

"He asked me to write that book to impress you, you know. He thought if you read about all the exciting adventures he's had, you'd be excited about him." Brooks' voice was hoarse from doing 10 radio interviews across the country that day to promote their book.

"All he had to do was grab me and kiss me."

Brooks shook his head. "No, no, that's never done in our politically correct era. Everyone's terrified of being sued. And in a workplace? Oh, my, the litigation."

"I'm not from this era. Never wanted to be."

Brooks took a gulp of scotch, thought a few moments. "And pursuing you too boldly might have been too much of a risk for even Tom Colt. There are about, I'd say, 100 things about you that enthrall him."

Brooks took another gulp of scotch.

"You're a fantastic writer, Brooks. Your book made me fall in love with Tom even more."

Brooks didn't hear the 'fall in love with Tom' part, only the 'fantastic writer' part.

"Thank you. But I'm starting to wonder whether my life, this so-called journalism career, was worth all the work, all the struggle to put it down on paper. Sure, I've travelled the world, met all the great sports stars of our era, blah, blah, blah, but what does it matter?"

Brooks stared moodily into his glass, then continued. "Look at tonight: all my chums at this fine Club are shunning me because I told the truth about them and their families in the book. I am abandoned to drink all alone. What's this thing called life about, lovely Carmen? Anything at all?"

That night was an example of why Carmen hated being substitute bartender. She was stuck there, behind the bar, with no avenue of escape. At least with waiting tables, you can walk away if the customer says something idiotic, something ridiculous, like now. She didn't have that critical bartending skill: patient, endlessly sympathetic listener and part-time philosopher.

"Bullshit," Carmen said crisply and directly.

Brooks looked at her with wounded, alcohol-clouded eyes. "What did you say?"

"You loved sticking it to the snobs. And it's bullshit because you are a seeker of truth—and that's important for all of our sakes. Which you well know."

Brooks was taken aback but thrilled at the same time. Carmen cared about him—now that's important.

"You are a woman of many facets, Carmen."

"That's the reason women love diamonds. We sparkle very much like them."

Brooks fumbled with his sportscoat pocket and retrieved his Intrepid Reporter's Notebook. "Good line. I'm going to borrow that one for my next book."

"You spent the whole day on the radio talking about how amazing Tom's life has been, and it made you wish that had been your life. But it's not. I listened to some of the interviews. It doesn't mean your life wasn't significant, it was just different from Tom's. Tom is the stuff of dreams. I still don't fully understand what he sees in me."

Brook about fell off his stool. "My turn: Bullshit!!!"

She cracked a slight smile that she didn't want him to see.

Brooks said, "In the words of the late, great Det. Ed Mathers, the problem with most of us is BTOB. Believing Their Own Bullshit."

One of Judge Wilkinson's innovations in the '60s had been to set up three furnished guest rooms on the 2nd floor of the Club, for members to stay overnight if they had too much to drink. This prevented the Judge getting a midnight phone call from Det. Mathers saying that one of his Club Members had been arrested for DUI, the most galling aspect which would have been the glee in Mathers' voice.

"To me, the honest journalist is a hero," Carmen said. "Remember the movie, *The Man Who Shot Liberty Valance*? Who did the outlaw try to silence—the honest journalist."

Brooks nodded. "Sure I remember that movie. He wasn't just honest, he was fearless."

"My grandpa Ernie was a stuntman in Duke's movies."

"He was? Cool beans!" Brooks exclaimed.

Carmen smiled. "That was one of Caroline Colt's favorite expressions."

Brooks lifted his glass: "To Caroline."

Brooks took a drink, set the glass down and sighed. He was about spent for one day.

He slid his glass over to her side of the bar and—unsteadily—got up from his chair.

He bowed to Carmen. "Goodnight lovely lady. I thank you for your kind words and your hospitality. If you wish to continue this conversation, I will be in Guest Room 3. Lovely view of the 18th hole. Quite romantic, I would say."

"Probably not," Carmen said.

"I knew that." Brooks leaned over and took his half-full glass back. At least he'd have that for company in his lonely, albeit luxurious room with high-speed Internet and fully stocked mini bar.

Raymond the Piano Man, observing this scene, couldn't help himself. He tried but just couldn't. He and Tom shared a trait: they were both rascals. So as Brooks toddled off, Raymond played and crooned Sinatra's melancholy barroom ballad, *Make it one for my baby (and one more for the road).*

"Not funny, piano man," Brooks said, suddenly grouchy. "I know she's Tom's baby, not mine."

"That fact is undisputed."

"Ray, the reviews of my book so far are all raves. The publisher says the pre-publication orders for it were amazing. They are ecstatic. I'm on my way to becoming a NYT bestselling author. People who don't really give a rat's ass about golf are even buying my book. My wildest dreams have come true. Why am I not happy, not satisfied?"

"You didn't get the girl."

"It's that simple."

"Always is."

***

Carmen's shift as substitute bartender ended at 11PM. At 11:05, there was a knock on the door at Guest Room 3.

Brooks opened it. "Carmen," he said with a note of hopeful astonishment in his voice. He was wearing an extra-large New York Jets jersey as a nightshirt.

"Brooks, you don't need these country club snobs to be your friends. You've got Tom...and me."

Brooks forgot for a moment that he was a cynical journalist who grew up on grim streets in New York before he found his way to the glorious West. He said simply, "Thank you, thank you."

"Goodnight," she said with what Brooks thought was the loveliest smile he had ever received.

As Brooks himself had once written, *her smile showed you the essence of your dreams before you ever dreamed them.*

He watched her walk away, then closed the door and walked back over to the desk where he had been working after returning from the bar. The thing about writers, they sober up quickly. Just like playing good golf, it's all about practice.

He picked up a sheet of paper with the schedule of radio interviews his publisher had set up for the next day to promote their book.

"Let me at 'em," Brooks said aloud, confidently, to a painting of golfing great Walter Hagen on the wall.

Deep in his 51-year-old bones Brooks Benton believed he still had a shot with Carmen.

***

Brooks Benton Continues Our Story:

March 17, 2005

Katrina knew Tom and Carmen were getting closer. Kat, on an evening walk in their condo development along the first fairway of Valley Vista CC, where she and Tom had lived for ten years, heard Tom and Carmen's voices on his patio, just three doors down from her own.

Katrina felt conflicting emotions. She wanted Tom, her best all-time friend and one of the men she truly admired, to find the happiness he deserved. And there was no way she would ever get married again, even to Tom. But a part of her didn't want Carmen to occupy too much space in Tom's heart.

She liked everything about her life at that moment. She liked her freedom, including financial freedom. But she adored the unscheduled, spontaneous intimacy she had with Tom. It was a key ingredient to her recipe for happiness in life. It suited her much better than being married. She was finally almost content, as content as an over-achiever like Katrina Stern ever could be.

The next day Katrina called Tom and asked him to meet her on the Club patio after work.

***

March 18, 2005

11PM On the Patio of Valley Vista CC

Tom and Katrina were the only ones left at the Club at that hour. Tom had raided the bar and retrieved a bottle of Burgundy and two glasses. It's OK, he owned the place.

Kat began, "I wrecked things for us on Bogey Island all those years ago. It's on me. I'm not going to grant myself some handy excuse like, well, I was just a young girl."

"It's a shame, Kat, that we can't know who we're going to be when we're 25. But we're expected to make the decisions that affect the rest of our lives."

"Look at this golf course. The design changes you made when you bought it were awesome. It's tough, but fair. Like life should be. This is THE CLUB to belong to in the Southwest. If it weren't so bloody hot here in June, they'd play the US Open at Valley Vista."

He didn't know where she was going with this. But he knew it was important to listen.

"Your life has been about making other people smile—whether it's with your stellar golf skill or saving them from possible harm in your private eye biz. Or being the life of the party, wherever the party is. Your sociable nature was part of you. I was too blinded by jealousy to see that. I'm not going to be selfish all over again, all these years later, and cling to you."

Tom refilled their glasses. He remained quiet. After a 40-year friendship you know when to let your best friend finish what they want to say.

"I'm still mad at myself for pushing you away all those years ago. But I would never try to keep you from your dream, even if I don't think the dream will last. Our game is the game that teaches you sportsmanship, honor, integrity, fair play. I drill that into my young students every time we meet for a lesson. And you've always been honorable to me."

"Thank you."

"On Bogey Island in '63, did you make love to Jilly Flannery?"

Tom was startled by the question. "No."

"Patti Boyle?"

Tom chuckled. "Nope."

"Julia?

"Nope."

"Amber Autumn?"

"It's Autumn Amber, but good grief, no."

"Who then? Just me, just your girl Katrina, on that glorious afternoon on the beach, one of the best afternoons of my life. I still think about that afternoon whenever I need cheering up. I acted like a spoiled child because you wouldn't quit your detective biz. And we lost something wonderful because of it."

"You were just being you. That's all you can do."

"No, sorry. I'm not going to be that easy on myself."

Tom thought, *wow, I would have never guessed that...*

Katrina continued, "And I will always hate that wretched place, Bogey Island. My misunderstanding of what happened there and my possessiveness ruined our chances of being together. I wish we'd never gone there in the first place. Your eyes used to shine with a...kind of glorious passion when you would see me. At my wedding to Stan, it all changed. It dimmed. I almost ran away from the altar. That's how important you are to me."

It was 10 minutes to midnight on March 18.

Kat opened her purse and pulled out a slender leather-bound book, 6"x9". It was their Friendship Book. Kat opened it to the inscription:

> *We renew the vows we first took in 1962, to treat each other with kindness, loyalty and respect. And to be there for each other, whenever one of us needs the other, whatever the circumstances. For each of us, the other is the Special One. And one year from today, if we mutually agree, we will extend this pact again.*

For the 43rd year in a row on March 18, Katrina Stern, then Tom Colt, signed their Friendship Book.

At midnight, Tom walked Kat back to her condo.

Kat took Tom's hand. "The strength of our relationship is that we let each other stretch our wings and fly where the breeze takes us."

Tom squeezed her hand in agreement.

"So go ahead. I don't think it will work out with you and young Carmen. But I've been wrong about so many things in my life—including the guy I married."

Tom's expression turned cloudy.

"It's not that you need attention from young women—you believe you are still young. In your mind, you and Carmen are the same age. You are remarkable that way. But I will wager that next March 18 you and I will be renewing our vows of friendship and signing Our Book."

Tom nodded 'yes' with certainty, which Kat recognized.

"When you turned 65, you thought the party might be over. I saw it in your eyes at your birthday dinner that night. I mean, isn't that what we are taught by society to believe, all our lives. Sixty-five is the end of the good things. We get put out to pasture at 65. It's even worse for professional athletes like us. Turning 40 seems like death." Kat paused, sighed.

"I'm sorry to make this long speech."

"Continue. Please."

"The truth is, lovely Carmen, with those long legs, mysterious dark eyes, and flirty smile, and sexy cowgirl voice, showed you the party is far from over. So I don't resent her. I wish I could thank her. I need you to be young. For me, not for her. In some capacity we will always be together."

"Absolutely."

Kat nodded. "Our friendship is amaranthine."

Tom shrugged. "Am-a-what? I'll have to ask Brooks Benton what that means."

"Everlasting, undying, deathless, unfading, is what that means."

A warm smile creased Tom's tanned face. "Yes, that's us."

"My sister Ingrid just retired from her business planning consulting career. She wants me to travel through Europe with her. I imagine Germany's changed a bit since my family left there in sort of a hurry in '45."

"How long will you be gone?"

"Six months seems about right."

Tom smiled. "Yes, it does."

They arrived at her back patio. They looked at each other like they always did—with passionate admiration.

Kat turned and went inside. Tom walked home, thinking about all that Kat had said, feeling blessed to have her friendship—blessed to have this life.

Chapter Thirty-Two
--A Quick Trip Back to 1963

At the Guest House with Tom and Caroline

In the kitchen at 4PM, Caroline was fairly stricken with stress. She was prepping for a dinner party there in two hours. Convinced she was behind schedule, she started to rush. She was chopping garlic and sliced her finger open.

Tom saw her wince and stepped into the kitchen. "Let me finish chopping while you bandage that. Tonight's recipe doesn't call for blood. I'll also get you a glass of wine. You seem to need it."

He poured the wine and she returned with a bandaged index finger.

"You might try and relax," Tom commented as he chopped a tidy bunch of rosemary leaves.

"If my dinner stinks, she wins."

"When did tonight's party become a competition?"

"A few minutes after I was born."

"It'll be fine. Have some more wine. You picked one of mom's best recipes. Although the dessert...tiramisu. You must be confident. Kind of a risky choice, don't you think. Very easy to chuck at each other." Tom smirked.

"Shut up," Caroline said, returning to work in the kitchen.

They combined the rosemary, garlic, salt & pepper, olive oil and balsamic vinegar—a wonderful marinade. The recipe called for marinating lamb chops, then grilling them over charcoal. Caroline substituted beef tenderloins for the lamb chops. She couldn't do lamb—it would be like serving up Bugs Bunny.

The wine worked its magic and Caroline calmed down. They chatted as they finished prepping the meal.

Caroline said, "The moral lesson from the Red Boyle Case was, how you treat others comes back around to you, for good or bad. Red Boyle was a material success, but a total failure as a person. Eventually, all the bad things he did to others—cheating them, abusing them, jerking them around—came back with a vengeance and took him down."

Tom nodded. "I remember talking to a rich guy's gardener during our first case, The Lisa Luck Murder. He pointed to the guy's mansion and said, 'Someday my people will live in houses like this, not just mow the lawns'. I thought, no you won't. And neither will I probably. I have no idea how you earn enough dough to buy one of these palaces. Now we consider Red Boyle, who owned dozens of spectacular properties, including mansions, hotels and golf resorts. How did he do it?"

Caroline had no answer. She took the tenderloins out of the refrigerator.

Tom said, "All the shit, the horrible things, venal things, people do just to get rich."

"Maybe you should re-evaluate your goals. Maybe not make being wealthy a priority."

"Let me consider that a moment." He paused, a mock-serious frown on his face. "Ok, I'm done considering. Hell, yes, I want to be rich. I hated it when we were poor."

"Now, THAT'S my brother. I just needed you to confirm the obvious truth. I love you Tom."

"I love you too, Caroline."

They laughed.

The doorbell rang.

"For whom the doorbell tolls," Caroline said ominously.

"Go ahead and answer it."

"No way. You answer it."

Tom did, and Laura Colt stepped into the guest house for the very first time since her son and daughter moved there.

She was smartly dressed in capri pants and a silky purple blouse. She had finished work early so she could get her hair done. She always admired Caroline's beautiful brown hair.

"Nifty, neat-o digs you've got here, kids."

Their mom, fortunately for all involved, seldom tried to sound 'hip'. When she did, they did their best to humor her.

Caroline was obviously nervous, which made Tom nervous. One of the perils of having a twin. Accompanied by Tom, Laura gave the guest house a quick tour, taking everything in with her sharp eyes.

"This house is bigger than the one I raised you two in!"

She went outside to the back patio. "A putting green! I bet you spend a lot of time out there practicing, Tom."

"Yes, even at night, when the neighbor girl comes over to play." Caroline had to chime in.

Tom threw a scowl at Caroline. She returned it with a wicked grin.

"You mean little Julia Wilkinson?"

"She's not so little anymore. Trust me," Caroline replied, chortling.

"Are you two succeeding as house mates? I was afraid that you'd be at each other's throats 24/7."

"Yes, we're succeeding really well," Tom said with a tad too much enthusiasm.

"And yes, we're at each other's throats," Caroline added with matching enthusiasm.

Laura said, "The dinner smells wonderful."

"It's your recipe, mom."

Laura smiled with great warmth—and a note of surprise.

***

How did the dinner go? Well, Caroline only let loose with cuss words twice. The only discussion of the twins' father was to share some fun memories they had of their dad taking them to see John Wayne movies at the Kachina Theater in Scottsdale. *At least,* Caroline reflected, *John Wayne is still with us.*

After the tiramisu was consumed, not tossed, they settled onto the patio and enjoyed the pretty view of the softly lit grounds of the Wilkinson estate.

A few minutes later, the mighty man himself, Judge Wilkinson, strolled down the path from the Main House.

"I heard a rumor you might be coming over for dinner, Laura. I had to come by and say hello."

To the mild shock of Tom and Caroline, their mom and the Judge embraced. A tight hug, with clearly the feeling of shared history.

"It's been too long, Roy."

"It has, much too long!"

"Some night we must all have dinner at my place." He pointed up the hill at the brightly lit mansion.

"I would love that," Laura said with eyes just as bright.

Tom gave the Judge a glass of wine, and they sat down on the patio. The Judge and Laura chose to sit together on the cushioned bench—the young detectives noted with curiosity.

"I thought that aroma was familiar. That dish—the grilled meat marinated in rosemary and balsamic vinegar. We dined on that in San Francisco all those years ago."

"Yes, we did. The aroma of great food can bring back fond memories."

Two sets of junior detective eyes were popping out of their heads—they detected the warmth between their mom and

The Judge. Laura had consumed enough wine to be uncharacteristically mellow.

When the conversation ebbed, Laura said, "I suppose I've had enough wine. I have to drive home, after all. But what a wonderful evening this was!"

The Judge said, "Relax, Laura. My man Duxbury will take you home when you're ready."

"He was Red Boyle's butler, wasn't he..." she said.

"Yes. I snapped him up. Old Red may have been a bastard in business, but he knew how to pick great people to work for him."

The Judge stood up, "Thank you for the wine, Tom. I have a few calls to make before the night is over."

"The King never rests," Laura remarked. The Judge and Laura exchanged smiles and he departed. Ten minutes later, Tom rang up the Judge to send Duxbury over with the car.

Laura thanked Tom and Caroline again and then stepped outside the front door.

Seeing Roy Wilkinson interacting with Tom, and particularly Caroline, Laura had a pleasant, nearly glorious flash of insight, which may not seem strange since she had given birth to not one, but two detectives.

Caroline was too curious to let the evening end this way. She followed Laura outside.

The wine had left her mother uncharacteristically gay and unfettered that night. She picked up on her daughter's quizzical expression.

"And you thought all this time it was only Tom that Roy wanted to take under his wing."

"What does that mean?" Caroline said incredulously.

"If it ends up, Caroline, that the only man you truly love in this world is Roy Wilkinson, you will have made a good choice. He adores you. You don't even seem to notice. Or maybe you pretend you don't. You two have that almost spiritual kind of love, *Agape* I think it's called."

Caroline sputtered. This conversation was too much for her to process.

"I once had the chance to make the same choice. But I didn't...I think I was afraid of him. You and I are so different. You're not afraid of anything. That's what always amazed me about you."

Caroline was thunderstruck by the enormity of what her mother had just said, *I once had the chance to make the same choice.*

Laura Colt was smirking with secret knowledge, it seemed to Caroline. Which irritated Caroline—she often displayed that same smirk to her own advantage.

"Mother! Tell me! Please!" On this night of firsts, it was the first time in a decade that Caroline did not say the word 'Mother' like it was a mild cuss word. Her voice was very much that of a little girl, pleading.

Laura shrugged her shoulders. Then waved an index finger like, no, no. "You're the celebrated detective. I've read about you in Bonnie Blunt's column in the *Arizona Republic* newspaper. You figure it out. And when you have this thing called life figured out, please explain it all to me."

Laura Colt sighed, but with evident happiness—almost bliss.

Caroline looked cross.

"I turn 50 years old this year. And all I have learned in that time is that life is about ROMANZA. Yes, that's it. Romanza. The other night I was reading a Zane Grey Western novel. He said, 'Romance is only another word for idealism; and I contend life without ideals is not worth living.' When I read that I wanted to stand up and cheer. It's so important to believe in ideals, in dreams. Tom already understands this. He always has. You, my beautiful and talented daughter, need to recognize it, too."

"I..." Caroline sputtered yet again.

"With all that has happened to me in my life, I still believe in 'romanza'. Why can't you?"

A limousine pulled into the driveway. Without another word, Laura got in the car and Duxbury drove her away.

Caroline might have stood out there on the driveway all night if Tom hadn't come out and taken her inside, by the hand.

"I was kinda hoping to solve mysteries, not live one," she said in a soft, hoarse voice.

***

One lovely evening in early November, the temperature still summer-like by the standards of the Midwest and East, Tom Colt was dressing for a night at the theater. He donned a light blue Munsingwear shirt and dark blue Izod slacks, and a new beige linen sport coat from his favorite downtown clothing store.

He was running late. He had to pick up his date in 25 minutes.

He reflected on the strange and often wondrous year of 1963 as he finished dressing and combing his blond hair, which he had grown out a bit more than usual that fall.

My goal for 1964: to earn an Invitation to the Masters Golf Tournament. I've got to play Augusta soon, while I'm at the top of my game (at least what I consider the top, even if the editors at Gentleman Golfer Monthly magazine don't).

I really think 1964 is going to be MY YEAR in golf. No more excuses, no more distractions. Maybe it's for the best that Katrina and I aren't together. I think we would have worn each other out. Our relationship was, is, too intense. I think my true love is still out there...MoniQue Jones has possibilities, but I'm still a poor boy in the eyes of the members at Valley Vista CC, and the eyes of the rich men's daughters.

Caroline says I should find a nice healthy ranch girl in Wickenburg. I have no idea where she comes up with these things. I don't even know how to ride a horse. And last year she told me I should marry a waitress, someone who works for a living. I didn't understand that, either.

Yes, my <u>total focus</u> will be on tournament golf in the upcoming year.

Unless Det. Mathers needs my help solving a murder. Or two.

Or Judge Wilkinson needs me to get one or more of his rich friends out of a jam.

Or I somehow find the perfect girl and embark on a whirlwind romance. Or the girl ends up breaking my heart.

Yes, <u>total focus.</u>

Sure, just like in '62, someone shot at me this year, but this time they missed. So all things considered, '63 was a good year.

Tom Colt checked himself in the mirror, was satisfied that he looked the part of the character he now played so well in public, Mr. Popularity. His mother had taught him to make sure to be careful with grooming, and always wear the smartest togs he could afford. Her advice regarding living amongst the rich: It's all about fitting in.

Tom went out to the driveway, got in his sporty red T-bird and picked up his date for the theater, the lovely Laura Colt.

***

Midtown Community Theater
Phoenix, AZ
Early November, 1963

Tom Continues Our Story:

People get involved with the performing arts for a variety of reasons. Tracy Amberson wanted fame and money. She saw it as a path to self-worth after enduring a childhood where her parents didn't love her. But the fame never came and the money was never enough to rid her of the anger she carried, to make her whole.

Autumn Amber simply wanted to entertain. And not just because she couldn't please her own mother so she sought to please strangers. When she brought joy to others through her work on stage and screen, it made her feel like her life had purpose. She was so lovely that her effect on men was not merely to bring lust to the surface, although that was surely a part of her appeal. They admired her like you would be inspired by seeing a beautiful rose-colored sunset or seeing a high-spirited doe running across a sun-kissed meadow.

My sister, Caroline Colt, through her theater performances in high school and beyond, sought to access and expiate the deep pain she carried inside. It was a kind of anodyne, of course, never a cure. I never understood how deep that pain was, or where it came from.

But that night, she was back in the spotlight, like she had been so often in those long-ago high school plays and musicals. Caroline needed that spotlight, even more than she knew, and possibly more than I needed it. And you know how vain I am. I'd rather read something negative about me in *Gentleman Golfer Monthly*, than find they said nothing at all.

Brooks Benton Continues Our Story:

Midtown Community Theater was performing a production of *West Side Story*. All 800 seats were filled that night. The production had received rave reviews in the local press. An extra week of performances were added to satisfy the unexpectedly robust demand for tickets.

Tom and Laura had enrolled Caroline in classes at the Boyle Academy of the Performing Arts. She excelled in the classes and was quickly sought after to perform in local theater.

Midtown was considered the most professional of the theater companies in the city at that time.

The last cast member to be introduced that night was the star, Caroline Colt, as Maria. The audience was on its feet. Caroline had earned a huge ovation. If this were a movie, we'd say CLOSE UP on Caroline's face, tears streaming down her cheeks, drinking in the applause as though it was a magic elixir. A tonic for all the pain she had felt in her life.

Tom never fully understood her pain. His attitude was that other folks have it a lot worse than the Colt family did.

When Caroline saw Tom, she gave him the thumbs up signal and winked.

Laura, Tom's mom, turned to him, with that special smile she reserved only for him, and said, "You really are a saint."

"Far from it, mom. I screw up all the time, one mistake after the other. I'm just a guy who gets up every day and tries to do his damnedest."

"Give me a better definition of a saint."

Chapter Thirty-Three
--A Brief Visit to March 2005   At Valley Vista CC
And This Adventure Comes to a Close

"Give me a better definition of a Saint," old-er Tom Colt recalled his mom's voice from long ago, still alive in his memory.

A round of golf on any fine course is a journey. On a great, tough course like Valley Vista Country Club, a round of golf reflects the journey of life. Adversity visits even the best players like Tom, testing not just their golf swing but their character. At Valley Vista, the journey ends on the 18th hole, a long hard uphill climb to the green, a full 570 yards from the tee. Many golfers arrive at the top of that hill weary, dejected, defeated.

Tom Colt, even on days he didn't play up to his lofty standards, always arrived exhilarated. To Tom, the journey was the joy. He looked forward to the next leg of his journey, tomorrow.

Tom Continues Our Story:

My mom's smile that night was one of tremendous appreciation, not for my success, my achievements, which were far from tremendous. But for how hard I tried, in this case trying to help my sister have the great life she deserved.

Success is impossible to measure, probably an illusion, and undoubtedly impermanent. Or, as I have come to believe, success is simply the tally of how many lives you touched in a positive way. My mom's smile that night after Caroline's magnificent performance has lived on in my memory, all the way down these many misty years—and lives on to this day.

I'd like to tell you that Caroline and our mom gave each other a big hug after the theater performance that night and all was well in my family from that time on. But our family's always been on a low-schmaltz diet, so that wasn't how things played out. Nonetheless, I felt satisfied. One thing that was wonderful about my relationship with Caroline: we always wanted to help each other succeed.

The recollection of that special night never fails to warm me, heal me, inspire me to keep going, no matter how bleak things might seem. Bleak is temporary. Happy memories last a lifetime. Defeat is temporary, too. There's always another tournament next week, another golf course to challenge us.

As I teed off that morning at Valley Vista CC, in my slightly biased opinion the greatest course in the entire Southwest, which was once the frontier West and, in many ways, still is, I was blessed with a beautiful cloudless day. Temp around 80. No headwinds worth mentioning.

"What A Lovely Day for Golf!" my mom would exclaim, if she were here with us.

What a stupid thing for me to say...she is. Her spirit is all around us, and will always be, at this magnificent place where both of us spent so much of our working lives. She earned her immortality by doing her absolute best for all of us every day of her life. I'm still laboring to earn even a semblance of that immortality of my own.

Isn't that what we all want, to be remembered? That, and of course, Romanza.

***

Brooks Benton, With the Last Words:

That same morning, Katrina Stern was at Valley Vista preparing for a long day of giving golf lessons to the Junior Girls, the up-and-coming little snobs. Katrina had taught golf to youngsters at Valley Vista ever since she retired from competition when she was 44.

She didn't need a job. Her naturally frugal nature, her success in golf and with product endorsements, and timely investments suggested by Tom, had left her a wealthy woman. She simply loved being close to the game she loved.

Although she enjoyed teaching golf, this generation of young girls made her feel old, or more precisely like she no longer belonged. Like she was 'out of it' as the girls themselves said.

They knew nothing of thrift, or struggle, or worry about money. They all had the most expensive golf equipment their parents could find for them, not to mention clothes that were the most fashionable and costly available.

The jewelry some of the young girls wore cost more than Katrina's first automobile in 1958, a six-year-old Dodge sedan she purchased for $169. Was Katrina jealous? Only in a sense. She knew all too well that the struggles had made her strong, damn near invincible.

That morning, Katrina opened her locker at Valley Vista and saw a small package on the top shelf. It was tied with a curled white satin ribbon over bright silver foil wrapping.

With her characteristic frowny face, this one born of curiosity, she took the package out and undid the ribbon, removed the wrapping.

It was from a well-known and frightfully expensive jewelry store in Scottsdale.

The box opened with an impressive snap.

Inside, a gold and diamond necklace. The tiny diamonds, sparkling in the warm rich lights, spelled 'AMARANTHINE'.

Katrina turned and leaned against the locker next to hers, closed her eyes.

She felt 26 again.

Tom.

--THE END--